Crazy Drama

Crazy Drama

D.A. Bourne

Copyright © 2007 by D.A. Bourne.

Library of Congress Control Number: 2007900473
ISBN : Hardcover 978-1-4257-5442-6
       Softcover 978-1-4257-5440-2

All rights reserved. No part of this book may be reproduced or transmitted in any form or by any means, electronic or mechanical, including photocopying, recording, or by any information storage and retrieval system, without permission in writing from the copyright owner.

This is a work of fiction. Names, characters, places and incidents either are the product of the author's imagination or are used fictitiously, and any resemblance to any actual persons, living or dead, events, or locales is entirely coincidental.

This book was printed in the United States of America.

To order additional copies of this book, contact:
Xlibris Corporation
1-888-795-4274
www.Xlibris.com
Orders@Xlibris.com

Prologue

August 2002

There he was. The ex-friend and hip-hop sidekick who slept with K.J's woman.

He was at the DJ booth signing autographs. It was Roderick Bailey, also known as Verbal Pain.

K.J Brar clenched his fist in rage. He did not care how much people were in the Toronto nightclub or how popular Roderick had become. He was ready to change his stage name from Verbal Pain to Physical Pain.

The Phat Five was at the bar counter waiting to purchase some drinks. K.J tapped his cousin Teddy Henderson on the shoulder.

"Yo, I'll be right back, Ted. Gotta use the washroom," he lied.

Teddy nodded his head without looking at him, failing to notice that K.J walked in the opposite direction of Club Oasis' main restroom.

If looks could kill, K.J would easily be sentenced to the electric chair. He pushed his way through the packed dance floor, never losing focus on his target. When he finally stood in front of Roderick, he and the ladies that were around him quickly noticed K.J's look of anger.

Trying to look cool and unnervous, Roderick smiled.

"What up, K.J? What's going on?"

K.J snapped. "You slept with Bianca!"

"What?"

Two seconds later, K.J swung his right fist at Roderick's face and sent him to the floor.

The music suddenly stopped, and people started leaving the bar counter toward the DJ booth.

"What's going on?" Teddy asked.

"Fight at the DJ booth!" Q exclaimed.

Teddy, Damon "Q" Quintino, Eros Alexander Jr., and Ajani Bethel quickly went to the action scene.

The guys had a difficult time observing the ruckus due to the huge crowd of people. Eros saw Roderick holding his face in extreme pain.

"Oh, snap!" he said. "Somebody just punched the crap outta Verbal Pain!"

"Dang!" Ajani yelled. "I don't know who did it, but a bouncer got some dude in a chokehold!"

He looked at Eros, Q, and Teddy and asked, "Yo, where's K.J?"

"He said he went to use the . . ." Teddy quickly remembered how his cousin looked at Roderick when he entered the club an hour prior. "Oh, no."

The four friends looked at each other and immediately knew who attacked Verbal Pain. They pushed their way through the crowd toward the fight like Warren Sapp through a herd of offensive linemen.

The bouncer, who looked like a poor man's Shaquille O'Neal, was choking K.J so hard that it looked like he was going to faint. A second bouncer was holding his legs while Roderick began to punch K.J in the stomach while holding his jaw. Teddy pushed him away from K.J while Ajani punched the Shaq look-alike in the face. Q and Eros joined the fight after a couple of men from Verbal Pain's crew entered the riot. It was a prime time mess in Toronto's hottest nightclub.

K.J put a bag of ice on his forehead.

"Guy, I'm sorry for ruining your going-away night," he said to Teddy.

He and the Phat Five were sitting on the sofas in Ajani's basement two hours after the incident.

Teddy replied, "Man, you think that I'm mad about a going-away evening? I'm mad that you went after Roderick without backup. You knew that he had security with him."

"Yeah, I know," he admitted, "but I was so freaking mad. If I told you that I was gonna fight him, y'all would've stopped me."

Eros held an ice pack on his right shoulder.

"Yeah, you're right. I ain't saying that to be punkish, but now we have a lifetime ban from Club Oasis, the booty palace of T.O!"

"Is that all you can think about?" K.J snapped. "Booty 24-7?"

"Guy, don't look at me. It was booty that caused you to start mess!"

K.J gave Eros the middle finger. Ajani shook his head.

"Normally, I don't give a flip about what you and Eros argue about, but you did let your emotions go too far, K.J. Shaq was taking you down before we stepped in."

K.J said, "That was my bad, bred-drin. But I messed up his jaw good, huh?"

Teddy laughed. "Man, I wish I could've seen that!"

"I punched him so hard; I think I sprained my hand in the process," he added as he shook his right hand in pain. "But it was worth it."

Q said, "I'm just glad that we aren't sitting in jail right now for assault."

"Roderick probably begged the club owner not to press charges," Ajani said. "He was already embarrassed that K.J beat him down and that two bouncers had to protect him. He would've lost his street cred."

"That, and the fact that the club owner likes Q," Eros said.

Q looked at his best friend. "Eros, what the hell do I have to do with this?"

"Man, don't act stupid. You're white and you're Damon Quintino, Canada's best ever college basketball player. That Italian dude is your biggest fan."

"Whatever. I'm just glad I don't have to call Trina from jail."

Teddy nodded in agreement. "I hear that. Janet would've been pissed."

Eros shook his head. "You guys are so whipped. Me and Ajah are the only cats who aren't controlled by the booty. Any chance we get, we're in another woman's panties."

Ajani said to Eros, "Lower your voice, guy! And speak for yourself. Savannah's upstairs, remember? I stopped macking for almost two months now."

"Whatever, if you say so," he said in disbelief as he pulled out a piece of paper. "As for me, I'm gonna call this girl Juanita, someone who gave me her digits before the fight. She looked so delicious, yo!"

"Who, Juanita Velez?" Teddy asked. "She was in my advertising class last semester. I'd be careful if I was you."

"Why?"

"Cause you're a player. And Juanita has a rep for getting sweet revenge on players."

"Like what?" Eros looked unconvinced.

"I heard that when she found out that her man cheated on her, she didn't cry or even confront him about it. He was an NHL hockey player and had a huge upcoming playoff game. A Game Seven in the first round. Juanita stayed sweet and made him lasagna and chocolate cake a half day before the game.

Little did he know that the meat sauce in the lasagna was dog food and the chocolate cake was made with Ex-Lax. Dude had chronic diarrhea and couldn't play the game. The team lost the game and was exited from the playoffs. When he got home from the hospital, Juanita left a note next to an empty dog food can and an empty Ex-Lax box which read, 'That's what you get for cheating on me, mother you-know-what!'"

Everyone was laughing hard by the time Teddy finished the story. Eros still did not look worried.

"Wow," he said. "I'll make sure that I don't stick around after I hit that."

After a few more laughs, Ajani got up from the sofa.

"Well, I gotta meet with Machete at the Irie Club to discuss some business, so I'll drop y'all home," he said.

They all got up from their seats with a struggle, complaining about their aches and bruises.

Teddy said, "As messed up as tonight was, I'm gonna miss these times with y'all when I move to Windsor."

K.J said, "I'm sure you'll stay quite busy, since you're a club freak and Windsor's a nightclub mecca."

Eros added, "Plus, I'm sure playing house with Janet will keep you quite occupied."

Teddy smiled. "Hey, I love me some Janet and I love me some clubbin'. But it ain't the same without the Phat Five."

"You got that right," K.J agreed. "Y'all came through for me tonight without hesitation."

"That's what we're all about," said Ajani. "Even though Club Oasis isn't the hangout anymore, we still know how to party, especially when it comes to . . ."

"JAM FEST!" yelled Q.

"JAM FEST!" the others repeated in unison.

"That's my number one reason for going to Windsor," Teddy said. "Not school, not Janet, but Jam Fest. And next year will be the best ever, especially once I join the committee. I guarantee it."

"Trust me," said Eros. "I'll remember what you just said."

The guys gave each other pounds as they left the basement.

Seven months later, Teddy entered his apartment in Windsor after a long day of classes and work. His girlfriend, Janet, left a note stating that she was at the library studying for a midterm exam, so he expected her to show up really late. That was not a problem for Teddy because he definitely needed to catch up on his studies, but not before doing some serious catching up on his e-mail.

Not surprisingly, his e-mail account was almost full, since he had not opened it in a couple of weeks. There was the usual junk mail, plenty of inspirational messages, and at least six e-mails from Eros that took up over half of his space. Teddy started deleting immediately.

I told Eros to stop sending me video clips from his dad's XXX movies, he thought. *I should just block his e-mail address.*

As he deleted messages, he noticed that there was mail from K.J. Eager to know what was up with his cousin, Teddy opened the letter.

From : "K.J" *(kellanjamal@csn.com)*
To : *t-henny@csn.com*

Message: w'happen?

    Yo, I know you a busy man and ting with school and trying to make this year's Jam Fest the best ever, but that don't mean you can't holla at somebody! None of the guys have heard from you in weeks, and its getting mad close to the big weekend. Holla at one of us soon! Let us know you're still breathing!

                                                            K.J

    Teddy stared at the message long after reading it. For the last three weeks, he eagerly wanted to talk to his crew. It was normal not to talk to Ajani, Q, or Eros on the phone, but not K.J, his cousin and best friend. They usually kept in contact once or twice a week since Teddy moved to Windsor. Although the whole Phat Five was tight, they were inseparable like Bert and Ernie. Yet Teddy did not know how to tell K.J that he was now a born-again Christian.

    He knew that it was something he should not hide. After all, when the spiritual transformation took place, it was the greatest day of his life. Never had Teddy felt so happy, so alive, and so free. For the first time in his life, he knew his purpose for living. But Teddy didn't know how to explain his experience to a quad of friends who believed that his mother gave birth to him in a nightclub. He was the party motivator of the Phat Five. Would they be ready for his announcement?

From : *t-henny@csn.com*
To : "K.J" *(kellanjamal@csn.com)*
Message: (none)

What up cuz,

    My bad for taking so long to holla back. I can't use the excuse of being too busy 'cause I've been busier in the past and still gave you a shout. Tell the Phat Five that I'm still alive and expecting y'all to crash my crib on Jam Fest weekend!

    The real reason why I haven't called or e-mailed you is because of the transition period I just went through. First of all, I quit the committee that's in charge of Jam Fest. Yes, I know that being on the Jam Fest staff was my main reason for coming to Windsor, but I had to resign due to the fact that I recently gave my life to Christ. Yes, your cousin is a Christian now! You guys might as well get the heads up now instead of getting shocked when you don't see T-Henny smoke any blunts or drink any forties or Guinness. Now I expect to hear from all four of y'all cause you probably don't believe me. That's understandable, but I'm serious as a car accident, guy . . .

Anyway, enough about me. You ready for the Freestyle Showcase, guy? This year is predicted to be huge based on the contestants on schedule to take the stage. But it don't matter 'cause you can beat them all without frustration. Looking forward to the day you win the crown, dog!

TTYL,
Ted

Before Teddy decided to send it, he read the message a second time. He made the announcement without beating around the bush, but suddenly he felt fear. That was unusual because Teddy never was afraid to tell the Phat Five anything. Did he feel nervous about revealing his newfound faith? Was it better to e-mail K.J about it or tell him over the phone?

Whatever the answer was, it would have to wait because the home phone was ringing. It was the Chinese food deliveryman wanting to get in the apartment. Perfect timing because the Lakers-Spurs basketball game was about to begin on television. Teddy signed out of his e-mail account without sending or saving the letter. He also never got around to giving his cousin a phone call.

March 2003
PART 1

THURSDAY

CHAPTER 1

AJANI

Very rarely do I drug deal and deliver for SpeedEx at the same time, but Thursday was the exception. Michael "Machete" Deverow, one of Toronto's biggest drug lords told me that he received a briefcase of counterfeit money from a client for a case of OxyContin, also known as Ghetto Heroin. My assignment was to get the money or the drugs back by any means necessary.

I was upset for four reasons. One, because receiving fake cash meant that I had to do extra work on a job that I hated. Two, because I hated having to kick the crap out of folks, but I was good at it, thanks to my black belt in marital arts. Reason number three was the fact that if I was behind on my SpeedEx delivery schedule, and it was not because of traffic or bad weather, I could lose my job. Finally, I just wanted to get the hell out of Toronto because it was the eve of Jam Fest weekend.

The house was located in the suburb area of Scarborough, a city in the Greater Toronto Area. The client was a Guyanese dude named Chester, an autoworker who worked the night shift and an OxyContin addict. It was his third time purchasing drugs from Machete, but the first time paying with counterfeit fifties. Chester seemed like an all right cat but business was business, and I wanted my cheddar.

I parked the SpeedEx truck a block away from the house. As I walked to the entrance, I told myself to complete the task in less than ten minutes. That was not a problem for me because I was a stubborn and impatient man who didn't beat around the bush.

I knocked hard on the front door, and then I hid myself on the right side and pulled out my seldom-used gun from my belt. There was no response after a minute, so I knocked again. I wasn't going to leave because his Jeep Cherokee was in the driveway. Finally, after another thirty seconds, Chester opened the door. That's when I pointed the gun to his temple, grabbed him by the arm, and pushed him back inside.

"Wha . . . what the hell is this about?" asked a very scared Chester.

"I'm here for the money, Chester," I said. "Got it for me?"

"Machete got it yesterday."

"No, Machete got some pieces of paper that looked like cash but burnt a pretty bluish-green. Nice trick, David Blaine. Where's the money?"

"B-b-believe me, Ajani, I . . . I didn't know the cash was fake! All I know . . ."

"Don't gimme that crap, Chester! Everyone knows how much you associate with them cats in Milton who've been making counterfeit bills since the day cassette tapes were cool! Now, you must have some real money stored somewhere in this lovely home. I mean, no one works for twenty years as a skilled tradesman for Chrysler and not have money put away for a rainy day, right?"

For a few seconds, Chester said nothing. I got impatient.

"Well?" I asked.

"I don't have any money," he replied, sounding weak.

"None? Don't lie, man! I know that Thursday's payday for Chrysler folk!"

"It all went to bills."

"Savings account?"

"Empty."

It was hard not to believe Chester was being truthful because the dude was shivering. It was a shame to hear that most of his money went to ghetto heroin. I told myself when I began drug dealing that I didn't want to know about the lives of my customers. It made the job way too difficult because I wasn't a ruthless guy. But, business was business, and I wanted to get paid. I had to think of another payment option because I didn't want to kill the man. I'd been involved in criminal activity since arriving to North America from Jamaica as a young teen, and I never had to commit murder. There were many close calls, but I decided that I wasn't going to kill anybody for something stupid. I knew too many cats that were behind bars for murder because of a few hundred bucks or someone bad-mouthing their chick. Stupid.

"Well, brah," I said, "Looks like you're gonna have to give me something in exchange for cash. I see a fifty inch plasma TV that I wouldn't mind putting in my living room."

"Ajani, give me at least a day to get you the money," he pleaded.

"I'm a busy man, Chester. I don't have a day to wait. Plus, my gun's very impatient!"

I pressed the gun harder at his head when I realized that I couldn't fit a fifty-inch TV in the SpeedEx truck. And I couldn't give the man another day to get the cash 'cause I was hours away from heading to Windsor. And I had to go to back to my regular job soon.

Guy, please don't make me have to use this gun!
I asked Chester how much credit he had on his plastic.
"Two hundred, max," he answered.
"Dang, you're making this difficult on you!"
"Man, I promise you that I'll have the real cash tomorrow! Plus interest!"
"I told you, I don't have a day . . ."
"Sir, please don't shoot my daddy!"

The voice scared the hell outta me. I looked behind me and saw a pretty little girl that didn't look older than seven. Wondered how long she was standing there. At first I thought why she wasn't at school, but then I remembered that it was March break for the kiddies. Our situation just got from bad to worse. The last thing I wanted was to traumatize a child. Suddenly I felt extremely embarrassed for the man.

"Sweetheart," cried Chester, "everything's okay. Just go back downstairs and watch TV."

My gun was still pointed at his head. I just wanted to put it down and disappear, but it was too late. The girl was old enough to call nine-one-one and tell cops what I look like. If I remembered that kids were home because of March break, I wouldn't have entered the man's home. Other dealers may not have cared less, but I wasn't the average. I had a soft heart for kids, unknown to the syndicate that I worked with.

I was a black belt in martial arts, tough as nails and fearless, yet I learnt how wonderful my life was as a father in 2001. When my son Ajani Jr. came into this world, I realized that I wanted him to have my confident personality but not to follow in my career footsteps. That's why my son and his mother knew nothing about my dealer lifestyle. Parents want their kids around good role models. I messed that up for Chester's daughter. She was witnessing her dad being dealt with, and terrified that he was about to die. If she thought that her dad was invincible before, I killed that reality quick.

I felt like crap that flies didn't even want to touch. I had to bounce ASAP.

"Let go of my daddy!" yelled the crying yet brave daughter.

Chester snapped, "Sasha! Go downstairs now!"

"Don't sweat it," I said as I moved the gun from his head. "I'll give you more time, despite orders from the boss."

Relieved, Chester started to breathe heavy. He grabbed Sasha and hugged her tight.

"I'll drop off the money at the Irie Club tomorrow around noon," he said to me.

"Hell no!" I replied. "Machete or Rancel can't know about this. I'll call you on Monday to meet somewhere."

"Monday? You sure? I mean . . ."

"You actually got a problem with that? You got three days to get me the money, thanks to your child! You're a helluva lucky man to have a daughter like her!"

They said nothing. I put the gun back on my belt and left, slamming the door behind me.

It was approaching four-thirty in the afternoon. My twelve-hour shift was nearly over. Trying to forget about the incident with Chester, I arrived at the SpeedEx headquarters, parked the truck, handed in my work material to the manager, and swiped out. My baby was waiting for me in the parking lot.

My baby was a brand new 2003 Cadillac Escalade, silver-colored with platinum chrome Sprewells, all leather interior, and a complete entertainment unit with a DVD, CD, cassette player and Playstation 2. It was a vehicle that I always dreamed of having, and was excited to see it happen. I stepped in the SUV, turned it on, and the *Reggae Gold 2003* CD was blazing through the speakers.

Taking my cell phone out of the charger, I turned the music down and started making calls. It was time to round up the fellas and head to Windsor.

CHAPTER 2

EROS

I thought that nobody could keep up with my sexual appetite. That idea changed after I hooked up with Juanita Velez. If she had her way, she would have sex more than five times a day. Of course, I didn't have a problem with that. The only difference between Juanita and I was that she liked to be a nymph with one man and I was monogamously challenged.

Juanita was quickly getting ready for work while I was lying under the sheets of her queen-size bed. I was going to Windsor in a few hours for Jam Fest and she was going to New York on Friday with her mother. Mrs. Velez deserved a thank you card from me, because there was no way in hell that I was going to take her to Windsor with me.

"I really wanted to go to Jam Fest this year," Juanita said while combing her straight jet-black hair. "But I can't turn down a weekend of shopping in Manhattan."

I said, "Sweetie, you made the right decision. Jam Fest is overrated. It's just a bunch of Toronto folk wanting to party in a different setting."

She stopped combing and looked at me with suspicion. I was lying and she caught it right away.

"Then why are you excited about going?" She asked.

"Baby, it's because of the Phat Five reunion. Me and the fellas: chilling, hanging, and hitting the clubs."

"Y'all ain't got any hoes waiting for you in Windsor?"

Every time Juanita questioned my faithfulness to her, I thought about the dog food and Ex-Lax story Teddy told me seven months ago. It kept me very alert.

"Why would I have a ho waiting for me when I get the best loving in the world from you?"

She went back to getting ready.

"You got that right," she said. "Nobody gives it better than this sexy Puerto Rican."

"Nobody! And you're pretty good yourself."

"Shut up!"

Juanita threw her brush and hit me in the forehead. At the same time, my cell phone rang.

"You're so lucky this phone rang, girl!" I yelled as I answered the phone, recognizing Ajani's phone number on the caller ID. "What up, Ajah?"

"Yo, it's four-thirty and I wanna be on the 401 highway by six, six-thirty at the latest."

When Ajani was serious, he never began conversations with a hello or what's up.

"Hello, Ajah. How are you?"

"Good. Where you at?"

"About to drop Nita off to her work, then I'm going home to pack."

"I'm leaving no later than 6:30."

"Guy, I heard you the first time."

"Yeah, but with you hearing don't mean doing. Brides on their wedding day get ready quicker than you."

The guys always cracked on me about how long I took to prepare for events. So what if I took long? I thought I was the sexiest man on the planet, and I refused to leave my house looking average.

"Whatever, Ajah. You picking me up last?"

"You wish. I'll get K.J first, then you, then Q. So be ready for six. Cool?"

"Fine. Later."

CHAPTER 3

Q

I knew that I'd only been married for nine months, but was choosing to go on a traditional get away with the guys rather than spending a much-needed weekend with the wife that bad?

That question ran through my mind the entire week. I made sure that I booked the weekend off for Jam Fest. Working seventy hours a week at the auto assembly plant was killing my marriage and me. I failed to spend more time with my wife Katrina earlier in the year, and when she realized that the upcoming weekend was free of work, she wanted me to focus on her. She deserved it, but Jam Fest only came once a year.

My body definitely wasn't in the mood for partying, and I really needed some rest. I was still trying to adjust to the blue-collar life after my basketball career ended with my fourth ankle injury. The dream of being the first Canadian drafted into the NBA from a Canadian college was shattered as well as a multi-million dollar contract. The day the doctor told me that I should not play basketball again was the worst day of my life.

I knew that life could be worse. Thanks to my father, Victor Quintino, a retired autoworker and union executive, he landed me a job as a foreman making close to a hundred grand a year. Of course, that wasn't close to a million dollars, but I promised Katrina before my injury that we would be rich and she wouldn't have to work. Two promises broken were worse than one, so I worked my butt off so that she could be a homemaker. Katrina had a degree in social work and wanted to work, but I insisted that it wasn't necessary. Little did she know I had second thoughts about my decision.

I lit up a cigarette as I cruised down the 403 highway going home from work. Smoking was the stupidest habit that I could pick up, especially as a well-known athlete. However, it was a stress reliever. While I tapped the ashes out of the car window, my cell phone rang. Not checking the caller ID, I knew that it would be either my wife or Ajani.

"Hello?"

"Q, you heading home?" Ajani asked.

"Yeah."

"Good. We'll be at your crib around six-fifteen."

"Ajah, I think I'm gonna stay here this weekend."

"What?"

I was about to get a lecture.

"You can't just back out of Jam Fest weekend, guy!" Ajani said. "This is our fourth year doing this. Teddy's expecting you. K.J's rapping in the freestyle showcase. It better be important for you to miss all the excitement."

I explained, "I haven't spent any time with Trina lately. I finally have a weekend off and she don't want me doing anything that doesn't include her."

"Guy, that's understandable, but this is Jam Fest. One weekend out of the year. When's the last time you spent a weekend with your wife?"

"The last time was Christmas when I had a week off from work."

"Christmas? That was three months ago! Guy, I work like a madman just like you, but making time with your woman is important. I deliver mail, deal drugs, work out at the gym, and make room for Savannah and my son. I knew that Jam Fest was approaching, so during the last few weeks, I treated her like a queen. Now, she knows that this weekend is all about what I want to do. You know what I'm sayin'?"

"I hear you."

I wished that Ajani had given me that advice six weeks ago. His lady Savannah was a good woman, and he treated her like royalty.

"So, I ain't telling you what to do, but you don't wanna miss Jam Fest this year. It should be off the chain, son!"

"True. I'll be ready at six-fifteen."

"Alright, then. Later."

We hung up. I threw my barely used cigarette outside. I wasn't looking forward to another argument at home.

CHAPTER 4

K.J.

It was so hard staying focused on cutting hair. I was two hours away from exiting Dark Fades Salon to the event called Jam Fest. I had spent so much time free styling and writing whenever I wasn't working or studying sociology and this was my season to shine at the Jam Fest Freestyle Showcase.

For the last two weeks, my fellow barbers and clients were giving me tons of encouragement. Not that I needed it, but it inspired me to get more prepared than ever. I felt like I was running for the mayor of Toronto.

Yo guy, is this the last cut I'm gonna get from you if you win this weekend?" asked the high school kid whom I was giving a cut.

"Trust me, I'll be back to work on Monday," I replied. "I have a big head on the stage, but I'll still be K.J from the block."

"Wow, guy. If you do that, you are good. If I won the showcase and a recording contract, I'd quit school and leave this SARS-infected city real quick."

Today's teenagers are something else. They think that rappers sign to a million dollar record deal, make a video, go on the TV show 106 & Park, and live happily ever after. I just shook my head and grinned.

As I tried to tell the boy about the importance of education and having power in the working world, the phone in the barbershop continuously rang. After the sixth ring, I stopped cutting.

"Clyde, you need a cordless phone in here," I said as I walked angrily to the phone at the desk. "'Cause you don't like walking over to answer it."

Clyde, who was a childhood friend and owner of the barbershop, just shrugged his shoulders and kept cutting hair.

I answered, "Dark Fades."

"How come y'all cats never answer the phone?" said Ajani.

"What else is new? When are you coming this way?"

"In about an hour, I gotta take care of some junk first."

"Cool. My stuff is here, so I'm ready to go."

"Seen, I'll be there soon."

"All right. Later."

As soon as I hung up the phone, Clyde walked towards me looking surprised and concerned at the same time.

"I meant to tell you about the call I got ten minutes ago, but I was busy," he said.

"What?" I asked. "Who called?"

"Bailey's coming for a cut in a half hour."

"Bailey?"

"Roderick Bailey, they call him Verbal Pain."

My eyes were ready to pop out of their sockets. I hadn't seen the guy since I jacked up his jaw seven months ago. I didn't know how to react because the news was unexpected.

I said, "He never comes here for a cut."

"Exactly," said Clyde. "So obviously he's coming for other reasons."

If Roderick wanted another beat down, I was ready to give it to him but I wasn't going to disrespect Clyde's place of business.

"Don't worry, Clyde. I won't let any crazy drama happen in here."

CHAPTER 5

Rancel Deverow's plan to kill Ajani Bethel was working out beautifully so far. He arrived at the Irie Club after completing sales in Scarborough and North York. While he delivered the OxyContin, Rancel spread the lie that Ajani and his cousin Machete Deverow agreed to go separate ways instead of working together. In addition, he also told clients that it was a positive break-up and Ajani's new business was an affiliate of Machete's. Rancel made a thousand business cards with Ajani's name, home address, and private cell phone number for every one of Machete's clients.

However, Rancel decided to tell Machete that Ajani started his own business and was trying to take away his clients. A few days earlier, he showed his cousin the business card. Machete took the news with difficulty because Ajani was like a little brother to him. When he started to doubt Ajani's actions, Rancel managed to convince him that he was telling the truth. Thursday was the day that Machete laid out the plan to take him out.

Rancel knew that his actions were ruthless, but he felt that it was well worth it. After all, Ajani was known as Machete's right-hand man after serving him for only three years. Rancel and Machete grew up together, from little boys getting in trouble in Kingston, Jamaica to starting a drug-dealing business from scratch that has turned into an empire.

He envied Ajani's youth, quickness, confidence and athleticism, but was fed up with him receiving special treatment. Many days he felt like killing Ajani, but Rancel was afraid of his plans backfiring. Thus, if the plan shifted to Machete wanting to kill him, Rancel would be off the hook. He was eager to hear his cousin's plan.

Machete felt betrayed. He sat behind his office desk looking and feeling stressed. People in the Scarborough neighborhood wanted him arrested or dead, but he did not care. Machete was hated by people of good moral his entire life. What he did care about were people he grew to love that ended up backstabbing him.

He remembered how eager Ajani was to make some money three years ago. He was twenty-three years old and Machete was thirty-three, so he knew that Ajani would have to be schooled in the art of drug dealing. With little experience, Ajani learned quickly and became fearless. Machete loved the fact that he knew martial arts and had great agility. Those attributes made Ajani more dependable than his cousin Rancel to get the jobs completed.

As he stared at the eight-by-ten picture of himself, Rancel and Ajani on the wall, Machete got more upset. He did not want to kill Ajani, but not taking him out would be dangerous.

Nobody's messing up the empire that I created, he thought. *Nobody.*

Rancel entered the office. Machete looked at his cousin and saw someone who appeared to be in a good mood. He knew that Rancel did not like Ajani. Machete also knew that Ajani was a greater asset to the business than Rancel, which created animosity. Thus, Machete really wanted to know if Rancel was telling the truth.

"So what's the deal with Ajah?" Rancel asked. "Is he on his way?"

"He's coming," replied Machete while watching CNN on the office's thirty-two inch flat screen.

"So what's the plan of attack? Will it be before or after his trip to Windsor?"

"During."

"Alright . . . what's the explanation? What are the—?"

"This crap you told me about Bethel is disturbing as hell, guy."

Rancel paused for a few seconds.

"Shoot, it should be, for the fact that he's been a massive asset for the business," he said. "But sometimes it's the most dependable that ends up being the biggest back stabber."

Machete looked directly at him.

"You know that I ain't afraid of anybody, and I won't hesitate to take a man out," he said. "Even though you're my cousin, I may kill you if I realize that you're lying about this. So, before I move on, I'm gonna ask you one more time: Are you B.S-ing about Ajani or are you telling the truth?"

Rancel walked closer to him and gave Machete a serious yet harsh expression.

"As much as I've been pissed about the fact that Ajah's had more favor in this firm than I, a man who you grew up with, I ain't lying about what I told you. Bethel is making plans to do his own thing and take what you started and break it down to pieces."

Both guys said nothing. Machete set his eyes back to the television.

A minute later, he said, "All right. Here's the plan . . ."

CHAPTER 6

AJANI

I didn't know who gave out my second cell phone number. I took it out of my briefcase under the back seat of my ride and the voice mail was full. What was even worse was the fact that all of the incoming calls displayed, "Private name, private number." I was so upset, I turned the phone off and tossed it towards the rear of the truck.

As I drove to the Irie Club, I tried to figure out who gave out the phone number. I carried two cell phones: all of my friends and family knew 416-555-2667, the number for cell phone one. Cell phone two was for drug operations only. Machete and Rancel were the only people that knew the number. Savannah, my girlfriend of four years didn't even know cell phone two existed. My guess was that player hater Rancel gave out my digits. After all, the man never liked me anyway.

It's frustrating when it takes all day to get in a good mood and have something as little as a cell phone turn the mood back to sour then add that to the fact that I took out money from my sacred savings account to cover Chester. I didn't have to do it, but I actually felt sorry for his daughter and I didn't want to make the drama any worse that what it already was. I just wanted to get the hell out of Toronto for a good three days without dealing with anything drug-related. Was that too much to ask?

I arrived at the Irie Club and my mouth started to water as soon as I stepped out of the SUV. The aroma of brown stew chicken escaped to the outside as I entered the back door that headed into the kitchen.

Rancel's wife Debra was cooking and I had been craving for the meat with rice and peas, coleslaw, plantain, and a Corona all day.

"Hello, beautiful," I said to Debra, who was preparing a plate of food. She looked like a caramel-skinned Angela Bassett.

"Hey, Ajah. How are you?" She asked.

"I'm good. That plate you're preparing is for me, right?"

"No," smiled Debra. "You want me to fix you one?"

"Yes, thank you, darling. Is Chete in the office?"

"Yes, him and Rancel."

"Seen."

I couldn't understand how a sweet woman like Debra ended up with a punk like Rancel. In my opinion, she deserved much better.

I stepped into the bar and restaurant and it was quiet. Just the way I enjoyed it. The Irie Club was only two years old and had a strong faithful clientele. Reggae music was always playing, and the four televisions were always on BET or international soccer during the daytime. Three of Machete's boys were playing dominoes in the dining area. When they saw me, they looked at me as if I was a modern-day Judas. They were expressions of anger, as if I betrayed someone. Why they stared at me like that was a mystery, and I didn't have time to find out the reason.

As I approached the office, which was located in the basement, Rancel was just leaving. He looked at me and nodded his head, but I didn't return the gesture. I hated his guts and I knew the feeling was mutual.

"Did you give out my number?" I snapped. "My freaking voice mail is full by some unidentified callers. I didn't want this number passed out, and I made that quite clear!"

"My bad, bred-drin," Rancel admitted, speaking in his usual low voice. "I couldn't remember the number to your other cell, so I gave it to one of your peoples who wanted to get in touch with you. I can't remember the man's name, though."

I knew the punk was lying. He knew who he gave my number to, and by the expression on his face, Rancel wasn't sorry that he did it.

I said, "Well, whoever it is, I ain't checking it. Actually, I'm changing the number on Monday. If you can't respect my privacy, I ain't telling or giving you jack. And nowadays, that's real easy for me to do."

Giving me a stern look, the rugged dude with long dreadlocks said, "Boy, you ain't nothing."

"Nobody knows that better than you. You ain't been nothing for the last three years."

I walked past him and entered the office.

The office looked stylish as usual with the black leather armchairs, sofa, flat-screen TV, mini-bar stand, and an eight-foot Jacuzzi twelve feet away from Machete's green marble desk. My boss was behind the desk staring at the TV and smoking a blunt.

There were some days that Machete looked pissed off and Thursday was one of those days. Two veins that were shaped like a V always showed off in the center of his forehead when he was mad. Looked like an angry, five foot two Mario Van Peebles.

"Did you get the money from Chester?" he asked as soon as he saw me walk towards the desk.

I took the envelope full of fifties out of my leather jacket and dropped it on the marble. Machete took out a fifty from the envelope, sniffed it, and put it under a fake money detector that rested on the far right side of the desk. He nodded his head.

"It's good," he said. "Cats oughta know by now that fake crap don't get past me. Did Chester put up a fight?"

"Of course," I replied. "But he surrendered to my demands and that's all that matters."

"Good. You're the man. Now I got another assignment for you."

Oh hell no, I thought. *Could I not have a weekend without criminal activity?*

"Chete, can't you give it to Rancel? This is a weekend I want to relax."

"This'll be easy, Bethel. And it pays double of the normal stuff you do."

He already had my attention. Machete pulled out a gold briefcase from behind the desk.

"I need you to take this case of OxyContin to Martinez," he said.

"In Detroit or Windsor?"

I wanted to know because I've never delivered drugs across the Windsor-Detroit tunnel. Went a number of times with Machete to Detroit to see Martinez, one of the city's biggest drug lords, but I spent most of the time observing. This would be a first time operation for me.

Machete answered, "You'll go over to Detroit. You need to be at the border between eleven thirty and eleven thirty-five tomorrow morning. Kwame Moss, the officer who always lets me bring drugs to the U.S, will be working one of the lanes."

"How do I know which lane is his?"

"You remember how I did it, right? I always went in the lane with the fastest flow of traffic. That's why you need to be there on time."

It sounded too easy.

"So that's it? Cross the border and give the case to Martinez?"

"That's it."

"But aren't you going to Detroit next week?"

"Yeah I am, but the Estafans want a case for the weekend before I take a trunk load on Tuesday."

He gave me the directions to the destination of Martinez and an envelope of cash.

"Here's a third of the money in advance," he said. "I know that you plan to gamble this weekend."

That was a definite yes in my plans for the weekend. Every time I went to Jam Fest, I spent a few hours at the city's mega casino. I loved to win at blackjack.

"You know money talks with everything I do," I said as I counted the bills. "I'll see you when I come back on Sunday night."

"You're a good man, Bethel," he said as he got out of his chair to shake my hand. "A lot of my success is because of fearless, determined, and honest cats like you."

I received the complement, but as I looked at Machete, he resembled a man who was ready to murder someone.

"Chete, you look pissed off."

He didn't respond. Instead, he walked to his bar counter and poured a glass of rum.

"Leave your cell phone on," said Machete. "Expect to hear from me tonight."

I didn't bother to tell him that I wanted nothing to do with my second cell phone. I just left the office, picked up my dinner from Debra, and headed home.

CHAPTER 7

EROS

I couldn't wait to finally drop Juanita at her work. She was a manager at a retail-clothing store and was running late due to our afternoon mattress recreation. I was speeding on the Don Valley Parkway in my 1996 Nissan Altima as if Juanita was ready to have a baby.

"Dang, guy!" She screamed. "I'm late, but you don't have to drive like a psycho! You're acting like you can't wait to get rid of me."

Juanita couldn't be any closer to the truth. I slowed down but still drove at a fast speed.

"I'm just trying to get you to work ASAP," I said. "Plus, I gotta get ready. Ajah's real anal when it comes to being on time."

"OK . . . So, Eros . . . if I was to go to Jam Fest, what do you think I'd like best about it?"

"The jams, baby! You're a music lover, so you'll be dancing all night long and the music's never whack."

"So that's why you're going, for the music?"

I could not believe that Juanita was bringing up the issue of trust again. This is a big reason why I hated relationships.

"Nita, there's no need to bring this up again. I already told you my reasons for going. Yes, there are some fine women at Jam Fest, and I will be looking at them but I don't wanna pick up any shallow club ho when I have a lady like you."

"Boy, you picked me up in the club, remember?"

"Of course, but you were a petite, sexy goddess in the midst of diva wannabes; A dime in the midst of nickels. You may have looked smaller, but you shined brighter and had twice the value of everybody else."

That complement shut her up for the rest of the drive. Juanita started blushing and gave a quiet giggle. She looked ready for another quickie, but obviously, that wasn't happening within the next seventy-two hours.

Five minutes later, we arrived at the mall. I gave Juanita a nice good-bye kiss.

"Have fun in New York," I said.

"I will," she replied. "Call me to let me know you got to Windsor safely."

"OK."

"Love you."

"Love you too."

I didn't drive away until she entered the store. Once Juanita was out of sight, I drove away and picked up my cell phone to make a long distance call.

"Hello?"

"W'zup, Whitney, its Eros."

"Hey. Nivea's in the kitchen cooking her booty off. She makin' baked salmon, wild rice, macaroni pie and acting as if Denzel Washington was coming over."

"Heh, heh, I'm close enough."

"Oh, is that so? You have any cute friends coming down with you?"

"You'll see when I get there tonight."

"Alright. Hold on, OK?"

I started singing the chorus of Ludicrous' *Area Codes* playing on Flow 93.5 FM while waiting for Nivea Davis to answer the phone.

"*'I got hoes, hoes, in every area code, area code . . .'*"

"Hey, Mr. Alexander."

"W'zup, baby? I heard you're working it in the kitchen."

Nivea laughed. "I'm just making some food for when you get here. Are you on your way?"

"Almost. I should be in Windsor by nine-thirty. Then we'll finally be face-to-face."

"Can't wait. I got a nice evening planned for us."

"Does it involve sleeping over?"

She laughed again. "You're coming over to sleep?"

I smiled. Nivea sounded like she was horny, and so was I.

"Nah. I don't even own pajamas."

"Alright, don't get me started too soon. Call me when you get in, OK?"

"Alright."

I hung up the phone, smiling as I thought about Nivea. She was sexy, chocolate-skinned, no taller than five foot five, and had one of the best ghetto booties I had ever seen. I met her in Toronto at a New Year's Eve party last December. Juanita went to her native country Puerto Rico for the Christmas holidays, and I went on a sex escapade. As a teacher's assistant at York University, I took the phone numbers of many gorgeous female students. From the first day of Christmas break to the day before New Year's Eve, I slept with two stunning Black women, a fine Italian who was a part-time cheerleader for the Toronto NBA team, and a Sri Lankan who paid her way through school as a stripper. My charm and personality opened the doors to their bedrooms and they really wanted A's in my marketing class.

Nivea was at a New Year's Eve house party in the city of Brampton. She looked so fine drinking her soberness away, and I wanted to start the New Year with sex. Thus, I spent three hours at the party trying to get to know her. I felt a sense of urgency to sleep with her because after New Year's Day, she was going back to school in Windsor, and I had no intentions of having a long-distance relationship.

Shortly after midnight, Nivea and I were already in a bedroom getting familiar with each other. She was hornier than I was, but she stopped me from undressing her. She told me that it was for feminine reasons. A very good lie for women not to have sex, but I actually believed her.

My consistent record of having one-night stands or sex on the first date was snapped. I really wanted to knock her boots, so we kept in touch over the phone for three months. Nivea was a sweet lady with an amazing personality. Yet, she would mean nothing to me after Jam Fest weekend . . . hopefully.

I took the 407 highway back to my apartment in Brampton. That was a rare move for me because it cost money to drive on it, but the road was clear, and I had little time to get ready. I couldn't wait to expand my sexual territory once again.

CHAPTER 8

Q

As I went up in the elevator to my apartment, I wondered how I was going to break the news of going to Windsor to my wife. It would be a miracle if an event suddenly came up and Katrina had to hang with her family or her girlfriends. I thought about telling her that I was a celebrity guest commentator for the Jam Fest Freestyle Showcase, but I would've mentioned it weeks ago and she would try to watch me on Much Music. Thus, I had no choice but to tell the truth. After all, marriage was about honesty and communication.

Before I opened my apartment door, I heard R. Kelly's "Bump n Grind" playing through the living room speakers. It was going to be tougher than I expected. I opened the door and the crib was candle-lit with rose petals all over the carpet. The atmosphere was definitely set for romance.

While I was taking off my shoes, I smelled the Angel perfume that I bought Katrina on Valentine's Day. She was standing about seven feet away me, and looked absolutely unbelievable. Katrina wore nothing but a thin strapless lavender bra that looked painted on her breasts and a matching thong. She had put in a brand new shoulder-length black weave earlier in the day. It complemented her Asian-like brown eyes and luscious big lips. I thanked God immediately for blessing me to marry a Black woman.

"Hey sexy," Katrina said softly as she slowly approached me.

I was already at full strength below and ready to have her for dessert, but I stayed cool.

"Hey," I responded.

Because I was almost seven inches taller than her, Katrina grabbed me by the shirt and pulled me down to kiss her. It was a warm and passionate kiss. I quickly picked her up and started walking to the living room.

"Ooooh," she smiled. "Looks like this outfit got you excited."

"Excited? All I can say is that I hope you're on the pill. If not, we're about to have triplets."

"If we do, we do. If we don't, we don't. Just take advantage of me, Big Q."

"With pleasure."

I laid her on the silver leather sofa before taking off my clothes. She took off her bra and I began the foreplay.

"Ohhh . . . that feels so good," she whispered.

"They taste wonderful," I replied.

"Did you miss this?"

"Oh yeah."

"I know you did. You've been working so hard lately. I was missing this so much."

"I know. I only work hard to make you happy, baby. I love you."

"I love you too."

"And now I'm about to make you real happy."

I began to do my specialty moves on her, which made her very excited. She enjoyed it so much she began to shake.

"Ohhhh . . . Damon . . . Victor . . . Quintino . . . you're really on point now!"

"Um hum."

"Are . . . you . . . ready to make some babies?"

"Uh hum."

"Are . . . you . . . ready to do this . . . all weekend long?"

I kept trying to please her because I couldn't speak. One of the hardest things I could ever do was lie to Katrina, even in the midst of foreplay. Unfortunately, she realized my silence and stopped shaking. That meant trouble.

"Oh, hell no," said my wife.

Her mood changed quicker than switching a TV channel. Katrina pushed me away from her.

"You're going to Jam Fest with the guys, huh?"

"Yeah," I answered.

She quickly got up from the sofa and walked towards the bedroom.

"Trina, wait . . ."

The door slammed and I heard it lock. I put on my boxers and walked to the door, trying to open it.

"Trina, let me in."

"WHY?"

"I want to see you when I talk to you."

"You should be used to not seeing me. You pretty much live at your workplace, remember?"

"Trina, let me in my bedroom!"

My wife swung the door open as if a harsh wind blew it. She wasted no time putting on a t-shirt and sweat pants. I had never seen her so angry.

She sat on our king-size bed and turned on the TV.

"You work seventy hours a week while I chill at home all day," snapped Katrina. "When you come home, you eat and fall asleep. When we make love, it's for two minutes. I let it go because I realize that you're a hard-working husband but damn Damon, what about me?"

"It's all about you, Trina, that's why I work so much, to make . . ."

"Cut the crap, Damon! You keep saying that you work so much to keep me happy, but that's crap. You work all the time to keep your mind off the fact that you're not playing in the NBA like you desired! Even worse, you've put on weight and started smoking. How pathetic!"

"Trina . . ."

"I'm not finished! Yes, I was looking forward to living rich, but you were injured *before* we got married, remember? I would've left you already if I was only into you for the money. Believe that! We've only been married nine months, and already we stopped going out on dates. When's the last time we went out to dinner or went to the movies? Where's the man that I fell in love with? I thought that this would be the weekend to rekindle the flames in our marriage but I was obviously wrong!"

Katrina had every reason to be upset with me. Ajani was so right. I should've taken another weekend off before Jam Fest. A romantic getaway or even just quality time at home would've eliminated this argument. Instead, I worked like a slave, and it only made my marriage worse. However, it was still Jam Fest weekend and the Phat Five was going to Windsor for the fourth straight year. I didn't want to be the first of the crew to break tradition.

"Trina, I have no excuse for the way I've neglected your needs lately. I am so sorry. You deserve so much better, and I will treat you better from now on. But baby . . . I booked this weekend for Jam Fest weeks ago. It's a tradition with the guys, Trina, you know that!"

As I spoke, Trina walked angrily towards the kitchen, pushing me out of her way. I followed her and shook my head as she slammed the fridge and cupboard doors while making a peanut butter and jelly sandwich.

"So now what, Jam Fest is more important than your wife?" she added. "Or are you afraid of reminding Eros that you're a married man and running after club hoes has been over for you since you met me?"

I knew that she would single out Eros. Katrina used to be cool with him until we were engaged. I made Eros the best man but he was upset that I surrendered to the monogamous penitentiary, as he called it. During the week of the wedding, Eros gave plenty of my former flings the home phone number. Of course, he didn't let them know that I was engaged and they left a lot of sexy messages on the voice mail. Katrina was pissed and demanded Eros to apologize. He did, but it wasn't enough for my wife to trust his actions again.

"Trina, Eros doesn't have jack to do with my decision. K.J's in the freestyle showcase and we're going to give him support. And we're staying at Teddy and Janet's apartment."

"Whatever. I don't care anymore."

Her response was quiet and cold.

I asked, "What you mean you don't care?"

"I don't care. You can do whatever the hell you want. As for me, I'm gonna party all weekend long . . . without you!"

She took her food, went back into the bedroom and slammed the door again. Frustrated and out of cigarettes, I went to the corner store to buy another pack of Virginia Slims.

CHAPTER 9

AJANI

I was so glad to arrive at my four-bedroom home in Richmond Hill. It wasn't because I lived in one of the nicest cities of the Greater Toronto Area, but my lady and son were waiting for me. They were the only things I loved more than money.

As soon as I parked the vehicle and walked into the house, A.J started walking towards me crying, wanting to be held, so I picked him up, wondering why he was looking so miserable.

"What's wrong, son?" I asked him softly.

A.J said, "I wanna watch videos."

Savannah walked into the hallway, looking tired and stressed. A.J obviously did something wrong.

She said to him, "Boy, didn't I tell you not to run to your daddy when I tell you that you can't do something?"

"What did he do?" I asked.

"I heard him say the word 'bitch' and I turned the TV off. That's why he's crying. I told A.J that the next time he says a bad word he would get punished."

I looked at my son, who I found to have difficulty punishing. He was a tough, handsome, and smart two-year old who looked just like me. Yet, I was determined not to spoil my children but give them tough love.

"A.J," I said, "those videos on BET are not for kids like you. They say bad words that you shouldn't say."

"But why, Daddy?" asked A.J.

"Because your mommy and I said so, now go and play with your toys."

I put him down and he slowly walked to the living room. While watching him play with his Sponge Bob Square Pants toy, I reached for Savannah and hugged her. She gave me a pretty smile.

"How was your day?" she asked me.

"Stressful, I'm glad work's over. But you look more tired than me, baby."

"I am, but its no big deal. A.J is just a busy boy. He's growing so quick, and his vocabulary is outstanding for his age. That's why your boys have to watch their language when they come over, he absorbs everything."

I kissed her on the cheek. To me, she looked like a young Phylicia Rashad with the size of Queen Latifah. I enjoyed watching Clair Huxtable on the *Cosby Show*, and when I first saw Savannah Shaw, it was an instant attraction. Hugging her everyday was more comfortable than air conditioning on a hot afternoon.

"Just relax for a little while, Vannah. I'll watch A.J a bit before I pack."

The phone rang and I picked up the cordless. It was Savannah's older sister so I gave her the phone.

I had never admired any woman as I did Savannah. She was a fifth-grade schoolteacher and was great with children. A.J could not have a greater mother. She was serious about being an excellent parent, a strong Black woman and pleasing her man. I truly believed that Savannah was my soul mate.

That's why it was a no-brainer for me to stop being a player. I was a nasty freak and slept with so many women, even Eros envied me. However, once I felt guilty for my actions, I actually told Savannah that I cheated on her. She took it really hard, but she eventually forgave me and gave me another chance. Thus, Savannah was the only woman in my life ever since, and I was ready to grow old with her.

Little did Savannah know that I had another big skeleton in my closet. She had no idea that I was a drug dealer. As far as she knew, I was just a hard worker and a good manager of money. To my advantage, Savannah grew up in a small Northern Ontario city where street life and crime were next to nil. Any other woman who grew up in Toronto might have figured me out by now.

When she questioned the home and the Escalade, I told her that I got the home with twenty percent down and super credit and that I wasn't paying tax or interest on the SUV, thanks to a great special offer from my job. The truth was that I was almost mortgage-free and I paid for the eighty-grand Escalade in cash.

I ran to A.J and began picking him up and throwing him in the air. We were having so much fun; I almost forgot that I had to get ready for my trip. Seeing A.J happy was my greatest stress reliever.

"A.J, guess what?" Savannah said, with excitement as she got off the phone. "We're going to Aunt Vanessa's house for the weekend!"

I joined in the fun, saying, "Alright! You get to play with your cousin Bobby!"

A.J jumped for joy. He loved going to his Aunt Vanessa's in Mississauga. Wish that I could say the same thing, but I couldn't take too much of Savannah's sister. She is a nice girl but she is a Christian who always talked about God and church. I shunned religion like it was SARS, but Savannah actually liked it.

"When are you going to your sister's?" I asked her.

"Tomorrow after work, I'll be there until Sunday," replied Savannah. "She wants me to go to a revival at her church to hear some prophet."

"Ooooh. Sounds like fun."

"Church really isn't that bad, Ajah. We need it more than ever with all the drugs and violence that's polluting Toronto."

I refused to comment on that issue. I took A.J with me to the bedroom as I packed my gear to go to Windsor.

Twenty minutes later, I put my sports bag in the SUV. Savannah and A.J followed me outside. I kissed my son on the cheek and my lady on the lips.

"I'll call you when I reach," I said to her.

"OK. Don't forget to bring me back some Victoria's Secret."

"Why?" I asked with sarcasm. "You have enough underwear."

"I want the scents and perfumes, guy. You know I can't get that stuff in Canada."

"Just playing. Anything for my Vannah. Love you."

"Love you too."

I drove away and headed towards Scarborough to pick up K.J.

CHAPTER 10

K.J.

Walking back to the barbershop after a ten-minute break, my heart was pounding rapidly. I honestly did not know how I was going to act if I saw Roderick. A part of me didn't want to talk to him. Part of me wanted to send him back to the hospital. None of me wanted to forgive him.

Roderick and I met in the ninth grade. Although he wasn't my best friend, we were pretty close because we had the same classes. Teddy and Ajani went to another school, and I didn't meet Q and Eros until high school. Hence, we hung out a lot. By the end of grade nine, we used our love for hip-hop and started a group called Phenomenal.

Before the group began, I started teaching Roderick how to write tight rhymes. He had great delivery but sucked at composing a verse. I rhymed very well but writing was my gift. Thus, until Roderick got better at writing verses, I played the role of ghostwriter for him and put together several tight songs.

Phenomenal was off the hook in the summer of 1995. Roderick had hook-ups with local producers, so our beats were nice. People loved my aggressive delivery and Roderick's smooth flow. We rocked the house parties, teen dances, and talent shows. Phenomenal was on its way towards something special.

The duo continued until the middle of our final high school year. Consistency was difficult because Roderick went to a different high school after moving from Scarborough to Brampton. In addition, he played basketball and I played football. Also, our parents insisted that we maintain good grades if Phenomenal was to continue.

We still received calls to perform, and the popularity was still steady. However, my mother Mavis Spencer-Brar was a strict single parent. She told me that my grades couldn't be lower than Bs and I got a C plus in Calculus. Mom forced me to quit the duo. I wanted to rebel, but I was scared of disobeying my militant mother. She believed that education was everything and anything not related to education was crap. Plus, her butt whooping was worse than losing a fight at school.

My mother was strict for good reasons. When I was three years old, my father Samuel Brar left us and moved back to Bombay, India. I barely remembered him being in my life. According to my mother, he was frustrated that he couldn't find success as a film director in Canada and wanted to pursue his dream in Bollywood. Mom said that there was no way in hell that the family was moving to India, because it was a huge cultural change and my father's family didn't approve of their marriage. Obviously, he chose his career over us. We have never heard from or seen him since. Thus, my mother had hatred for the entertainment industry, and I didn't want her to think that I was gonna be exactly like her ex-husband.

Roderick was upset, but I promised him that Phenomenal would continue after high school. Unfortunately, he couldn't wait for me, so he tried going the solo route. I gave him my blessings with no hard feelings.

Phenomenal never got back together, but Roderick and I stayed in touch. Things weren't going great for him as a soloist due to his weak writing skills, so he actually offered me eighty bucks for every song that I wrote for him. I was a broke college student at York University, so I gladly wrote him five songs. As for myself, I had moved on and concentrated only on my studies. That is until I met Bianca.

Bianca James was the female version of Teddy. She was a charismatic woman who lived for entertainment and the nightlife. I loved her beauty and the fact that she was in love with Phenomenal during our high school days. It was an instant attraction. She loved the hip-hop culture and her goal was to be a model for rap magazines and videos. She was shallow, but I was in love with her. We were together for over two years, and during that time, she encouraged me to re-pursue a career in hip-hop.

Because I loved Bianca and hip-hop, I started writing rhymes for myself and prepared to make a comeback. However, my time management was poor and because I was partying with her and the Phat Five frequently, my grades fell dramatically and I was on the verge of failing my sophomore year in sociology. Once again, I put my hip-hop dream on hold to get my grades back on track.

Meanwhile, Roderick no longer needed my rhymes and actually became a tight solo rapper. Bianca and I went to a few events where he performed, and were very impressed. It was harder to keep in touch with him, but he definitely stayed in my thoughts. Bianca talked about Roderick often and always wanted to know more about him and the days of Phenomenal. I shared everything with her, being very clueless of her intentions.

Roderick won the 2002 Jam Fest Freestyle Showcase. By then, his ego was gigantic. He had his own crew and took no time to acknowledge me when I wanted to congratulate him after his victory. I told Bianca what happened and she was disappointed. Not in Roderick for acting stuck-up, but in me because I didn't push hard enough to be as successful as my former partner was. That was the beginning of the end of our relationship.

She and I saw each other less, and when we got together, it was mostly sex and little conversation. I was still in love with her, but she became distant. Weeks later, rumors spread in Toronto's hip-hop community that Bianca and Roderick were an item. That led to the big fight at Club Oasis.

Of course, I broke up with Bianca and broke Roderick's jaw. With the both of them out of my life, I focused on my grades and they reached the vitamin As and Bs again, and I worked hard at my rhymes again. I was ready to win the 2003 Freestyle Showcase.

I walked into Dark Fades Salon, and the place was packed. Everybody started to look at me as if I was ready to create some drama. That made me upset.

"What's everybody looking at?" I snapped. "I ain't startin' nothing!"

Some guy was sitting in my barber chair and turned around to face me. It was Roderick. His crew was lounging in the sofas, prepared to back their guy if stuff went down. I told myself that I wasn't gonna hurt him, so I decided to give him a fade. I really wanted to know his intentions.

"K.J," he said with a grin. "What's going on, chief?"

Looked at Roderick but I said nothing. Instead, I grabbed my clippers and turned it on.

"What do you want?" I asked as I sprayed the gadget.

"Just touch-up the goatee and edges."

I proceeded.

"You know, K.J, I oughta thank you for breaking my jaw and delaying my debut album by three months."

"Hey, don't mention it. There's plenty of whoop-ass available if you want some more."

"Alright, I deserved that remark and what you did. I screwed Bianca and that was a foul move. But, if you didn't know, she approached me, wanting me to break her off."

Furious at his remark, I turned off the clippers and glared at him.

"Alright, Roderick, obviously you didn't come here to get a touch-up or just to tell me this crap. What do you want?"

He answered, "I heard that you were entering the showcase."

As I turned the clippers back on, I said, "I am. What's it to you?"

"Well, I entered that last year and got my breakthrough. I'm a recording artist now on a major label, something that Phenomenal always wanted to achieve. So now, I want to offer you an alternative."

Not interested, whatever the hell you're offering.

"Alternative?" I asked, wanting to know his plot.

"You don't need to enter the showcase. Pass it up and I'll offer you a guest appearance on my album."

What? If he offered this a year ago, I would be excited. But I don't trust this. He's up to something.

"I broke your jaw, you freaked my woman, and you want to reunite for a song?" I said. "This can't be your idea. If you had the look of sincerity, I'd believe you. But you look like you don't wanna do this."

Roderick looked at me through the mirror. He knew that I was telling the truth.

"You're right," he said. "This is the idea of Pacific Records, plus people want a Phenomenal reunion, despite what happened between us."

"Let me think about it for a bit . . . uh, no. OK?"

My voice rose higher than usual, but I didn't care. I was ready to expose him.

I added, "You may think that my decision is based on Bianca, but its more. We were a team that was tight like Krazy Glue. Yes, we went our separate ways, but I always rooted for your success. You on the other hand, acted as if your crap never stinks. I went to give you props after you won, but you played me off like I was a racist. This is what I got after I ghost wrote for you for years!"

People began to react in surprise. I'd never let the public know about Roderick's inability to write good songs. It was finally revealed, and I felt good saying it. However, he was furious because he was exposed. Roderick looked like he wanted to kill me.

"Why did you have to go there?" He asked. "I paid you to keep that confidential."

"That's usually an agreement between business partners or friends. I ain't your business partner, and I'm definitely not your friend."

I finished touching up his fade.

"That'll be five dollars," I concluded.

Roderick got up, slapped a five in my hand, and gave me a cold stare.

"Well, in that case, forget you, Kellan Jamal. I got an announcement to make."

He stood in the center of the barbershop and raised his hands to get everyone's attention.

"W'zup, y'all, I have an announcement to make," he yelled. "In this year's Jam Fest Freestyle Showcase, I will be aiming to repeat as the champion!"

I couldn't believe my ears, but I should've expected it. Roderick always loved drama, and as Verbal Pain, he was even worse. The crowd became ecstatic.

Clyde, who was one of my biggest supporters, said to Roderick, "You already got a record deal. Why compete again?"

"For bragging rights, guy," he replied. "I won't win nothing if I repeat, but no one's ever won or even attempted to win back-to-back. Until this weekend."

"You're dreaming, boy. K.J's taking the crown this year!"

All of the barbers and some customers began cheering for me. I stayed serious, but I loved the encouragement.

Roderick said to me, "Well, we'll see who the better rapper in Phenomenal is, if you even make the finals."

I replied, "Oh, I'll be there, and I hope it's against you. You'll wish you never entered the battle, especially when I destroy you on national TV!"

"Save the B.S for second place. See you in Windsor."

Roderick and his crew exited the building. I stayed cool while people couldn't stop talking about the upcoming event. Escaping to the washroom, I dreamed about defeating the ex-friend that I loved to hate.

CHAPTER 11

AJANI

I have never been someone who enjoys being noticed. I still had to get used to people staring at the Escalade and me. When I parked across the street from Dark Fades Salon in Scarborough, folks looked at my ride as if it was Jennifer Lopez. It felt good to be admired, but at the same time, I didn't want to stand out like a nun at a nudist beach. It was something that I had to get used to.

"Excuse me, dawg!"

As soon as I stepped out of my vehicle, somebody tried to get my attention. I turned around and saw a Filipino man who stood no taller than five foot six. He sported a brown leather jacket, short hair and a goatee. He didn't look familiar at all.

"W'zup, man, I'm looking for a guy named *Ah-jan-nee*."

He was looking at a business card when he said my name incorrectly. Everyone who knew me called me *Ah-ja-nigh*. In addition, the last person that said my name wrong was an undercover cop, so I was really suspicious.

"*Ah-jan-nee*?" I asked. "No, I don't know anybody by that name."

"Really?" he replied, sounding unconvinced. "Somebody told me that a dude name *Ah-jan-nee* drove a hot looking Escalade with Sprewell's . . ."

"Look, I'm not the cat you're looking for, aight?" I snapped as I walked towards the barbershop.

"Then what is your name?"

"Stephen, but that's none of your freaking business."

Stephen was my middle name.

The Filipino caught up to me as I made it across the street.

"My bad, man," he said. "I'm just looking for some G.H for the weekend, that's all."

G.H, or ghetto heroin, was the nickname for OxyContin after the drug got popular in the urban neighborhoods. I decided to tell him that he could go to Rancel Deverow for the stuff, and I gave him his cell phone number. It was the least I could do for someone who betrayed me by giving strangers my seven digits.

"That's spelled R-A-N-C-E-L." I added. "He always has his phone on."

"Alright, cool. Thanks, chief."

He gave me a pound and left. I went into the salon.

I had never seen Dark Fades so packed. People were chatting about some event that had just occurred, but I didn't pay too much attention. I was sure K.J would give me the raw details. I said hello to Clyde and a few other cats that were either clients or just friends from high school. K.J came out of the back room with a knapsack and a sports bag. He looked crazy eager to leave the area.

"Let's bounce, guy," he said after giving me the nod.

Outside the barbershop, I saw the Filipino again, who seemed to be staring at me while sitting in a parked Mercury Cougar. I had to ask K.J if he knew him.

"I've seen him a couple of times," K.J answered. "He came to the shop for a cut two days ago, but I don't know who he is. Why?"

I said, "He just looks suspect, that's all. So, what's with all the brethren in the shop? They weren't all there for a haircut!"

"Guy, you won't believe what just happened!"

We headed towards Eros' apartment in Brampton as K.J gave me full details about Verbal Pain's visit. Hearing about the crazy drama made me briefly forget about my daily adventure, which was what I needed for the time being.

CHAPTER 12

EROS

Sometimes I believed that God made me perfect, even though nobody else agreed with me. Maybe I believed it because I didn't care if my boys saw me as a strange cat. I loved being me, and everyone else in my opinion except my father was strange people.

K.J for example, came to my condominium to make sure that I was ready to go while Ajani waited in the SUV. As much as I loved my boys, K.J was the most annoying. Him and me were as different as a virgin and a prostitute, and rarely agreed on anything.

First, he complains that I wasn't totally ready to go. Then, K.J rants about the amount of luggage I was taking to Windsor. So what if I had a sports bag that was big enough to hold football equipment and a knapsack for only three nights? Pretty boys need to have more than enough of everything, so I pack well for whatever.

K.J was disgusted by the hundreds of XXX videos and DVDs he saw and called me sick. I thought that he was frustrated because he hadn't had sex since he and Bianca broke up. It wasn't my fault that my father was a famous adult video producer. He lived in Los Angeles most of the time and allowed me to stay in his condominium in Brampton, rent-free with unlimited access to porn. If a man couldn't enjoy that, I thought that he was too tense and conservative. Like K.J.

Ajani got on my nerves sometimes as well, especially when K.J and I heard him honking the car horn while I was getting ready. We looked out the balcony window and the dude was taking off. K.J yelled his name and Ajani stopped, cursing us out for taking so long. He was the most impatient person I ever met. Punctuality is good, but I hated rushing, unless I wanted to rush. Ignorant as that may seem, that was just me, Eros Alexander, Jr.

On the way to Q's crib, K.J told me about the drama that went down with him and Roderick at the barber shop. That got me geeked about the weekend even more. Then Ajani broke the news that Q was having complications with going to Jam Fest.

"What?" I exclaimed. "Didn't he book the time off?"

"He did," Ajani answered, "but it's his first weekend off in three months and Trina wants him to stay at home."

Immediately I started to get angry.

"See? That's what he gets for not listening to me last year. I told him not to get married."

K.J, who was in the passenger's seat, looked back at me.

"Guy, you still bugging about that? He's been married nine months now."

"So?" I continued. "She's messing with tradition! We've been going to Jam Fest for five years straight and none of us have missed a single event. See, that's why I hate freaking relationships, 'cause its all about commitment. I don't kiss anyone's booty."

"Oh, OK!" K.J yelled with sarcasm. "So what do you call your connection with Juanita?"

"Hot sex on a platter, buffet-style but I keep humping around, unlike Q. He's whipped like a disobedient slave. As for Ajah, I still think he's a player."

Once again, Ajani disagreed and said, "Told you already, guy, I'm done with that junk."

"Whatever, if you say so."

We arrived at Q's apartment. I thought Ajani was gonna act the fool and be impatient, but he needed to take a piss and so did K.J. I didn't want to go in, but I changed my mind because I was in the mood to tick off Katrina.

I thought that I would accept the fact that my best friend was married, but I was still bitter. Q and I were the dynamic duo of macking. As Canada's best college basketball player and the looks of a Backstreet Boy, girls were on him like flies to garbage. I really didn't need his help to get a woman, but when I was with Q, sleeping with them was ridiculously easy. However, the fun ended when Q met Katrina, and I still held a grudge until the present moment. Probably because I looked forward to Q making the NBA as a single man and meeting hot celebrities like Tyra Banks. My goal was to sleep with her before my life was over.

Q opened the door, and he looked upset. It was obvious that he had a fight with his wife.

"Come in," he said. "I'm almost ready."

I smiled, "So that means you're going."

"With a price to pay."

"Well, at least you're going, that's all that matters."

I walked towards the living room, not wanting to hear any details. I was just glad that Q didn't give into his wife.

While Ajani and K.J took turns using the washroom, Katrina came out of their bedroom. She said hi to Ajani and K.J, but she acted as if Q and I didn't exist. We talked very little as she made herself a protein shake in the kitchen. After completion, she came into the living room.

"Make sure that you leave your MasterCard for me before you leave," she said to her husband.

"OK," replied Q.

As she walked back into the bedroom, I gave her an ignorant look before turning to Q.

"Q, I thought you were a man!" I snapped. "How could you let a woman tell you what to do with your s . . . ? OW!"

K.J was sitting next to me, and he gave me a big slap on the back of my head. I was mad.

"What the hell, man?" I said to him.

"Lower your voice and mind your business, guy!" K.J snapped back. "Q ain't you, and thank God for that."

I sucked my teeth. I just wanted to leave already.

Ajani came out of the washroom and said, "Alright, let's bounce. Eros, you got the directions to get to Teddy's crib?"

"Directions?" I asked him. "I was supposed to have it?"

"Remember, guy? You said that you'd call him to get directions."

I completely forgot about Wednesday's conversation.

"Can't we just call him when we get to Windsor?"

"What if he isn't home?" asked K.J.

"Where else would he be? And why don't you have directions? You're his cousin. When's the last time you talked to him?"

"Three weeks ago. I left him a message a week ago, but he never called me back. He ain't even returned my e-mails."

What K.J said was news to me. He and Teddy always communicated, more than the rest of us did. Now we didn't know our accommodation status.

Q said, "Call him from our phone so we can know what's up before we leave."

I nodded and grabbed the Quintino cordless phone. K.J could've easily called him, but I wanted to talk to Ted. Presently, he seemed like the coolest Phat Fiver other than me. Teddy was the ultimate party animal who was all about getting high, tipsy, and enjoying the nightlife.

"What's the number?" I asked K.J.

"519-555-2894," he replied as I dialed.

CHAPTER 13

TEDDY

If anybody would've told me a month ago that I would be in a church on the eve of Jam Fest weekend, I would've laughed. Yet, it was Thursday evening, and instead of going to the beer store to buy forties, I was watching my girlfriend Janet's praise dance rehearsal at Kingdom Workers Fellowship a church in downtown Windsor. Who would've thought that I would become a born-again Christian?

I sat in the front row in the sanctuary, reminiscing about how I arrived at this stage in my life. God really worked in a mysterious way. I intended to be a staff member of Canada's biggest college party weekend. That was my reason for moving to Windsor, that and being closer to Janet. If it weren't for Janet, I wouldn't have changed spiritually.

She and I were living together while attending Windsor University. We were also quite involved with the social scene because we both were club fanatics. I became the assistant promotions director for the Jam Fest committee and Janet was the president of Swerve, the university's off-the-hook hip-hop dance club. Thus, we kept busy studying, going to class, working, partying, and being intimate with each other. During the weekends, I had a part-time job at an auto factory that paid very good money. As long as I had the time and money to party, I was happy.

Things began to change at the beginning of 2003. It was the start of the second semester, which meant attending new classes. While Janet was taking anthropology, she met a classmate named Kaitlyn Fuentes. She was a zealous Christian woman who invited my girlfriend to a Sunday morning service. A brand new Janet Watters came back from church that day.

Physically, Janet looked the same when she walked in the apartment. The same dark skin, jet-black hair, big eyes, juicy lips, and incredible body didn't change, but her overall presence was different. It was as if she got humbled from her proud mentality. With tears of joy, she hugged me and told me that she gave her life to Christ.

I hugged her back as if I was happy for her, but I wondered if Janet was only going through a phase. I was so far from the truth. Within a month of being saved, Janet stopped going to clubs and resigned from Swerve. Her resignation shocked everyone because dancing was her passion. I tried to talk her out of it, but she was serious about her decision. Instead of dancing and clubbing as a pastime, Janet went with Kaitlyn to Tuesday cell meetings, Friday youth nights, and Sunday morning and evening services.

Janet also gave up something that greatly pissed me off, which was sex. We made love twice after she was saved, but afterwards she would start crying, demanding that we shouldn't have sex until marriage. As a result, we stopped sleeping in the same bed. The longer the sex drought, the more I resented her walk with God.

To be rebellious, I partied harder than ever. I drank a lot on Saturday nights so that when Janet invited me to go to church on Sunday, the hangover was my excuse so I didn't have to go with her. Of course, that hindered our relationship. Janet threatened to leave me, saying that she would rather be single than date a man who didn't serve God. At first, I didn't believe her, but I thought of what she already gave up for God. She loved dancing just as much as she loved me. I became nervous because I loved my Jan-Jan. We dated for five years, and I wasn't ready to throw in the towel.

It wasn't until the end of February when I decided to go to church with her and that Sunday was the first day of the rest of my life. I heard a powerful salvation sermon by Pastor Harvey Jackson of Kingdom Workers Fellowship. It seemed as if Janet told him our business, because it felt as if the pastor was speaking directly to me. Pastor Jackson spoke about people who do things excessively to fill a void of emptiness in their lives, yet they were not happy. I was one of those people. As much as I partied, I always wanted more out of clubs and jams, yet I didn't know what it was. The *word* helped me realize that I needed Christ for complete joy. I gave my life to the Lord after the sermon.

Apparently, Janet, Kaitlyn, and Minister Tyrone Carter, who was also called Min-T, were praying for my salvation and it worked. I stopped going to clubs, smoking weed, and drinking. I didn't resign from the Jam Fest committee, but I stopped going to the meetings. It wasn't easy, but my baby was a great encouragement, as well as Min-T, who was also Kingdom Workers Fellowship's youth leader. I went from being hyped for Jam Fest to getting prayed up for the first annual Bless Fest weekend.

Bless Fest was the new nemesis of Jam Fest. It's goal was to have a spiritual alternative to Jam Fest on the same weekend. I was going to be a part of history, and I felt excited. There was going to be a talent/fashion show, a mega concert featuring popular gospel artists and a youth Sunday afternoon service. Pastor Jackson welcomed the idea of Janet starting a gospel dance group for Bless Fest, which was great news for her. She was willing to give up dancing and yours truly for God, and He blessed her by saving me and opening the doors for a dance ministry.

Everything seemed all right except that I felt like I punked out on my four best friends. Since I was saved, I hadn't spoken to K.J, Ajani, Q, or Eros. K.J left me a voice mail a week ago, but I didn't return it. I wouldn't answer his e-mails. It was the longest time span ever from communicating with my cousin or the Phat Five. I just didn't know how to break the news that I was born-again with no intentions of attending Jam Fest.

I hoped that if I didn't call them, they wouldn't try to come to Windsor, but what was I thinking? Jam Fest was our biggest tradition. They would travel through a blizzard to reach the event. A part of me missed hanging out with them and another part told me to avoid them in order to resist temptations.

I prayed, "Lord, if it be your will, let my friends make different plans this weekend. I know that I promised them that they could stay at the apartment, but that was before you changed my life around. I know that you're a way-maker, and if you do this, I'll be extremely grateful. In Jesus' name, Amen."

As soon as I started to feel good about my prayer, my cell phone started vibrating. I looked at the caller ID:

Q
905-555-6113

I refused to answer it, hoping that Q wouldn't leave a message or not call back. *God is going to answer my prayer! I can feel it!*

Fat chance. I felt a short vibration a minute later, which meant that he left a message.

> "Yo, what up T-Henny, it's Eros. Where you at, guy? We're about to head to Windsor, but we don't know where the heck you live. Call me on my cell, 416-555-1818. I was gonna turn it off, but I'll leave it on for you to call. Call as soon as you hear this, guy! Out!"

I erased the message. God didn't answer my prayer.

CHAPTER 14

EROS

"Got Ted's voice mail, there's no use waiting for him to call back," I told the guys.

It was odd that none of us were able to get in touch with Teddy. K.J called his home number, and there was no answer there as well.

"This is unlike my cuz," K.J said. "I hope everything's cool."

Ajani replied, "Well, the only way to find out is to head to Windsor. Hopefully he'll call on the way there."

Q grabbed his sports bag and we headed through the door to leave. As we walked down the hallway towards the elevator, I had the sudden urge to release.

"Yo, Q, give me your keys, I gotta pee," I said.

"Guy, what's wrong with you?" asked Q, looking at me as if I was stupid. "Why wait until I lock up to use the toilet?"

"Just gimme the keys, man. I'll meet y'all outside."

As I walked back to the apartment, Q yelled, "Eros, I left my cell on the kitchen counter. Bring it with you."

"Aight."

I used the washroom as quick as possible in order to avoid contact with Katrina and almost left the crib without grabbing Q's phone. Walking back to the kitchen, I saw two cell phones on the counter. One was silver and the other was blue. I had no idea which phone belonged to Q. Choosing not to ask his grumpy wife, who was watching TV in the bedroom, I grabbed the silver phone and bounced.

Twenty minutes later, we were well on our way to Windsor. Again, we talked about Verbal Pain and reminisced about last year's fight at Club Oasis.

K.J busted with laughter, saying, "Ted was the funniest fighter I'd ever seen in my life. The boy thought he was Jet Li that night!"

Everybody started to laugh.

Ajani added, "Yeah, but he looked more like Jackie Chan on crack. Yet, he still dropped some licks."

"For real? Man, he's gonna trip when I tell him that Roderick's in the showcase. But then again, he probably knows that already."

My cell started ringing. I noticed a 519 area code.

"Speak of the rude boy!" I exclaimed as I answered. "We just finished talking about your crazy self."

"What up, Eros?"

"What up? What the heck's up with you, Ted? Sell us out and can't call nobody?"

He laughed. "Sorry, man, I've been making some changes and adjustments with stuff recently. I didn't forget about y'all coming down though."

"I'm glad you didn't, 'cause we're about to get stupid this weekend! You got the V.I.P passes, right?"

"I'm working something out."

"I hope that's a yes. Anyway, what's your address?"

"You know where Ouellette Avenue is, right?"

"Who doesn't know Ouellette? That's downtown."

"1410 Ouellette, apartment 604. We live across the street from 7-Eleven."

"Alright, I'll remember that. You wanna chat with any of the crew?"

"Nah, I'll talk to them when y'all get here, 'cause I'm busy right now. When are y'all getting here?"

"About nine-thirty if the traffic stays flowing."

"Alright. Holla."

"Late."

I hung up. K.J looked at me with his usual expression of frustration.

"Why you hang up already?" he snapped. "I wanted to ask him why he can't return messages."

"Relax, he had to bounce," I said. "Said he was busy. Y'know I can understand T-Henny being too busy to chat. He is on the committee of the country's biggest party. He must be making sure stuff is real tight for the weekend."

CHAPTER 15

TEDDY

I didn't feel any better after talking to Eros. Homey still expected me to hook the fellas up with V.I.P passes for Jam Fest. Normally I kept a promise, but that one was unlikely. I scratched my Afro. Stress was creeping, which Janet easily noticed as she walked towards me.

"Uh oh," she said while wiping her forehead with a rag after sweating during dance rehearsal. "Bear's scratching the afro. What's wrong, baby?"

Bear was Janet's nickname for me while everyone else called me Teddy, Ted, or T-Henny. I smiled at her.

"They're on their way, and they're staying at our place."

She knew exactly whom I was talking about. "You okay with that?"

"Of course," I lied. "Why wouldn't I be?"

Janet looked at me as if I stole money.

"Because Bear, you're a different person now. The guys are coming for Jam Fest and you're involved with Bless Fest. You know how they get down."

"That doesn't mean that I'll give in to what they wanna do."

"Do they know yet?"

"What, about my salvation? No . . . I haven't told them yet."

Min-T and Kaitlyn approached Janet and I. I didn't want to talk about the issue around them, but Janet didn't mind.

"Well, you can't keep it a secret," she said. "They'll notice a change in you."

"Janet, I know that. I'll tell them when they get here, OK?"

"What's going on?" Kaitlyn asked us.

Janet answered, "Teddy's friends are coming down from Toronto for the weekend."

"Cool. Are you bringing them to Bless Fest?"

With a sarcastic chuckle, I replied, "My boys don't know a thing about Bless Fest."

"Oh. Well, hopefully they'll follow you to this event after they hear how awesome it's going to be."

If only she knew the Phat Five. The only way they would step in a church is if I paid them in advance.

"Well, Kaitlyn, it'll be a miracle if they even consider it," I replied.

"Well, Ted," Min-T said, "that's a challenge that you'll have to face. You know, I never told you this, but on the day you were saved, I heard the Holy Spirit saying to me that you will have a strong evangelistic spirit. This weekend might be confirmation."

They all smiled at me. I didn't know what to do or say except give a little smile in return. That was the first prophetic message ever given to me about evangelism. It felt strange to me because I had thoughts about it, but my focus was on reaching out to children or family members. I never thought about the Phat Five.

"We'll just have to wait and see, I guess," I told him with a lack of confidence in my statement.

"We are going to touch and agree that God will use you to reach out to your friends this weekend."

"Amen," Janet and Kaitlyn agreed.

I nodded and smiled. I wasn't fully convinced, but perhaps something great would happen. Only God knew what was in store. My greatest concern was whether I could resist smoking a blunt, drinking a forty, or setting foot in a nightclub with the Phat Five in my midst.

CHAPTER 16

Ike Trencio parked his car in front of The Irie Club, where Rancel told him to meet when they spoke on the phone earlier. He got out of his brand new Mercury Cougar and walked into the facility.

So far, things were going well for the undercover narcotic cop. The Jamaican, who Ike strongly believed was the drug dealer Ajani, gave him the information of Rancel Deverow, cousin of drug lord Michael "Machete" Deverow. He made arrangements for getting a case of Ghetto Heroin and Ike only hoped that he was getting closer to taking down the crew that was destroying the streets of Toronto.

He walked towards the bar counter and saw a man who looked like an older version of actor Omar Epps with dreads and smoking a cigarette.

"Rancel?" He asked as the man looked back and nodded his head. "Rex Marcos."

Rancel shook his hand and smiled. "The brother of the late Luke Marcos, have a seat."

Ike and the Toronto police department were well prepared for the case. Luke Marcos was a drug lord who controlled the streets of Vancouver in the early nineties. He had an incarcerated brother named Rex who resembled Ike's appearance. The department retrieved all the information needed to make the identity highly effective.

"So I heard that you're the man with the connections for some G.H," said Ike.

"I got the hook-up, but first I need to know some stuff about you," Rancel replied. "First of all, how long have you been out?"

"Almost two years. Served a solid decade and was released for good behavior."

"I see. So how did you end up living in Toronto?"

"I needed a change, plus I got link-ups to an accounting firm through a relative. I've been a white-collar accountant in downtown Toronto making the honest paycheck, know what I'm sayin'?"

"Sounds like a decent life. So what can I do for you?"

"I don't make the good cash like I used to make with my brother, so I'm looking to deal what's hot now, which is G.H."

Ike looked at Rancel's expressions. It was hard to tell if he was buying his story. Rancel kept looking serious.

"So you're not just wanting the pills for yourself," said Rancel. "You wanna be an affiliate."

"No doubt," said Ike. "I have connections to a large number of accountants as well as the Filipino community."

"I see. What I'll do is let Machete know about this and arrange a meeting."

"Good. How soon can this happen?"

"Tomorrow morning. He's putting together a pancake breakfast for the community of Scarborough at the London Community Center."

Hilarious, thought Ike. *A drug-lord who's concerned about the community.*

Rancel concluded, "I'll call you tonight with the details."

They both got up from their seats and Ike gave him a business card with Rex's fake information.

"Sounds good," said Ike as he shook his hand and left the club.

CHAPTER 17

TEDDY

After the dance rehearsal and helping Min-T set up the sanctuary for Bless Fest, Janet and I arrived at our apartment. Immediately I started cleaning up, as I prepared myself for the best and the worst. The best was that the Phat Five were on their way. They were the greatest quad of friends I ever had. The worst was totally unpredictable. I had no idea how they were going to react to my new direction.

Janet was packing clothes for the weekend. She agreed to stay at Kaitlyn's until Sunday, but it was actually a pre-permanent move. At the end of March, she was officially going to become Kaitlyn's roommate. Janet believed that the best way for us not to have sex was to live in separate addresses. I didn't like the decision, but it made good sense.

"OK, I think I have everything," Janet said as she came out of the bedroom with a suit bag, suitcase, and a cosmetics kit.

"You think?" I replied with sarcasm. "Looks like you're moving out already. Need some help?"

"What do you think? Come down with me, Kate's already waiting downstairs."

Grabbing the suitcase and suit bag, we took the elevator to the ground level. Before she left, I gave her a goodnight kiss.

Janet said, "Don't forget what I told you. I'm still living in the apartment until the end of the month."

"I know," I concurred. "The crib will be the same way that you left it."

In other words, if the fellas wanted to drink or smoke, they had to do serious clean up afterward or find another setting to do it. The latter seemed like the best solution.

While I swept and mopped the kitchen floor, I played my new favorite CD. Min-T made me a mixed CD of different Gospel R & B, Hip-Hop, and Reggae artists. I wasn't fully used to the praise and worship at Kingdom Workers Fellowship and being a strong listener of FM 98, Detroit's Hip-Hop/R & B station, the CD was exactly what I needed.

Listening to the Cross Movement, Tonex, Papa San and many other gospel artists kept my head nodding and mind focused on God. Every time I played the CD, I thanked him for Min-T. To me, he was the perfect example of a Christian young man, and his words of wisdom kept me pursuing for righteousness.

It didn't take me too long to finish cleaning. It was eight forty-five, forty-five minutes before I expected them to arrive. I went to the living room, dropped myself on the sofa, and fell asleep watching a stupid episode of *Scrubs*.

The sound of my phone woke me. It was indicating that someone wanted to get into the apartment. I answered it and immediately pressed six, which opened the ground lobby entrance. I didn't expect anyone other than my boys, so I knew they were on their way up.

Two minutes later, the Phat Five reunited. I hugged them all like I just won ten thousand dollars. Wasting no time, we put their bags in the living room and we headed to Rude Boy's, Windsor's best West Indian restaurant and the official restaurant of Jam Fest.

The place was packed with college students, but it didn't take long for us to get a table. All of us were energetic and ready to talk some smack. Right away, I complemented Ajani on his new SUV. It was the best vehicle I'd ever set foot in.

Ajani smiled. "You should've been in the ride on the 401. It was so smooth; the drive didn't even feel like three hours."

That was all he said about his Escalade. Ajani wasn't a bragger and always made sure his actions were louder than his words.

We all ordered beverages. Surprisingly, nobody questioned the fact that I ordered a Sprite while they all ordered a beer. I thought that would be the gateway to proclaiming my faith, but it wasn't. Next, we all ordered a dinner except for Eros. I had to ask him why.

"Why spend nine dollars and ninety-five cents on food when there's a baked salmon dinner waiting for me as I speak?" Eros grinned.

I asked, "Who's the special woman now?"

"Nivea Davis. You've seen her before. She's on her way to pick me up."

"Is that the girl from the New Year's Eve party?"

"Yep."

"You're actually still with her after a week?"

"I didn't hit it yet. I will this weekend, and then she's history."

Eros was still Eros, the proud son of a porn movie producer.

K.J shook his head. "If God only gave us a limited supply of sperm, Eros would've been dry a long time ago."

"Yeah, well we're not made that way," Eros, replied. "Lots of sex eases the mind. That's why you're so tense, 'cause you're not getting any."

"Oh yeah, that's in your book Life According to Eros Alexander, Jr., I remember that page because I used it for toilet paper."

Ajani and Q almost spit out their drinks because of laughter. I just smiled and shook my head. Nobody could diss each other like K.J and Eros.

Eros sucked his teeth. "Whatever. You're a funny guy."

"Guy!" I said to K.J, deciding to change the subject. "You shocked me when you said Roderick's going in the showcase again!"

K.J said, "I thought you'd know before me. You are on the committee, right?"

Technically yes. I quit, but I never officially resigned.

"Yeah, but I missed the last few meetings. Plus, I worked with promotions more than putting the showcase together."

"Well, I'm just glad that you hooked me up with the right cats to get in the tournament. I owe you, cuz."

"It was nothing, man. At least you got your demo in before the January deadline."

And before I got saved.

"I wasn't gonna miss that due date for submissions," K.J grinned. "My hard work is gonna pay off. It's gonna feel so good to beat Verbal Pain on national TV."

Ajani added, "And it's going to feel good seeing it live in the club as well. But I did ask Savannah to set the VCR and record it."

I asked Ajani, "Speaking of, how is Vannah and A.J?"

He smiled. "Vannah's great, man. A.J's growing up real fast. Ted, my son's so smart . . . you need to see him."

"Yeah, I do. I miss my godson. How does Vannah like the Escalade?"

"She loves it, especially now that she can drive my Dodge Durango all the time instead of her old Toyota Corolla."

"She didn't question how you paid for it?"

I was getting nosy, but I didn't care because I felt that Ajani, Savannah, and A.J were family.

Ajani answered, "Vannah did at first, but I told her that it was a great employee discount special. Plus, she knows that I'm a good saver."

I wanted to know how long he thought he could keep his drug dealing a secret before quitting, being arrested, or killed, God forbid. Thankfully, the arrival of the dinners interrupted the discussion. I was mad hungry and anxious to eat my ox-tail, rice and peas, stir-fry, and festival.

Eros gave us an envious look as we enjoyed our food. While we were eating and talking smack, all he did was sip his beer and look at his watch.

"Yo, where this girl at? Being horny and hungry at the same time's not a good combination?"

"Serves you right for ditching your boys on the first night," I said, although I wasn't surprised because Eros was just being Eros.

"I just wanna do Nivea and move on. I'll be with y'all in the morning anyway when we go to Detroit."

Somebody's cell phone started ringing, which sounded loud and very annoying.

After a few seconds, K.J yelled, "Answer your pimp phone, Eros! That ring is bugging."

"That's not my phone," denied Eros. "I turned it off after I called Juanita to tell her I arrived in Windsor."

"But it's coming from your jacket."

"Oh, snap!" shouted Q with his mouth full. "I forgot I asked you to bring my phone, but that doesn't sound like my . . . man, pass me the phone!"

Eros grabbed the silver phone out of his jacket and gave it to Q.

"Man, hurry up and answer it," he said. "It sounds like its sick."

"You crack head! You took Trina's phone instead of mine! Now she's calling to see where it is!"

"Guy, you never told me your phone was blue!"

K.J snapped, "Just answer the stinking phone, yo!"

Q answered it. "Hello? . . . No, no, I asked Eros to grab my phone and he took yours by accident . . . I'm sorry, that's my bad . . . I could've called you when I reached to let you know I got here safe, but I thought you didn't wanna talk to me . . . Well if you didn't wanna talk to me then why should I call?"

Obviously, Q and Katrina were arguing. I tried to tune out, but it was tough with him sitting across from me.

He continued, "I'm not at the club, I'm in a restaurant with the guys . . . You're going to the club tonight? Good for you! Have fun! I don't care if you find a nice man. Tell him your husband says hi!"

When Q said that, all four of us were looking at him with curiosity.

"You think that I'm at Jam Fest to meet other girls, so I think that you're clubbing to meet men," Q added. "If it's for spite, go ahead and do your thing . . . Bye!"

He hung up the phone and saw that we were all staring at him.

Eros asked, "You told Trina that it's OK to see to talk to other men?"

Q sucked his teeth. "I didn't mean it. She pissed me off 'cause she wants to be spiteful because I came here for Jam Fest."

I asked, "What's going on?"

Ajani answered, "Trina's mad 'cause Q decided to come to Jam Fest instead of spending a weekend with her."

"Q, when's the last time you and Trina spent a weekend together?"

"It's been a while," Q said softly.

"Now you made things worse, telling her she can see other men," K.J said.

Q looked at K.J. "So what?"

Eros raised his hand like a student eager to answer a teacher.

"Ooh, ooh, ooh!" he yelled. "K.J, lemme answer this! Q, first of all, if your woman says to go ahead and see other girls, we go against their request just to prove them wrong."

We all stared at Eros with confusion.

"Well," he continued, "I'll do it anyway. But if we tell our women to see other men, trust me Q, they'll do it just to piss you off!"

Q said, "But I was . . ."

"Hold on, I'm not done. Secondly, although you are Damon Quintino, national sport celebrity, you are still a White man."

"Italian."

"Italian, White, whatever. You're still pale-skinned. You married a fine-looking Black woman. You made many Black men real jealous."

I nodded. "Trina's good-looking for real."

Eros concluded, "Black men would love to make your wife regret marrying a White man."

Q said, "Italian."

"Whatever."

K.J said, "Wow. For once, I actually agree with Eros. You better hope for the best, Q."

Q picked up his wife's phone. "Maybe I should call her back and apologize."

Eros exclaimed, "Forget that! The damage is done. She's made up her mind to meet with the opposite sex, so you need to do the same."

I said, "Oh, Lord. Eros, you're something else."

"What?"

K.J shook his head. "I knew that you couldn't make sense for very long."

Q snapped, "For real! What the hell kind of advice is . . ."

"Yo, yo, yo, yo, yo!" Ajani yelled. "What is this? I know that none of us came to Jam Fest to deal with crazy drama. At least I didn't! Q, wait until you're away from us to handle the situation. None of us has been married before, especially Eros. On the real though, all we should be doing this weekend is hanging out and partying. Y'all feel me?"

I said nothing. K.J and Q continued eating. Eros sipped and beer and looked at his watch again.

"Shoot, where this girl at?" said Eros. "I'm about to order some food if she don't hurry up. Anyways . . . T-Henny, you hooked us up with the V.I.P passes, right?"

Right then I felt nervous, knowing that it was my time to confess my faith. Caught up in the moment I almost forgot my intentions.

If I'm changed for the better, why am I feeling fear? I thought. *Teddy, do it now while the time's good.*

"Man," I said, "I would have the passes, but I quit the committee three weeks ago."

Everyone looked at me like I told them I was a woman.

"Shut up," Eros grinned.

"I'm serious."

K.J said, "But I thought being on the committee was the reason you came to Windsor."

"I know," I agreed.

Ajani asked, "So why did you quit?"

"I got saved," I said.

Q asked, "From what?"

"I became a Christian."

It was Eros' turn to spit out beer in laughter.

"Yo, Ted, that was good," he chuckled. "I almost believed you."

"Believe it, Eros."

K.J looked directly into my eyes. "He's telling the truth. There's no vein in his forehead, which is usually an automatic giveaway that he's lying."

Q asked, "When did this happen?"

"About three weeks ago," I said. "Six weeks after Jan-Jan did it."

Ajani said in shock, "Janet did it too? That's serious."

Eros shook his head. "It figures. It takes a woman to encourage a man to do that."

I glared at him. "That's ignorant, guy!"

"Guy, I'm just shocked! Nobody parties and goes clubbing more than you."

Q said, "For real! You still go to clubs?"

"No, and it hasn't been that bad," I replied. "I realized that I partied plenty because I felt empty, but God filled that void in my life and I feel really good. Really good."

I was happy that it was out in the open. Now I had to deal with the consequences.

Ajani asked, "So what else have you given up?"

"Drinking," I said, holding up my Sprite as evidence. "Weed too. Going to church a lot helps me forget about them also. Speaking of church, the one I attend is holding a huge event called Bless Fest, which is the gospel version of Jam Fest. Y'all should check it out."

"Sorry. I don't do church."

"I go to church three times a year," Q said. "Christmas, Easter, and the annual BBQ at a Church Of God In Christ church in Mississauga. Best chicken and ribs on the planet."

"Bred-drin," K.J said to me, "I admire your decision and act of consciousness. Nuff respect."

My cousin gave me a pound. His words made me feel good.

Then he asked, "So, does this mean that you're not gonna watch me in the showcase?"

Before I could answer, Eros stepped in. "He'll be there. I guarantee it."

I glared at him again. "So what make you think that, Alexander?"

"Can you honestly tell me that you don't miss clubbing?"

"I don't miss it."

"You're lying. Christians shouldn't lie."

"Nobody should lie."

"That's not the point. The point is that during the short three weeks that you've been saved, Jam Fest wasn't around. It's here now. Temptations, brah."

I liked and disliked Eros at the same time. He could be a pessimist and devil's advocate, yet he would make me think of issues that I sometimes overlook. Honestly, I didn't think about whether or not Jam Fest was still in my blood.

"I got faith that I won't give into Jam Fest weekend."

"And I have faith that in twenty-four hours, you'll be partying with us in the club. I still think that you'll hook us up with the V.I.P passes as well."

Q asked Eros, "Is that your girl coming towards us?"

We turned around and saw two pretty ladies in jogging suits. The short dark-skinned girl with a solid body was Nivea Davis. Her friend was someone I recognized on campus, but I didn't know her. She resembled a dark-skinned version of the late singer Aaliyah.

After Eros got his hug on with Nivea, he introduced us to her and her roommate Whitney.

"Hey," Nivea said shyly as we waved at them both.

Whitney said hello but it seemed as if her eyes were fixed on Q. Q seemed to be clueless to her observations.

"Ajah, I need my stuff from your trunk," said Eros.

Ajani pulled out his keys and pressed a button. "Lift gate's open."

I started at his keys, amazed at what he pulled off.

"Works from two hundred feet," he confirmed.

Eros said, "Cool. I'm out. See y'all cats tomorrow."

Ajani said, "I'm leaving at eleven sharp, with or without you."

"Got it."

When Eros and the ladies left the restaurant, I turned to Q. "Guy, that girl's eyes were all over you. You notice?"

He seemed uninspired. "Really? So what, you want me to take Eros' advice?"

"Of course not, I just wanted to know if you were aware of her, that's all."

"Hey, if I wasn't married, that'd be a good thing. K.J's the only cat without a woman."

Ajani grinned. "Ask Eros for a phone number out of his black book."

"HAH!" K.J roared. "I'm single, but not desperate."

I said, "If you win the showcase this weekend, you'll have to pull women off like leeches."

"I'm not worried. I learned from Bianca that I need to be much more picky in choosing who I date. If a girl's not *the one*, I'm not interested."

Q asked K.J, "'The One?' How do you know who's the one if you don't date?"

"Trust me, Q. I'll know."

We continued to talk smack as we finished eating. I was so glad to reveal my faith to my boys. It gave me more confidence about getting through the weekend, despite Eros' bet.

CHAPTER 18

"I thought Rex Marcos was still in prison," Machete said as he searched for articles on Luke Marcos on the Google search engine through the Internet.

"I thought so, too," Rancel said. "But I was talking to him, face-to-face. He seems legit."

"He better be. I'll find out for myself tomorrow."

Rancel gave Machete the full detail about his encounter with the former drug dealer, but other matters were of greater concern. Confirming the setup for Ajani's arrest was the current top priority.

"Did you get through to Moss?" asked Rancel.

Machete picked up the cordless phone. "That's what I'm about to do."

"Hello."

"Kwame Moss," Machete replied.

"Deverow, what's going on? When are you coming back to Motown?"

"Early next week but I need your help before that?"

"What's going on?"

"What's your schedule at the tunnel like for tomorrow?"

"Six a.m. to six p.m."

"Seen. One of my men named Ajani Bethel will be going across the border at eleven-thirty sharp. Does that work for you?"

"Yeah, no doubt. It'll be the same routine. My lane will be the fastest to drive through."

"I don't want you to let him through."

"Say what?"

"That's your job, right?" asked Machete, "To stop anyone who tries to bring narcotics into the U.S?"

Kwame said nothing.

"Is that a problem?"

"No, but it'll cost you extra."

"But that's your responsibility as an American," he exclaimed.

"Forget that! It means extra work that I don't wanna do. It's easy to let cats with guns or drugs go through. I don't give a crap and plus I get mad loot under the table for it. You also need to realize that if I make a legit arrest, word will hit the underground that I can't be trusted. I could lose mad clientele; know what I'm sayin'?"

Machete was silent, realizing that Kwame stressed a valid point.

"Alright, I'll pay you double the usual amount. Half of it you'll get through Western Union tonight."

"That'll work, but only because you always come through with my cash on time."

"Just don't mess this up, I'm dead serious. My name shouldn't be involved in this operation whatsoever."

"I'll come through. Just make sure you e-mail me the full descriptions of the man, vehicle, and . . . will he be traveling solo or with a crew?"

Shoot, thought Machete, *Bethel might be with his boys.*

"I don't know. I'll find out and get back to you tonight."

He hung up the phone and made a call to Ajani.

CHAPTER 19

TEDDY

It was eleven-thirty when we left Rude Boy's. There was a jam that was taking place at Windsor University, but the fellas surprisingly didn't want to go. Fatigue was the main reason, and eating heavy West Indian food didn't help the situation. My mind was made up not to go, and perhaps my shocking confession changed their thinking as well. Nevertheless, we proceeded back to my place.

The Phat Five reunion felt so good. I expressed my joy to Janet on the phone while Ajani discussed business on his cell and Q and K.J played games on the X-Box. I told her that Ajani was all right, except for the fact that he was still pushing drugs. I also mentioned that Eros was still a Hugh Hefner wannabe and K.J was the same conscious-minded hip-hopper on a mission. Q in my opinion changed the most. The once proud basketball star seemed frustrated, oppressed, overweight, and in love with nicotine. Friendship wise, however, Q was still my dog.

We ended the phone conversation by agreeing in prayer for Bless Fest, and that it would reach those who needed salvation, without mentioning any names. It made me feel really good about the weekend. I told my baby that I loved her and hung up the phone.

Before I left the bedroom to hang with the guys, I thanked God for giving me the courage to tell the Phat Five that I was born-again. It was easier than I expected. I honestly believed that Friday and the rest of the weekend would be smooth sailing. It felt good to be confident about my walk with God.

PART 2

FRIDAY

CHAPTER 20

Undercover police investigations had gone to new technological levels, and Ike Trencio was going to be a part of the latest gadget in the Toronto Police Department. He had a pair of contact lenses that had digital video cameras built in them. It was incredible to Ike because they were the same size as his regular contacts, but with microscopic cameras unseen to the human eye. The lenses would eventually expose the evidence of drug-lord Machete Deverow and lock him up behind bars for a long time.

Ike put on the lenses, left the police headquarters, and headed towards his vehicle. He had confidence that the gadget would not malfunction and that they would see all the evidence live, and recorded. They designed them specifically for Ike because he was far-sighted. Ten minutes earlier, he had a chance to see the television screen that connected to the cameras by remote. Everything that Ike looked at presented itself on the screen. The device was perfect except that it felt slightly uncomfortable in Ike's eyes, but as long as the discomfort was not noticeable, everything would be all right.

It was a twenty-five minute drive from the police station to the Landsdowne Community Center, the place where Ike, disguised as Rex Marcos, would meet up with Rancel and Machete. It was seven forty-five in the morning, and apparently, they were organizing a large charity pancake breakfast for the community. Machete did charity events four times a year to win the hearts of city citizens who threatened to destroy him. The events helped to keep some mouths silent, but not enough for narcotic investigators to discover what was really going on. It was time for real answers and the whole truth.

The community center filled to capacity. People lined up from the entrance, through the hallway, and into the auditorium for a free plate of pancakes, turkey bacon, scrambled eggs, and orange juice. Ike somehow managed his way through the crowd to see a group of sharply dressed people serving with smiles on their faces. Rancel was pouring juice into plastic cups and greeting every person that passed by as though he actually enjoyed it. Next to Rancel, was a short, muscular Black man wearing a silver and white apron and serving pancakes. It was Machete, the head honcho.

"There's our man," Ike said, knowing that his fellow police officers were seeing and hearing the situation from their headquarters.

He walked behind the serving table towards Rancel, who turned around to greet him.

"Mr. Marcos, you're here early and that's a good sign. Want some breakfast?"

Ike replied, "Nah, I'm straight, just ready to do business."

"Alright, let's get to it. Debra, take over for me."

His wife was right next to him and began serving drinks without questions or hesitation. Rancel walked over to Machete, who looked at Ike and immediately stopped what he was doing.

"Rex Marcos, Machete Deverow," he said as they shook hands. "Rancel tells me that you're interested in working a deal with us."

"Working a deal?" Ike asked. "I'm interested in more than a deal. I'm the answer towards making your enterprise stronger."

Machete nodded. "You come with plenty of confidence, just like your brother. I met him once in Vancouver over fourteen years ago. What was the name of that joint he loved to eat at all the time?"

Whoa, Ike thought. *Dude is testing me already to see if I'm really Luke's brother. The chief only mentioned one place he always hung out at.*

"Luigi's Steakhouse," he answered. "That was his church, he ate there religiously."

"No doubt. That joint was off the hook! Anyways, let's leave this noise and head out to my headquarters. Just follow me and Rancel."

Ike followed the cousins through the back exit of the auditorium, thankful that he got the right answer to the question.

Whatever metals were contained in the contacts were not detected when Ike was searched. This was another break, another step closer towards more evidence unfolding to authorities. They entered a warehouse that was in the industrial area of Scarborough.

The scene was incredible. The inside of the warehouse looked like a biochemistry lab. There were seven people dressed in scrubs counting OxyContin pills and placing them into plastic containers and jars. The prescription pill that was available only in the pharmacy and drugstores is now being manufactured and distributed illegally by Machete Deverow.

"Welcome to my enterprise," Machete said with pride. "Consider yourself one of the elite and very few to witness what takes place behind these walls. Without Rancel's approval of you, Mr. Marcos, you wouldn't even know this place existed."

"The place is well put together," said Ike while observing the entire area.

"It's only the best. Why should I have to rob pharmacies for the fastest growing new drug in the country like other third-class dealers when I can organize my own operation? I contacted the right sources and eventually started my own distribution. Now, the third-class dealers are coming to me for the drug to sell on the street, and the price is high, considering the fact that cats don't have to rob their neighborhood pharmacy for the stuff."

Rancel led them towards another room, which looked like a computer lab. He sat down at a computer desk and began to open a program on the PC for Ike to observe.

"This is the info-tech room," Machete continued. "What Rancel just opened is a program that handles the distribution of the OxyContin. We know exactly how many pills were sent out, what dealers are selling, how much they sold, and most importantly, what money is coming in.

You see, we still have the issue of giving a man a drug to sell and waiting for the payback. Things need to be done in decency and in order. I'm sure your brother knew about decency and order, right?"

Ike agreed. "No doubt, Luke took pride in every thing he put his hands to do."

"Seen. You see, Rex, when it comes to drugs, I've dealt them all: weed, crack, heroin, you name it. I knew about OxyContin or Hillbilly Heroin for a while, but I didn't deal it because it was only popular in the rural areas, and I'm living in Toronto. However, as news spread about the unbelievable high that OxyContin provided, all of a sudden crack-heads and club owners were asking me about the pill. I had to get what the people wanted, and now I'm making mad dollars from these bad boys. I changed the name from Hillbilly Heroin to what cats call G.H or Ghetto Heroin. It's the high of the twenty-first century."

Ike smiled and agreed with everything that Machete was saying. The investigation was going perfect until the left contact started to fall out of position in his eye. It started to get painful, but Ike tried his best to make it unnoticeable.

"So, Mr. Marcos, how can you be an asset to this empire?" asked Machete.

"Well," Ike replied, blinking rapidly, "like I said to Rancel yesterday, being an accountant and working exclusively with the Filipino community in the G.T.A, I could give you . . ."

"What's wrong with your eyes, guy?" Rancel asked as he looked at Ike as if he was crazy.

"Nothing, it's just these contacts. My eyes aren't used to them yet 'cause they're brand new."

"They didn't seem to bother you yesterday."

Ike noticed how observant Rancel was, and he had to lie well in order to make it out of the place alive.

"Trust me; they were in pain when I wore them yesterday. I had them adjusted last night, but now . . . I don't know . . . I'll be alright."

With force, Ike stopped blinking. Rancel looked at him seriously for a few seconds before re-focusing his attention on the computer. Machete was quiet, observing every one of Ike's actions.

"You were saying, Mr. Marcos . . ." he said anxiously.

"Yes, I was saying that I got links to the Filipino community from Markham to Mississauga, and trust me, both upper and lower classes are looking for this pill and I can be their link."

"And I'm guessing that you come at a hefty price. You see, Mr. Marcos, your brother was one of the best drug-lords ever, and I bet that you're good at what you do, but I don't trust anybody, at least not lately."

"I understand, but . . ."

"I've had cats come to me and tell me that they would be the top dog to get cash in for me, make the right deals, and do excellent networking. However, I will let you know now that those in the past who backstabbed me and didn't follow my guidelines are six feet under right now. I know you hear what I'm saying, right?"

Rancel said, "Cats who messed with us have been dealt with or are in the midst of it right now."

Someone messed them up recently, Ike wondered. *Could it be the guy in the Escalade I saw yesterday?*

"Look, I'm not trying to be a front-page headline," said Ike, "so when I talk business, I mean business."

Ike was ready to leave. His eye was feeling worse, and he was praying that the pain would not become more evident.

"Good," replied Machete. "That still doesn't mean that I trust you, so you'll need to leave your cell number and social insurance number. We do security checks on everyone before any deals are made. If we find anything that makes us suspicious, like anything government-related, we'll kill you. No questions asked."

Ike gave him the social insurance number of Rex Marcos. The police department found the number and changed information in the database to fit the physical attributes of Ike. Rancel immediately began the search through the computer.

Ten minutes later, Machete and Rancel escorted Ike out of the warehouse. Their security was waiting at the door.

"Well Rex, everything will be set to go after closing time tonight at the Irie Club," Machete said as he shook Ike's hand. "Welcome aboard."

Ike also shook Rancel's hand, and then headed towards his vehicle, with two men dressed in black leather leading him to the parking lot. He quickly drove away.

Machete looked at Ike's vehicle until it was completely out of sight. He turned to his cousin and asked him how he and Ike hooked up.

"Ike said that a West Indian man with an Escalade gave him my number," replied Rancel. "It had to be Ajani."

"I knew Luke Marcos for a long time, but it wasn't until we checked the history that I was convinced that he really has a younger brother named Rex."

"He seems confident that he's the man to do business with."

"Yeah, he seems confident, but I'm watching him. If he's legit, he can replace Bethel. However, if this cat ain't for real, there's hell to pay, and trust me, that includes you. In the meantime, we need to make sure that Bethel is busted at the border. The last thing I need right now is for that operation to mess up."

"Oh my God!" Ike screamed in relief as he stopped at the corner ten blocks away from the warehouse. He quickly took out the contacts and put on his glasses from the glove compartment.

"I need some serious Visine right now!" he yelled as he took out his cell phone to call his boss.

"Good job, Trencio! We almost have Deverow for good now!"

"I deserve a good raise for just wearing these things in my eyes," Ike said in anger. "After tonight, I ain't putting these contacts on again!"

He was only hoping that he was right.

CHAPTER 21

It was nine forty-five in the morning, and Katrina was not in the mood to get out of bed. She did not get home until four in the morning and she had an entire king-size bed to herself. However, the argument that she had with Q still made her upset, which kept her from sleeping properly. There was a guest in the living room that she could not wait to fellowship with so she forced herself to get out of bed.

Hanging out with her girlfriends in downtown Toronto was the most fun that Katrina had since getting married. She danced and drank Long Island iced teas all night, just like her college days. However, it was not the same because during college, Katrina constantly flirted with men and there were a few fine-looking men that approached her at the club. The chance of a one-night stand was great. Nevertheless, the massive diamond on her wedding ring was shining bright on Thursday night, and Katrina changed her mind. She only hoped that her husband had the same conviction.

Even though a one-night stand did not take place, Katrina still brought a man into the Quintino home, and she wanted to make him some breakfast. She walked in the living room and saw that he was already awake and taking a shower in the washroom. Katrina opened the fridge in the kitchen and saw very little. They would have to go to Denny's for a Grand Slam breakfast.

Ten minutes later, Katrina was watching TV in the living room. Leron Brown came out of the bathroom wearing a white undershirt, brown corduroy pants, and a towel around his neck. They both smiled.

"What up, Trina?" he asked with a deep voice that would make Barry White proud.

"Nuttin' much, cousin," answered Katrina. "It's about time you came back to Toronto for a visit."

"It's been a long time, huh?"

"Four years! Since you moved to New York, Aunt Maggie, Uncle Randy, and your sisters have come back to visit, but not you."

Katrina and Leron were close since elementary school. Leron's parents, both retired corporate lawyers, moved to Syracuse, New York after he received a football scholarship at Syracuse University. That was two years before Katrina met Q.

"Yeah, it's been too long," he said. "School and football keeps me so busy."

"I still can't believe you missed my wedding."

"Trina, I was so upset that I couldn't make it. I was in the middle of training camp."

"I see," said Katrina, looking at his huge chiseled body. "You must've gained fifty pounds of muscle since I last saw you!"

"I had to work my butt off to get the starting middle linebacker position, and the work has paid off. I'm entering the NFL draft next month."

"And I'm so proud and happy for you! My God, Leron, you surprised my girls big time when you walked in the club and came to our table," she exclaimed as she squeezed his biceps.

"Yeah, I saw their eyes looking me up and down," Leron said with pride. "Trust me, instead of being a gentleman, I could've been a dog like I was in my freshman year and pull off a sweet one-nighter but I wouldn't do that to your girls, and I've gotten pickier lately. There's not much women as all-around beautiful like a Katrina Brown."

Katrina smiled. If she and Leron were not related, they might have married each other. Because they were best friends, they always compared the opposite sex to each other's qualities. Katrina wanted a man like Leron: athletic, dark-skinned, tall, and sensitive. Then she met a college basketball star named Damon Quintino. Three of the four qualities that she was looking for were still more than pleasing.

"Remember, my last name has changed," she said.

Leron grinned. "Oh yeah, you're half Italian now. I've been anxiously waiting to meet your husband and now that I'm in town, he's not here!"

"Well, if you would've called me before Thursday, I could have stopped Q from going to Windsor. He's been waiting to meet you too."

"My bad. This visit was a last-minute decision. So how's married life, Trina? I want details."

Katrina grabbed a towel from the linen closet. "Well, I want breakfast. After I get ready, I'll give you details while we eat a Grand Slam at Denny's. You down?"

"Ha, ha! You know I'm game with that!"

CHAPTER 22

EROS

Why am I such a freak?
That was my thought when I woke up after only four hours of sleep. I acted as if I hadn't had sex in years. The thought of getting with Nivea was finally a reality, and when the opportunity arrived on Thursday night, we went wild.

Nivea was sleeping really hard. Seeing that made me feel proud about my stamina and the way that I could make women feel physically exhausted. I could only thank hereditary, because Eros Alexander, Sr. had the same gift.

I was twelve years old when my dad revealed the explicit details of his job as an adult video producer. Since then, I saw or heard of at least eighty women that he had slept with, most of them in the industry. It was my father's polygamous actions that made me want to be a player. Thus, after sleeping with Nivea, I was ready to move on with someone else.

If Juanita found out that I was such a dog, she would try to do something vicious and nasty to me. Teddy warned me about her, but I was confident about my game. She has never caught me with another woman in Toronto, and my time with Nivea was in another area code. In addition, I had no intention of dealing with Nivea after the weekend.

It was ten minutes to ten. I wanted to take a shower before Nivea woke up, because if she did, I would want a quickie. Tried to sneak out of the bed, but the squeaky noise of the mattress woke her up.

"Where are you going?" She asked in her high soprano voice.

I looked at her and smiled. "Remember, baby? I'm going with the boys to Detroit. You have to drop me at Teddy's."

Her dark chocolate skin was turning me on, and looking at her, big innocent eyes. She crawled towards me and started to cuddle.

"Why do you have to leave me already? You just got here," Nivea begged while caressing my chest. "I was gonna make you breakfast and take you shopping."

I said nothing as I highly considered ditching my boys to get some gifts from this beauty. Then I quickly reminded myself that I didn't travel to Windsor to get whipped by another woman. Plus, I pleased her so good that I did not need to be with her all day for her to reward me.

She said, "I must be changing your mind 'cause you aren't saying nothing."

"Oh . . . sorry, baby. I was just considering my options. I gotta roll with the boys to Detroit. We do it every year, and Ajani is leaving in an hour. That dude's so punctual, he almost left me in Toronto yesterday! That cat be acting crazy sometimes."

Laughing, she said, "Well, I'll still go to the mall after I drop you and surprise you with something nice."

"Like some stain-resistant Dockers? They're on sale at Sears."

"I said it'll be a surprise. Get ready, and make sure you take your entire ID. Immigration's not playing since that war began in Iraq."

"Alright, baby."

I kissed her cheek as she released her warm hug. As I got off the bed, I looked at her and smiled. Nivea was so sweet. She would make an excellent wife, but marriage to me was worse than saying the F-word.

As I opened the bedroom door, her roommate Whitney was standing at the entrance holding a cordless phone to her ear.

"He's right here, OK? Hold on," she said with a pleasant voice. "Eros, it's for you. It's Q."

I grabbed the phone from her. "Q? How'd he get this number?"

"Is that your white friend?"

"Yeah, why, you like him?" I asked, already knowing the answer from just staring at Whitney's smile.

She looked at Nivea, grinned, and then looked at me again, telling me that my boy looks fine.

I answered the phone. "Yo, what's going on? How'd you get this number?"

"Four one one," Q said.

"Tell Ajah to relax, I'll be there in a half hour."

"This ain't about that. Man . . . I think Trina's cheating on me, guy!"

"What? For real, guy? How . . . how do you know? How'd you find out?"

"Remember yesterday when she called me to see if I had her phone? Well, we know each other's password, so I checked her messages this morning just in case she called after I turned the phone off."

"Uh huh."

Q was highly upset, but I was excited. Finally, he had a good reason to cheat on Katrina. I kept a serious look because the women were in the bedroom.

"Anyway, the message on her phone was from a cat in New York who went to T.O just to see Trina! Some guy with a deep voice, sounded like Barry White. Didn't leave a name, but obviously he knows my wife. She's cheating on me, guy! This is my punishment for working too hard and coming to Windsor. Yo . . . I'm so pissed right now . . . Hello?"

"Still here. Dang, man, that's some drama. Did you call her?"

"Not yet. I just heard the message and I called you. The other guys don't even know yet."

Inside, I was laughing, but I still felt bad for my best friend. To hear Q stress out was the reason why I had little respect for women. I believed that women played guys better than we played them. Q was one of a few men that were starting to get a clue.

"Don't call her yet," I told him. "Wait until I get there."

"Why? What are you gonna do?"

"Just wait, dog. I'll be there in twenty minutes."

As I hung up the phone, I noticed the ladies looking at me with serious concern.

"Is everything alright?" asked Nivea.

I needed to lie. "No, a friend of mine and Q's fellow employee just got that new virus in Toronto."

"Oh no! SARS?" cried Whitney.

"Yeah. Q just found out this morning. We're gonna call her family once I get to Ted's crib so we can get her address to send her a get-well package."

"Ahh, that's real thoughtful," Nivea said. "I'm sorry to hear that. I'm doing a case study on SARS. I hope that none of your boys have any of the symptoms."

I said, "No, baby. We're all clean."

"I hope Q's family doesn't have it, or his girlfriend," added Whitney.

"F.Y.I, Q ain't seeing anybody right now, Whitney," I lied again.

She gave me a shy smile, took the phone and left the bedroom.

"I see that your roommate's feeling my boy," I said to Nivea.

Nivea replied, "She loves dating White boys. Whitney's attracted to Eminem, Bubba Sparxxx, Justin Timberlake, Michael Jackson . . ."

"Michael Jackson?"

"Don't ask."

"I saw Q checking her out last night. We should hook them up."

She looked at me with a glare. "I hope Q's not a player."

"Q? Ha, ha, of course not."

Not yet, anyway.

CHAPTER 23

TEDDY

Don't worry about a thang
He's gonna handle everything
Don't you worry about a thang
He's gonna handle it, He'll handle it
So don't worry about a thang

The music and lyrics of gospel singer Tonex was encouraging me as I was getting dressed.

I don't need to worry about nothing, I thought. *Ain't no crazy drama's gonna happen this weekend. God won't put me through more than I can bear.*

As I went in the kitchen, I noticed that Ajani wasn't in the apartment and his keys were gone. Q was taking a shower. K.J was already dressed and watching CNN.

"What up, cuz?" I asked K.J.

"Yo, guy, what the world is coming to?" he exclaimed. "There's war in Iraq that makes no sense, a disease out of nowhere that's hitting Toronto like a plague, plus anti-war protests all over the place. It's like the world needs a spiritual cleansing or a whopping from God."

"That's because the world needs God, straight up."

"It needs something. All I know is that if one has peace in their heart and mind, solutions will come forth without hostility or violence."

"Prayer is a major factor as well."

"True, but God don't seem to be answering any prayers at the moment, probably because of the evils in society today. I just hope He'll come through for me tonight in the freestyle showcase."

Over the last few years, I'd noticed that K.J had become more intelligent and conscious-minded due to extensive reading and news watching. He memorized quotes from Martin Luther King, Jr., Malcolm X, Louis Farrakhan, and even Bishop T.D. Jakes. However, because of what he knew and studied, I felt that the extensive research was the reason for his universal belief of religion. I really wanted him to visit Kingdom Workers Fellowship Church and discover the real purpose of life.

I turned the volume up on the stereo.

I said, "Yo, man, check this track out. This artist is nice."

K.J started nodding his head to the bass-thumping beat.

"Beat's nice," he said. "Who is this?"

"His name's X-Secula."

"Who?"

"A gospel rapper. Listen."

> *God blessed me with a talent so I had to release this*
> *Had a hard-head but the Lord broke me down to many pieces*
> *So now, my rhymes got on thesis and its all about Jesus*
> *Needs to be a smash hit like the Broadway play Grease is*

After hearing the song, K.J seemed impressed. "Kid's tight. He needs to get signed."

"X-Secula is signed and he has an album," I said.

"How come I never heard of him? I read all the Hip-Hop magazines."

"They hardly ever feature Christian rappers, even though they're in the hundreds across North America. But *The Source* did an article on *Grits* a few months ago."

"Oh . . . I overlooked that article 'cause I never heard their music. So, all of this X-guy's music is Christian? No explicit joints?"

"Nope. You wanna see him live? He'll be at our church tomorrow night."

K.J paused. "I plan to be in the finals tomorrow night."

"C'mon, that's at eleven-thirty if you make it. The concert's at eight."

"I can't promise that I'll be there. And I'll ignore the fact that you said 'if'!"

We had a Phat Five original breakfast that consisted of Cap'n Crunch, Froot Loops, Frosted Flakes, bananas, and milk all in a large mixing bowl. K.J asked about the artist of every song he heard on the mix CD, and I was gladly providing the info. It was good to see a non-gospel music listener enjoying the grooves of urban gospel. I looked at the living room clock and noticed that Ajani had not returned. It was twenty minutes to eleven.

"We're supposed to be leaving at eleven, right?" I asked. "Where's Ajah?"

K.J replied, "He said he was going to get gas and wash the ride but you know how he is. Ajani will be here right before its time to go, like 10:58."

"For real. That's Ajah all right."
"Yo, is Q still in the bathroom? I've been waiting a long time to take a . . ."
"OWWWW!"
That was Q's yell and few F-words coming from the washroom.

CHAPTER 24

AJANI

I was feeling extremely uneasy as I parked in front of Teddy's apartment building. Couldn't sleep on Thursday night 'cause I felt like something was shady. Everything was on my mind: Machete, his punk cousin Rancel, the drug delivery to the U.S, Savannah and A.J. The crazy amount of messages on my phone and the Filipino who spoke to me in Scarborough. This was enough drama for me to swallow four cups of Tim Horton's coffee.

Since Thursday the only plus factor for me was receiving a nice chunk of cash from Machete for the delivery. Money was my obsession, and other than my woman and son, the only thing that was more enjoyable than cash was having more cash but the task seemed too suspect. Machete always made the international deliveries because he went to Detroit frequently. However, the assignment was handed over to me. Did Machete really trust me to get the job completed?

I used to feel like I earned his trust. After all, I always got the deals completed, I never was arrested, and surprisingly never had to kill anyone. However, I saw a different side of Machete on Thursday, a look that I hadn't seen since I met him four years ago. The, "I'm-watching-your-every-move" look confused me. Must have pissed him off, but I had no idea how and when.

More and more questions roamed through my mind. Would I get in the right tunnel lane to get to Kwame Moss? Was it a good idea to take my boys across the border, knowing that they will be arrested if my SUV was searched? Why couldn't the two briefcases of G.H be sent through express mail? When some people made international drug deals, especially to and from the U.S, SpeedEx was the cheapest and easiest route. The drugs would be wrapped and sealed as tight as possible so that it wouldn't be sniffed or detected. As an employee, I could've sent the package free of charge. The delivery was making lesser sense by the minute.

I concluded that the quicker I completed the job, the better for keeping my sanity. Drug dealing was a major stress, and if it wasn't paying so well, I would've finished the game years ago but it was all about the cash. Money was everything.

I checked the back of the Escalade one last time to make sure that the briefcases were not visible. When I closed the lift gate, a car parked behind me. It was Eros' new gal dropping him off.

"My God!" I said in a surprising tone as Eros stepped out of the car. "You're here on time! I thought you would get left for sure."

"Not me," he replied. "I need some tight gear for tonight. Plus, I have to catch the drama!"

"What drama?"

"Q said Trina's screwing another man."

CHAPTER 25

Q

I almost gave myself a double chin while shaving. A wet cloth pressed on my cut to stop the bleeding. It was easily one of the worst mornings of my entire life.

"Guy, are you sure that the guy's not one of her relatives?" Teddy asked after I told him and K.J about the situation. "Perhaps it was an out-of-town cousin."

I thought of that possibility, but I met almost everyone from Trina's family, and none of them had a deep voice. Maybe it was her cousin Leron, but I doubted it. If he was visiting T.O, she would've told me in advance 'cause I've never met him.

"Yeah, I'm sure," I replied to Teddy, but I still was very unsure. "Man, I need a smoke."

"Dang, you started that crap again?" K.J exclaimed. "I thought you quit!"

"I started it again when work was stressing me out," I said as I put on a t-shirt.

"Man, you're always stressing out."

I snapped. "Excuse me? Look at the crap I gotta deal with!"

Teddy said, "Q, I know you're mad, but calm down. Try calling her again, 'cause it could be a misunderstanding."

I replied, "Yeah, it could be, but she could be getting back at me for not spending quality time with her. I've been working almost everyday, and she was missing me. I take a weekend off, and now I'm in Windsor away from her again. I messed up."

"Just call her already, guy!"

I tried calling her for the fifth time that hour. There was no answer on the home phone and my cell that she had was off. As I hung up the phone, Ajani and Eros came into the apartment.

"Guy, I told you not to get married!" Eros shouted.

"Oh, Lord," K.J sighed. "Here come words of wisdom."

"Q," Eros began, trying not to laugh at my pain, "you know that you're my boy and I got mad love for you. But if I was Trina, I would've cheated on you too."

I glared at him with rage.

"What? It's the truth," he continued. "How long can adult toys make a woman happy? She wanted your goods, but you were too tired to please her. Hey, I'm just being real with ya."

The bleeding finally stopped on my chin and I placed a huge bandage on the cut.

Ajani asked, "Yo, what happened to you?"

"Shaving," I sighed. "This cut's the only thing I can easily fix. My B-ball career is finished, my marriage is messed up and my life sucks big time."

"Have you talked to Trina about it?"

"Nope. Can't get a hold of her."

Teddy suggested that I leave a message on our voice mail. My stress level was rising like yeast in donuts, which was why I didn't want to leave a message. I was afraid of saying something extremely hurtful. However, I had to get in touch with her, so I dialed the number again. Suddenly, Eros took the phone away from my hand.

I yelled, "Yo, what's your problem? Give me the phone!"

Eros said, "Don't call her, guy."

"Give me the freaking phone!"

"No." He turned the phone off and put it in his pant pocket.

"Give me the phone." I was ready to hit him hard in his face.

K.J snapped, "What's wrong with you, Eros? Give the man his phone!"

"Q, the proof is in the pudding," said Eros. "An unknown dude that leaves a message to see your wife means that Trina's playing you. We agreed last night that we don't want any drama this weekend. Deal with your wife when you get back on Sunday. In the meantime, get yourself some booty! You're in a different area code, and the harvest is good. If you took my advice on having a one-nighter before, you wouldn't feel so crappy now."

Ajani said, "Hey bred-drin, whatever's going on right now, we need to take it to Detroit. It's eleven o' clock. I'm out." He exited the apartment.

Teddy put his keys on the kitchen counter. "Whoever's leaving last, please lock up." He followed Ajani.

Eros gave me back the phone. "Hey, if you wanna stay whipped and played out a flat-top haircut, call your wife. But if I were you, I wouldn't waste my time."

K.J said to Eros, "You know that you're a natural born jackass, right?"

"And you have a left hand as a best friend 'cause you don't have a woman."

"Whatever," K.J grinned. "Your comments don't faze me. Just don't be surprised when consequences beat you down because of your actions."

K.J's comment stayed in my mind as I put away the cell phone. I had to call Katrina, but I put it off because I dying for more nicotine.

CHAPTER 26

A fresh bundle of hundred-dollar bills was always an incentive to do unusual work, especially for Kwame Moss. Before he started work at six in the morning, he stopped at a Western Union to pick up half of the money promised by Machete for the tunnel drug bust. It was ten minutes after eleven, twenty minutes before Ajani Bethel would try to make an entrance into the U.S.

Kwame hated sitting in a booth that looked like a long, skinny box. He would sit in a seat, investigate thousands of Canadians and Americans, and input data on a slow computer. "What's your citizenship?" "How long will you be in the U.S?" "How long were you away?" "Do you have anything to declare?" were just a few questions that Kwame asked people all day and everyday. It was crazy, repetitive, and boring at times, but he enjoyed having authority.

Kwame's appearance intimidated people. He was dark, tall, and had evil-looking eyes that would make actor Christopher Walken look like a nice guy. His voice was deep, so when he asked questions, people gave short, immediate answers. He made people park their vehicles to be investigated, interrogated, and sometimes arrested. However, situations changed when the tunnel was busy, which made full searches tedious, or when people paid him to allow them into the U.S without investigation.

Allowing drug dealers and people with firearms to cross the border was his second income. Criminals contacted him on his off-work hours to arrange a time when he was on duty to enter the country. Clients knew that Kwame's lane was the one that was the fastest. It was the best procedure because the booth windows were tinted to the point where no outsiders knew who was in what booth. That eliminated racial profiling and favoritism.

Because of the war in Iraq and the increased security at the border, he raised his rates by thirty percent. He was making double his average border officer salary during the period. If his superiors ever found out about his actions, it would result in a jail sentence. He knew of the risks, which is why he was slightly relieved to be paid by Machete for an arrest instead of an entrance. He took out the list of details that he needed to look for:

> VEHICLE—2004 Cadillac Escalade SUV
> COLOR: silver FEATURES: dark tinted windows, platinum Sprewell rims
> LICENSE PLATE—ANMC 509
> DRIVER—Ajani Bethel—Jamaican landed immigrant in Canada, dark brown skin, five foot eight, age twenty-six, bald
>
> SECONDARY INFO
> PASSENGERS
>
> Theodore Henderson—African-Canadian, medium brown skin, five foot ten, age twenty-four, afro
> Kellen Brar—African-Canadian/Indian, dark brown skin, six feet even, age twenty-four, low-fade haircut
> Eros Alexander, Jr.—Afro/Puerto Rican (US/Can. Citizen), light brown skin, five foot ten, age twenty-five, cornrow braids
> Damon Quintino—Italian-Canadian, six foot four, age twenty-four, Caucasian, short hair

Kwame hoped that Ajani would come through alone. More people meant extra work, but he was not complaining. Machete was one of his best clients, and he was determined not to let him down. It was time for action. His booth was lane three, and he increased the flow of traffic.

CHAPTER 27

"I hate this stinking job!" Georgina Tucker mumbled as she stepped into the booth of lane two.

Not only did she hate working the evening shift, which started at three in the afternoon, but also her boss asked her to start four hours early. Georgina was angry that she said yes, but she needed the money.

She was taking care of her three teenage boys with no support from their father, who was serving time in a Michigan prison. She stayed up until six in the morning taking care of the youngest who was suffering with the stomach flu. Her time of the month arrived on Thursday and she was craving chocolate, but she began her Atkins diet and she was bothered by hemorrhoids. Thus, Georgina was not in the mood for any more drama.

For the first fifteen minutes of her shift, Georgina did what she was required to do as a customs officer. Did she care if some Canadians tried to enter the U.S without proper identification? Did Georgina care that her country was in the midst of a war and the possibility of terrorists entering without interrogation? Did she care if people tried to bring drugs or firearms into Detroit? Usually, but today she decided to make her job much easier.

"Citizenship?" Georgina asked the following driver of the vehicle.

The driver replied, "Canadian."

"What's the purpose of your trip?"

"Pleasure. Just going to do some shopping at the . . ."

"Go ahead."

The traffic in lane two was smoother than downtown driving at four in the morning.

CHAPTER 28

There was no comparison between Teddy's ten-year-old Honda Accord and Ajani's Escalade. Teddy thought that the SUV was excellent and was enjoying the ride and its interior features. He had the passenger seat, while Eros was sitting between K.J and Q in the back.

Eros was making fun of Ajani, saying that the customs officer would be ignorant to think that he was an Arabic terrorist because of his unusual name. The cousins were laughing, but Ajani was serious and did not react to the comment. Teddy strongly believed that he was up to something, and wanted to know before entering the U.S.

After Ajani paid the toll, Teddy looked at Q, who threw his cigarette out the window before entering the tunnel. He thought it was pathetic to see his athletic friend with a smoking habit, but he also felt sorry for him. If Janet ever cheated on him, Teddy would probably feel the same as Q. He thanked God that he was saved, because his beautiful girlfriend could have been with another man if he was still the old Teddy Henderson.

Perhaps Q was more paranoid than he had to be about the phone message. He did tell Katrina over the phone on Thursday that he did not care if she saw another man, although Teddy felt that he did not mean it. It was probably true that Q was not spending enough time with her. Nevertheless, Teddy prayed that God would comfort him, fix their marriage, and give him enough conviction to quit smoking.

Eros changed the conversation to his favorite subject.

"Yo, I like going over to Detroit, y'know," he said. "Some D-Town women have some of the biggest, firmest onions that I've ever seen, and trust me, I've seen plenty! It must be the chitlins and Coney hot dogs they be eating. Ajah, remember that stripper from Southfield that you dealt with last year? Her booty was so rotund, she'd make J.Lo say, 'Dang, she got a big booty.'"

Ajani didn't respond to Eros.

"Ajah? What's wrong with you? Somebody ticked you off?

"No," he answered.

"Then why you bugging and why are you so concerned about getting to the mall on time?"

"I'm not. I got business to take care of in Dearborn."

Teddy looked at Ajani.

"You picking up or delivering?" Eros asked.

"Both."

K.J stopped mimicking the song playing in the car stereo and stared at Ajani.

"What do you mean 'both'?" he asked.

"I got two briefcases of G.H. in the back that I'm delivering to some Latinos."

Teddy felt a headache approaching, which seemed to happen whenever he started to panic. Although he had known Ajani since junior high, it still amazed him how blunt he could be no matter how serious the issue. Ajani seemed to be fearless when it came to honesty, minus telling his lady about his second occupation.

"Yo, why'd you pick now to take drugs through immigration, guy?" Teddy snapped.

"I know what I'm doing!" Ajani snapped back. "So relax!"

"Why? You've sent drugs across the border before?"

"No, but everything's cool. I got connections."

K.J exclaimed, "Like what? There's a war going on in the Middle East, and Bush thinks that terrorists might come from Canada. What if they search us?"

"Yeah, what if they got dogs sniffing the cars?" Q asked.

Eros said, "Guy, if you got business to do, that's fine but why you putting us at risk though? Yeah, we'll probably get through, but what if they pull us over? I won't make it in jail, man! There's too much men there, I'll go crazy!"

K.J yelled, "Ajah, you better not freak this up! You know my mama don't like you already, and Lord knows if we get arrested . . ."

"YO, EVERYBODY SHUT UP, SHUT UP, SHUT UP!" Ajani was outraged. "All y'all want to get in a crazy panic mode before I explain what's going on! My boss knows one of the officers named Kwame Moss and arranged with him to allow me across without a search. I'll know which booth he's in according to the fastest lane. It's as easy as that."

Teddy said, "Ajah, I'm telling you, this better be legit. None of us should be a part of your drug functions."

Ajani shook his head and looked ahead as the tunnel exit was approaching.

"Look, everything's cool, bred-drin. Y'all have nothing to do with my dealings. I wouldn't have brought y'all with me if things weren't safe."

Teddy wanted to believe his friend, but in his heart, he believed that something was not right. For the first time since Janet warned him, he began to wonder if hanging out with his unsaved friends was a good idea. He started praying that God would prevent them from being arrested of drug possession.

It was one minute to eleven-thirty on Kwame's watch. He looked anxious as he was speeding the traffic in his lane, but he just wanted to get the task finished. After he allowed the last vehicle to go through, Kwame stepped out of the booth to get a clearer vision of the traffic flow.

Looking at the long line of vehicles, he saw a silver Escalade behind eight other automobiles. Kwame was relieved that Ajani was punctual. However, he wanted a quick view of the people in the SUV, but the front window was very tinted.

It must be a Canadian vehicle, he thought, *'cause no vehicle in the U.S can get away with windows that dark.*

He went back into the booth to continue his task.

As they exited the tunnel, Ajani saw a vehicle ahead of him that immediately caught his attention. The sight of it got him angry.

"You got to be kidding me," he said. "Somebody's driving my ride!"

K.J said, "And? I see Escalades all the time. You ain't the only cat with a phat ride."

"I know that, I'm not stupid, K.J. Look closely at that ride. The spinning rims are the exact replica of mine."

Q added, "For real, guy! That ride looks exactly like yours."

"And it has an Ontario license plate and . . . oh my God, I must be tripping. The license plate is identical except for a letter scramble. That's messed up!"

Ajani finally understood how a woman felt when she bought an expensive outfit for a party, only to see another wear the same wardrobe. He spent thousands of dollars on his Escalade to make it unlike any other vehicle in Toronto. He shook his head in disbelief.

"I wish that I could see who's driving, but their windows are crazy tinted."

"Ajah," Teddy said, "you have G.H in the truck, and you're pissed off about another Escalade? Concentrate, guy!"

"I am! I'm staying right behind this copycat 'cause this is the fastest lane."

Ajani looked to his left and saw another lane with the same speed.

"What the . . . ? Lanes two and three are moving quick! Which one is Kwame's?" he asked himself.

Eros asked, "Guy, don't you know which one's the right lane?"

"Of course," he lied. "I was given clues."

"Well, I'm glad that you can tell the difference, 'cause the left lane looks faster than . . ."

"Look, do any of you cats wanna take over and do this? Huh? All right then! Let me do what I have to do, so everybody shut up and let me concentrate! What I plan to do is stay behind this clone 'cause it is the fastest lane to me. You don't like it? I don't give a crap!"

Thoughts of Friday evening created anticipation in Kwame's mind. He was definitely in the mood for hedonism. All he needed was the rest of money from Machete, and he was ready to feast in some adult entertainment and a night at the Hilton hotel in Windsor. He was less than two minutes away from making the arrest.

Kwame was able to see the Escalade's license plate and it resembled what he was supposed to know. The information was in his knapsack, but he did not feel the need to retrieve it. After all, Cadillac Escalades were not as popular as Dodge Caravans or Toyota Camry's. It was a luxury vehicle, and Kwame could count the amount that came through daily on one hand. Instead, he grabbed the orange slips of paper from his desk, which was important for placing on the car's windshield if the passengers needed to be searched.

In less than two minutes, Kwame allowed a Nissan Altima, Chevy Cavalier, and a silver SUV enter the U.S. It was finally the moment for him to meet Ajani for the first and last time.

The driver's window rolled down, and he took a good look at the suspect . . .

The person in the tunnel booth was a complete surprise to Ajani. He expected an African-American male but the officer was a full-sized African-American woman. She wore glasses, had a long weave, and looked miserable. Ajani was upset at his last-second decision to move to lane two from lane three. Drivers were honking their horns 'cause he was disrupting traffic flow. He shocked his boys, who more than likely thought that his mind was set on staying in the third lane.

I made a stupid move, he thought. *What's done is done. I gotta hope for a break.*

Teddy had collected everybody's ID and gave them to Ajani.

The woman asked, "What's everybody's citizenship?"

Ajani replied, "Three Canadians, one Jamaican landed immigrant, and a dual U.S/Canada citizen."

She looked at each person and began pressing buttons on her computer. Ajani held the pieces of ID for her to grab, but she ignored them.

"What's the purpose of your trip?"

"We're going to Fairlane Mall and . . ."

"Have a nice day."

Ajani wanted to ask, "That's it?" but he did not. The woman gave her approval, and it was time to move. He waved good-bye, but she did not return the gesture.

A beautiful middle-aged woman rolled down the driver's window of her Escalade. She looked like she was prepared to go to church, wearing a shiny cornflower blue outfit.

Kwame thought to himself in anger. *How in the world could this vehicle not be the target? What the hell's going on here?*

"Good morning, ma'am," he said. "What's your citizenship?"

"Canadian," the woman answered in a polite and pleasant voice.

He asked her for identification. He looked at the woman's ID and her name was Michelle Lynette Walker. Obviously, she was not the person that he supposed to arrest, but something seemed extremely suspicious. The vehicle looked exactly the way Machete described it. He had to know who owned the SUV.

She replied, "It belongs to my husband, Pastor Randall Walker. I drove this vehicle from Toronto and I'm going to a woman's conference in Detroit."

"May I see the papers for the vehicle?"

"Sure."

He reviewed the papers and sure enough, Randall Walker owned the vehicle. His head started to ache severely. He had to find out what went wrong.

"Here you go," he said as he gave her back the papers and ID. "You're free to go."

"Thank you," she said with a big smile. "God bless you and have a good day."

As soon as she drove away, he looked at her license plate again: AMNC 509. He quickly went back into the booth and opened his knapsack to find the paper with Ajani's information. As he reviewed it, he saw that the license plate number for Ajani's ride was ANMC 509. He had focused his attention on the wrong vehicle.

Another car approached the booth. He ignored it and turned on the stop light to indicate to the drivers in line that lane three is closed. It was against procedure to make that move, but he did not care. He looked at the cars that were exiting immigration and behold, the ANMC 509 was driving away from lane two.

He looked at the sky and yelled an F-blast.

Georgina was allowing another vehicle to enter the country when she heard the telephone ringing.

"Who wants to vent about something now?" she asked as she picked up the phone. "Officer Tucker speaking."

"Georgina! Was it you who allowed that Escalade through just now?"

It was Kwame, and Georgina knew that he was in a hot mood.

"What? The one with the Canadians in it?"

"I don't have to explain it! It just happened a minute ago!"

"Yeah, I did. Why?"

"Why are you letting cars pass through without full investigation?"

"Excuse me? Look who's talking! You got people going through faster in your lane!"

"'Cause I was trying to get those cats you let through and you . . . Never mind, forget it!"

"What are you venting about, and how can I freak up something for you when I don't know what the hell's going on?"

"Look, never mind alright, just do your freaking job properly!"

"Boy, I swear . . . If I wasn't working right now . . . How dare you!"

Georgina saw the people in the car looking at her strangely. She slammed the phone down.

I don't care if I let Saddam get through right now. I hate this job.

CHAPTER 29

TEDDY

If there was anything new that I learnt since becoming a Christian, it was the belief that there was no such thing as luck. I didn't understand Ajani's drug smuggling arrangement, but I knew that it was the grace of God that allowed us to cross the border without a hassle. I was glad that I prayed and thankful that God answered it.

I looked at Ajani. He looked relieved that we made it through, but he hated to be wrong and he wasn't going to admit his fault. At least not in front of the Phat Five. I stayed cool because I didn't want to get him upset, but Eros felt the need to speak his mind.

"So," he said to Ajani, "I didn't know Kwame was a woman's name. I've heard of unisex names like Robin, Dale, even Shirley. But Kwame? Dang, her parents must've been mad that she wasn't a boy!"

Ajani said, "Shut up, Eros. You talk too much."

"At least I don't mess up arrangements and deal with the wrong people."

"Look! We made it through without issues, right? We weren't sniffed out by dogs or racially profiled. Even if we were, that ain't half as messed up as situations that I've dealt with before."

K.J said, "Well, we don't live your lifestyle, Ajah. I ain't trying to be somebody's whore behind bars."

Q, who was really quiet during the entire ride, said, "We should've gotten pulled over. I might as well go to jail, 'cause I'll probably be there after the beat-down I give to whoever's sexing Trina."

There was an unexpected silence after his comment. All of a sudden, Ajani burst out laughing, and we all followed. Q's face was red like ketchup. I didn't want to laugh at him, but I couldn't help it.

"Q, I'm sorry man, but you aren't gonna beat up nobody. You don't want bad press, and we don't want another Club Oasis situation."

Q smiled, but he didn't look amused. "Man, forget you punks!"

"Relax, guy," said Eros. "I'm gonna help you avoid doing something stupid. I got some booty lined up for ya."

"What? This weekend? With who?"

"I'll give you details later. Just trust me on this one."

I wanted to argue with Eros, but I stayed quiet. How was having an affair going to solve anything for Q? Doing something stupid to avoid doing something else stupid seemed extra stupid. Especially if Q wasn't completely sure that Katrina cheated on him.

K.J decided to bring back the subject of drug dealing.

"So, Ajah," he asked, "where's the exclusive drug behind this border drama?"

Ajani replied that the briefcases holding the ghetto heroin was under the back seat. K.J pulled out a large black leather briefcase that looked more valuable than the drug itself. When he opened it, there were about two dozen containers of OxyContin, which looked like extra-strength Tylenol pills.

"So this is the crap called Ghetto Heroin," K.J said while pouring out a few pills in his hand.

"Yeah, that's the crap," replied Ajani.

It looked so plain and unappealing to the naked eye. I asked Ajani what was so special about it.

He said, "The high is like crack and heroin, except that it's cheaper, which explains the name 'Ghetto Heroin.' It's really called Hillbilly Heroin 'cause country folk were all up on it like black on tar. Somebody brought the junk to the streets of T.O, and the rest is history."

Eros asked, "How do you inhale it? Is it that powerful?"

"I don't know, guy, I just sell it. I don't have a clue as to how it feels. A successful dealer never messes with his merchandise but from what I hear, cats boil it and inject it like crack, grind the pill and sniff it, or just plain swallow it.

Machete took full advantage of the hype. He connected with a pharmacist that hooks him up with strongest OxyContin in North America, which is what y'all are looking at now. People are paying mad loot for the high it gives."

"How much?" I asked.

"A lot."

"How much?"

"Let's just say if I do this full-time, I'd be rich before I'm thirty."

"Whoa, nuff said," K.J., said as he quickly put the pills back in the case. "You should have enough loot to pay all our student loans, guy."

"Nobody knows how much money I have, and even though y'all are my boys, you'll never know how much I'm worth," said Ajani very seriously. "I will let you know that my ride is fully paid and my credit is mint. I can finish paying for my house, but I'm not trying to make it obvious to Savannah."

I nodded, but I had the hardest time believing that Savannah was clueless about Ajani's wealth. Did she really think that he was living well off as a SpeedEx driver? Ajani had to be the greatest liar ever.

More than ever, I was concerned about the focus and direction of my long-time friend.

"Ajah," I asked, "when you deal, do you ever think about the people you sell it to and how it affects them in the future, especially your own people?"

My cousin said, "Oooh, Ted, that's deep. All right, Ajah, you're in the hot seat. How do you respond? Inquiring minds want to know."

"Alright, I'll be blunt with ya," said Ajani. "I used to think about the customer, but not anymore. If I think about the overdoses, the crack-heads robbing their families to pay me, the broken and dysfunctional homes, and the newborn crack babies, that would stop me from making thousands of tax-free dollars. If I wanted to make a limited income and be concerned about my community, then I would be a social worker. My community consists of three: A.J, Savannah, and me. I came from Jamaica to North America to get rich, and I have to do whatever it takes to fulfill my goal. Good, honest people with university degrees are driving taxicabs, while some white-collar workers are drug dealing just to make more cash, which proves that the economy sucks, society is messed up, and education is highly overrated. Of course, this is only my opinion. I don't hate anyone who tries to get an education. Shoot, my woman is a schoolteacher, A.J has a college fund but I am in the drug game because life is short and I want lots of money now. Any more questions?"

I didn't say a word for the rest of the journey to the mall. Ajani's thoughts were so strong that I couldn't respond right away. However, a Bible verse came to my memory right away, **"What *does it profit a man to gain the whole world and lose his soul?*"** I couldn't remember where the verse was found in the Bible, but it was one of a few verses that always stuck with me.

I truly believed that Ajani was more than obsessed with having money. Money was his poison. Suddenly, I had a fear that the drug game was gonna kill Ajani really soon, which meant that I had to witness to him as soon as possible. He was definitely on the route to Hades in my opinion, and it was up to me to pray for a one-eighty in Ajani's life.

CHAPTER 30

Q

It was shortly after noon when we arrived at Fairlane Mall in Dearborn, Michigan. Ajani dropped us at one of the mall entrances and told us that he would meet us in the food court at two. For me, that was too long because I wasn't interested in shopping. What I wanted to buy was a bottle of vodka for passing-out purpose, but it made more sense to buy it in Windsor. Thus, I decided to window shop, because no material item could take my mind away from my marital issues.

Teddy and K.J went to Sam Goody to buy some CDs while I followed Eros into a men's clothing store. I wasn't in the mood to deal with his arrogance, but I was somewhat curious as to what he wanted to discuss with me, even though I was ninety-nine percent sure that it probably involved sex.

"Eros Alexander, Jr., you are so fine!"

Eros tried on a Sean John leather jacket and posed in the store mirror. He admired himself for at least five minutes.

"God, you knew what you were doing when you made me! I can see why women love me so much, why they want to buy me gifts, why they want my lips to kiss them from head to toe, why . . ."

"Dang, Eros!" I snapped while staring at some designer sweaters. "Get a room and take that mirror with you. People in here don't need to hear all that!"

He ignored my comment.

"Man, I don't understand why I haven't gotten paid for sex yet. With this fit body, great looks, and super stamina, I should be rolling just like Ajah. Forget my low-paying job as a teacher's assistant. I should be paid for sex."

I said, "The reason why you haven't been paid for sex is because it's tough nowadays to live off of five bucks an hour."

"Hee hee, you got jokes, huh? You know that I could rebound with a comment to make you feel shame, but you're going through drama, so I'll leave you alone."

"Anyways . . . what's this news that you want to tell me?"

Eros looked at me with a kid-in-a-candy-store grin.

"Ah, thanks for reminding me. How bad do you want to know?"

With a serious look, I said, "I only want to know because you mentioned it like it was big news."

"It is big news if you're in the mood for it."

"What I'm in the mood for is a serious blunt and some heavy liquor, anything to get my mind off Katrina."

He turned towards the mirror and said, "Oh well, suit yourself."

I shook my head. I was so used to Eros messing around with me, especially when it involved a hook-up with another woman.

"All right, I'm interested," I said with no enthusiasm. "Who is it?"

"Guy, its Nivea's roommate, Whitney."

"You serious? The other guys were saying the same thing."

"Well, it's the truth. Nivea says that she loves Caucasian men with soul."

"Well, that's nice."

"That's nice?" Eros exclaimed. "Is that all you can say? Q, Nivea looks nice, but Whitney is off the hook! Although Nivea is a sweetie and great in the bedroom, if I knew that her roommate was that fine, I wouldn't be checking for Nivea at all."

"Well, if she's so fine, then go for her. I'm a married man, you're not. You have no problems being polygamous."

"And neither did you before you got whipped! If you weren't my best friend, yes, I would give Whitney the night of her life and not care less about Nivea but the girl wants you, and you just got played by your wife. How in the world can you refuse *get back at your woman in a different area code* sex?"

I knew that Whitney was pretty, and it was nice to know that she liked me, but I wasn't ready to stoop to Eros' level.

"Look," I snapped. "I'm not fully sure that Trina's cheating on me yet!"

"Whatever . . . and SARS is not contagious. If an unknown Barry White sound-alike called my girl's cell phone to come over from N.Y to T.O, you best believe that they weren't playing Scrabble. The truth hurts, man!"

"And so does my head right now. You done?"

Eros saw that I was mad and frustrated, so he took off the jacket he was trying on.

"Yeah, I'm done," he answered. "I ain't making pimp dollars yet, so this jacket will have to wait."

We exited the retail store.

While walking up the mall escalator, Eros asked, "Guy, do you remember Stacy?"

Stacy? I thought. *He hasn't mentioned that name in years.*

"How can I forget Stacy, the only girl in history that actually cheated on you?"

"That's right, the only one. I was thirteen years old when that happened. When Stacy dumped me, I was depressed for three weeks because I was in love with her."

Just thinking about that junior high memory made me laugh out loud. I started singing the chorus of Slick Rick's *Teenage Love*. Eros gave me an annoyed expression.

I started imitating him, saying, "'Oh Stacy, let me carry your books for you.' 'Oh Stacy, let me do your homework!' Meanwhile, you did her work and got D's on all your assignments!"

Eros said, "Yeah, I was pretty stupid back then. But now I can thank Stacy 'cause she helped me become the player that I am today. Since that break-up, I promised myself that I'll never let another woman play me again. So far, so good. I had mastered the art of not being caught and not falling in love. I also learnt a lot from my father. He dates the most beautiful women in the adult film industry. Some of them, unbelievably, wanted to marry him, but my dad refused to commit. The last woman that he committed to treated him like dirt. That woman brought me into this world.

Q, what's the big deal about love? Love is like liquor: at first it tastes and feels real good. You think it's all good when you consume a lot of it, but the end result is that you feel like crap."

That was the harshest comment that I ever heard about love. I stopped smiling and didn't react to it at all. Was I happier as a player and a rising basketball star? Will having an affair take away my misery?

Eros put his hand on my shoulder.

"Dog, I'm just trying to give advice. If you enjoy the thought of Katrina getting busy with another man, then I'll leave you alone. If not, you can come with me to Nivea's crib at seven tonight. Whitney will be anticipating your arrival."

CHAPTER 31

AJANI

I turned off my secondary cell phone in disgust. It was ringing constantly and the voice mail was completely full. I refused to answer it unless it was from Machete, but I got so sick of the rings that I threw the phone at the back seat.

Situations weren't making sense, and I was ready to cuss out my boss. The drama at the tunnel was unorganized and unprofessional, and the more I tried to understand it, the least it made sense. Yet, I would be less upset once I got the drug money from Martinez.

Martinez Estafan was a forty-five year old, no-nonsense drug lord who had a good working relationship with Machete. Machete traveled to Detroit at least three times a year to negotiate deals, and Martinez always returned the favor. However, because of the SARS epidemic in Toronto, Martinez refused to travel to Canada. Yet it didn't bother Machete because he loved his Cuban business partner like a big brother.

I wondered why Martinez wanted a rush order of G.H when Machete was coming to Detroit after the weekend. Was the drug *really* that hard to get in Motown? It didn't make sense, but at least I was making some extra loot as a result.

The directions to the location weren't a problem because I'd been there previously. The place, The Real Feel, was Detroit's largest ethnic strip club located on the popular Eight Mile road. I parked on the side of the street, turned on the car alarm, and walked towards the back entrance of the club with the briefcases.

Knocked on the steel door a few times, but there was no response. Deals were made through the back entrance, so I had no intentions of going through the main door. The place was full of people, so I knocked again, this time with a few pounds.

Someone with a strong Latino accent yelled through the intercom, "Who is it?"

I said that I was looking for Martinez.

"And who are you?"

"Ajani from Toronto. I work for Machete Deverow."

"You that Jamaican cat?"

I sighed. "Yeah, the Jamaican cat."

Dude didn't respond. It seemed like I was unexpected. Twenty seconds later, I heard his voice again.

"What's the password?"

Oh yeah. Almost forgot about it. I was glad that I had a good memory because Machete failed to remind me about Martinez's password system. A year ago, I came with Machete and Rancel to the club and Martinez said that he had six children. Every two months, the password was the middle name of one of the kids in descending order.

Let's see . . . its March, which means that its Martinez's second child. Dang, I think their first names are English and the middle names are Latino. There's Jennifer Maria, David Pedro, Leann Juanita . . . but which one is the second oldest? Oh, I know! It's Daniel . . .

"What's the password?"

"Hold on!" I yelled back. "I know this . . . its Jesus."

The door unlocked by a loud buzzer.

"That's why I just sell the drugs and never use them," I said quietly as I breathed a sigh of relief.

A short, muscular Cuban man stood at the entrance. I recognized him right away but I didn't know his name. His four front teeth were platinum-plated.

"If you said *Gee-zus* instead of *Hey-Zeus*, I wouldn't have opened this door," he said without smiling.

"What's going on? Everything cool?" I asked when I shook his hand.

"Yeah, man but this is a surprise, yo. Martinez didn't say you were coming. Where's your boss?"

"In Toronto. It's just me."

He pulled out a gun from his jacket.

"I swear, if you sneeze on me, I'll kill you! That's a promise!" he panicked.

"Forget you, dog; I ain't got no SARS, just a briefcase of goodies. Where's Martinez?"

"He won't be back until later. Like I said, we didn't know you was coming and he didn't say jack."

I was surprised and confused. How could these cats not know that I was coming with their stuff? I asked the guy if Ricardo, Martinez's younger brother was available.

"He's in the office," he said, "but he's higher than a kite right now and probably with some stripper. Let's go and find out."

Obviously, he had no problem spoiling Ricardo's party. That was good, because I wanted my money.

During conversation, we walked through the kitchen and into the club's main area. The club filled with men eating five-dollar steak lunches and stuffing dollar bills into thong panties of beautiful women dancing on tables and around stage poles. The *Real Feel* almost encouraged me to open a strip club in Toronto, but my mind changed immediately after finding out that Savannah was pregnant with A.J.

From the main area, we proceeded towards the basement, where the office and the V.I.P lounge was located. Mr. Platinum Teeth knocked on the office door.

"Ricardo! Ricardo!" he yelled.

Hearing no response, he took out his keys and unlocked the door. We saw Ricardo leaning back on in a recliner chair with a stripper on his lap. Whenever Martinez was away, he was in charge of the club and all deals. However, once I saw the weed on his desk and his moaning expressions, I knew that business was the last thing on his mind.

Ricardo snapped. "Jose! What the . . . Ajani? What the hell are you doing in Detroit?"

I replied, "Business, Ricardo. Why wasn't anybody informed that I was coming? Machete sent me."

Before he responded, he looked at his mistress and told her to get out. She got off his lap, grabbed her clothes and exited the office.

"Yo," said Ricardo while zipping his pants, "a dealer can't even get high and laid without having to deal with business. Now, somebody tell me what the hell's going on here?"

I didn't like to do business when the other party was under the influence. Somebody usually ended up being ripped off or highly frustrated because their mind was not in full function. On a normal day, I would've re-scheduled the appointment but the trip was international, and I wasn't going back to Canada without the loot.

"Apparently, Machete and Martinez negotiated a deal for some G.H next week," I explained. "I was told by Machete that your brother wanted a rush order this weekend. So I have the stuff here and I'm ready to collect."

Looking confused, Ricardo got up from his seat and walked to the liquor cabinet to pour himself a glass of vodka. He offered me a drink, but I refused.

After taking a sip, he asked Jose, "Did Martinez tell you about this?"

He replied, "No! I swear this is news to me, too."

I was glad that I had a decent working relationship with the Estafan brothers. They were short, intimidating Cubans and not to be messed with. Dealers came correct with their business or they were severely dealt with, but I wasn't worried. Machete sat well with the brothers for years, and I felt that a slight misunderstanding wouldn't ruin anything. At least I hoped it wouldn't.

"My brother lets us know beforehand about any pre-arrangements," said Ricardo. "If I knew you were coming, I wouldn't have gotten freaked up like this. Is that the G.H in your briefcases?"

I placed one of the briefcases on the desk and opened it.

"The best, baby," I answered.

Ricardo opened one of the capsules and poured out the pills on the desk. He looked at them as if he wanted another high.

"Looks like the real thing," he said. "Cats in D-Town would rob their family for this."

I said, "This stuff in T.O is hotter than J.Lo sweating in a hot tub. I got the details of what I'm supposed to get from you."

I handed Ricardo a piece of paper from my jacket side pocket. He studied the information.

Ricardo said, "Like I said, Martinez ain't told me jack about this. All I know is that he and Deverow are meeting next week. I don't set no deals unless it's approved by my brother."

I snapped. "Bred-drin, what you think this is? I don't make any decisions unless it's pre-approved by Machete. Y'all cats know how we represent! Y'all know our stuff is legit! I didn't drive for four hours from another country for a lap dance. I can get that in Toronto where the booty is nicer and the women look better! Therefore, I ain't leaving without the cash!"

"Son, you're lucky that I'm high and that I actually got respect for you, otherwise you'll be lucky to leave this room alive! Maybe Martinez forgot to tell me, which I highly doubt, but because y'all sell the best G.H and you got a good rep, we'll work something out. I would call Martinez, but he's with his daughter and wants no interruptions today. So I'll give you half of what Machete's asking for now, and the rest when he comes down next week."

"That's crap, Ricardo. I ain't leaving without at least seventy-five percent."

"Say what you want, but I won't give you more that sixty. And that's pushing it, considering that you're making me work on my day off!"

I didn't care if he was in the midst of heart surgery at that point. I was upset that arrangements weren't properly made, and as I result I was looking suspect. However, sixty percent was still a decent chunk of money.

"Alright," I agreed, "sixty percent it is, only because of miscommunication."

"It's all good, Ajani, its all good."

Ricardo sat down on the top of his desk and pulled a gun from the top drawer.

He said, "Martinez will be here tonight and I'll tell him what went down. If he and Machete made this deal, then everything's chill. However, if this deal was a load of crap, you'll know about it and be dealt with. That's a guarantee."

I didn't waste any time getting in my truck. I made sure that nobody was observing my actions before I took out the money. Indeed, some cash was better than no cash, but I felt like I was the victim of other people's screw-ups. I was frustrated, had no answers, and very pissed off. The plan for me was to wait until I arrived in Windsor to call Machete, but I changed my mind. Situations had to be cleared up now.

CHAPTER 32

"What you mean you didn't get him?"

Machete could not believe what he was hearing through his hands-free phone. Kwame revealed the news of not being able to capture Ajani.

"Man, you're a funny brother," said Machete. "You sure know how to tell jokes in a serious tone. You got me good."

"I wish I was joking, man," Kwame said. "I didn't arrest him."

Machete was silent for a few seconds. He walked into his office in the warehouse and shut the door.

"Moss, you mind telling me how the hell you messed up something so freaking easy?"

"Chete, let me explain . . ."

"I'm waiting! And this better be real good!"

"I sped up the line, and your boy was about to drive through it. All of a sudden, the guy turns into another lane that was going just as fast as mine! It was unplanned and definitely unexpected."

"And why couldn't you tell the other officer to slow his lane down and pull Ajani over? Isn't that why you have walkie-talkies?"

Machete was furious. Things obviously were not going as planned. He wanted answers and believed that Kwame was hiding some information.

"Yeah, we have walkie-talkies, but . . . I can't explain how the plan messed up, man. This has never happened before, 'cause I usually have this crap under control. I don't what to say but . . ."

"You freaked up! This was the best chance to nail someone who's out to mess up my business, and you failed!"

Machete picked up a coffee mug from his desk and smashed it on the floor.

"You have no idea how pissed off I am, Moss! I hope you're at Western Union sending my money back!"

Rancel walked into the office, staring at his cousin with curiosity.

"Your money?" Kwame asked, sounding surprised. "Who said you were getting this money back? I don't guarantee anything when I make deals!"

"And I don't give four-digit figures to people that mess up operations!"

"I told you beforehand that I never got paid to arrest someone for drug trafficking! I messed up, but I can get some cats in Detroit to track him and take him down!"

"Nah, forget it! I don't work with cats who mess up more than once with me. Just send me my money today, before situations are real messed up! I'll deal with Ajani myself!"

"Oh, how quickly you forget that I'm the man that let's you get into the U.S without hassle!"

"And you forgot that I got enough connections to get you arrested for allowing international criminal activity in your country. You can take me down, but I'll bring you with me!"

Kwame was silent.

"Alright, Deverow, you win. I'll send your money back tonight."

Machete hung up the phone. He turned around and saw Rancel, but decided to ignore him. He folded his arms and stared at the wall with rage. Machete hated failed operations with a passion.

Rancel asked, "What's going on?"

"Bethel got through," replied Machete after ten seconds of silence.

"How the . . . I thought you paid that fool to arrest him!"

"Forget Kwame. My focus is on getting Ajani and preventing him from taking me down."

Machete's cell phone started ringing. He looked at the caller ID.

"Speaking of . . . Bethel's calling me now," he said before answering. "What's going on, Bethel?"

Ajani snapped. "Yo, I can't believe you didn't have your crap together!"

Machete raised his eyebrows in reaction to the way Ajani spoke to him. The man sounded angry, and he had to pretend that he was clueless.

"What's the problem?"

"Everything! First of all, your boy Mr. Kwame Moss confused the hell outta me at the border! You said his entrance lane would be the fastest, but there were two freaking lanes going the same speed, and I had to eeney-meeney-miney-moe my way through it! I picked one of the lanes, and it was the wrong one! Instead of Mr. Moss, I get this grumpy sister who actually let me through without hassle. What the hell, man? I could've sworn y'all were trying to mess me up on purpose!"

Guy's not stupid, thought Machete.

"I just spoke to Kwame, and he apologized for the tunnel screw-up. I'm just glad that you made it through. I'm not trying to mess you up."

"Oh yeah? Well how do you explain what happened next? After finally getting through, I made it to *The Real Feel* only to go through a verbal showdown with Ricardo Estafan 'cause he didn't know I was coming! Apparently, Martinez ain't said jack to him about the deal. What the hell, Chete? Of the three years I've worked with you, you always had your stuff together. Guy, if those cats didn't associate me with you, I'd probably be dead right now! So, what the hell is going on?"

"Your guess is as good as mine," lied the drug-lord.

Ajani was not supposed to reach the strip club, and the only arrangement that was made with Martinez was for after the weekend.

"I specifically told Martinez that you were bringing a case of G.H on Friday," he continued. "I'll have to talk to him about that. Did you at least get the money?"

"Yeah, I got some money. Only sixty percent of it! They were only gonna give me half, because Ricardo claimed he didn't know nothing about the deal. You're gonna have to get the rest when you come down 'cause I'm sick of this crap. It's one thing to live as a dealer, and another to deal with unorganized business. I'm sick of it!"

"Bethel, relax. You'll get the cash you deserve once I talk to Martinez. Have I ever let you down when it comes to you getting your money? I look out for my peoples when they look out for me."

"Yo, I ain't sure about nothing anymore. Before this, I wouldn't even sweat it. Now, I don't know what's going on now. I just do what I have to do to be paid. Dang, if more crap happens like this, I might have to bounce. This is unnecessary stress!"

Maybe Rancel was right after all. Bethel is up to something and I gotta take him out before he goes ballistic.

"Bred-drin, enjoy the rest of the weekend," Machete concluded. "Spend some money and get some booty. Smoke some weed, gamble with some money. You accomplished your task, so we'll talk on Sunday when you come back to T.O."

"Yeah, whatever, I'm out. By the way, I'm still pissed about these unidentified calls on my cell phone! Tell Rancel that he better fix this crap ASAP!"

They hung up. Rancel was looking at him in shock.

"You told him to enjoy his weekend?" he snapped. "That punk just messed up our plans!"

"I'm not worried," Machete replied calmly. "If there's one thing you know about me, when plan A doesn't work, plan B is already into effect."

"What's plan B? Going to Windsor to kill him?"

"Guy, please. That's the last resort. Bethel will be dead before the day is over, and it won't be by us."

Machete took out a jar of pills from his desk drawer and showed one of the pills to his cousin.

"Look at the pill real closely," he said. "It's the same kind I gave Ajani. It looks like OxyContin, but it's weaker than a Tylenol. He's a dead man once the Estafans realize that the drug's counterfeit."

CHAPTER 33

TEDDY

"So Teddy, is there a lot women that go to your church?" Eros asked me while I was sipping a chocolate milkshake.

We were sitting at a table in the mall's food court eating and talking as we waited for Ajani to appear. The subjects ranged from the upcoming NBA playoffs to shoes to music and now churchwomen. I actually stopped thinking about the U.S border incident and began to enjoy fellowshipping with my boys.

I asked Eros why he wanted to know about the ladies at Kingdom Workers Fellowship, as if I didn't know what his answer would be.

"Just curious," he replied. "I know that women are unstable creatures and need to be inspired frequently."

"How do you know this? When's the last time you went to church?"

"If a Donnie McClurkin concert counts, it was last year. I'm telling you, I ain't ever seen so much women cry in one setting."

K.J asked Eros, "Why were you at a Donnie McClurkin concert? I know that it wasn't your idea."

"Of course not," he answered. "I was tutoring a chick who happened to have free tickets. You know me; I was just trying to get on her good side and in her bedroom."

I shook my head. Eros' dating stories always had the same conclusion, sex. Being platonic was a sin in his world.

"At the concert," he continued, "the girl was clapping her hands, praising, and crying, even hours afterward. After she laid down her burdens, she just wanted somebody to hold her, and that's what I did. Of course, one thing led to another, and . . ."

"And you're thinking that it's easy to get into a church lady's dress," I interrupted. "Guy, I hate to burst your bubble, but most Christian women aren't that easy."

I saw Q nodding his head while chomping on a bacon double cheeseburger.

"Although I don't go to church, I agree," he said with a full mouth. "Member, Eros? Before Trina, I went out with a girl in high school that was so Christian she didn't even let me kiss her."

"Oh, please! Marilyn Johnson?" asked Eros. "That girl became a nun right after she graduated. That doesn't count. I'm talking about the average single woman who goes to church every Sunday."

I pointed a French fry in his face.

"How could you, of all people, jump to that conclusion after seeing just one church girl?" I asked. "I'll guarantee you that if Janet was single and I wasn't seeing her, you couldn't sleep with her."

"Guy, that doesn't count. I wouldn't date Janet 'cause I see her too much as a sister. My theory is that God created sex and He created hormones and sex drives. Churchwomen may be born-again, but they never stop thinking about sex in my opinion. You call yourself a Christian, but you still crave sex. Am I right?"

I didn't want to say yes, but the dude was right.

"Yes, but . . ."

"And," Eros continued, "don't even lie to me with this question, T-Henny. You and Janet still have sex, right?"

"No, we don't," I answered, not expecting him to believe me.

"Guy, you're a Christian and you're lying to me like that?" Eros sipped his drink and shook his head. "You're still doing it, man. Don't deny it."

"Believe it, guy!" K.J said, eager to defend me. "Trust me; this is coming from someone who probably has the longest sex drought of all five of us. I'm not bragging about it, but I know that some people who are not gay, good-looking, can go months and years without sex. Gospel divas like Yolanda Adams and Mary Mary probably waited until marriage to get their freak on. It sure as hell ain't easy, but it can be done."

Eros asked, "So, are you saying that you'll wait until marriage to have sex?"

"Well . . . I never said that I'd go that far."

Q and Eros started laughing, followed by my cousin letting out a few chuckles. I continued eating, revealing the expression that I didn't want to continue the discussion. Since I became a Christian, not a day went by when I didn't think about making love to Janet. Avoiding pre-marital sex was more difficult than reading Japanese, and I felt that my boys wouldn't fully understand my reasons for not giving in.

Q, who was sitting across from me, looked up and grinned.

"Well, at least he's still alive," he said, looking at someone behind me.

I turned around and saw Ajani carrying two large Victoria's Secret bags. As usual, the man was on time, two minutes before two pm.

"Y'all ready to go?" he asked us, looking very serious. He looked more upset than he did before we crossed the border.

"Aren't you gonna get something to eat?" I asked him. "What's the hurry?"

"Man, I already ate. Let's just get back to Windsor. I did what I had to do, I got Savannah her beauty stuff, and I don't like walking around with two pink bags."

"It's all good," said Eros. "That stuff is the answer for getting booty. It never fails."

"Oh, really?" Ajani asked. "And when do you actually take the time to buy stuff for women?"

"Only when the girl is mad, and right now, ain't any ladies ticked off at me, as far as I know. When they're happy, they use their debit and credit cards on me. I ain't got my time to spend my little money on . . ."

Q interrupted him while getting out of his seat. "Anyways, let's head out! Let's get to Windsor before rush hour traffic."

We all got up quickly as an indicator that we didn't care what Eros had to say.

As we walked away, I heard him yell, "All y'all cats hating on a true player! Forget y'all!"

CHAPTER 34

AJANI

I decided to take the Detroit-Windsor Ambassador Bridge instead of the tunnel heading back to Canada. I was glad that I didn't have anymore drug business to deal with for the weekend, but I still didn't feel right about what took place at *The Real Feel*. It was stressing me, but the real thing I didn't want was my boys finding out the drama. In addition, I felt like I owed my boys for putting up with the tunnel incident, so I had a plan.

"Ajah! We're almost at the entrance," Teddy said. "You're clear of all drugs in this ride, right?"

Man, shut up, I thought as I looked at him, but he looked serious. I looked behind and saw that Q, K.J, and Eros also looked concerned.

"Relax," I said with a grin, "the Escalade is clear of all narcotics. I told you that I got my stuff together."

"Then why are you taking the bridge instead of the tunnel?"

"'Cause I want to. Got a problem with that?" I said it in a tone that indicated that I was sick of Teddy's paranoia.

"My bad, guy. But can you blame my paranoia? You put us at risk today!"

Eros said, "For real! Therefore, Ajah, how are you going to repay us for our stress now that you have some more Benjamins? Convert that to Canadian dollars and you can do more for us!"

"I don't know about y'all, but all I want right now is some weed," Q said. "That's the only fulfilling thing for me at this moment."

"Relax, children," I said as I paid the bridge toll. "Don't think that I wasn't looking out for y'all when I was doing business today. I'm gonna reserve an executive suite at Casino Windsor for tomorrow. How about that?"

Eros got excited. "What? Are you serious? How much does that cost?"

"Does it matter? Should I reconsider?"

"Forget Eros, Ajah," said Teddy. "We'll take it! I ain't never stayed in an executive suite before."

Q said, "Guy, all is forgiven with whatever happened before. You the man."

"Yeah, I know," I replied.

Other than spending time with my family, hanging with the Phat Five was the best solution to forgetting about the drug game. Just as it was a joy to focus on the interests of the family, I decided for once to focus less on myself at the moment and more on the fellas.

K.J didn't here my announcement. He was nodding his head while listening to a Discman.

"K.J!" I shouted. "What's the deal, man?"

"Huh?" he shouted back as he took off the headphones.

"What's the deal, man? You ready for tonight?"

"The showcase?" K.J. sucked his teeth. "Of course I'm ready."

"Well then, pass me your CD with the beats and let's hear you rip something."

K.J. gave Teddy his CD to put in the car stereo. The first beat that played sounded addictive with a hard bass and melodic piano riffs. It was so tight, it made me want to rhyme, and I couldn't even rap old school.

"C'mon, cuzin!" Teddy exclaimed. "Spit something."

K.J. started to nod his head and said, "Yo, cats ain't ready for this! Uh . . . come on . . .

> Listen to the music, you ask 'who loop this?'
> Roll with the Phat Five, that's who my troop is
> Mr. Rapper, I sound better than any rhyme that you did
> So much intellect, it'll make Bill Gates feel stupid!

After hearing the fourth bar, everybody went nuts with excitement. It inspired K.J to freestyle all the way to immigration. I wasn't the biggest hip-hop fan, but he was the best rapper I'd ever heard. K.J had me looking forward to the showcase.

We entered Windsor without hassle from the border officer. Thank God.

Teddy said to me, "Yo, before we go to the crib, let's stop at my church."

I gave him another crazy look. I was craving a blunt, and he wanted to go to church? He definitely wasn't the Teddy I knew in Toronto.

"You're joking, right?" I asked him. "I'm not going to any church."

Eros said to Teddy, "Why are you going to church on a Friday afternoon? And why you wanna drag us with you?"

"I just want y'all to meet some people, that's all," Teddy answered. "Plus, y'all wanna see Janet, right?"

"Not that bad. I'm staying in the ride."

I agreed with Eros. If I wasn't going to church with Savannah, I wasn't going to church with anybody. Yet, I didn't want to be a jerk either.

"Alright, we'll go, but only for a hot minute. But I'm staying in the truck."

CHAPTER 35

K.J.

"This is a real nice building," I said as I looked at the church headquarters called Kingdom Workers Fellowship.

I was the only guy who came out of the SUV with Teddy. My cousin was a spiritual cat unlike the past, so I was very interested in his place of worship and I was impressed, because the building wasn't too flashy and definitely not ghetto.

I asked him how many people attended the church.

"About six hundred and fifty," said Teddy. "About half of them are college students, and way more than half of the students are women. *Beautiful, single, blessed women of God!*"

"Wow, you emphasized that last sentence! What are you trying to say?"

"Nothing, guy. Just giving you some choices since you're more single than Kraft cheese. Ain't no better place to look for a lady than the house of God," he said, trying to sound serious but couldn't stop grinning.

"Look, Theodore," I replied smiling, "I don't need anybody rushing me. I'm gonna take my time in choosing my woman. Trust me, when I find the one, you'll know."

Man, Teddy wouldn't quit the matchmaking game. He was even trying to find a woman for me in the mall. I couldn't care less about any girl at the present moment, no matter how available the lady or lovely the body. I was on a mission.

We entered the gates of the sanctuary. I looked around the facility as we moved closer to the pulpit platform. The place looked outstanding. The sanctuary consisted of theater-style blue and gold chairs and a center aisle. The windows were stained and the walls were decorated with flags and scripture banners. Looking at Ted's face, I could tell that he enjoyed being a part of the church.

We sat in the front row and waited quietly as Janet's dance group gathered in a circle holding hands and praying on the stage.

"Ah, man, they finished rehearsal," Teddy said with disappointment. "I was hoping we'd get to catch some of the routines. This group is off the hook."

I said, "They sound like they're full of energy, especially the way that they're praying."

They were all praying at the same time. It was the first time that I saw energetic prayer like that so up close and personal. I didn't know how to react to it. As I sat and watched them do their thing, I heard a powerful female voice take over the prayer session. I didn't know who she was, and I couldn't see her face because she was facing the wall and her head was bowed. It was a voice that I could listen to all day long and not get tired of.

She was dressed in a light blue business suit with the boots to match. The clothes definitely complemented her body, which didn't look thin or overweight. Her figure seemed ideal for her height, which looked about five foot ten. I couldn't wait to see her face. I thought that if her face were as great as her voice, she would be outstanding but I didn't want to be too optimistic because eye and ear candy were as different as apples and oranges.

The prayer ended, and the lady turned around to talk to one of the dancers. Her face was caramel-colored, and her hair was jet black and long. Looked like it was her own, but that didn't matter to me 'cause I was in awe of her appearance. Her face looked very similar to Denzel Washington's mistress in the film *Training Day*. She was absolutely beautiful, a drop-dead gorgeous Latina woman. She gave me goose bumps, that is how pretty she was. I'd never had this feeling for a woman before. Not even Bianca.

Teddy began to walk onto the stage, and I was right behind him. My eyes were still on the lady until I heard a familiar voice call me. It was Janet, and I gave her a big hug.

"What up, girl?" I said to her. "How are you?"

"I'm doing well," Janet, answered with her pretty smile. "It's so good to see you!"

Then she looked at her man and asked him if he had a good time in Detroit.

"Different," Teddy replied.

"Why, what happened?"

"It's a long story. Talk to you about it later."

"True. So, K.J, I heard that you're in the Freestyle Showcase. You ready?"

With confidence, I replied, "Girl, what you think? They're not ready for K.J."

"I bet they're not. I would be there to see you but . . . you know."

"No need to explain, J. You're born-again now. I'm happy for you and Ted."

Janet put her arm around Teddy's waist and said, "Yeah, Bear and I won't be at Jam Fest or those other parties anymore, unless they're Christ-operated."

I looked at Teddy and he had a semi-grin on his face. If my cousin were going to the showcase, he would have to go through Janet and judging by Ted's expression, his decisions for Friday night weren't finalized.

The lady that blew my mind approached us. I started feeling warmer than a humid day in July.

"Hi, Ted," she said with her beautiful voice.

"Hey, Kaitlyn," said Teddy. "I'd like for you to meet someone."

Good looking out, cousin.

Kaitlyn looked at me and smiled. I smiled back.

Oh my God, she looks incredible. Is she the one? Man, its hot in this church!

Teddy said, "Kaitlyn, this is my cousin, K.J. K.J, this is Kaitlyn, oh pardon me, Minister Kaitlyn Fuentes."

She and I shook hands.

"Nice to meet you, K.J. Are you going to be a part of our Bless Fest weekend?"

I was speechless.

Say something, stupid.

"Well . . . I uh . . ."

"Yeah, he'll be here," Teddy interrupted. "We'll be here tonight, Lord willing."

"Wonderful!" Kaitlyn said. "K.J, you won't regret it. It'll be awesome!"

I loved her spirit. She was full of joy and zeal.

My tongue started functioning again and I said, "I think I'll have to check it out. It looks like it'll be exciting."

I wanted to get to know Kaitlyn. I had to know more about her. Yes, I was in Windsor to kick booty in the freestyle showcase, but now, it seemed so secondary. The only thing I knew about this lady was her name, but she already had my heart. Unbelievable.

Janet asked, "Bear, where are the other guys? The apartment?"

"No, they're outside," said Teddy. "None of them wanted to come in. Let's go and see them. You gotta see Ajah's new ride, its ridiculous!"

"Alright. Kaitlyn, I'll be back in a sec."

Kaitlyn nodded. "No problem. I'll still be here."

I followed the couple towards the exit. Gave Minister Kaitlyn Fuentes a wave and she did the same. I felt like a kid walking away from a brand new X-Box because it was bedtime. I was not ready to leave.

Tapping Teddy on the shoulder, I asked him quietly, "Yo, guy, why didn't you tell me about her?"

He said, "Wasn't it you who just told me, 'I don't need nobody rushing me. I'm gonna take my time in choosing my woman.'"

"Well, I took all the time I need. Is she single?"

"As far as I know," he said smiling. "She's five star quality, man."

"She's the one, guy. I'll meet you at the truck."

She's the one. My search is over.

I walked back to the stage. Just in case I didn't have another opportunity to speak to Minister Kaitlyn, I wanted to release my thoughts about her at the present moment. She was talking to one of the dancers who noticed that I was approaching. Once she notified the minister, she turned around and gave me a surprised look.

"Hey," I said to her.

"Hi," she replied.

Start talking, K.J. And don't make yourself look stupid.

"Minister Kaitlyn, you probably have heard what I have to say from many men, but I'll say it anyway: you are absolutely beautiful. If I never get the chance to see or talk to you again, at least I will feel better letting you know how I feel about you. All I know about you is your name, but there is no doubt in my mind that your inner and outer beauty is outstanding. You are a gift from God that cannot be copied or duplicated. Don't you ever think twice about it."

She was blushing with embarrassment. The dancer that heard me started to fan herself with her hand. I felt like the corniest man on the planet.

"Why, thank you," replied Kaitlyn. "That's so sweet."

"You're welcome. Take care."

I walked away without looking back. I couldn't bear to turn around and see her reaction.

When I arrived to the parking lot, I noticed the Phat Five and Janet laughing and talking. When they saw me approaching, they wanted details. Obviously, Teddy told them that I found the one, but I gave no information. I still felt embarrassed, and I got upset at myself for losing focus on my mission. The headphones went back on my ears and I tried to re-focus on hip-hop domination.

CHAPTER 36

EROS

We finally left Teddy's church. It was great to see Janet, but I didn't enjoy being around churches for more than a few minutes, even if it was only the parking lot. I just felt that church folk always shunned wannabe gigolos like me.

I still had a few hours before Q and I had to go to Nivea and Whitney's apartment. Teddy was going back to the church to do who knows what, so he was in and out of his crib in five minutes. K.J and Q decided to stay at the apartment, but I wanted more action. Thus, I went with Ajani to Casino Windsor.

At that time, Ajani was the only person that I wanted to hang with. As much as I loved my boys, I was relieved not to argue with K.J, listen to Q's marital problems, and tolerate Ted's newfound zeal for Christianity.

"Ajah, I need to know when you realized that you were ready for commitment," I said during the drive.

"When I realized that Savannah was the most down-to-earth woman that I've ever met," replied Ajani. "That, and Ajani, Jr. I want my son to have a visible and supporting mother and father in his life."

"Oh, okay."

"Why? You thinking about settling down?"

Without hesitation I answered, "Never! I was just being curious. I can't stand being somebody's boyfriend. Juanita wants me to call her so we can just *talk*. Nivea wants to show me off to her girls. It's just so annoying."

Ajani started laughing, but I was being very serious.

"You think its funny, but I ain't joking," I continued. "Canada is a country of freedom, and commitment in my opinion is the opposite of freedom. I live in Canada. Thus, I choose to be free."

"I'll leave that comment alone," said Ajani.

"Why can't I just meet a fine woman who likes men and women, has a girlfriend, and just wants a man for an occasional threesome? I've slept with every race and ethnicity on this planet and never had a ménage et trois."

"Never? You, of all people?"

I gave him a look of envy and surprise.

"What and you have? How come you never told me this?"

"You never asked. I've had it several times."

"WHAT?" I shouted. "Wow, Ajah! I know it was good, huh?"

"If you're the nasty type, like I used to be," he said calmly as if I asked him a normal question. "It was fun for while . . . until this thug fell in love."

I turned my head towards the passenger window. Love was a word that I shunned daily. To me, it was a wasted feeling. Having love for a girl during junior high school seemed wasted after the chick cheated on me. That brief couple of weeks was the first and last time I ever loved a female. I firmly believed that love was the worst four-letter word in the English language.

"Guy, is Savannah the first woman you ever loved?" I asked.

Ajani answered, "Other than my mother, yeah. Some say that you'll treat your woman like you treat your mama."

"I hate my mother," I grumbled. "I've never met her, and I don't want to. I never want to see her as long as I'm breathing."

I couldn't believe how easy that came out of my mouth. Ajani helped me open a can of worms.

"I think Q told me a while ago why your mother's not in your life, but it wasn't in too much detail," said Ajani. "Why do you hate your moms? You sound like Eminem."

"I can relate to how he feels," I said. "The woman who gave birth to me was a Puerto-Rican porn actress. My dad had just begun photography in the industry. They began seeing each other and of course became bed buddies. One day however, they didn't use birth control and she became pregnant. Neither of them was ready to be a parent. She especially didn't want a baby because she was at the prime of her career. She wanted to abort me so that she could continue making films without a long absence. My dad surprisingly wanted to keep me. He promised her that if she had me, he would be a good father, pay the cash to remove any stretch marks, and she wouldn't lose her status as an adult film star. She agreed. However, that still didn't change the fact that she didn't want to be a mother. She wasn't working after she got big and quickly became depressed. She smoked weed and drank during the full nine months. The witch tried to kill me, but I survived, and it still blows my mind that I'm not physically messed up! I was born and she named me after my father, Eros Andre Alexander. My dad and this woman were living together well before my birth. Two weeks after I was born, my dad woke up one morning and noticed that she wasn't in the apartment. She never returned, and my dad never heard from her again."

I used to be ashamed to tell that story, until I realized that I wanted cats to know that my mother was the worst human being ever.

"Ouch," Ajani said quietly. "Now I see why you hate to love women."

"Uh huh. My pops told me all of this when I was only twelve. For as long as I can remember, my dad has played and screwed tons of women without regret. He's my hero and role model, no matter what anyone thinks of him and his morals."

CHAPTER 37

AJANI

We arrived at the front entrance of Casino Windsor. Came out and had the Escalade valet parked. Before Eros and I went into the gaming area, we went to the casino's hotel to reserve the executive suite for Saturday.

"Yo, guy," Eros said as we approached the front desk, "you need some cash to help cover the room? Just holler if you do."

"I'm paying for an executive suite, not a Big Mac combo," I said. "Go and win your broke self some money."

"Whatever, man. I'll be in the game room." Eros walked away.

"Can I help you?" asked the front desk clerk.

"Yes, sir, I would like to reserve the executive suite for Saturday night," I answered.

They actually had one still available. I smiled as I reserved the room. The money that I received two hours prior felt good, but I frowned after remembering what I went through to get the cash from the Estafans. The entire drug deal seemed very suspect to me, and until the deal was approved by Machete and Martinez, I wasn't going to spend a single dollar of the cash. Thus, I decided that I would charge the expenses on my gold MasterCard when it was time to pay.

I then proceeded to the game room to play blackjack, my favorite game. I grew up watching my late father in Jamaica collect thousands of dollars from winning as a player and a dealer. Once I was at the legal age to gamble, I used my daddy's tactics to win cash in Windsor, Atlantic City, and Las Vegas. However, this time, I wanted to try other games for a change.

My goal for the afternoon was to win cash from as many games as possible. Once I won money at blackjack, I would move to Roulette. After Roulette, I'd go to Caribbean Stud, and so on. I studied the rules of all the casino games and I was ready to test my luck. My mission was to come out with double, if not more than my fifteen hundred dollar budget.

CHAPTER 38

EROS

Within fifteen minutes of playing the one-dollar slot machines, I lost twenty-five dollars. Man that ticked me off, plus it didn't help that a middle-aged man who smelled like Ben-Gay used a slot machine next to mine and won twenty grand.

"I won! I won!" the man shouted in my face. "And I only spent five dollars!"

"Wonderful!" I said. "But unless you're giving me some of it, I couldn't care less!"

Then I walked away.

I really wasn't pleased with the eye candy in the casino. After all, that was the true reason why I made the trip. I saw a few okay-looking women, but none of them could come close to Nivea or Juanita. All I wanted was a one-night stand or better yet a threesome this weekend. I'd kick Juanita and Nivea to the curb to get that opportunity within the next two days.

While I was walking towards Ajani at another slot machine area, I saw a waitress with cocktails and decided to buy one. As I was taking money out of my wallet, I was hit from behind. All of my coins spilled on the floor.

"What the . . ." I snapped as I turned to see who hit me.

"I'm so sorry . . . oh my God, I didn't mean to hit you," said a caramel-skinned lady that looked so gorgeous I had to bite my fist.

She had all the body features that I loved on a woman. A beautiful face with juicy lips and platinum blond hair, honeydew-sized breasts, A J.Lo behind, legs like Beyonce and she was just an inch or two shorter than I was with high heels on. It was amazing what I noticed in two seconds. She also wore a tight dress, which allowed me to picture her naked.

"Are you okay?" she asked.

I said, "Never been better."

We stared at each other as if we just found diamonds. Then she blinked.

"That's good, I'm glad that I didn't hurt you . . . I'm in a hurry, I have to run."

She quickly headed towards the lobby.

Am I really letting this fine lady get away? I thought before the waitress re-captured my attention.

I paid her for the drink and quickly walked towards the lobby, hoping to catch up with the woman. She approached the lobby exit and greeted another fine woman. Her friend was Asian with a Halle Berry haircut and a very fit body. I had joy when I saw them kiss each other as they left the lobby. However, they stepped inside a stretch limousine and drove away.

That was my missed opportunity to get with two women who enjoyed both sexes. I was crushed, yet I remembered seeing that caramel beauty somewhere previously, but I didn't know where. It could've been a men's magazine or even an adult film. I couldn't remember, but I was determined to find out so I made my way to the front desk.

"Sir, do you know those ladies?" I asked the clerk.

"She looks fine, eh?" he replied. "I can't remember their names, but I know that the caramel one is the niece of a casino executive."

Good clue.

"Is she a model?"

"I think she is . . . she's been in *Maxim,* or was it *FHM*? No, someone told me it was *King Magazine*. It was one of those three, that's all I know."

Whatever, guy, you have no idea.

"They're staying at this hotel, right?"

"Yes, sir."

I felt more joy as I pulled out a twenty from my pocket.

"Look, my friend, I'll give you this if you tell me what room she's staying in."

He laughed, "Please! That's not enough to even tell you her floor."

"I'll give you forty."

"One hundred."

"Man, forget you!"

I walked back to the gaming area, saying, "I'm gonna see those girls again. I'll find out who she is, 'cause this player's got resources."

Checking all of the floors that have a game room, I couldn't find Ajani. I was surprised that he was done gambling in less than an hour, 'cause he usually takes three. Tired of looking for him after twenty minutes, I sat down near the cash redemption center. It was there I saw Ajani in the lineup holding four buckets of tokens. I rushed to the line, eager to know how much he won and to tell him about the eye candies.

"Guy, how much money did you win?" I asked.

Ajani said, "About eight grand."

Dude was as cool as the actor Morgan Freeman. It was so obvious that he was a man who always had money.

"And you won that from blackjack?"

"Not all of it. I started with blackjack, played for twenty minutes, won three games and thirteen hundred bucks then left immediately, went to Caribbean Stud, played a half hour, won three grand, left immediately after that. Then I played fifteen minutes on the slots and won another thirty-six hundred, and here I am now. This new *win-and-move* method of gambling is working for me."

It's true, I thought. *The rich get richer. Ajah ain't wealthy, but his earnings keep increasing daily. Me? The weekend's just started and I'm almost broke.*

I patted him on the shoulder and said, "You're the man for real. So, can you reserve me a regular hotel room for Saturday while you cats stay in the executive suite?"

"Yeah, no doubt, I can reserve it," he answered.

That was too easy.

I asked, "Will you pay for it?"

"No."

"Dang! And I thought I was cheap!"

"Guy, you know I don't like beggars. I like giving at will, and if I get you a room, the other guys will want something from me, and so on. So enjoy the executive suite tomorrow like it's your last day on earth."

"Alright, alright, it's all good. Guess what? I believe that I just saw the sexiest woman ever, yo!"

"Oh yeah?" Ajani sounded so uninterested.

"I'm serious, guy! Right here in the casino! She's crazy fine, plus she has a girlfriend!"

"And that makes you happy?"

"Of course! If I see her again and get to talk to her, I could finally get my first three-some!"

"Where are they from?"

"Don't know. One of them looked mad familiar though."

"What's her name?"

"Don't know."

Ajani looked at me. "Guy, what do you know about them?"

"All I know is that she has an uncle who's an executive in this casino, according to the hotel desk clerk."

"Ooooh, that's so much info."

"Trust me, I'll see her again. Her and her partner, then you'll see I'm on point with my game."

"Well, if you introduce me to them, then I'll pay for a room for you."

I gave a big grin. "Wow, Ajah, for real?"

He grinned back. "Dream on."

"Forget you. Don't need nothing from you anyway."

"Not even some good reefer that I have in my truck?"

"Well, except that. Weed's the best thing other than sex right now."

Ajani cashed in his tokens and we headed back to Teddy's crib. There was no doubt in my mind that I was going to see those ladies before the end of the weekend, even if I had no idea who they were.

CHAPTER 39

TEDDY

I went back to Kingdom Workers Fellowship to help my brothers and sisters finish decorating for Friday night's talent/fashion show. Thankfully, everything was finished in under an hour. Afterwards, Janet and I headed towards the church parking lot and we talked about some of the day's events.

"Keep Q and Trina in your prayers, baby," I said to her. "Judging on what Q's been telling us, they might need counseling, 'cause they're quickly heading downhill."

"Sounds like no communication to me," said Janet. "I'd be really surprised if Trina cheated on Q. She's a really good woman."

"I'd be surprised too, but we'll see what happens. On the opposite note, though, K.J's digging Kaitlyn big time."

"I know, ain't that something?" Janet said smiling. "That's funny, 'cause both of them haven't been in a serious relationship for a long time."

"Plus they're smart, confident, out-spoken, and gifted. They're ideal for each other."

She suddenly became serious. "But K.J's not born-again."

"I know that," I said, getting defensive for my cousin. "When you got saved, I wasn't born-again yet."

"But Bear, this is a different situation. I was already going out with you before I was saved. Kaitlyn's last relationship was with a man who wasn't a believer, and she was born-again. To make a long story short, they had spiritual differences, but they were in love. He wouldn't be saved, and she had to break up with him. It was the toughest thing she ever had to do.

Kaitlyn wants to be with a God-fearing man, someone who can encourage her and knows how to handle struggles and temptations when they approach."

"K.J definitely respects God, and he knows the importance of trying to live righteous."

"Yes, baby, I know that . . . but does he *try* to live righteous according to society, or God's will? I think you know the answer to that."

I paused as I thought about what my lady said. Janet was so right. Spiritually, she was growing in God very quickly.

"Janet, do you struggle with temptation?"

"I'd be lying if I said that I didn't," she replied. "I struggle with it every day. However, I have to remind myself how to deal with temptation when it approaches. Why do you ask?"

I didn't want to go into specific detail with Janet, especially with what took place earlier in the day but I could tell that she knew that it had to do with the Phat Five.

"I guess this weekend will be a test of how I can resist temptation," I said. "You know what I'm talking about: the junk that I was doing with the guys for so long."

"Well, Bear, our pastor said it many times; don't try to handle situations yourself, but let God take control, and that's through prayer and asking for His presence."

"I wish it was as easy as saying it."

"It's not."

Janet moved closer to me, lowering her voice. "How do you think I had to deal with us always having sex? I had to move in with Kaitlyn. Who said being a Christian is easy? It's joyful, but definitely not easy."

I opened the car door and sat in the driver's seat. She gave me an intellectual gold nugget to think about.

I asked, "Do you want me to bring any stuff from the crib that you may need for tonight?"

"Um . . . no, I think I'm good for now. If I do need anything, I'll just ask Kaitlyn to take me there."

"Ok, baby. I'll see you tonight." I kissed her on the lips. "Love you."

Janet smiled. "Love you too."

CHAPTER 40

Q

"Why won't she answer the stinkin' phone?"

I was really mad when I closed the cell phone. My wife turned off my cell phone and she wasn't answering the home phone. I wanted to punch a punching bag until its insides spilled out but there wasn't one around, so I did the next best thing and lit up a cigarette.

"Guy, just settle as best as you can," K.J said while playing NBA Live 2003 on the X-Box. "It's tough as hell. Trust me, I've been there, and there's nothing that you can do until Trina calls you back . . . and why are you smoking in the apartment?"

"Oh, snap, I forgot," I said, putting the ashes in an empty Pepsi can. "I'm not thinking straight right now. I hope Ted's got some potpourri."

It still hadn't hit me that Teddy was a Christian. Plus I should've known better, because I don't even smoke in my own crib. As I began to look for a Lysol or Glade can, Ajani and Eros entered the apartment.

"Who's ready to get lifted?" sang Eros. "We got the weed!"

That was sweet music to my ears.

Ignoring Eros, K.J asked Ajani how he did at the casino.

"Seventy-eight hundred, baby!" answered Ajani. "The games did me very nice!"

"That's tight," K.J said. "You need to rub some of that luck on your boy."

"Yeah, Ajah, no doubt!" I said, giving him a pound, which involved connecting our fists.

Eros said, "And I saw the finest shortie that ever walked in this country."

"Yeah, whatever," I told him while spraying Glade in the atmosphere. "That's what you say every week. You guys really got some weed?"

"Q, I'm serious this time! This girl was recently in one of the men's magazine, which I'm about to find out through the Web. I'm telling you, her booty was like . . ."

"Guy, does it look like I care? I am stressed the hell out! Where's the reefer?"

Ajani replied, "It's in the ride. I'm going down to light one after I use the washroom."

"Yo, as much as I don't want to touch weed this weekend, I'm mad anxious right now," said K.J as he turned off the game to put on his jacket. "I'm joining you."

"I hear that," I agreed, willing to do anything to take my mind off Katrina Brown-Quintino.

While Eros turned on the Internet on Teddy's PC, he said, "Ajah, bring the stuff up here. We ain't going nowhere. Why should we be all cooped up in the SUV if we're not driving?"

Ajani answered, "'Cause we shouldn't smoke in here."

"Why not?"

K.J said, "'Cause Teddy might not be cool with it, that's why. I just told Q to put out his cancer stick."

"So what if T-Henny's a Jesus freak now?" asked Eros. "That doesn't mean we need to be frontin' like we're a bunch of holy folk in his crib."

I kept my mouth shut because Eros was getting ignorant again.

"Yeah, but Janet lives here too, and she's a Christian as well," Ajani said. "It's a sign of disrespect."

I nodded my head, although I really wanted to smoke in the living room instead of the parking lot. Eros turned his eyes away from the computer and faced us.

"My brothers, Janet is not coming here this weekend," he said. "Plus, Teddy never said that we couldn't smoke in his crib because he's a Christian. This is the same T-Henny who used to out-party us, smoke the most weed, and drink the most Labatt's not too long ago. Do you think he expects us to change just because he claims to be living for God? I don't think so. In addition, we are the Phat-freaking-Five! We're down for each other, and we have each other's back. If Ted doesn't want weed in the crib, we'll smoke in the truck. How will we know that he minds it if we don't start doing it? We're in this together, right?"

I just looked at Eros. He had to be the world's greatest devil's advocate, who always wanted his ideas to become corporate.

To my surprise, Ajani said, "Open all the windows. Q, take out every potpourri and disinfectants in the house. I just want to relax on the sofa right now."

K.J shook his head while taking off his jacket.

"Alright, whatever," he said. "But if Teddy's pissed off, I'm saying that Eros smoked the first blunt."

I yelled, "No doubt! I ain't taking the blame for this one."

"Me neither," agreed Ajani as he went into the washroom.

"Punks," Eros said to us. "It's like y'all ain't heard a word I said."

CHAPTER 41

TEDDY

As I came out of my Honda Accord, I noticed Ajani's truck in the visitor's parking lot. For the first time ever, I was actually worried about what my four friends were up to and it wasn't a good feeling at all.

Going up the elevator, I said to myself, "I used to be down with everything the Phat Five was doing. Now I'm worried about what I'm getting myself into. But hey, I'll be alright, 'cause God will never give me more than I can handle."

I stepped out of the elevator and immediately smelt marijuana.

Oh man, I'm saved now, and I still like the smell of weed! Not good.

Then I detected where the smell was coming from, and I wasn't pleased.

Oh Lord, I hope that is not coming from my crib. God, why now?

I opened the door to find the fellas sitting in the living room, rolling up joints and smoking them.

Lord, I beg you, please keep Janet as far away from here as possible.

Eros yelled, "T-HENNY! What up, dog?"

I said nothing.

"Yo, man, do you mind us doing this?" Ajani asked me. "It's your call if you don't want us to smoke in here."

I still said nothing.

Q added, "We don't want to disrespect the fact that you're religious now, but . . . I guess we're too late."

Uh, yeah.

I still stayed muted.

My cousin asked, "Janet's still coming to the crib? Don't worry, cuzin, we'll take care of the smell . . . for real."

I thought I prepared myself for this. It wasn't supposed to be a big deal, right. What would Jesus do? Dang, Ted, say something!

I said, "Man, I really gotta pee," and rushed to the washroom, closing the door behind me.

I leaned over the sink.

"I can handle this!" I said. "These are my bred-drin. Janet won't find out what's happening here if she doesn't show up, and she said she probably won't come here today. I'll be alright. It's all good, Ted, its all good."

The guys were looking at me when I came out of the bathroom.

"You cats know you're wrong with this," I said to them smiling, not trying to show disappointment. "Y'all couldn't wait to puff up, and now you wanna know if I'm cool with it?"

"It's all Eros' fault, Ted," Q said with no shame.

Eros replied, "Bite me, Q! I ain't held a gun to nobody's head. All I said was that Teddy shouldn't mind us smoking even though he doesn't do it anymore."

"It's not that," I explained. "What if I brought some people over from my church? How you think this will look?"

"Messed up. I see what you're saying," said K.J. "Is Janet coming anytime soon?"

"No, and thank God . . . she'd trip if she found out. Just promise me that this living room will be spotless when y'all are done!"

"No doubt, Yo," Ajani said, offering me a pound. I responded, showing my boys that I was a good sport.

"Man, it's about time this movie finished downloading," said Eros.

I didn't notice him walking from the sofa to my computer. Looking at the monitor, I saw a clip of two women and a man having hardcore sex. I was outraged and aroused at the same time. Being that I missed having sex, my eyes were enjoying the film. However, I quickly reminded myself that I was a Christian and the video would have to be deleted.

"What the hell did you download on my PC, guy?" I yelled.

"This is the latest stuff from my dad, Yo," Eros replied, unfazed by my anger. "This video hasn't even hit the stores yet!"

All of the guys gathered around my computer. Eros turned up the volume on the speakers to hear the screams and moans.

Q said, "I can't see how your pops can film this and not explode! He must have to think about sports."

Ajani responded, "As long as it isn't co-ed wrestling."

I grabbed control of the mouse and stopped the video.

"Alright, that's enough!" I snapped. "Watch this crap at your own crib. I already let y'all get away with too much!"

The guys headed back to the living room.

"Damn, Ted!" said Eros. "If sex is so wrong to act and watch, why did God create it?"

I answered, "He created it for marriage and not before."

"Ridiculous. That's like a ten-year old getting the keys to a brand new car and being told that he can't drive it for at least six years."

Forty minutes later, we were all lounging in the living room talking smack. I was excited to hear more of K.J's freestyles and all about Ajani's winnings. As usual, I didn't care about the new woman that Eros wanted to seduce. Nevertheless, I was having a good time and I stopped worrying about whether or not Janet would show up.

I began to feel proud of the fact that I wasn't giving into the marijuana, even though it wasn't easy. The presence of weed filled the entire apartment, and I found myself staring at the joints as the guys inhaled them. Every time I looked at a joint, I noticed Eros looking at me as if he wanted me to give into the plant.

Taunt me all you want, Alexander. **I got things under control.**

K.J took a puff and smiled. "Yo, I don't need weed to help me rhyme, but man, there's something about it that gets me buggin'."

"Bugging about what?" asked Q. "I'm feeling real nice right now."

"For real," Ajani added, "ain't no better stress reliever than weed, especially after you get through some crazy drama."

"I know that," K.J continued, "but I be thinking about life issues and coming up with my own psychological terms and theories. It's wild."

"Like what?" I asked my cousin.

"Like the vibe of necessity. Hear me on this; it's when you do or have something in life that gives you a mental or emotional sensation. In other words, the vibe of necessity is something other than people that you need and can't live without."

"Man, are you for real?" asked Eros. "I didn't come here this weekend for a psych lecture."

"Guy, its more than psych, it's about real issues and real life."

I suggested that since it was his theory, that K.J should give us the first example.

"Alright, fine," replied K.J. "My vibe of necessity is control. I can't do anything in life without it."

Ajani said, "So? All of us like control. It's a desire."

"I know that, but most of us don't have control. I have to be in control. I'm obsessed with it. I cut hair at a barbershop because not only am I good at it, but because I control my own hours. Fast food jobs and working at the mall were options that I always refused. That's why I love rapping so much. When I grab the mic, the stage belongs to me. Either the crowd will receive you or they won't and the only way the crown receives you is when you dominate with your lyrics but that's not what gives me control. Control is when I'm at the top of my game and no one else can stop me!"

"Control is taking down Verbal Pain this weekend!" I yelled.

"No doubt!" he yelled in agreement.

Q asked, "So K.J, why did Bianca cheat on you? Did she think you were too controlling?"

K.J grinned, "No. She was just a shallow, materialistic, hoe!"

We all started laughing. The scent of weed smelled better and the temptation of getting high was stronger. Instead of giving in, I continued the conversation.

"So cuz, would you be a controlling man with a woman like Kaitlyn?" I asked.

He smiled. "Kaitlyn, just looking at her tells me that she's a real woman. I would have to raise my standards just to be with her, like no more weed smoking. Don't get me wrong when I say that I want control, 'cause I would not order my lady around or lay hands on her but a real woman wants a man to take charge, and I have no problem with that. Anyway, y'all know what the vibe of necessity is now, right?"

"I hear ya," Q said with a big grin. "I see where you're coming from."

"Dang, Q!" exclaimed Ajani. "You got a grin wider than Julia Roberts."

"That's because I'm feeling real nice right now. As soon as K.J explained the necessity vibe, I knew what mine was . . . or is."

"And what is it?"

"Security, I long for it because many times I feel the opposite. I mean . . . when great things were going on, I felt secure, especially on the basketball court. I averaged thirty-seven points a game in my junior year and I was close to becoming the first Canadian drafted in the NBA without attending a U.S college. I was terrified of breaking my ankle because the doctors said if I broke it a third time, my B-ball career was done. I was careful, but not to the point of paranoia. My optimism was at an all-time high!

"Then, y'all know what happened: the dunk, the fall, the injury. It was the worst day of my life."

Eros said, "Guy that was painful to watch."

"My confidence has never been close to what it used to be since then," Q continued. "I mean, I promised Trina a seven-digit income. Now, I'm working sixty hours a week on a job I hate just so I can get the material things I still want. The fact that I'm insecure about my future is the reason why I started smoking after quitting ten years ago. I ask myself, is working in an auto plant my real future? Will Trina stick with me through thick and thin? Can I ever return to basketball? Finally, is Trina really cheating on me?"

I said, "Q, I'm no marriage expert, but perhaps if you stopped worrying so much and concentrated more on your wife, you wouldn't be stressing so much now. She did marry you after knowing you weren't going to play ball, right?"

Q nodded and continued to smoke.

Eros cried, "What is this, Dr. Phil? Sex is always the answer in my opinion. Q, you didn't give it, and now Trina's getting it elsewhere. I already told you that you need to do the same."

"All rightly, who's next?" K.J asked, and then looked at Eros. "I think we already know your answer, but spit it out anyway. What's your vibe of necessity?"

"The beautiful S-word. I live for it; I'll probably die having it too. I'll be ninety years old and still working it, even if I have to take Viagra four times a day."

Wow. Big surprise.

I asked Eros if sex was really the most important thing in his life.

"Look, T-Henny, don't get me wrong," he explained. "Money's always needed, plus security, power, and in your case, religion. They're all good to have in life according to the situation but man, I can have all of that and be the grumpiest cat alive without some good, wonderful sex! It's a drug for me, and I gots to have it frequently!

We all want it often, even if we don't admit it. You can call me an addict or say I'm like this because my dad produces porn, but I'm just keeping it real. Sex with fine women is the bomb and everything else is just firecrackers."

K.J said, "None of us ever said we didn't need or want sex. It's just that you're so ridiculously vocal about it."

Ajani added, "I've been under many panties, but I choose not to boast about it."

"And that's your prerogative," said Eros. "Sex is my life, and I'm not ashamed of it. I'll have it anywhere with no respect of time or place. And before the year is up, I'm gonna start getting paid for it."

I was surprised at Eros' comment. I shouldn't have been, but I was.

"Are you for real?" I asked. "You want to be a pimp?"

"No, but enough respect to the pimps worldwide," Eros said, raising his fist as a salute. "I have two choices: one, become a maintenance man, which is an upper class escort, or . . ."

K.J interrupted, "You're joking now, right? You wanna be a ho?"

"Call it what you want, but think about it involves. There are some rich sexy women in Toronto that just want a sexy man for an evening, willing to pay at least a grand for it, tax-free."

"That's a waste of money."

"Not if they can afford it. Not if they want a classy man who runs like Duracell in the bedroom."

Q asked him what the second option was.

"Adult porn star," Eros answered.

That was the first time I ever knew someone that openly admitted a desire so outrageous.

K.J started coughing. "Now I know that you're high and talking crap!"

I said, "Your father works behind the scenes. Why do you want to work in front of them?"

Eros replied, "'Cause I have stamina, physique, and looks. Women will want to work with me. I'll make crazy money."

Q asked, "Would you change your name?"

K.J snapped, "*Dang, let's move on already!*"

Eros started laughing at him. "Guy, you really are sexually frustrated with a reaction like that."

"No, I'm just tired of hearing you run on about what you can do, and how good you are and . . . dang, you sound like me."

We all laughed. I couldn't believe how open we were about life issues. It was more than a "reveal-all-when-you're-high" experience, but an indication of how tight we were as friends. Yet, I was glad that the subject of sex had ended. As if being tempted by the weed wasn't enough, my mind began thinking about sexing Janet again. The porn discussion made my thoughts even more explicit.

Perhaps I should light a joint for the very last time, 'cause I need to relax. I really shouldn't, but I need it. God will forgive me.

"Guy," K.J said to me, "your turn."

"Man, I wanna think about mine for a minute," I said, not ready to talk in the spiritual. "Ajah, you go first."

Ajani grumbled, "Man, forget this, I'm hungry!"

K.J said, "Just say what your vibe is, man!"

"Money, what else would it be? The world revolves around it, and I can't get enough of it. Because I love it, I'll do crazy crap to obtain more of it and with Savannah and A.J in my life, I really need more."

"Would you give up the drug game right now if it meant your girl and son's happiness?" I asked him.

Ajani paused for a few seconds and replied, "Yes, I would."

"What took you so long to answer?"

"No reason . . . I'm just mad hungry, guy! Let's get some pizza or something!"

That was a good excuse for Ajani. His answer wasn't convincing to me at all.

Q picked up the phone and ordered two extra large pepperoni and pineapple pizzas from Domino's. While Eros used the washroom and the other three focused on a Lil' Jon video on BET, I picked up Eros' joint from the empty porcelain plate on the coffee table. It looked so inviting. I moved it closer and closer to my lips. Took a quick drag, it was really good. Sinfully good. I quickly put the blunt back on the plate.

I can't believe I gave in! What have I done?

I pushed the plate away from me, only to bring it back towards me. I smoked the joint again, enjoying the second puff better than the first.

Oh man, I missed this! If this is the last blunt I ever smoke, I won't be disappointed.

The guys were still caught up in the video when I exhaled the smoke and put the blunt away. Eros came back from the washroom and sat on the sofa.

"Teddy boy, last but not least," K.J said as he finished watching the video. "What's your vibe of necessity?"

I thought about how crazy my life was before I accepted Christ as my Savior. I was just like my boys, thinking that a worldly action or object was the answer to happiness. Being born-again was wonderful, despite the struggles and temptations. Once again, it was time to express my faith.

"You know . . . living the fast life used to be my number one love," I began. "However, that chapter in my life is done. Money is a great need, but I don't love it. Security is very important, and its great to have power, but I don't have much of a competitive spirit. As for sex, well, let's just say I'm trying my best not to think about it."

"Janet's not giving up the goods, huh?" Eros laughed.

Jerk.

I continued, "Since I got saved, I learnt so much about the love of God, his peace, and having joy during tough situations. God is teaching me how to be set apart from what I used to do. Therefore, I guess that my vibe of necessity is Christ. He's my all and everything."

K.J nodded his head and mumbled, "That's tight."

Q said "seen" very quietly, and Ajani continued to smoke in silence. For the next thirty seconds, nobody said anything until the stereo started playing the latest CD by hip-hop artist Nas.

"Yo, this CD's real tough," K.J, said as he began nodding his head and rapping the lyrics.

Eros replied, "Yeah, it's tight . . . so Ted, you're a different cat now, right?"

I nodded. "No doubt."

He was ready to debate. So ready, I could see it in his red eyes.

"And God is teaching you how to be set apart from the stuff that we do?"

"Well, I'm still learning."

"Obviously, you're still learning, because right now, you're dying to smoke more of my joint."

All eyes were suddenly focused on me. I saw their "are you for real" expressions and I started to feel conviction.

I asked, "What makes you think I smoked your joint?"

"Guy, I'm not stupid," Eros argued, "you did it while I was in the bathroom! My blunt was not this small before I went!"

He held up his blunt for the others to notice.

"Y'all didn't see Henderson smoke this?" he asked the guys.

My cousin said, "Nah, I was watching the Lil' Jon video."

Q added, "I was ordering the pizzas and watching the video. Ted, you really took a puff, huh?"

Ajani looked at me. "Your eyes do look red. Lips are ashy, too."

I wasn't ready to tell the truth.

"So?" I shouted. "That's because I'm in the midst of second-hand smoke!"

"Guy, just admit it," said Eros. "You took a puff of my reefer. Thou shalt not lie, remember?"

I was hot with embarrassment; I was busted by Eros Alexander, Jr., the wannabe porn star. I gave into temptation and I had to be a man and confess, even though my integrity was at stake. Eros put the joint back on the plate, and I foolishly picked it up again.

"Yes, I gave into the smell and took a couple of puffs," I admitted. "I thought that it wouldn't tempt me, but it did and I was stupid enough to give in. Eros, you can look at me and think that I'm a hypocrite, but I meant everything that I just said about my relationship with God."

Putting his hand on my shoulder, Eros said, "Dawg, I know that you're a believer and trying to live right. But you know, and at least I know that deep down inside, you're still the same old T-Henny."

If looks could kill, Eros shot me in the head. My mind started to mess with me. Was I faking the funk? Spiritually, was I just going through the motions? Did I really change? Was I *really* born-again?

I looked at Ajani, K.J, and Q, but their eyes were looking at the front door.

"Sounds like the pizza man's trying to get in," Q said.

Ajani got up and walked towards the door.

"Yo, I never knew Domino's was so quick," he said. "But, dang, why the hell are they trying to open the door without knocking?"

I said, "They probably knocked but we couldn't hear them because of the music. K.J, turn it down, man!"

My cousin turned the volume down with the remote control. I walked towards the door as Ajani unlocked it. He opened the door. The embarrassment that I felt two minutes prior was nothing compared to my current state.

It was Janet, with a very shocked and angry expression and I was still holding the blunt between my fingers.

CHAPTER 42

TEDDY

Ajani stood at the door and looked at my woman like he saw a ghost.

"Oh my God," he said. "What up, Janet?"

She walked past him as if he was invisible. Janet was mad. So mad that she wouldn't even look at me. I quickly threw the blunt in the kitchen trashcan.

Janet didn't say a word as she observed the premises. When I looked at her, immediately I pictured Jesus disgusted at the people who turned the church into a flea market. She looked more than ready to wreck everything in sight. K.J was spraying potpourri like an exterminator trying to kill cockroaches. Eros began emptying ashes in the trash, and Q rushed to the storage closet to get the vacuum cleaner. All three of them were speechless, which was a good thing.

She went into the bedroom and slammed the door. As much as I didn't want to go in after her, I knew that I had to be a man and admit my mistakes. I slowly walked in the room and closed the door. Janet was pulling clothes out of the closet and packing them in her suitcase.

Glaring at me, she mumbled, "Lord, please help me not to curse this boy out!"

I began, "Baby, I can explain . . ."

"Unless the doctor gave y'all a note saying that you guys have a chronic illness and need weed to cure it, I don't wanna hear jack!" she yelled.

"I know what you're thinking about seeing me with a joint, and it's not what you think!"

"Oh, whatever! I'm supposed to think that your intentions are good when I see you holding a blunt? Boy, get out of my way!"

Janet pushed me aside and walked out of the bedroom with her bag. Leaving the apartment without saying anything to the guys, she headed towards the elevator, ignoring the fact that I was behind her.

"Janet, I'm very sorry that you had to see what you saw. I experimented with it, but . . ."

"But what?" she asked. "You're like Bill Clinton, 'you didn't inhale'. Man, I'm really pissed off and disappointed in you. You let your boys smoke in our apartment, and you didn't even make a stand as a Christian. I'm so glad I didn't bring up Kaitlyn with me. I would've been so embarrassed."

She was about to enter the elevator, but I grabbed her arm.

"Look, I made a mistake," I said. "I gave into temptation. It was stupid and it won't happen again."

"You got that right! Ted, you need a lot of maturing, more than you realize."

That comment made me upset. I thought that she was trying to belittle me because I was a baby saint.

"Excuse me, Ms. Watters, but only Christ was perfect! Don't act like I'm not saved and you're perfect since you found God. You caught me in my sin, but who knows what you be thinking or doing behind closed doors!"

It came out a little harsh, but we both knew that I was right. However, the apartment and I still reeked of marijuana, and Janet was too stubborn and angry to admit that her comment was unnecessary.

"Look, just make sure that crap is out of there and everything is smelling fresh by the time I return," she said while entering the elevator. "Anything that still smells like weed, I'm throwing out! Understood?"

I didn't reply as the elevator closed. All I cared about was getting on my knees and asking God for forgiveness and wisdom to get through the rest of the day.

CHAPTER 43

Martinez Estafan rarely smiled at anything or anyone. Whenever he smiled, it was a day when he spent time with his six children. Friday was one of those days.

His oldest daughter had just turned sixteen, and Martinez took her to an auto dealership for her gift. Jennifer was extremely excited when her father gave her keys to a brand new Chrysler Sebring convertible. It brought great joy to Martinez, and spending time with Jennifer and his other children took his mind off his drug empire.

It was five in the afternoon, and Martinez was already at the Real Feel. He had not planned on arriving, after all, it was a day that he devoted to family and his cell phone stayed off. However, it was on the way to his second baby mother's house, and he wanted to check and see if the club had enough inventory for its biggest night of the week.

Martinez parked his black Jaguar in his reserved parking spot. He was still smiling as he got out of the car and into the back entrance. While walking to his office, he greeted the chefs, showed affection to one of his sexy waitresses and a stripper that was off-stage. They all gave big grins when they saw Martinez in an unusual cheerful mood. Everyone that knew Martinez knew that he was a short, tough-looking Cuban that was very serious about his business but very generous to those who worked their behinds off for him. If anyone wasted Martinez's time, the result was mostly fatal, and it took plenty of pleading and begging to get him to change his mind.

Bad news was definitely something Martinez didn't want to hear on a good Friday afternoon, but as soon as he saw his brother Ricardo in his office, he knew something was wrong. Ricardo looked both frustrated and confused.

"Why don't you answer your phone?" he snapped. "What if stuff was going down over here?"

Martinez snapped back. "Can I spend one day with my daughter without interruption? What's the problem?"

"Miscommunication! Why you ain't tell me that Jamaican boy from Toronto was making a visit?"

"Ajani Bethel?" he asked with surprise. "What did he want? Was Machete with him?"

"He came by himself."

Martinez looked at his little brother and knew that he was high.

"Brother, you look like crap," he said.

"I feel like it too! I'm in the other office, high as a kite and getting some booty and all of a sudden, I get a visit from Machete's boy. Why you ain't told me he was coming early?"

"I can't answer you 'cause I don't know what's going on!"

Ricardo explained that Ajani came to the club with two cases of G.H and said that Martinez wanted a rush order for the weekend.

"That's ridiculous," replied Martinez. "I talked to Machete yesterday, and he's coming here on Monday and he didn't ask for nothing a day sooner."

"He was mad serious when he said that Machete sent him here. I told him we didn't know jack and the boy went off! If he wasn't Machete's boy, I would've smoked him!"

"So what happened?"

"I gave him sixty percent of what he was asking for. I figured it must've been legit since he drove from Toronto. Plus, I figured that having some G.H for the weekend won't hurt, since it's the hottest drug right now and cats can't get enough of it anyway."

Martinez had a great reason to be upset. He went to the liquor cabinet and poured a glass of tequila before sitting behind his desk. He loved Ricardo to death, but Martinez was frustrated by the way he did not follow instruction. It was an easy rule: if Martinez did not pre-authorize a deal, do not make one, and it did not matter who it was. He was a man of order, and was disturbed at what took place.

"How . . . many . . . times do I have to tell you that if you haven't heard word from me beforehand to do something, DON'T DO IT! It's common freaking sense, and I know you have it 'cause you're an Estafan. I don't wanna repeat this B.S again!

You know that Machete is like family to us, and he wouldn't pull a stunt like sending Ajani here to make a deal without me knowing about it. That's too shady. Otherwise, I'll have to call him about this. Where's the case?"

Ricardo grabbed the briefcase and placed it on the desk.

Opening it, Martinez asked, "You said you paid sixty percent for this?"

"Exactly," replied Ricardo. "At least the stuff looks legit."

"Well, we'll see about that."

Martinez took out a container of the G.H. He poured the contents in his hand and took a close look at one of the pills. After sniffing it a few times, he looked at his little brother.

"This is fake," he said quietly.

"What?" Ricardo asked.

"THIS IS FAKE!" Martinez roared, throwing the open container at him. "YOU JUST PURCHASED A CASE OF ASPIRIN!"

"How . . . what the . . . how can you tell? It looks like the real s—"

"Of course it looks like the real thing, but that's why you gotta smell it! Crap smells like Flintstone vitamins! OxyContin don't smell like Flintstone vitamins!"

Ricardo sniffed a pill he picked up from the floor.

"That Jamaican punked me, yo!" he snapped.

"That's right, you got punked! You gave that cat plenty of my money for some aspirin and you better get it back!"

As Martinez picked up the telephone on the desk, he said, "I'm about to call Machete to find out where this boy is at!"

CHAPTER 44

Machete was relaxing in a bubble-filled Jacuzzi with a female companion. Marvin Gaye was playing in the background and they were getting physical when the cell phone rang. He grabbed the phone in the midst of their action and saw *The Real Feel's* number on the display. He softly pushed the woman off him and answered the phone.

"Martinez Estafan!" he exclaimed.

"Machete," replied Martinez. "What's going on, brother?"

"Just here. What's up?"

He knew immediately that something happened between the Estafans and Ajani. Thus, Machete had his answers pre-planned.

"Chete, you know you're like family to me, right?"

"No doubt. We've been through plenty of good and bad times."

"I helped you become highly successful by giving you American clientele, and you did the same by giving me a Canadian market."

Machete hummed in agreement.

"When I come to Canada, you treat me like royalty. My family loves you, and my girl Le Ann is your god daughter."

"Of course. Is everything alright?"

"I wish it was, brother. We did make an agreement to meet on Monday for the G.H, am I right?"

"That's correct."

"Then why the hell did Ajani come to my club selling counterfeit OxyContin and told my brother that we arranged a rush order?"

"Martinez, let me explain. The . . ."

"Why would you try to sabotage what I thought was a good relationship between us? You know what I do to people who try to pull fast ones on me!"

"Ajani is a backstabber trying to take me down," Machete explained. "Word from Rancel and around Toronto is that he's working for me and trying to take my clientele for himself so that he can start his own empire."

"OK. Go on."

Machete continued by stating how he loved Ajani like a little brother and did not want to kill him personally, thus arranging a drug smuggling arrest at the U.S border. He also mentioned that he did not expect Ajani to get past Martinez with the fake G.H.

"He didn't," said Martinez. "Bethel got past Ricardo who didn't check the pills to see if they were legit. Now that cat's got my cash and I want it back!"

"What do you need to know?"

"Are you and him finished business?"

"According to me, yes."

"In other words . . ."

"If you want to take him out, that's fine with me," smiled Machete. "He's still in Windsor."

Martinez asked him where Ajani would be hanging out. Machete suggested the Jam Fest locations and the casino as his main spots.

"If he's anywhere else familiar, I'll let you know."

"Good. If you can tell by my tone, I'm highly pissed right now."

Machete knew that he was furious, but he hoped that their friendship and business relationship was not tarnished.

"Other than that, everything's cool?" he asked.

"Everything's still cool brother, just as long as this crap doesn't happen again."

Machete hung up the phone and got out of the Jacuzzi, leaving his companion in the tub. He had local business to finish, such as the upcoming deal with Rex Marcos.

"Alright, Ricardo," said Martinez as he hung up the phone. "You screwed this up, so it's on you to get my cash back."

Ricardo asked, "How do you want it done?"

"I *don't care*! Call Big Cement and send him to Jam Fest and the Windsor Casino, wherever Ajani may be. I want my money tonight! Do I always need to spoon-feed you? Just do it!"

CHAPTER 45

TEDDY

"Dang, Ted, I've never seen your woman that mad before," Ajani said to me. "That was our bad for real."

I continued sweeping the kitchen floor in silence. I was angry about my failure to stop my boys from smoking in the crib, my submission to temptation, and Janet making me feel like a heathen. The Phat Five reunion weekend was worse than I expected.

"Ted! Say something, dog!" K.J commanded. "I feel bad too. Not just for you, but now Janet's gonna tell Kaitlyn that I smoke weed. Then she won't want to get to know me."

I broke my silence. "She won't say anything to Kaitlyn. Janet doesn't gossip like that."

"Well, she still won't recommend me to her. Kaitlyn looks like a strong godly woman."

Ajani added, "And so is Janet. Guy, your girl has changed for real. I don't know what would happen if Savannah got serious like her. She's at some church function in Mississauga this weekend."

That was encouraging to hear.

"That's good," I said. "Trust me, when you have a woman that fears God, they start praying for you a lot. Then unusual things start to happen. I'm evidence of that."

"Damn," mumbled Ajani as he ate a slice of pizza.

Wow, I thought as I looked at him. *Ajah really wants nothing to do with God. Probably because it means that, he has to live an honest lifestyle.*

Changing the subject, he asked, "Yo, you eating any of this pizza? There's only two slices left."

Two extra large pizzas had twelve slices each. Having the munchies after blunting, the guys ate like they were victims of a famine. Once Janet caught me in the act, I instantly lost my appetite. I told him that I wasn't hungry at the moment and I may eat it later.

"Oh well, suit yourself," Ajani said with a full mouth. "Look, the apartment is spic and span like how we met it. Janet's like a sister to me, and I don't want her to stay mad at me."

"Me, neither," agreed K.J. "Let's chip in some loot and buy her something to show we're sorry."

I shook my head and smiled. As much as the Phat Five had corporate and individual issues to deal with, we always looked out for each other. I agreed to K.J's idea, thinking that it would be great to get her something nice from the mall.

Q came out of the living room to join the conversation. He was with Eros, who was chatting with one of his flings on the phone.

"Yo, when it comes to *I'm sorry* gifts, I know them all," he bragged. "I'll show you the best stores to pick up something really thoughtful."

"Not right now you won't!" yelled Eros to Q as he hung up the phone. "Nivea and Whitney are waiting for us at their place. I told them that we're heading there right now."

Ajani said, "Q, I knew that girl was checking you out at Rude Boy's yesterday."

I added, "That girl is fine, but not as fine as *your wife*!"

"I'm just going to visit," Q denied.

K.J shook his head. "Q, who're you fooling? We all know Eros is once again leading you into the world of adultery."

Eros looked at K.J. "It's not as bad as you think. Affairs are refreshing, a change from the usual. Just ask Bianca."

We all stared at Eros after that comment. Why did he have to strike a nerve again with that remark? K.J looked like he wanted to smack him upside his head.

"What goes around comes around, Eros," my cousin replied. "That's all I gotta say."

"Whatever," Eros said. "It's sexually frustrated cats like you that make this world a tense and angry place."

I continued to sweep. Thank God, wannabe porn stars didn't operate the world.

CHAPTER 46

Q

Ajani dropped off Eros and me at Nivea and Whitney's apartment building. I didn't want to visit another woman, let alone be a victim of a matchmaker game. Katrina was steadily on my mind. Did she cheat on me? Was she about to cheat on me? Was this the beginning of the end of my marriage? Those questions kept running in my head, and I looked at my wife's cell phone, eager to give her a call.

"Guy, keep that phone off," Eros commanded. "Thinking about your wife is the worst thing to do right now."

"I can't believe I let you talk me into this," I said in frustration.

Once again, I allowed Eros to include me in his polygamous antics. I've never cheated on my wife, but I had many opportunities thanks to my fame and Eros' open houses of adultery with fine women. I thought that he would've left me alone after a year of marriage, but its almost impossible to teach old dogs new tricks.

Eros ignored my comment and pressed the apartment number in the lobby. Nivea answered through the intercom and opened the entrance.

While waiting for the elevator, he said, "Guy, this will do you good. Remember, this is one weekend and you're almost four hours away from home and, your wife's dealing with a New York man right now. Where do you think they may have been last night, the Hilton, Holiday Inn, your bedroom?"

Sometimes I believed that Eros was the devil. He would say things that would make me upset about being married, and his comment created a hot rush of anger. I prayed that Trina wasn't screwing another dude, especially in our condo that cost too much to rent monthly. No doubt, Eros opened up another can of worms.

Going up the elevator Eros asked, "Q, remember when you called me this morning about your crazy drama?"

I nodded and asked him why.

"Well," he answered, "I had to tell them why you called 'cause they were in the room and they thought it was serious. I told them that you found out an employee of yours got infected by SARS and you were feeling down about it."

How did this guy ever become my best friend?

I snapped. "What kind of stupid story is that?"

"A good one. What'd you want me to tell them, the truth?"

"That would be nice for once. Then I won't be involved in your games!"

"Well, the story worked, and Whitney was touched when I said that you sent a nice get-well package to your workmate. The ball is in your hands now, Q! Are you gonna pass or score?"

"Do I have much of a choice, Eros? I'm known for dishing out serious assists, but obviously the defense has covered all of my possible options, so I have to score."

I decided to play along, because he gave me a headache whenever I tried to be logical.

"That's what I'm talking about!" Eros smiled, waiting for me to give him a five. "You gonna shoot a three or attack the rim?"

I sucked my teeth, leaving my hands in my pockets. "Slam dunk it, or course."

"That's my dog!"

"Whatever."

Nivea opened the door to greet us. Of course, Eros gave her a tight hug and caressed her below the waist. She smiled, but quickly moved his hands away.

"Stop that!" she said. "Behave yourself. How are you, Q?"

I replied with a friendly greeting. I couldn't believe how high-pitched her voice was. She seemed very perky as well. Looking like she was only five-foot-two, she stared upward at me as if I was Mount Everest.

"Dang," said Nivea, "I know that you were tall because you play basketball, but standing next to you . . . wow!"

"Yeah, I know," I said. "I get that often. People are shocked when they see how tall six-foot-five really is."

"For real."

"Girl, I didn't bring Q here for you," said an envious Eros. "Where's Whitney?"

"She's in her room," Nivea answered. "She'll be out. You guys have a seat."

I saw their eyes flirting as Nivea went to get her roommate. Freaks.

Looking at the apartment scenery, I knew for sure that college students rented it. It was nicely decorated and smelt pretty, but it lacked the material items that I craved. The TV was only thirteen inches, the sofa looked second-hand, there was no entertainment unit, a small CD portable stereo, a VCR on top of the TV, but no DVD player. It reminded me of Katrina's apartment while she was in school.

She often reminded me while we were courting that I was spoiled because I'd never lived without having nice things. My family lived upper-middle class with my parents making six-figure annual salaries as union executives in the auto industry. Thus, I never had to struggle to pay tuition, get a student loan, or worry about being broke. I guess I'd always been financially blessed.

Yet, I decided that I wanted to think and act shallow as a poor excuse to be disinterested in Whitney. The choices were little otherwise. My other two options were faking a sickness or tell the truth. However, both options wouldn't cure my anger about Katrina, and Eros would be an angry dude. Man, I wished that I didn't have a good conscience.

Eros was in a annoyingly good mood. He stared at me and said that I looked good.

"Huh?" I asked.

"You're looking good, guy."

I was already dressed to go to Jam Fest just in case we weren't going to Teddy's beforehand. Yes, I was flossing a Phat Farm shirt, Dockers pants, and a pair of Air Force Ones, but I didn't need Eros' approval. Couldn't care less of his opinions at that point.

"Man, I know I look good," I said. "Just shut up."

"Chill, Q! I'm just trying to boost your confidence, that's all."

"Well, I don't need you to do any more stuff for me . . ."

"What's up, Whitney?"

I turned around and wondered how in the world I overlooked that beauty of Thursday night. Her jet-black weave made her look similar to the late singer Aaliyah, except that she was slightly darker in complexion. Whitney gave us a smile that made me grin like a four-year-old watching Sponge Bob Square Pants.

"W'zup, Eros," she said before looking at me. "Hi, Q. Remember me from yesterday?"

Yes, but I never met your two friends and the booty.

"Of course!" I answered. "How are you doing?"

From what I remembered at Rude Boy's, Whitney wore an oversized sweater and baggy blue sweat pants. She was dressed as if she was making a quick stop at Seven-Eleven to buy a Slurpee. Presently, she was wearing make-up, a short-sleeved white t-shirt that read "110% Woman" and a tight, baby blue jogger pants. Whitney looked really good.

"I'm doing good," she said. "I'm sorry to hear about your workmate catching SARS. That must be horrible."

"Huh? Oh, right, right, it is. I was in great shock when I found out about it," I lied. "The person who called me was in great panic because my workmate showed similar symptoms of SARS. But so far it's not official."

"Ah, man, let's hope its not," said Whitney as she sat down between us. "But Eros told me you sent a get-well package, which I thought was really sweet."

"Hey, the main thing is that he recovers one hundred percent. Hopefully he didn't catch the virus."

I wanted to kick Eros through a wall. I hated lying. It made me sweat plenty. That is why I couldn't continue being a player. It meant lying to women on a consistent basis, which Eros was an expert at, but not me. I started to worry. What would happen if Whitney tried to find out about this lie through the newspaper or TV? Nivea came into the living room with a gift bag from Sears. She sat next to Eros with excitement.

"Baby, I got you something," she said.

Acting surprised, Eros took the bag and looked inside of it.

"For me?" he asked. "Nivey, you shouldn't have!"

It was a pair of stain-resistant Dockers pants.

"For real, Nivea, you shouldn't have!" I said sarcastically, but I really meant it.

"I wanted to get it 'cause he really wanted it, and he's my baby," said Nivea with love and sincerity.

Eros gave her the silliest grin and said thank you to her. I just gave a small grin, wondering how many gifts he had received from clueless women. They must have been plenty.

Whitney asked if anyone wanted a glass of white wine.

"Yes!" I said, excited. "I mean, sure . . . that would be nice."

That sounded desperate and anxious, but it was the best question I heard all day.

Laughing, she said, "Wow . . . its coming right up. Be right back."

Nivea followed her and added, "I'll help you bring the glasses."

We stared at them as they walked away.

"Q, relax!" Eros whispered. "Whitney already likes you. My goodness, she's so fine. I need to take Nivea to her bedroom so I can stop looking at her so much."

"I hate lying, man!" I whispered back. "I'm not like you, and I'll never become like you! I don't know how you do it, but a skunk can't stay looking pretty and not expose its odor."

"Shhh! They might be listening! Look, you just got lifted two hours ago. Drink a few glasses of wine, and you'll feel real good. Remember, you're real close to *new area code* sex. Think of these five words: Trina, another man, your bedroom."

Eros was a wicked man.

Three glasses of wine and forty-five minutes later, I was feeling much more comfortable. The buzz allowed me to relax around Whitney. Eros and Nivea were in a bedroom doing whatever, so the two of us got to know each other better.

We talked about school, relationships, music, my college basketball experience, and Whitney's desire to become a dentist. The more we talked, the more she reminded me of my wife. It felt so much like the first time I took Katrina on a date. That was over two years ago, the best date of my life.

CHAPTER 47

AJANI

The cousins and I went to a video store in Windsor's Devonshire Mall. I was interested in buying some DVDs and Teddy still didn't know what to get Janet, so I made a suggestion that might have benefited us both.

My favorite movies were kung fu, and I found five to add to my collection of over two hundred and fifty. Teddy walked towards me, and he was holding a DVD collection.

"Like you really need more DVDs," Teddy said to me. "How much do you own now, a thousand?"

"One day," I replied. "I have to collect all the kung fu flicks I watched as a kid in Jamaica. This is the stuff that inspired me to earn a black belt in martial arts."

"True. I found this collection of DVDs for Janet. It's the first season of the TV show *Fame*, which costs about eighty bucks."

"That's fine. I'm charging it to my card anyway."

Teddy pulled out a couple of twenties from his wallet. He attempted to give me his money, but I refused.

"Keep your money. We were at fault, remember?"

K.J approached us and took out a twenty as well.

He asked, "Who am I giving this money to?"

I said to him, "Look, I told Ted, and now I'm telling you, I got this. You know I'm stubborn when I'm sent on doing something, so don't bother me!"

Teddy shook his head as he put his cash back in his wallet.

K.J raised his hands in agreement. "That's fine with me!"

"Wow," said Teddy, "as much as you guys can tick me off, we stay inseparable. You cats are my true boys."

I smiled, "Man, we know that already. Shut up with that sappy crap and let's bounce."

We walked through the food court on the way to the mall exit. Teddy finally got hungry and wanted to buy something from KFC. I was full from the pizza and kinda sleepy, so I just wanted to leave.

K.J sucked his teeth. "Guy, you see that line-up? Let's just stop at a drive-thru."

Teddy said, "Man, I can't wait that long. I need something now!"

I said, "You should eat right after smoking like normal weed heads. We'll be in the ride."

He walked towards the line and said, "Nah, man, wait for me. It won't take long."

Without a big fuss, K.J and I sat down in the dining area.

"Guy, I know we're all boys, but I swear, Eros gets on my last nerves!" K.J said in frustration. "I wanted to hit him hard a few times already this weekend."

I shook my head. Who could disagree?

"That's just Eros, man," I replied. "I just tune him out when he starts thinking with his privates."

"I mean, it's been a while since Bianca slept with Roderick, but that topic still strikes a nerve. I won't be over it until I take him down in the showcase. My hate for him and her are still strong."

Hate. I could relate to his pain. I hated Rancel the same way.

K.J added, "Ted told me earlier today that I should forgive and let go. He means well, but guy, I think that's called punking out!"

I agreed. "That's Ted's opinion. Revenge is sweet like sugar. Beat Roderick down in the showcase tonight!"

He smiled and gave me a pound. "That's what I'm talking about!"

"AHHHH! OH MY GOD! SOMEBODY HELP!"

That scream came from a woman. We quickly turned behind us to see what was going on. About four feet away, a young boy fell on the floor. Everyone who was in the food court heard the scream by the young lady and gathered around the scene.

The boy was having a difficult time breathing and his face was turning blue. Saliva was exiting the side of his mouth. I knew immediately that something was blocking his airway. K.J and I made our way towards him. He asked the lady what happened to the boy, although I already knew the answer. She was resting his head on her lap while sitting on the floor.

"My son was eating while I was feeding my baby in the stroller," she said with a strong Latino accent, "and he just fell to the ground. I don't know what to do! Somebody call 911!"

There was no need for that because I knew first aid. I rushed behind the child.

"Back up!" I yelled to the several folk who were standing too close to them. "Miss, I know what to do."

I grabbed the child from the lady's lap. "Something big is in his throat and it needs to be pushed out!"

This was my first real opportunity to use the Heimlich maneuver. I wrapped my arms around the boy's small waist and moved my fists towards the bottom of his rib cage.

"Do you know what you're doing to my son?" she asked in panic.

"Yes, ma'am, I've done this before."

In practice, but you don't need to know that now.

As I did the maneuver, it seemed like nothing was happening because the boy was choking louder. I repeated the procedure four more times and he was starting to cough clearer and show better skin color. The fifth time was the last. The boy gasped a *PTOOOH* as a fat, three-inch chicken bone shot out of his mouth. Trying to catch his breath, I pulled him up and sat him in a chair. The lady hugged her son, lifted him up and put him in her lap as she sat down.

I thought the mother looked unique. She had short dark brown hair, slim yet muscular, pretty, and sported a nose and tongue earring. It seemed like I knew her from somewhere, but I couldn't remember nor tried to remember.

"Make sure you take him home so that he can rest," I recommended. "He needs some fresh air as well, 'cause he's breathing hard and still in shock."

A first aid crew rushed to the scene and asked the lady if everything was alright.

"Yes, everything's fine," she answered. "This man saved my son's life."

She then looked at me and smiled. "Thank you so much, I am so grateful. My name is Carla, and this is my son Paulo."

"My name's Ajani, and you're very welcome."

I looked at Paulo, who didn't look older than five, and patted his head.

"How are you, Paulo?" I asked.

Softly and shyly, he replied, "Good. Thank you, sir."

"You're welcome. Just remember to eat slowly from now on, OK?"

"OK."

Carla said, "Thank you so much once again."

"You're welcome again. Take care."

When I turned around, I saw a big group of people including Teddy and K.J looking happy and inspired by what had just occurred. It just made me feel good to lend a helping hand, especially when it came to children. I didn't like the attention, though. I barely smiled when people said "great job", "way to go" and "God bless you" to me. I could never be a celebrity due to that factor.

"That was tight, dog," said K.J, patting me on the back. "I know now that I must learn first aid for unexpected situations like that."

Teddy added, "That was scary and a blessing to witness at the same time. Good job, guy. See, you had to wait for me for a reason."

Leaving the mall, I felt extremely good. I felt so lucky that I wanted to go back to the casino and win more cash but as I thought of Carla and Paulo, I thought of my undying love for Savannah and A.J. I had to call them just to hear their voices and tell them that I loved and missed them.

CHAPTER 48

TEDDY

Like the average person, I hated to be wrong. I was glad that Eros wasn't around to tell me "I told you so", because I made up my mind to go to Jam Fest on Friday night. It wasn't an easy decision, but I had to watch my cousin compete in the freestyle showcase. K.J in my opinion was the second coming of Nas, and I wanted to witness the coming-out party.

However, I wasn't going to miss Bless Fest, because the plan was to attend for at least two hours. K.J agreed to go with me to watch the festival's talent/fashion show, largely because he was eager to see Kaitlyn Fuentes again. However, he told me that we had to leave no later than nine pm, because he needed "pre-domination" time.

Dressed to impress and ready to roll out, I grabbed Janet's gift off the kitchen table as K.J and I left the crib at exactly seven o'clock. The plan of the evening was simple: The Phat Five would meet at Club V around nine-thirty. Ajani went to the casino so K.J and I would take the Accord to the club. Eros and Q would meet us there with Nivea and Whitney. I was ready to put the drama of the day in the history books and move on. It was time to have some fun.

As soon as we arrived at Kingdom Workers Fellowship, we saw a silver Dodge Durango drive into the parking spot reserved for the pastor.

"That's Pastor Jackson's car," I said with pride. "He's an awesome man of God and he has an incredible wife. I want you to meet them."

We got out of our car the same time Bishop and his wife got out of theirs. I was shocked to see them in casual attire, even though it was a youth event. They were both sporting his and her Detroit Pistons jogging outfits and looked very cool for couple in their fifties. I greeted them both and gave them a hug.

"Y'all are looking real tight in that gear," I said with sincerity. "Real tight!"

Lady Jackson said, "Why, thank you baby!" She always enjoyed a complement about her appearance.

Pastor Jackson asked me how I was doing and who the guest was that accompanied me. I gladly introduced them to my cousin.

"God bless you, sir and madam," K.J replied politely as he shook their hands.

"It's so nice to have you here, Brother K.J," said Pastor with a joyous expression. "You're doing the right thing, Brother Ted. If every member brings a guest tonight, this event will be standing room only."

I agreed. "No doubt, sir. I'm really looking forward to this Bless Fest, now that it's finally here."

"We are too," replied the First Lady. "We've lost so many young people in the past due to Jam Fest. They are so caught up in that heathen event, and they don't come back to church. I'm so glad you guys are coming here and not to those parties. God is good!"

K.J and I looked at each other, but said nothing.

Conviction, I thought. *Does it ever go away?*

The show hadn't started yet, so K.J and I went to the church basement. In the basement's recreation room, Janet and Kaitlyn were going over the show program while dancers and models went over their routines. We greeted each other and of course, Kaitlyn seemed shy because of what K.J said to her earlier, but nonetheless, there was a small chemistry brewing between them.

Right away, I said, "Jan, we need to talk."

Janet sighed and replied, "Alright, but not here. Let's go in one of the Sunday school rooms."

We found an empty classroom and closed the door. My woman was upset, anxious, and pressed for time, so I went straight to the point.

"I have something for you," I said, giving her a bag with the gift. "This is a little something from me and the guys to say that we're sorry for smoking weed in the apartment."

Janet sighed again. She looked as if she wanted to stay angry, but once she opened the bag, she was full of joy.

"Oh my gosh, it's the whole first season of *Fame* on DVD! I can't believe you remembered how much I wanted to see this! You do listen!"

"Yes I do, baby. I saw it in the store and I had to get it for you."

She gave me a warm hug. "Oh, thank you, Bear. You guys are so sweet and . . . I'm sorry that I said you were immature. I'm no better than you because you smoked weed. We both have different struggles, so we just need to pray that we both stay in God's will."

I told her that I forgave her, and what she saw in the apartment wouldn't happen again. Janet agreed, but she stopped smiling.

"You better believe it won't!" she snapped. "Man, Bear, the mad West Indian woman was so alive in me when I saw the place! Oooh, that place better be spotless when I come back on Sunday. Did you clean up?"

"Everybody helped with the cleaning. The place is crisp."

"I'll be the judge of that. You know that I'm a neater person than you. I'm gonna wash the stench off my clothes when I get back." She looked at her watch. "Alright, I gotta meet with the team before the show starts."

"Are you guys ready to go?"

"We'll see. They've worked really hard for this weekend. They don't want to let anybody down."

I smiled and looked into Janet's big brown eyes. "Well, if they can dance one-third as good as you, it will be a success."

She smiled. Janet knew that I was her biggest supporter when it came to dancing.

"Thanks, baby. Hey! Let's go to Rude Boy's after the show with Kaitlyn and K.J. I'm seriously craving their BBQ chicken right about now."

Suddenly, I remembered that I didn't tell her my change of plans.

"Oh, yeah, that's another thing that I have to tell you. K.J and I are only staying until nine. I'm gonna watch him in the showcase at Club V tonight."

Janet gave me a look of disappointment. She didn't respond.

I continued, "J, I know what you're thinking, but I'm only going to support my cousin, and that's it. I'm not going there to party. K.J came tonight to support this, even though he's performing in a few hours."

"Bear, I think Kaitlyn may be a huge reason why K.J's here, and you know that."

"True," I agreed, not trying to argue that point. "Are you upset with my decision?"

Janet wasn't my mama, and I felt that I wasn't wrapped around her finger, but her opinions meant a lot to me. However, I wasn't planning on changing my mind on going to the club.

She said, "Look . . . I don't have time to be angry. As I said, I have to go. I'm not going to make your choices for you. I love to dance, and because of that, I loved the nightlife but I know its influence on me isn't positive, so I chose to stay away.

You know how much you can handle, better than anyone, except God. Let His spirit lead you and guide you wherever you go."

We left the classroom and went back into the recreation room. Based on Janet's words of wisdom, I still didn't change my mind, but I wasn't confident about my choice.

CHAPTER 49

K.J

"So, Teddy tells me that you're an excellent rapper," Kaitlyn said.

We had decided to sit and chat in the basement recreation room until Teddy and Janet showed up. I told her that I was very confident about my skills, and that I was someone who put hours of work towards perfecting my craft of rhyming.

"I hear you," she said. "So what do you talk about in your lyrics?"

I loved the fact that she seemed so interested in my music. Bianca my ex only cared about the fame and bling-bling, like a real video chick.

I answered, "I speak about life issues, desires . . . you know . . . social topics."

"K.J, I know that we're in a church, but what do you really talk about? Be specific."

"Alright, you got me. I talk about power, domination, wack M.Cs, making money, women . . . but don't get me wrong though. I'm not like the average rapper on BET. I stay on the conscious tip."

She smiled. "Ok, I got it. Don't worry, I'm not going to rebuke you for your taste. I just want to know the man behind the microphone. What's your ultimate goal in life?"

I paused. Didn't expect a question like that from her so soon. Then again, that was the first time I ever tried to get with a minister. I wanted to give her a short, yet confident answer, something to impress such an incredible woman.

"My goal is to have a school that's entirely focused on empowering the youth of the present and future through the Hip-Hop culture."

I never shared that long-term goal with anyone before. She had to be my soul mate to get that out of me.

Kaitlyn's eyes lit up. "Are you serious? That's an out-the-box idea. I think that's awesome."

"And of course, I want a beautiful, God-fearing woman by my side as well."

My comment made her lower her head. Once again, I made Kaitlyn blush. However, she was ready to throw another challenging question at me.

"Are you a God-fearing man?" she asked.

With pride, I answered, "I love God. I love God and respect Him."

"No, no, you didn't answer my question. We can love and respect our brother, our cousin, our parents, but are you a God-fearing man?"

Paused again. Did I really fear God; especially to the point where I could do everything, he wants of me according to the Bible? I was just thankful to be a gifted, healthy, and smart Black man.

"Not as much as I should," I admitted. "I guess that's because I'm still learning more about who God really is."

"Well, I believe that I'm a God-fearing woman and the man that I choose to marry one day will be a God-fearing man, someone who is led by the Holy Spirit."

Spiritually, Kaitlyn wanted more than I could offer. However, did she want to marry a preacher? I never saw myself on a pulpit. I just liked going to the occasional Sunday service to give God his props. Maybe she just wanted me to step up my game and learn more about God before I even tried to pursue her as a potential girlfriend.

I just wanted to spend more time with Kaitlyn Fuentes. I felt a presence around her that I never felt around Bianca. Kaitlyn stimulated my mind, and we seemed comfortable around each other. It was too bad that we both had other priorities to deal with for the entire weekend.

"I want you to come to Bless Fest tomorrow night," Kaitlyn said. "I know that you have the showcase, but if you can, you have to hear X-Secula."

"X-Secular? Teddy played me one of his songs today. It sounded pretty tight."

"Well, that's nothing compared to seeing him live. The ministry of this man is incredible. You won't be the same after seeing him."

Teddy and Janet came towards us.

I said, "I'll try to come. I won't promise, but I'll try my best."

Kaitlyn and Janet went upstairs to the sanctuary, waving good-bye to Teddy and me. I looked at my cousin with a serious grin.

"Guy, on the real . . . I'm not smoking weed anymore," I admitted.

Teddy gave me a pound. "Amen to that."

CHAPTER 50

AJANI

What started as a messed-up day turned out to be a very good day for me. My first visit to the casino made me seventy-eight hundred dollars richer and I saved a young boy's life. A.J and Savannah were having a good time with their relatives, and I was already making more money on blackjack.

Upon twenty minutes of my return to the casino, I lost two hundred dollars but it only took thirty minutes for me to earn it back, plus an extra five hundred. I was ready to win big money, and nobody could tell me that luck wasn't on my side. Concentration was even on my side because nobody accompanied me, and I gambled best alone. Like the first visit, I proceeded to the next game after winning at another. The method wasn't broke, so it didn't need fixing.

Two hours had passed, and I had twelve thousand dollars from four games. Besides the half grand from blackjack, I won four thousand from Caribbean Stud, fifteen hundred from Roulette, and six grand from my new favorite, Baccarat. The way luck and favor poured on me, it easily became one of the greatest moments of my life. I felt like a champion, and was ready to leave the casino like one.

During my winnings, three beautiful escorts, all Italian and in their twenties, approached me at different times once they found out about my earnings. Although I was tempted, I shunned all three offers. I shook my head when I realized how easy it was for me nowadays to refuse sex. It was still great, but a very distant third to having money and my family.

I couldn't wait to deposit my cash after leaving the coin redemption booth. Unlike other drug dealers who carried lots of paper with them, I never liked to have more than five hundred in my wallet. If I needed more, a bank machine was never too far away. I was the type of man that never enjoyed attention, with the exception of my Escalade.

Most importantly, I had a closet paranoia, especially when I felt that someone was watching me. I was suspicious of anyone that looked like an undercover cop, dealer, hit man, or guys who wanted to rob me. Since my first winnings at the blackjack table, I observed the moves of a three-hundred pound, six-foot Latino. He looked familiar, but like the mother in the mall, no name, time, or place came to mind. Whoever he was, he looked as if he could crush someone into coffee crystals.

When I played Caribbean Stud, the man was twenty feet away. During Roulette and Baccarat, he always sat at a table that was across the aisle. The dude was watching sports at a bar counter in the same restaurant that I ate a steak dinner. Was I being paranoid, or was someone on my tail waiting to take me down?

I headed towards the valet parking exit.

It couldn't be about the money that I got from the Estafans. Even if the delivery wasn't arranged, Ricardo still got two cases of G.H for a forty percent discount.

I turned around and scoped the lobby before leaving. Didn't see the man.

Maybe I'm just trippin'. That's what happens to me when situations are going really good. I always prepare for the worst to happen.

When the parking attendant arrived with my truck, I took off as fast as possible, making sure that I wasn't being followed. For the moment, I wanted to be around lots of people, and what better place could that be than Club V, the hottest nightclub in the city.

CHAPTER 51

TEDDY

The first night of Bless fest was off the hook. The Kingdom Workers Fellowship sanctuary was designed with colorful spotlights, a dazzling Bless Fest logo behind the stage, and a twenty-foot catwalk in the middle of the aisle for the fashion show. Four hundred youth including K.J and I were dressed in street apparel, getting with the program to the fullest. I'd never seen anything like it before.

Min-T and Kaitlyn were the hosts of the show, and they did an excellent job of pumping up the audience. I was very impressed with the fashion show, because I had no idea that there were Christians making designer clothing that looked just as tight as Sean John or Phat Farm. The guys were sharply dressed without having to wear platinum chains and the ladies looked gorgeous without having to show cleavage or wear tight pants. This was the classiest fashion show I had ever seen.

Without question, the best part of the show was seeing my baby dance for the Lord. Janet and seven other dancers rocked the house while dancing to *Holla* by Trin-i-tee 5:7 and Mary Mary's *Incredible*. The crowd gave them a much-deserved standing ovation. I was so proud of her. She showed so much love and passion in her dancing. I prayed that God would open doors for Janet to dance for him around the world.

K.J tapped me on the shoulder, indicating that it was time to leave. Nine o' clock came so fast. I know my cousin enjoyed watching Kaitlyn, I mean the program, but he kept looking at his watch every five minutes. I didn't want to go, but I wasn't going to let K.J down. We quietly left the church and drove to the club.

"Dang, Ted, that service was good," said K.J, sounding surprised that church folks could actually have fun. "It's too bad that it had to be on my night, otherwise I would've stayed."

"I know," I said, pleased at his comment. "You nervous?"
"If I said no, would you believe me?"
"No."
"Well, what about anxious-infected?"
"Who wouldn't be? There'll be almost fifteen hundred heads at Club V tonight and forget about the judges, the crowd'll be the real critics. They make Simon from American Idol seem nice."
"Well, that's fine with me. I've never been a victim of intimidation. Cats don't know that I'm the sleeper in the showcase, and when they hear K.J, it's over!"

When we arrived at Club V, the line of people waiting outside was two blocks long. Parking was nowhere to be found except for the club's lot, which was charging money.
"Man, you know Jam Fest is getting huge when they charge twenty bucks to park," K.J complained.
I told him not to worry about it as I took out my Jam Fest V.I.P pass badge from the glove compartment. As we drove to the parking entrance, I showed it to the attendant. After inspecting the badge, he allowed us through. Hallelujah.
"Praise the Lord!" I shouted.
"No doubt," said K.J. "I didn't know you had a V.I.P pass."
"They gave me this way before the event. When I got saved and quit the committee shortly after, they didn't ask me to give the badge back."
Instead of waiting on the end of the line to get in the building, we decided to walk to the front since I had a pass and K.J was in the showcase. We were almost at the front when somebody yelled, "PHAT FIVE!" Turning around, we saw Ajani, Eros, and Q with Nivea and Whitney, all waiting to get in.
After we all greeted each other, Ajani showed us a finger in his right hand and two fingers in his left.
"This is how much grand I won at the casino!"
"Nice!" I said in shock. "Twice in one day, that's crazy!"
K.J gave him a pound. "Wow, you save a kid's life and win cash? Wow, you need to rub some of that karma on me, dog."
"Yet, this guy won't buy us V.I.P passes to get in before everyone else," complained Eros.
"Yo, call me cheap, but I won't even pay seventy-five bucks for myself to get in," Ajani responded. "Twenty-five is alright, but seventy-five to stand up and sweat?"
"Well, let me see if I can get us in," I grinned as I showed them my badge. "Be right back."
K.J and I went to the front and I saw a short Indian guy with a long ponytail talking to the bouncer. It was my Guyanese buddy from school.

"Yo, that's my boy, Lego," I said. "He's the vice-president of Nubians United, the campus group organizing Jam Fest."

Approaching Lego, I didn't know how he would react. I joined Nubians United in September, and after meeting him, we instantly became friends. We were both nightclub fanatics and toured every jam and club in Windsor. Lego appointed me as the PR representative for Jam Fest, and I did the job with joy. We were both committed to making Jam Fest 2003 the best ever.

Things changed, however, when I was saved. I immediately quit my PR job and stopped hanging out with Lego without proper explanation. I felt bad about not returning his phone calls, but I was afraid of giving into the temptation of smoking weed, drinking, and clubbing. I just hoped that there would be no hard feelings between us.

"What up, Lego," I said to him.

Dude looked very surprised to see me.

"What the—?" he yelled. "Looks like the freaks still come out at night! What up, T-Henny?"

I gave him a pound. "Long time no see."

"You telling me? You're the one who stopped hanging out."

"Guy, I apologize about that. It was a spiritual move, and hanging out in clubs isn't my thing anymore. I just didn't know how to explain it."

"What you said just now would've been fine, man. I may not understand it, but at least I can respect your decision."

Ouch. I felt a lump in my throat. Lego was absolutely right. Why did I think that every guy thought like Eros?

"So," continued Lego, "if you don't hang out in clubs anymore, what are you doing here?"

I told him that I was here to support my cousin, which followed by an introduction between K.J and Lego. They shook hands and said, "What up."

"You can go right in, guy," Lego said to K.J. "Much Music is interviewing the contestants in the V.I.P lounge on the, third floor."

"Cool, cool," replied K.J as he headed towards the entrance. "Holla, Ted."

"Yeah, cuz," I said.

Lego gave me a feisty smile. "No lie, Ted; you just came because you couldn't resist Jam Fest. Partying's in your blood."

Dang. Now he sounds like Eros.

"I'm serious, Lego. I came to watch my cousin."

"Whatever, guy. You can go in 'cause you're eager to get your freak on."

I ignored his wise crack and asked him if I could take my boys and their female companions with me. I pointed to the five individuals, letting Lego know that the tall white boy was Damon Quintino, Canadian college B-ball superstar. He just shook his head.

"That's cool Damon's here," said Lego, "but Ted, you're something else. You ain't hung out with me in two months, and now you want favors."

I grinned and showed him the badge. "I still got this."

"I should've taken it from you after you quit but you did work your butt off trying to promote this. All right, they can go in, but only for tonight! No favors tomorrow!"

I smiled. "I owe you, dog."

"Just go before I change my mind."

After being carded by the bouncer, the group and I went inside to pay admission. Ajani gladly paid twenty-five bucks a pass for everyone except me, who didn't need to pay.

Eros looked at me and said, "Repeat these words; 'I-was-so-wrong-and-you-were-so-right, Eros.'"

I pretended as if I didn't know what he was talking about.

"Oh, how soon you forget," said Eros. "Last night, I guaranteed that you would be at this jam tonight even though you denied it."

'Whatever," I replied.

"Deny it all you want, guy. Deep down inside, you're the same old T-Henny."

That was the second time in the day that Eros said that. I wanted to believe that I did the right thing by attending the club, but it didn't feel right. From Lady Jackson's comment to Janet's advice to Lego's judging and Eros just being Eros, I quickly started to believe that I should have stayed at Bless Fest.

CHAPTER 52

AJANI

The attendance at Club V was ridiculous. There were so many people to the point where finding an open seat was like finding Osama bin Laden. It was only forty-five degrees Fahrenheit outside, but the air conditioning was on due to the heat that the crowd generated. People kept coming in, and nobody was attempting to leave, even if they were desperate for fresh air. It was Jam Fest, the biggest party weekend of the year.

Soca music was blazing through the speakers. The dance floor was a can of sardines. The group of us was standing in a corner, admiring the atmosphere. Nivea and Whitney were winding their booties in front of Eros and Q while Teddy and I remained in GQ composure. Nobody did much talking 'cause the music was crazy overbearing.

I felt my personal cell phone vibrating. I looked at the number on the caller ID and saw that it belonged to Savannah's sister. It was too loud to try and talk and I assumed that it wasn't important, so I didn't answer.

If its important, she'll leave a message.

The phone vibrated once a minute later. Savannah left a message.

"Guy, I'll be back!" I screamed at Teddy. "Gotta make a call!"

He nodded and I made my way to the washroom.

In the men's room, the music was still loud but at least it wasn't too loud to make a call. I found an available toilet stall and went inside to hear the message. To my surprise, my son was the messenger.

"Hi, Daddy, this is A.J . . . I just called to say hi and . . . I miss you. I'm having lots of fun and . . . Mommy is too. OK, that's all I have to say . . . Love you! Bye."

I smiled as I saved the message. I was going to wait until Saturday to talk to my pride and joy, but I couldn't resist.

"Hello?" It was Joselyn, Savannah's sister.

"Hey Josey, what's up?"

"Hi, Ajah. How are you?"

"Chillin', is my son still awake?"

"Yeah, he's right here watching Blue's Clues. Hold on."

"Hi, Daddy!" answered A.J. "Did you get my message?"

"Hey, Lil Man, yes I got your message. I'm calling because I miss you."

My son said he missed me too, but wasn't worried because I was coming home soon. The way he expressed it made him sound so bright for a two-year old. All I could do is smile.

I said, "Yes, son. I'll be back really soon. Where's Mummy?"

"She's here. Mummy fell on the ground at church tonight."

My smile left. The last thing that I wanted was my woman or son getting hurt while I was away.

Why wasn't I called about this?

"Fell on the ground?" I panicked. "How? Is she there? Put Mummy on the phone."

A.J said nothing and just yelled for his mother.

"Hey, baby," said Savannah.

"Vannah, what's going on? What happened?"

She laughed. "Baby, I'm fine. In fact, I've never been better."

I was confused. "What happened that made you fall at church?"

"It wasn't a bad fall. The preacher laid hands on my head and the Holy Spirit allowed me to drop. I didn't get hurt."

The Holy what? What's this woman talking about?

"Huh? Laid hands on you? Why?" I got upset.

"Well . . . I guess it's what they do when someone gets saved. I gave my heart to the Lord tonight."

"Gave your heart?"

"I'm a born-again Christian now."

I said nothing. What was going on? Everyone around me seemed to be turning into Christians. First, it was Joselyn, then Janet and Teddy, and now Savannah. Why would anybody want to serve any religion?

"Ajah, you still there?"

"Yeah, it's just real noisy at this club. So you really did it, huh?"

"Yep! I'm just so happy now, I can't even explain it! Oh, Ajah, it was great. So many people were saved, including this one guy who used to deal drugs in downtown T.O. Yesterday, he was a part of a major cartel and today he gave it all up for God. Isn't that amazing?"

That was the last thing I needed to hear.

"Yeah . . . that's good."

"The game almost killed him and his kids. He said that if God spared their lives, he was going to give up the drug life. Well, God came through, and he left the game and then some!"

Savannah continued the story, saying that the dude's wife also gave her testimony, praying that her man would give up the dangerous lifestyle. I was ready to tune Savannah out until she said that she admired the wife for putting up with his crap, because she wouldn't know what to do if she had to deal with it. I received her statement as a warning that it was best that Savannah never found out about my shady business. I would have to quit the game forever before telling her.

As a good man, I listened to her wonderful night at church, but my mind was tripping. Why did Savannah have to tell me that story? Did she suspect my actions or was she still clueless? The more she spoke, the more rotten I felt as her man and a father. I had to end the conversation quickly.

"Vannah, the phone's breaking up," I lied. "I'll call you tomorrow. Tell A.J. I love him."

"OK, I will. Love you."

"Love you too."

I went to the bar to order a Guinness. As I waited to be served, I had a strong feeling that crazy drama was about to happen. I had good reason to be paranoid, because in the midst of the huge crowd, I saw the same large Latino from the casino.

CHAPTER 53

EROS

The more women I saw in the jam, the more I wished that I wasn't Nivea's date. Sure, Nivea was pretty and her body features impressed me, but I wasn't in Windsor for a relationship. There were too many fish in the ocean of Jam Fest to choose.

I liked it when Nivea pushed her backside in front of me, and it wasn't because it made me feel good. She was facing the crowd, which gave me the freedom to observe God's creation. The bootylicious Ebony women, the White women that looked good enough to be in any Hip-Hop video, the very fine Latinas and the petite yet sweet Filipino girls. Yet, all I could do is just look, look, and look.

When we finished dancing to Beyonce's new single, I told Nivea that I was going to buy us a couple of Long Island iced teas.

"Oooh, that's my favorite," she admitted. "I swear the freak in me comes out when I drink it."

I gave her a surprised look. As much as I wanted to move on, at least Nivea Davis loved bedroom activity. Good for me if I didn't get any new prospects.

I saw Ajani drinking a Guinness at the bar counter. Something was bugging him 'cause the dude was looking serious once again.

"Yo, you're staring hard at something, man," I told him.

Ajani said, "It's all these fine women! If only I was single and crazy again . . . dang. It's ridiculous in here."

That's not what was on his mind, but I definitely agreed with him.

"No doubt," I said.

"Especially that eye candy on the floor dancing with another woman."

I looked where Ajani was pointing and gasped. It was *them*. The woman who bumped me at the casino and her lady friend. They looked sexier than earlier as they danced up a sweat. It was arousing.

"Guy, that caramel-skinned girl is the one I saw in the casino!" I shouted. "The Asian girl was also with her. She's fine too, but man, God couldn't chisel a finer masterpiece than her friend. Dang, why did I have to be here with Nivea?"

Ajani said, "Even if you weren't with Nivea, it'd be hard to get between those two. Look at the way they're dancing. You can tell they're a couple."

They were touching each other and not paying attention to any people on the dance floor. Being the type of dude I was, it turned me on, and the men in the club were fascinated as well. The thought of having both of them at the same time almost made me drool.

"They may be together, but I know they wouldn't turn me down," I said. "The way that Miss Caramel looked at me today, I know she wants me."

As I looked at the two beauties, the light one saw me through the crowd and smiled. She showed me to her friend and she smiled as well. They were smiles of passion directed right at me. Miss Caramel licked her lips slowly and gave me the signal to approach her.

"Me?" I asked by pointing to myself.

She nodded. I left the bar stand and pressed my way towards the ridiculously packed dance floor.

The Asian diva allowed me to make my move on Miss Caramel by stepping aside, but not too far, 'cause I wanted her as well. I grabbed her waist. She placed her hands on my shoulders. The song *Hot in Here* by Nelly began playing and our feet started grooving. As our eyes stayed connected to each other, she moved her hands slowly down my chest. I glided my hands towards her south. The lower her hands moved, the more aroused I became. Immediately we were steady on second base.

Suddenly, I felt two more arms on my waist. It was her friend, and her warm, firm body stimulated me even more. She began to caress me from behind while I continued to kiss Miss Caramel. Then the roles between the ladies switched. I smiled with joy, knowing that I was the greatest player ever. I was on the road towards having my very first threesome.

Then all of a sudden, Miss Caramel yelled "Fifteen" with a manly voice. That shocked the crap outta me. How could a beautiful woman speak with such ruggedness? I would have a heart attack if I were dancing with two men!

I looked at her and asked, "What'd you say?"

"I said fifteen dollars!"

A frustrated male bartender was looking at me, waiting for his money. The two Long Island iced teas were seven-fifty a drink.

"Oh yeah," I said as I gave him a twenty and told him to keep the change.

I was still at the bar counter and the two women were no longer dancing. Ajani was still next to me, looking like his mind was on anything but the jam.

"Ajah," I asked, "why does it seem like doing something immoral and unethical feels so right?"

Ajani thought about the question for a few seconds, without asking me about my intentions. My boys knew me way too well.

He answered, "Because you don't care if what you're doing is right or wrong. You just want it."

Words from a man with experience. Thank you, Ajah.

I was tired of playing boyfriend. It was time for me to take my game to the next level. After the jam, I was going to ask Nivea if she was cool with us and one of her girls getting it on. If she wasn't, then I would fulfill my desire elsewhere.

CHAPTER 54

Q

A young man approached the table that Whitney and I were sitting at. This was the seventh person in the last half hour. He said that I was the baddest white boy ever to play college basketball and I would have been a star in the NBA if I hadn't been injured. I had to shake his hand for giving me such great props.

"Thank you," I said. "That means a lot to me. Appreciate it."

The man nodded his head and left.

Whitney looked at me with admiration. "Wow, aren't you popular in here! How does it feel when people approach you like that?"

"Trust me, I still find it overwhelming," I answered. "I just wish that I could've given them more than what they anticipated."

"You have, Q. You showed them a player of integrity and someone they could look up to."

Integrity was a word I didn't need to hear at that moment. It made me think of how dishonest I was acting. Little did Whitney know that I was on the road towards adultery. Did I need to put on my wedding ring? Did she need to know that I was married? Of course not, because I was only going to hang out with her until the end of the weekend. Yet, my mind was still on Katrina, and I needed to call her.

"If you'll excuse me, Whitney, I have to use the washroom. Be back soon."

"Alright," she sang. "Hurry back, 'cause I wanna dance."

Searching through Katrina's cell for the umpteenth time, I noticed that she didn't try to call me. I hated that with a passion. Whenever my wife was angry with me, it usually took her two days to get over the issue. I thought it was immature, but I always let her actions slide away from my mind without confronting her about it but I couldn't take the suspense of the unknown Barry White-sounding man any longer.

I called home, but the phone just rang so I decided to hang up before the answering machine came on before re-dialing the number. It was the same result three straight times. Tried the cell number again, but it was off. I felt that if Katrina saw the cell number appear on the caller ID, she would know that I called.

My feelings were of anger, frustration, anxiety, and confusion. Where was my wife? Did she go clubbing with her girls again? Did she visit family or was she with another man? I squeezed my fist so hard that I almost cracked the phone.

If Katrina was cheating on me as Eros suggested, she couldn't have picked a better weekend but what if she's been cheating for weeks already? Was she that fed up with our marriage? I was only trying to make our lives financially better. As I sat in the toilet stall in the club washroom, I began to look at the situation from her perspective. I did work seventy hours a week while she complained how bored she was being a housewife. When she wanted sex, I wanted to catch up on sleep. Yet, I got upset when Katrina bought a vibrator. Our social life decreased dramatically from going to the movies or dinner twice a week to once in the last four months. Finally, she wasn't pleased with my smoking after being physically fit and healthy for our entire relationship. I was a bad example of a loving husband.

If my wife was cheating on me, I understood her reasons. However, an affair would make her just as bad as me, if not worse. I pictured my wife having sex with another man. She was enjoying every second of it. I wanted to scream in horror, as if it was actually happening.

How could she enjoy cheating on me . . . ? How, how?

Instead of losing my composure in a public washroom, I took a deep breath. I remembered that a fine woman named Whitney was waiting to dance with me. She was a beautiful Black woman who loved dating Caucasian boys like yours truly and yes I, Damon Quintino, wanted to sleep with her.

If Trina can sleep with someone else, so can I. I am not going back home feeling like doggy crap.

I turned off the cell phone and left the washroom with a smile of revenge.

CHAPTER 55

TEDDY

When I was a clubber, I flirted with women when Janet wasn't with me. It was fun, and I did it only to get a dance or two. A lady was sitting at the bar counter flirting with me, and all I wanted was a ginger ale.

The woman was pretty with her dark skin, natural afro, and big sexy lips, but she wasn't a Janet Watters. Unlike my baby, she had a tongue ring and exposed too much skin. Since when did that turn me off? God really did change my lifestyle.

I saw Ajani get his drink on and Eros and Q get their groove on with their dates. For the first time in my life, I felt out of place in a nightclub. Club V used to be my church, but now it felt like wet socks . . . very uncomfortable.

Just six weeks prior, everything about Windsor's hottest nightclub was great to me. The hot music, the gorgeous women, the coolest guys to hang out with and the aroma of liquor and tobacco all seemed much better when I entered the jam high and tipsy. It was the highlight of my weekends.

Presently, the event that I highly anticipated was very overrated. The beats of the music was tight, but the lyrics were garbage. The cursing in Hip-Hop bugged me more than ever. The rappers talked about having things clubbers only dreamed about owning. The guys would recite the verses as if they wrote the song, yet the majority of them couldn't relate to the artists because they were broke college students. I used to do the same thing.

I also noticed how the men in the club tried to pick up women. The guys that were known for borrowing ten dollars for a haircut tried to pick up the ladies known as gold-diggers. I thought that if they would be themselves and not a bootleg resemblance of Morris Chestnut, 50 Cent, or Ludacris, the women might take them more seriously. However, that still didn't guarantee a girl's seven digits.

I shook my head and grinned at the gold-digging girls. They looked sexy and wore revealing outfits yet shunned every guy that came in their proximity. Yes, the men were broke students, but so were they! Instead of going for a future doctor or engineer, they wanted a thug with a Benz and a suspect occupation. I reached the conclusion that materialism was a sickness instead of a choice.

As for the smell that used to be highly tolerable, the liquor and cigarettes now had a disgusting odor. Only the Holy Spirit could change me from adoring the smell of weed to choking from cigarette smoke in a span of a few hours. Who would've thought that?

My mind was set. Jam Fest wasn't my cup of tea anymore. If Janet could avoid it, so could I. The difference between Bless Fest and Jam Fest was so obvious. The joy I had at the talent/fashion show was gone and I wanted it back.

I looked at my watch it was ten minutes to eleven. The freestyle showcase was almost ready to begin, and I felt more relieved.

C'mon, K.J. Do your thing so I can get outta here.

CHAPTER 56

K.J.

It was less than ten minutes until my time to shine. I sat in the large black leather sofa in Club V's V.I.P lounge, trying to look relaxed but anxiety was driving me crazy. One hour earlier, I spoke big about beating Verbal Pain on Much Music, so I couldn't afford to lose. Otherwise, I would forever be known as the Phenomenal rapper that never lived up to the hype.

Although Verbal Pain was thought by many Jam Festers to repeat as the showcase's freestyle champ, there were six rappers other than me that were ready to prove them wrong. Sitting to my left was a bald-headed Latino named Material. I never heard him rap, but I heard people say that the Detroit native flowed as fast as the Hip-Hop artist Twista did. Fast rappers didn't impress me though. They were either hard to understand or spoke too much nonsense for rhyming sake.

Next to Material at the sofa arm was an Afro-Canadian, dread-wearing dude called Three-Dollar Bill, the hometown favorite. I assumed that the Windsorite gave himself that name because he thought he was unbelievable. However, in the showcase's five-year history, there was never a winner from Windsor due to its strong competition from the U.S and Toronto. I heard his stuff once at a jam in T.O.; he sounded tight, but not enough to beat me in a battle.

Sitting to my right was a large White boy from Cleveland by the name of Willy Black. The name sounded slightly corny, but I realized that since the entrance of Eminem in the late nineties, White rappers strongly elevated their game.

Standing next to him smoking a big blunt was a Detroiter called Triple E. The dude placed third in last year's showcase and looked like he wanted to murder somebody. He was easily the most explicit rapper I ever heard, and because of that, he didn't impress me whatsoever.

The final two contenders were sitting at the other side of the lounge. J-Thrill, a light-skinned Jamaican from T.O, had excellent delivery. There were large rumors that he had fake ID and was really seventeen instead of the minimum contestant age of nineteen. I thought that the issue would only make noise if he won the showcase, but I believed it wasn't going to happen. Didn't know much about Flow Daddy, other than he was a short, dark-skinned guy from Chicago who had an afro bigger than Ben Wallace.

Nobody was speaking to each other, which was fine by me because I only had words for the stage. Every rapper looked anxious and tense; expect Verbal Pain, who was being interviewed by The Source magazine. He looked so arrogant I wanted to slap him. Bianca was next to him, trying to look important being Roderick's woman. As much as I stared at them, they acted as though I wasn't in the room.

My mind was full of anger and disgust. That was the first time I ever saw my ex-friend/partner and ex-girlfriend as a couple. Feelings of hate grew stronger as I thought about how they betrayed me. I hated thinking that way after being in church a couple of hours earlier, but I couldn't help it.

That punk and that hoe will pay, I thought. *They'll wish that they never met me.*

"Ladies and gentlemen, welcome to the high-adrenaline, action-packed, drama-filled, super-lyrical, Jam Fest Freestyle Showcase!"

Sho'nuff, host of Flava Unlimited, North America's hottest new Hip-Hop show, got the crowd roaring. During the intro, all eight of us rappers stepped on the stage. I looked at the crowd and saw the Phat Five cheering me on. Their rants made me feel like a superstar, and I was determined not to disappoint them.

"As you can see," the dread-wearing host said, "this is being shown live on Urban TV for the first time ever!"

The audience yelled and applauded.

"So," he added, "if you thought that the pressure to shine was tough in the past, add this hostile crowd plus a few million!"

I smiled. *If cats can't take the heat, get out the kitchen now!*

"Also," Sho'nuff continued, "being live also brings up the question asked by many; will cursing be eliminated from the showcase? Well, we can't stop anyone from saying the N-bomb, F-bomb, or the S-word, right?"

The crowd cheered as if they heard news that all Club V's drinks were half-price. The contestants already knew the rules before showtime. Sho'nuff waited until the people stopped yelling before explaining the rest of the game's guidelines.

"We can't stop them from cussing in their rhymes, but . . . if a rapper lets one out, they will be disqualified from the showcase!"

Reactions were mixed with boos and applause. I laughed, thinking about Triple E. I wasn't worried because my mother was watching, who slapped me hard when I was a Pinckney if I even thought about cursing.

The host concluded the rules, stating that each M.C had ninety seconds to out rhyme their opponent. The five judges, who were all record executives, each gave a score out of ten, with fifty being a perfect score. The winners of the first round would go to the final four, and the winners of that would enter the Saturday night championship.

Sho'nuff added, "Of course, the winner of the showcase will get a record deal, if they can beat last year's champion, *Ver-Bal Pain!*"

In the midst of the applause, the Phat Five were screaming my name repeatedly. I tried to stay serious, but I had to grin. I had the best four friends on the planet.

"Only time will tell!" he ended. "But until then, let's make history. Let the battles begin!"

Five minutes later, the first battle of round one began.

"The first battle will be Windsor's own Three-Dollar Bill against Material from *Dee-troit*, Michigan!" the host yelled.

The cheers were loud because of the crowd majority being from the border cities. Sho'nuff flipped a coin after the two contestants stepped on the stage. Material won the toss and wanted to go second.

Usually, the first free stylist of the contest was the most nervous, and Three-Dollar Bill wasn't an exception. For the first thirty seconds, his rhymes sounded unoriginal and out-of-flow, but he improved as he went along. He threw strong disses at Material, saying that he was, "so broke, his gold tooth was penny copper." The crowd went nuts when he concluded that Material needed to quit the showcase because "Twista is trippin' and he wants all his lyrics back." The judges gave him a respectable thirty-five out of fifty points.

Good, but not great. Let's see what Material can do.

When I heard Material flow, I realized what people said about him was true. He was the second coming of Twista, 'cause he had a machine-gun flow and pronounced every word clearly. He was destroying Three-Dollar, shocking folks and well on his way to a victory. However, Material's glory came to an abrupt end when he spit out an F-bomb with only twenty seconds left. One of the judges pressed a siren button and the music stopped. Battle over.

"The winner by disqualification; Three-Dollar Bill!"

The people booed and Material was arguing with the judges. It was obvious that they hated the no-swearing rule. Three-Dollar walked off the stage with his hands in the air.

"Gotta respect the rules, baby!" he shouted.

"The second battle will be J-Thrill from Toronto and Chicago's own Flow Daddy!"

Battle two was a walk in the park for J-Thrill. The young rapper, who lost the coin toss and had to rhyme first, did a freestyle so tight that he scored a forty-five.

Flow Daddy looked as if he regretted his decision to go second. When it was his turn, he didn't make it past thirty seconds 'cause the loud boos from the crowd ruined his concentration. He walked off the stage in total embarrassment.

"And the winner of battle two goes to J-Thrill!"

Sho'nuff started laughing as he looked at the winner. "Boy, I heard rumors that yous a youngin'. I don't care how tight you are, if them rumors are true, I will call your mama in Toronto so she can whoop your . . ."

The audience laughed as J-Thrill tried to show the host his ID.

Sho'nuff ignored it and said, "Whatever, son."

I lowered my head and closed my eyes; I had a strong feeling that my turn was next. I didn't want to battle Roderick in the first round because of the big chance that the battle may be fixed. Verbal Pain was the defending champ and his employer Pacific Records was a huge sponsor of the event. Anything less than making the Finals could greatly affect the sales of his upcoming debut album. Thus, I didn't want to be judged unfairly.

"And now for battle number three! Returning to the showcase for a second time is Detroit's own Triple E, versus a newcomer to the stage, Toronto's own K.J!"

Thank you, God.

As I stepped on the stage, I heard my boys scream my name, but I ignored them. Looking at Triple E, I saw terror. His eyes were larger than Joan's from the sitcom *Girlfriends*. He was trying to intimidate me, but it wasn't working.

"Save that look for Osama bin Laden," I whispered. "I'm gonna tear you apart."

Sho'nuff tossed the coin. "Triple E, what do you call?"

"Heads," he replied, still staring hard at me.

"It's tails. K.J, you win the toss. You wanna go first or second?"

I looked at Triple E with a devilish grin. I knew exactly what to say to him. "I'll go first," I said.

"Ladies and gentlemen, K.J has agreed to go first! D.J, run the track!"

The beat that played was *Grindin'* by the group Clipse, one of my favorites. It was a simple bass-heavy track that was perfect for free styling. It was time for domination!

> "Yo, yo, yo, yo,
> You lookin' at my face as if you really hate me
> Big ol' ugly eyes trying to intimidate me
> Man, you couldn't scare a newborn baby
> You look sick as if you were infected with rabies
> What the heck is Triple E? I've heard of Triple A
> But I can tow you outta this battle in any way
> What's Triple E? Boy, lemme give you some trivia
> The only Tripoli is the capital of Libya
> I remember when you were rhyming last year

CRAZY DRAMA

> Sounding like Kool G Rap during his post rap career
> Fire breathing dragon, looking so serious
> Mouth more dirty than Eddie Murphy's Delirious
> But this year my friend, the rules have changed
> And I doubt that you have your lyrics re-arranged
> Without the F-word, you can't go very far
> I bet you get kicked out by the sixteenth bar
> I've urinated on your quest to blow up like Nelly
> But to do that, you need to pray that you can defeat me
> So look at me all you want like Ike did to Tina
> My presence is blinding, I'll burn out your retina
> But now its time for me to look at my final score
> But you need a janitor to sweep your spilled ego of the floor
> YEAH!"

I could've rapped for another fifteen seconds, but it wasn't necessary. The damage was done. Triple E was sweating more than an MC Hammer dancer. Three of the five judges were out of their seats in awe. The crowd was roaring. The Phat Five cheered like they had no common sense. Now it was up to the judges' score and seeing if Triple E had a miracle verse to defeat me.

The first judge from Much Music gave me a nine. The second judge from Columbia Records gave a nine as well. Vibe and XXL Magazine had judges as well, and they surprised the crowd and me with two tens. The only bad score came from Pacific Records, go figure. Their judge gave me a seven, yet my final score was still a strong forty-five.

I kept my cool, but inside I felt very excited and confident. Triple E would need to think about flowers just to avoid swearing. Could he do that and get a better score? Not if I could help it.

The beat played again and it was his turn to rhyme. I wanted to really tick him off so I started to grin like J.J from *Good Times*. It was an out-the-box plan of intimidation.

> "Yo, why the hell are you smiling? You ain't win this yet
> That's like saying you won the lotto without placing a bet
> You dumb rookie! How in the world you get so cocky?
> Grin standing out like a Black man playing hockey
> I chew and spit people like you and throw them in the trash
> Win competitions and a pocket full of cash
> Make the six-figures without pulling any triggers
> You figure all Detroit has is a bunch of crazy niggas?
> You Toronto cats ain't got—"
> BEEP BEEP BEEP BEEP BEEP BEEP BEEP BEEP BEEP BEEP

I gave a wicked laugh as the siren went off.

I overestimated him! Dude only went eight bars!

Triple E turned to the judges. "What? What did I say? I didn't curse!"

The judge from Vibe who pulled the siren replied, "You can't say the N-bomb on TV. Disqualified!"

Proving to everyone that he had anger issues, Triple E threw the mike on the ground and yelled the F-bomb as he left the stage. Boos followed him for his un-sportsmanlike conduct, but once I raised my hands in victory, the cheers returned.

Sho'nuff shouted, "The easy winner by default, K.J!"

I looked at my boys and gave them the Phat Five symbol; a left fist and five fingers on the right. The guys, acting like junior high teenagers, returned the gesture.

As I went backstage, I walked past my former buddy, who patted me on the shoulder.

"Guy, that was so tight, it sounded written," he said without stopping to look at me like a real man.

I stopped and turned around. He was already near the stage. Thank God, 'cause I was ready to say something really vicious to him.

I stayed backstage while Verbal Pain battled Willy Black. Watching it on the TV screen, Verbal lost the coin toss, rapped first and gave a crowd-pleasing rhyme. However, the surprise was Willy Black and his competitive spirit. The White boy shocked everyone but fell short of an upset win. The final score was a very close forty-seven to forty-five in Verbal Pain's favor.

There was a fifteen-minute intermission before the semi-finals. I could've talked smack with the guys during the break, but instead I went into a washroom stall, put on my Discman, and prepared for more domination.

CHAPTER 57

K.J.

"We're ready to begin the Final Four!" Sho'nuff exclaimed while the crowd cheered in anticipation. "The four cats remaining are Windsor's Three-Dollar Bill, K.J from Toronto, J-Thrill from Toronto, and last year's champ, Verbal Pain from Toronto! An all-Canadian semi-final! How did this happen?"

There was a mixture of cheers and boos. I knew that much of the audience was patriotic, but when it came to hip-hop, all I cared about was skills. My opponents could be from Mars, and my number one concern would still be to defeat them.

I was anxious to know my next opponent. My desire was to reach the Finals facing my former partner-in-rhyme. Anything less would be disappointing. I felt that there might have been a conspiracy taking place with Verbal Pain and the judges. Any one that challenged him would have to be flawless just to pull an upset. I heard "boo's" from some people when Verbal defeated Willy Black. Many thought that the boy from C-Town should've won. I'm glad he didn't, 'cause it would've spoiled my revenge.

"The first battle of round two should be real hot! Real hot! We have the underage suspect J-Thrill versus Mr. Smiley Face K.J! M.C's, step on the stage!"

They didn't put me against Roderick, which was great, but I had a fierce match-up against a cocky and talented youngin'. As I looked at J-Thrill, I saw a confident kid but one that was never challenged by an above average rapper like yours truly.

Hope you're ready, boy. You might get your feelings hurt.

The coin was tossed. I called tails and won. My choice was to go second because I really wanted to hear what J-Thrill had in store for me. Ludicris' Southern Hospitality was the beat chosen for the battle. I decided that I wouldn't grin while J rapped. Instead, I folded my arms and looked at him with sarcastic admiration, as if he was the late Malcolm X. I was in an extra-good mood.

Wasting no time, J-Thrill began the freestyle:

> "Yo, where's that stupid grin that you had during the first round?
> My thought is that you looked like a constipated clown
> Hold on, dog! Word'll soon get around
> That I make your rhymes sound like farting sounds
> Where did you learn to rap? Hip-hop summer camp?
> I wouldn't buy your album if you only charged food stamps
> Couldn't spark a fire with a kerosene lamp
> Your style would give my grandmother menstrual cramps
> I heard you and Verbal Pain was a hip-hop group
> Now he's blown up and you're just some doggy poop
> Now you want a record deal 'cause you started playa hatin'
> This won't be your season, keep anticipatin'
> Keep dreaming in your own imaginary world
> You ain't got jack, Verbal Pain even has your ex-girl
> So you can look at me like I'm just a young child
> while you read my book, *How to Really Freestyle!*"

J-Thrill didn't use the full ninety seconds, but it wasn't needed. The audience cheered loudly. I kept the same look that I posed before the rhyme began, but it was tough 'cause I was mad.

I never spoke to J-Thrill in my life, yet the boy knew about my past. That didn't surprise me because the whole Toronto Hip-Hop community knew about my feud with Roderick. I was shocked at how happy he looked to attack me, as if I hurt him in the past and he wanted revenge. The crowd was impressed with J's references to Verbal Pain and Bianca, as well as the "constipated clown" and "menstrual cramps" remarks. The judges gave him a serious forty-six points.

When I free styled, I liked to use big words and similes to blow the minds of my opponents and other people listening. I was never very explicit, and tried not to be very rude. However, this little rude boy came tough, and I had to respond tougher.

Forgive me, Lord for what I'm about to do. Forgive me, Mom, forgive me, Ted, forgive me, Kaitlyn. I'm about to lyrically murder this kid!

"K.J, Take him down!"

"Your stuff's tighter than that crap!"

I heard the cries of the Phat Five. I was ready to respond.

"Run that beat! I'm ready!" I told the host. "Run that track!"

Sho'nuff gave the DJ the signal. Showtime!

> "Bred-drin, how did you find out about my past drama?
> I guess that what happens when I sleep with your mama!

Yeah, she was real good, I'm glad I got with her
But I have a question for you: Where's your babysitter?
Everybody in this joint knows you're only seventeen
I changed your picture ID with a delete machine
And it worked, 'cause the bouncers let your butt pass
And you're up here, waiting for me to kick your . . .
Ha ha! Thought I was gonna slip? Not that easy
You gave a good rhyme, but I can also get teasy
I came from an era when lyrics were artistic
Before the cats like you got materialistic
You don't even know who is 'A Tribe Called Quest"
I was free styling while you were still sucking on your mama's breasts
So you can trip on me like your name was Ron Artest
And I'll still smack the two little hairs off your chest
Then you can kiss my Lugz and say 'K.J's blessed'
And go straight to your room after you lose this contest
Think about how K.J became the over taker
While you take your freshie self on a boat back to Jamaica
Listen to the crowd and you'll know I came sweet
So put the mike down and sit in your booster seat!"

It was the rudest and most offensive freestyle that I ever performed and it was live on national TV but if it was the rhyme to beat J-Pickney, then I believed that it was worth it.

The crowd cheered with equal response to J-Thrill's freestyle. He looked slightly embarrassed during my performance, but he kept his composure the entire time. I think it was the first time he ever got schooled. I nodded my head at the young rapper, giving him a *that's-what-you-get-when-you-get-personal* look. I noticed my boys, who were giving each other high-five as well as to other spectators who enjoyed my comeback.

"Whoa!" screamed Sho'nuff. "Free styling at its finest, baby! This is a real close call. Can K.J beat J-Thrill's score of forty-six? Let's see what the judges came up with!"

Twirling my thumbs in anticipation, I knew that I came tough, and my delivery would be the deciding factor for a victory. Much Music gave me a nine compared to a ten for J-Thrill. Columbia Records gave both of us a ten. Vibe gave me a ten compared to a nine for my opponent. XXL gave J an eight, but thought my rhyme was a ten.

The final score belonged to the judge from Pacific. He gave me the worst score in the first round. He gave the kid a nine. Would he give me my due respect or keep hating because I had beef with their beloved artist?

Pacific gave me an eight, the lowest of the judges. He was hating, but I didn't care once I saw the final score. I had forty-seven points!

"The final score is K.J with forty-seven and J-Thrill forty-six. K.J advances to the Freestyle Showcase championship!" the host screamed.

I gave J-Thrill a small brotherly hug to show that I was a good sport. He didn't look at me, proving that he was highly disappointed. The reaction from the audience was mixed as expected because pre-Showcase, J-Thrill was the favorite to beat Verbal Pain in the Finals. Not anymore.

I gave my boys the Phat Five salute again. They acted as if the Toronto Raptors won the NBA championship. As I went backstage, many heads congratulated me in the VIP lounge. I proceeded to the washroom, gave God thanks, and went to watch the other battle on the lounge's Trinitron.

Verbal Pain destroyed Three-Dollar Bill by a score of forty-four to thirty-five. It was a walk in the park for him because he wasn't challenged. Nevertheless, my wish was fulfilled. The battle of Phenomenal would take place on Saturday night.

Sho'nuff announced that the two finalists would each do a solo performance at the Jam Fest fashion show on Saturday afternoon. Eleven o'clock would be the time for the ultimate showdown.

I left the stage and spent the rest of the time with the Phat Five. Never before had I received so much high-fives, pounds, and handshakes from unknown people. It was one of the best nights of my life.

CHAPTER 58

Q

"Well, I hope you had a good time tonight," I said to Whitney as we walked out of Club V ahead of the gang. "I really enjoyed myself."

"So did I," she replied. "I still can't believe how tight your boy was on that stage!"

"Yep, that's K.J! Tonight was his coming-out party. So what are you gonna be up to now?"

"What you mean, when I get home? Guy, it's two in the morning, and I like my sleep. It's way past my bedtime, believe it or not."

I wasn't surprised by Whitney's response. Thought that it wouldn't hurt to ask, just in case she wanted to invite me back to her place. The night was great for a one-nighter, but I respected her for not inviting me and it made the night less convicting.

"Yeah, it is late," I said. "I hope that you don't think that I was . . . y'know, trying to . . ."

"Q, if you weren't trying to get with me, I would've thought you were either gay or married."

We both laughed at the same time. I hoped that comment never came up. I wiped my sweaty forehead.

We arrived at Nivea's Honda Civic, waiting for Eros and Nivea to arrive. I looked in her eyes as I grabbed her hand.

"Let me take you out for lunch and a movie tomorrow," I suggested. "I don't know the best places to go in Windsor, so you can choose your favorite."

"Alright," she smiled. "Let's go after the fashion show. I know a great place where we can get to know each other some more."

"So it sounds like a date."

"I guess so."

I wasn't going to do it, but I felt that the moment was right. I approached Whitney with a kiss and she didn't turn it down. It was a three-second smooch with no intentions of giving tongue. Felt like a young teenager on my first date, which was scary because it was identical to my first kiss with Katrina.

"Here comes Nivea now. Good night, Q, see you tomorrow."

"Can't wait."

CHAPTER 59

AJANI

"Yo, I'll check you cats tomorrow," Eros told the cousins and me. "I'm about to bang this girl one more time and move on."

I asked him, "You really wanna get with those lesbians?"

"You mean bisexual. There's no way they'll turn me down if I got my A-game on, especially the caramel one. Dang, she's fine!"

"You think that you'll see them tomorrow?" Teddy asked.

"If you pray about it, I'll see them for sure," joked Eros.

"I don't think God will answer a prayer for a friend to get an opportunity to have pre-marital sex with two gay women while committing adultery."

"No comment."

The guys started laughing the usual *I'm-tired-or-drunk-and-I'll-laugh-at-anything* chuckle. I was still watching my back, I didn't see the big Latino follow me out of Club V and I felt relieved. Yet, I was ready to leave the area just in case I was still being watched.

"Is Q coming back to the crib tonight?" Teddy asked.

"Boy, I hope not," replied Eros. "I hope he's coming this way to say good night."

K.J said, "Look at him. He's never been so happy-looking since his wedding."

Q arrived at the Escalade and said to Eros that Nivea was waiting for him.

Eros looked surprised. "What, you're not coming with us?"

"No."

"Why not?"

"Cause Whitney's a lady and I'm taking things smooth."

"Why? It's not like you live in Windsor. That girl is horny, and I'd be in that car if I was checking her."

While they continued to talk smack, I observed the many people that were still exiting the club. There was no big Latino in sight. I saw the many vehicles that were slowly leaving the parking lot and there was no big Latino driving away.

Lastly, I viewed the cars that were still parked in the lot and next to the street. There were close to fifty cars and only three of them didn't have their outside lights on. One of them was Teddy's car, the second was a bright yellow Ford F-150 truck, and the third was a black Toyota Sequoia with a Michigan license plate. Maybe nobody was in the ride, maybe he was in the ride, or maybe it was someone else.

I wanted to leave . . . immediately!

"Ajah!" Eros yelled.

Startled, I quickly looked at Eros and the guys who were staring at me. "What?"

"Later." He shook my hand and left.

Teddy asked, "Ajah, you alright?"

I didn't respond. Instead, I noticed Q getting into the passenger side of my ride.

"Q, I need you to go with Ted in his car. I'm gonna make a stop at the casino," I lied.

"Yo, that's cool," Q replied. "I don't mind playing a few games of blackjack."

"I'm not going to gamble. It's business."

"That's alright, I'll play while you . . ."

K.J interrupted, "Q, roll with us."

At least K.J figured it out. Q saw my serious look, apologized, and stepped out of my truck.

Teddy said to me, "I don't have an extra key, so you'll have to get buzzed into the apartment building when you arrive."

I nodded my head and got into my ride.

I waited until Teddy drove his car out of the parking lot before starting the engine. Immediately I lowered the stereo volume. Trying to drive behind Teddy's Accord, I looked in the rear view mirror and saw the Sequoia leaving the lot as well. Had a strong feeling that it was him, I was about five vehicles ahead of it. Club V was located on the east side of Windsor and very close to the city's main expressway. Teddy took it to get to his apartment located in the downtown area. I continued to follow him and look out for the SUV. Once we were on the E.C Row freeway, we increased acceleration.

I was getting quite impatient driving behind Teddy. His car was struggling to push eighty miles an hour and I had to drive faster. However, I didn't panic because the Sequoia was still a good distance behind. My next task was to take an unpopular exit and see if the truck would do the same. I had to do it soon because it was getting closer.

"Don't mean to disrespect your ride, Ted, but your hooptie's in my way," I said.

Got in the left lane, zoomed past my boys like they were strangers, and cruised the freeway at one hundred and five. Suddenly, the Sequoia was only two cars behind. There was no doubt in my mind that it was the big Latino. Looked in my rear view mirror and saw a blue Dodge Neon between us. The driver of it looked frustrated because the Sequoia was tailgating him hard. He finally gave in and moved to the right lane. Crap! Now it was a real car chase. The big Latino was on my butt like jerk sauce on chicken.

"I knew that I wasn't having paranoia!" I yelled as I floored the speed to more than one-twenty. "I don't know what he wants, but I bet he's linked to the Estafans!"

Saw the street for the Dominion road exit. Because the freeway traffic died down, I didn't have to maneuver around many slow cars. That was a good and bad thing because the Sequoia remained on my tail. I had no choice but to keep speeding. Made the exit and turned left on Dominion road, which headed towards the outskirts of Windsor.

"Good thing there's no cars, 'cause I'm busting through every red light!"

Had no knowledge of the area and I didn't care. If I had to, I would drive the Escalade until it ran out of gas, and it was three-quarters full. I had no choice because it was obvious that this hit man was on a serious mission. Suddenly, I saw an arm and a gun in the side mirror. A shot fired, which almost made lose control of the wheel. I didn't know if it was aimed for my head or not, but I just kept pushing forward. He fired another shot, and this time it hit the left corner of my fender. This time, it caught it me off-guard as I almost drove off the road. Dude was trying to bust a tire, so I assumed that he didn't want me dead.

What the hell does this man want from me?
TWANG!

A third shot fired and it bounced off the Sprewell of the rear left tire. It was real close, but no bull's eye! I had to throw the hit man off his shots, so at the next traffic light, I made a quick right turn. It didn't help a great deal cause he stayed right behind me.

I kept increasing my speed. Not long after my turn, I saw flashing red lights and gates lowered.

"Oh hell no! A train's the last thing I need!"

The train had not crossed the street, but it was quickly approaching. I didn't slow down and neither did the Sequoia. One watching this would think that we were on a suicide run. A U-turn wasn't a good option because the man could take a clear shot at my forehead, if he wanted me dead. There wasn't another street to turn on, and if I stopped, he would have me at his fingertips. Hence, my only choice was to beat the train. Either I would make it over and escape him, or funeral arrangements would be made for me on Saturday.

I knew that I wasn't a stunt man. Maybe I watched too much action movies. It didn't matter at the moment because I was determined to cross the tracks.

I yelled out a scream of rage.

Still going about a hundred, I made a quick left to avoid the first gate. I kept screaming. Whoever was driving the train made a horrendous siren noise. My scream continued as I swerved to the right to avoid the second gate. The train missed me by millimeters! I had truly escaped death once again as I ended the scariest moment of my life!

I kept driving. I stopped screaming cause I had the hardest time breathing properly. Refused to look back, but the one thing I knew for sure was that I escaped the Sequoia. A stop light was ahead, so I quickly slowed down. Once I made a complete stop, I put the truck in park on the empty road and looked back at the train. It was a lengthy one, thank God. I actually had a few minutes to figure out my next move.

Two options came to my mind as I tried to re-gain my breath. One option was to drive back to Teddy's and call it a night. However, I would still be hunted, and if found I could put my boys in danger as well. Option two was to settle the matter at hand. Catch the big Latino off-guard and get some answers. Option one sounded great, but I was an angry man and borderline crazy. Somebody was going to pay for this adventure.

I put the car in drive and headed straight to the 401 highway. Once I was out of the city, I pulled my ride to the side of the road and turned the engine and lights off. Through darkness, I grabbed my Louisville slugger from the trunk. Finally, I left the truck and hid in the ditch. I hoped that the hit man would continue looking for me once the train passed, see the Escalade, and try to find me. Only time would tell.

Twenty minutes later, I wondered if the man turned around and went back to Detroit. About twenty cars drove by and none of them stopped in curiosity. I laid flat in the cold mud and grass, alert yet very tired. My mind was reminding me why I entered the lifestyle, and wondered if it was worth the ridiculous drama. I was so ready to escape to a place where nobody knew me except my woman and son.

As soon as I decided to make my way back to Windsor, I saw some headlights and got back in my original position. The beams were so bright and big that I knew it was an SUV. The vehicle was driving slow and eventually parked about fifteen feet behind my truck. It had to be the hit man.

Sure enough, it was the Sequoia. The big Latino turned off the truck, kept the lights on, and stepped out. I gripped my bat real tight and stayed deep into the ditch, hoping that he wouldn't see me. He had his gun and searched my ride entirely. Once he couldn't find me, he attempted to shoot my tires. That was my cue to make a move.

I silently crept behind him and swung my bat across the back of his head.

"Peek-a-boo!" I shouted.

Wobbling as he turned around, the hit man tried to shoot me, but instead he fell face first on the ground. Now he was in my hands.

CHAPTER 60

AJANI

I drove down highway three, a country road outside of the city. The hit man was behind the back seat with his wrist and ankles tied together with rope I had in my trunk.

Putting a three-hundred plus man in my truck felt like lifting a Smart car, but I managed to do it. After the hit that knocked him out, I gave him a few kicks to the face and ribs for confirmation. It wasn't necessary, but I was in a furious mood. What was supposed to be a getaway weekend turned out to be a mega-dramatic event in a span of less than thirty hours. I was ready for answers and willing to wait until the big Latino regained consciousness.

When we were finally in an area with only trees and open fields, I pulled on the roadside. I got out, opened the lift-gate and began pulling him out by the legs. He was like a dead horse, but I kept pulling until he landed on the ground. That's when he started to awake.

I slapped him across the face. "Wake up!"

He gave me a vicious look. With blood rushing down his left temple, it was obvious that his head was feeling serious pain.

"Where the hell am I, and where the hell's my truck?" He asked with a rugged and thick Spanish accent.

"I'm asking the questions, chief! Who sent you to get me?"

He said nothing. I slapped his face again.

"Answer me!"

He said that I owe Martinez some money. Of course, I wanted to know why.

"They told me you gave them fake G.H," he replied.

"That's crap! I don't deliver anything that's counterfeit! All they had to do was call me or Machete to fix the situation!"

Unless this is confirmation that I am being framed!

"This is all I know. I was hired to get the cash back or take you down."

"And you can't do either. Ain't that unfortunate?"

Dude went on the rude tip and called me a refugee N-bomb from the bushes. I kicked him in the nuts for the unnecessary remark. The man yelled in agony and said something in Spanish that was probably another curse word or racial slur.

"Watch your mouth in English or Spanish, chief!"

He said, "Whether I get outta this dead or alive, your hours are numbered."

Tell me something that I haven't thought about.

I grabbed his wallet, car keys, and cell phone out of his pockets. I already had his gun, but I didn't plan on using it 'cause I wasn't going to kill him, unless I really, really had to. His wallet was thick with fifties and hundreds, but I didn't need his money. Looking at his plastic, I discovered that his name was Cortez Estafan. I then remembered him from my last trip to Detroit several months ago.

"Oh, so you're a cousin to the Estafans, huh? The notorious Big Concrete, the one they all brag about."

"It's Big Cement."

"Whatever," I said as I closed the wallet and threw that and the keys in the bushes. "I could've taken your cash and credit cards, but I'm not a thief. Don't want your truck either, 'cause my ride is better anyway. You can play hide and seek later if you ever get loose."

Then I broke his cell phone in half just to add misery.

Again, he asked, "Where the hell did you bring me?"

"It's called the bushes, remember? That's where you said I was from. It is outside of Windsor and a few miles away from *I-don't-give-a-crap*."

I ended the torture by pushing Big Cement in the ditch. Thirty seconds was the length of time I pushed his face in the cold dirt.

"Nobody messes with Ajani Bethel. Remember that!"

"You are so dead," he said as he spit mud from his mouth.

I went in my Escalade and headed back to the city, knowing that situations just got much worse than better.

CHAPTER 61

The deal was finally completed. Rex Marcos, a.k.a. Ike Trencio was in Machete's office at the Irie Club receiving a briefcase of ghetto heroin in exchange for plenty of brown and green Canadian bills. Everything recorded through the microscopic camera located in the cop's contact lens. If Ike made it out of the club alive, he would soon be responsible for the biggest OxyContin drug arrest in Toronto history.

Machete was highly professional in dealing with clientele. He took all of Ike's information, which of course were the records of Rex Marcos of Vancouver, brother of the late Sam Marcos the notorious drug-lord. The information was then recorded in a customer database that Machete said was one hundred percent confidential. Ike kept looking at Machete's expressions and it seemed as if he was not fully convinced that he was not an undercover police officer but the important thing was, the deal was settled.

"Alright, Mr. Marcos," said Machete, "you're in the database now. Pleasure doing business with you."

Ike shook his hand as well as Rancel's, who was right behind his cousin.

"Likewise," he replied. "And I'll be back soon once I get an exact number of accountants who want your product."

"Excellent. We'll keep in touch. Rancel, escort Mr. Marcos out the building."

Ike drove for twenty minutes before he used his cell phone. Once again, he had to make sure that he was not being followed. He continued to rub his eyes after taking out the camera contacts. Even though the police department gave him another pair that was a better fit, they were still heavy for the eyes. Nevertheless, the mission was accomplished.

"Chief, we got him. It's all on video . . . Well, viewing footage is a whole lot easier to do than wearing this crap! I'm never putting these things in my eyes again! This'll be the bust of the year when we nail Deverow . . . Huh, I definitely deserve a vacation after this is done . . . ."

"Man, I really thought that Rex was still incarcerated after all he went through with his brother," said Rancel as he sat across from Machete in the office. "Don't you think it's surprising that he's free already?"

Machete, who was laying back in his recliner replied, "Yes and no, the Marcos family have some of the smartest lawyers in the country. Rex probably received a shorter sentence due to a lack of evidence."

"Well, we can't say that we didn't search the man down. Everything seemed legit."

Machete's mind was on the situation in Windsor. He had yet to hear a confirmation from the Estafans that Ajani was dealt with.

"It's after three in the morning and no word from Martinez," he said.

"About Ajani? That boy's dead, Chete."

"Sez who? How could you be so confident about that? Bethel's one of the toughest bred-drin in Toronto."

"So? We're talking about the Estafan family in Detroit. We're talking about Big Cement, who weighs three-fifty and all muscle! Ajah can't compete with that!"

"Listen to yourself. That's why I don't put in full charge of my operations. You assume too much. This time, I ain't taking your word for jack."

Rancel stopped talking, which was a relief for Machete. He decided to call Martinez instead of waiting any longer. Ajani was a hustler and warrior, and no matter who his opponent was, he was not to be taken lightly. Machete needed assurance.

"Chete."

"Martinez, what's the word?"

"Haven't heard from Big C yet."

"What? It's been eight hours!"

"I know. He talked to Ricardo over an hour ago, said he was still working on it, and then hung up."

Machete said nothing.

"Big C always gets the job done. This is unusual, but once this is completed, you'll hear from me."

They hung up.

Machete began tapping his fingers on the desk. He felt that Ajani was still alive. He was just like Machete in that he always found ways out of crucial situations. If Martinez's best hit man could not beat him, then Machete would have to use the next best option. He would take care of it himself.

"What's going on?" asked Rancel.

"They ain't heard from Cement. I got a strong feeling Bethel's still alive. That dread's smarter than you think."

"Well, I'm going to Windsor in the morning, so I can make sure that . . ."

"Forget that! See, that is what I just finished saying about you. I can never put you in full charge of nothing. You don't work with urgency 'cause you assume that everything is alright! I'm calling Romano."

Romano was the man that Machete called whenever he wanted to rent a first-class vehicle. Machete owned four automobiles, but he rented for trips just in case police tapped one of his vehicles. He dialed his number.

"You're calling him now?" asked a surprised Rancel.

"Urgency calls," Machete said. "I'm going to Windsor A.S.A.P. If you're down, I'm leaving in an hour. Romano? Sorry to bother you, but I need a ride . . . Yes, right now, 'cause I have to go south. I'll pay you double if you can get me one ready in a half-hour . . . You're a good man, Romano . . . Late."

After hanging up, Machete pulled out a gun from his dresser and walked towards his cousin.

Looking at him, he said, "Sometimes, I have to oversee crap to make sure things go my way."

He walked out of the office.

CHAPTER 62

It was almost three in the morning, and Juanita Velez was still awake. She ended up not going to New York because her mother became sick with the flu on Thursday night. Thus, after taking the weekend off from work and Eros escaping to Windsor, she found herself bored watching *The Cosby Show* marathon on TBS.

Juanita could not believe that Eros had his cell phone off. She called him almost every hour on Friday and his voice message always came on right away. Not trying to be an annoying girlfriend, Juanita only left one message, saying that she did not end up going to New York and she missed him, nothing more, and nothing less.

Is Eros trying to avoid me?

That question was going through Juanita's mind frequently. Despite the opinions of her friends, she trusted Eros until proven guilty. Yes, he loved to look at other women, but of the seven months being together, Eros never smelt like another woman's perfume, or had any unknown panties in his apartment. There were not any missing or used condoms in his garbage can so; Eros was either a faithful man or the best player she had ever met.

Her girls were curious as to how Juanita could date a man who loved collecting porn. It would have bothered her if Eros was fat, unattractive, and had zero social skills, but he was the opposite. Eros was a fine Afro-Puerto Rican and a man who was just as freaky as herself. They even watched a few movies while making out. Juanita borrowed one of his DVDs and felt the urge to watch it, but she dropped the idea when her roommate Shanice entered the apartment.

Shanice and Juanita became instant friends while attending the University of Toronto. She was a woman's studies major and lived the life of a renaissance woman. Juanita thought she was like Oprah without the big bucks and talk show. Shanice believed in living life to the fullest yet being a "highly respectable minority woman." The roommates agreed on many issues and opinions, but their difference of opinion was the fact that Shanice could not stand Eros Alexander, Jr.

She had a big smile on her face as she took off her high heels.

Wow, she looks happy, thought Juanita. *It must be because Eros isn't here.*

Shanice said, "Oh, it's so good to be in a place of peace and quiet."

Juanita asked, "How was the club?"

"It sucked. The attendance was lower than usual, and the best DJ's were at Jam Fest. Looks like enough people went to Windsor this weekend."

"Yet we're still here."

"For real!" Shanice agreed as she sat down in the sofa. "Something's wrong with this picture."

"Clubbing in T.O is the worst during Jam Fest weekend. I'd rather watch TV all night than go to a lame club during this time."

"Girl, it gets worse! Not only are the DJ's whack, but it seems like all the straight men left too. Nita, tonight I saw the finest looking brother in a very long time. All the women were staring at him, especially in shock when he started grooving with another man!"

"Wow. The same thing is going on with some Latino men as well. Single women got it tough finding a good man. Most of the good are either—"

"Gay, ugly, or married, and they wonder why we are bitter."

"For real."

The roommates watched the television.

Shanice asked, "Oh, is this the episode when Cliff dreams that he's pregnant?"

"Uh huh," answered Juanita. "And Theo gives birth to a car while Cliff delivers a ten-foot sandwich."

She laughed. "Classic show."

"Girl, you working tomorrow?"

"Nope. You took the weekend off for New York, right?"

"Yeah. Mama's feeling better, but we're not going there for just one night."

"I hear you." Shanice smiled. "Wanna go to Windsor?"

Juanita looked at her. "You serious? I'm down, but where are we gonna stay? Hotels will be booked up, right?"

"I spoke to my friend last week who goes to school there. She said her living room's available."

"She's not gonna mind you bringing a friend?"

"Please. My girl's real down-to-earth. You'll love her."

Juanita gained excitement. She had never been to Jam Fest and she wanted to see what all the hype was about. In addition, she could surprise Eros, if she ever got in touch with him.

"I'm down, Shanice," she said, giving her a five. "Why should everybody else have fun and not us?"

"Exactly." Shanice turned serious. "I hope you're not excited to go because your man's down there. He should've taken you with him."

"I'm not checking for Eros this weekend," Juanita lied. "Boy won't return my calls. If I see him, great, if I don't, I'm still getting my groove on."

CHAPTER 63

TEDDY

It was approaching four in the morning, and I was still waiting for Ajani. I knew that if I was to fall asleep, chances were good that I wouldn't hear the buzzer. Q and K.J were victims of heavy West Indian food, thanks to the Rude Boy take-out dinners. I resisted sleep by playing a few games of NBA Live on the X-Box.

After all the drama that took place on Friday, I should've at least spent fifteen minutes with the Lord. I definitely needed to talk to him, but I really didn't feel like praying. Condemnation surrounded my mind as I thought about my actions. I barely avoided being arrested, gave into smoking weed, and partied at the nightclub. In addition, to my day of sin, I retrieved the porn flick that Eros downloaded from the computers recycle bin. After the guys fell asleep, I watched it for ten minutes and let out my sexual frustration in the washroom.

Saints in Kingdom Workers Fellowship warned me that being born-again wasn't easy, but this seemed ridiculous. Was I supposed to hang out with only saved folk in order to stay saved? I couldn't just stop hanging with my crew, but hanging with them wasn't helping me to grow as a Christian. Therefore, I needed guidance to get through the weekend without stressing. The Word of God was available at my fingertips, but I wasn't in the mood to do any reading.

Ajani finally buzzed, and I let him in the building. He opened the door, and it looked like he was involved with some serious crazy drama. Dude had mud and grass stains on his clothes, and he looked oppressed. I asked Ajani what happened, and he said it was a long story. That meant his story involved the drug game and he wasn't going to discuss anything about it. I left it alone and got ready for bed.

I really wanted to call my Jan-Jan, but it was already past four. Wanted to know how the first night of Bless fest went. I knew for sure that I wanted to be a part of it on Saturday no matter what. My only concern was whether Saturday would be just as wild as Friday, if not worse . . . Especially with friends like mine.

PART 3

SATURDAY

CHAPTER 64

AJANI

Chilling in the basement of my house in Richmond Hill, I was enjoying a retro Jet Li movie on my fifty-seven inch flat-screen TV. I hadn't felt so carefree in a very long time. I wished that every day was like this, but they rarely came, and when they did, I had to savor the moment.

My son came from upstairs. A.J was still in his pajamas, since it was only nine in the morning. He liked to lie next to me in the sofa, and I loved it, especially for the fact that I barely relaxed. I always looked forward to bonding with my son.

However, when A.J approached me, he looked very different. His eyes were red, and his face looked surprisingly rugged for a two-year old. Yet, A.J was smiling while hiding something behind his back.

I quickly sat up and knelt down to observe my boy.

"Lil Man!" I cried. "My God, are you okay? What's wrong?"

"I'm fine, Daddy," said A.J.

I felt his forehead. It wasn't warm, but he looked sickly. I started to panic, ready to take him to a hospital.

"SAVANNAH!"

"I'm fine, Daddy! Plus, Mommy's sleeping anyway."

That surprised me. Savannah never slept past eight on a Saturday morning. What surprised me even more was that I took A.J's word as the truth and continued to watch the movie.

Suddenly, my son asked, "Daddy, can I have some of your pills?"

That scared the hell outta me. How did A.J know about G.H? Did Savannah know about it, too? Who got to my son?

"A.J, what are you talking about?"

"Your Ghetto Heroin, Daddy, the stuff you deal every day. Can I have some?"

"I don't know what you're talking about, son."

A.J pulled out a gun from behind his back.

"Stop playing with me, Dad! Where are the pills?" he said in anger.

It felt like my heart stopped beating. My worst nightmare had come true! My son was a drug addict! I jumped out of my seat, ready to give my two-year old a whooping that he would feel for the rest of his life.

"What the—? You give me that gun boy!"

I squeezed his wrists and tried to pick him up, but I couldn't lift him! A.J started laughing. I tried to pull him up, but he wouldn't budge or let go of the gun. My son had superhuman strength!

A.J swung his little leg between mines and hit me in the you-know-where. It felt like a kick from a grown man. The pain was so excruciating that I let go of A.J and fell to the carpet face first. Then, my pride and joy stepped on my neck and pointed the gun to my temple. I was in so much pain and shock to the point where I couldn't defend myself.

"Now, Daddy, I need those pills!" A.J snapped. "I'm gonna ask you one more time: Where are they?"

I said, "Boy, as long as I live, I will never support your addiction! You can do what you want to me, but I'll never give you drugs! *NEVER!*"

"Is that so? Oh well, suit yourself!"

BANG!

I arose from my nightmare, soaked in sweat. Instead of my basement, I was on the carpeted living room floor in Teddy's apartment.

The clock on the wall read seven am. K.J and Q were passed out on the two sofas. I pinched myself to make sure that I was awake. My heart was beating rapidly and my eyes were wide open despite having only two and a half hour of sleep. I was shaken up big time.

That dream seemed way too real. Just the thought of A.J being a drug addict or following my footsteps scared the hell out of me. I wanted to quit the game. I had to quit the game, but I was in too deep to escape. My obsession with money brought me to the point where I was in little control of my destiny. Someone wanted me dead, and it felt like I had no one on my side to help my defense plus, I couldn't express this pain to my loved ones. Not my girl and not even my crew. I was doomed.

CHAPTER 65

EROS

It was the same girl, same bedroom, same horizontal action. Deja vu.

It was noon on Saturday and I was still with Nivea. I wanted to move on the day before, but the present desire to leave was even greater. She was getting on my nerves big time. Nivea spent the entire morning talking about her desire to marry a sexy brown man who could give her humor, joy, and endless sexual pleasure. She should've just said Eros Alexander, Jr., 'cause that's who she meant. Juanita dated me for seven months and mentioned marriage twice at the most. I had to escape Ms. Davis by any sensible means necessary.

" . . . and that's why I need to help Teddy tonight at his church," I concluded.

Nivea said, "I didn't know you were a sound technician."

"Well, I know enough to get a party started. And Teddy's a part of that Bless fest event, and I thought that it'd be great for me to be involved with it as well," I lied.

"What about seeing your boy in the Finals tonight?"

"I'll try to come to the club in time to watch K.J, but if I don't make it, he'll understand. After all, it's a shame to wrong a man for choosing church over a jam, right?"

"Right. Gosh, Eros, it's hard to find good men like you nowadays. I feel like going with you tonight, especially for the fact that I need some church, but my girlfriend and her roommate are coming down from Toronto and they want to hit Jam Fest tonight."

That was music to my ears.

"That's OK, baby, I understand," I said while kissing her on the cheek. "Show your girls a good time."

"You'll at least come back here after the fashion show to meet my friend, right? You'll love her, Eros, she's so sweet."

"We'll see."

Not if I could help it.

Nivea looked at the clock in her bedroom.

"Dang, its past noon, Eros!" she panicked. "We're lying in bed and the fashion show starts at one! We gotta leave soon if we want good seats!"

Nivea, Whitney and I arrived at the Capitol Theatre in downtown Windsor at exactly one o'clock. She was right about the attendance, 'cause there was a huge lineup of people waiting to enter the building. I didn't see the Phat Five, which meant that they were already inside. That sucked because I wanted Teddy to sneak us in or Ajani to pay for our tickets. Yes, I was cheap, but the two-hour program cost twenty bucks per person. I still paid for three tickets nonetheless, because even if I thought cheap, a player should never act cheap.

We went inside the auditorium and there weren't any empty seats on the main floor. As soon as I started to head towards the balcony, Whitney informed me that she saw Q looking out for us from the front rows. He was with Teddy, Ajani, and to my surprise, Janet and they reserved three seats for us.

After the usual greetings, I introduced Nivea to Janet, who knew that I was a dog but still treated me like a brother.

"Nice to meet you," Janet said to Nivea in a polite manner, but she was obviously disturbed about seeing Q with Whitney. They were looking like a couple more than friends, and Janet obviously knew that Q and Katrina were having marital issues.

"Kind of surprised to see you here," I said to her. "I thought you didn't like this stuff anymore."

Janet explained that she was only present to support Kaitlyn, the Christian girl that K.J was digging. Every year at the fashion show, the program always featured a brief gospel selection, which kinda seemed out of place. Kaitlyn was scheduled to sing, which meant I was going to see what kind of taste my boy had after being dumped by a video hoochie wannabe.

Nivea said to her, "Eros is going to your church to be a volunteer tonight."

"He is? I mean, you are, Eros?" Janet asked with great surprise.

Since when did I need a spokesperson?

"Yeah, I'll be there tonight," I lied with total calmness.

She looked at Teddy. "Bear, you didn't tell me Eros was coming to Bless fest tonight."

Teddy couldn't have looked more clueless. He stared at me and I gave him a wink to play along.

He caught on right away.

"Oh yeah," he said, "Eros and I talked about it, but I didn't have an answer yet."

"Well, I'm coming tonight," I lied again. "Count me in, brother."

Teddy saw through me like x-ray glasses but he smiled and shook his head. I sat in my seat, not wanting to engage in any more discussions about church. Nivea should've kept her big mouth shut.

As expected, the fashion show started late. The pretty caramel-skinned girl with the wild hair from Much Music was the host, and she did a admirable job keeping the show in a nice flow. The first segment was a runway featuring models wearing urban clothing by Karl Kani. It was nice, but not great. Maybe it was great, but my mind was on Miss Caramel and her friend.

Next, there was the gospel selection by Kaitlyn. As soon as she stepped on stage, I could see why K.J really liked her. Girl looked so much like Eva Mendes from *Training Day*, and she could sing! Kaitlyn ripped up the hugely popular *His Eye is on the Sparrow*, well enough for a standing ovation. It actually made me forget about the girls for a hot minute.

There were a couple more model segments and a special number by a whack R & B group that tried to sound like B2K. Thankfully, the host introduced K.J afterwards, the last selection before intermission.

"Ladies and gentleman," she shouted, "If you weren't blown away by this cat last night, you must've been passed out! This brother was last seen as half of the rap duo Phenomenal, but now he has taken the game to a new level. Performing to you now before battling his former partner in the showcase tonight, give it up for K.J!"

The applause from the crowd was greater than Friday night, since they knew what K.J brought to the stage. K.J appeared as the beat began, dressed in a plain black turtleneck sweater and brown corduroy pants. No designer wear, jewelry, or two hundred dollar shoes. Obviously, he was ready for his lyrics to speak louder than his material image.

The beat was solid, with a typical East Coast flavor. Had no idea who produced his music or if he made it himself. The song was called *Move Over*, as he rapped about the re-emergence of true hip-hop and the task to overthrow pop-star wannabe rappers. What stood out about K.J were his tight delivery and his crazy tight one-liners. The one-liners that received the most reactions were the disses aimed directly at Verbal Pain. He was bringing it better than Reggie Miller was at clutch time.

Of the entire Phat Five, I liked K.J the least. We were like oil and water when it came to agreeing on things. We dissed each other frequently, but deep, deep down inside I had respect for him and I was glad that he stood for integrity. Would I ever tell him that? Absolutely never. Dissing K.J was a joy for me but I was very proud of him as he showcased his talents to the Hip-Hop world.

Intermission was fifteen minutes long. K.J and Kaitlyn joined us, looking like best friends. Q and Whitney were chatting and getting more acquainted. Ted and Janet were acting like husband and wife, and I pretended to be into Nivea, who I was getting more tired of by the second. I almost started missing Juanita.

Ajani was the only guy without a woman, but couldn't care less if he looked like the ninth wheel. Something was bugging him huge according to his facial expressions, but in the midst of a loud theatre, I wasn't going to ask what was wrong.

The second half was about to begin. Thank God. Nivea was chatting away about why she wanted to be a nurse and I needed an interruption.

Verbal Pain opened the second half performing his debut single, *The Pain U Love*, featuring a surprise guest appearance by Jazmine, his label mate and R & B sensation that was escalating on the Billboard charts. Of course, the crowd was fully into it. The nine of us just watched, shook heads, and grinned. Dude was trying to look tough on stage, but all I could picture was a cocky Roderick Bailey getting his jaw broken by K.J. The Club Oasis incident was a classic, and that fight was worth the lifetime ban.

After the song, people cheered, but a small group of people started yelling, "K.J! K.J!" continuously. Our group joined the chant, and before Verbal Pain left the stage, it seemed like half the audience joined the party. It was great to hear.

Trying not to look embarrassed, he shouted, "I will repeat as champion tonight!" Then he made his exit with quickness.

The host said, "It's gonna be a classic tonight! Eleven pm at Club V, live on Urban TV and Much Music! Expect a battle to the finish!"

There was another model segment and a dance selection before the presentation that the crowd was anxiously waiting for: the lingerie show. Women could scream at muscular men in tight briefs and the men can holler at the beauties in silk wear. There was a rumor that a lady would show her full frontal, which would remain to be seen. That rumor showed up at every Jam Fest fashion show in the past, and it had yet to come true. Nevertheless, I was ready for the eye candy.

It was real nice. Of course, I wasn't checking for the guys, but the shorties were off the chain. Silk was a wonderful thing, especially when it was thin and fully embraced the breasts and booty. I remained cool and enjoyed God's creation in front of my eyes.

Each of the five female models had fit bodies. I examined every one of them and tried to figure out which lady would show her twin friends and when. The presentation was almost ending, and once again, I was ready to call it a disappointment. During the entire lingerie set, my mind wasn't thinking about the two lesbians. Suddenly, a brand new gorgeous beauty appeared on the catwalk, wearing a pink sexy nightgown. My mind was tripping with joy, 'cause it was Miss Caramel again! She worked that supermodel walk in her pink high heels like Tyra Banks doing Victoria's Secret. When she reached the end of the catwalk, she started to untie the gown. Men in the crowd were roaring with anticipation. That's when everything started to move in slow motion.

My mind couldn't take the anxiety. Miss Caramel was about to show her priceless possessions! My eyes were glued. The mystery of what was behind the gown had my heart beating faster than an Uzi.

She dropped the gown. I saw the breasts. Round and beautiful. Immediately I remembered her name and where I originally saw her.

Crystal Quinn. Men's Fantasy Magazine, issue 17, May 2002.

The fact that I could recognize a woman by their breasts easier than the face proved that I was a true male hoe.

The fellas hollered like the chorus of Baha Men's *Who Let the Dogs Out*. Nivea said something critical but I acted as if she didn't exist. Ajani was in a bad mood, but he had to raise his eyebrows. K.J, Teddy, and Q acted like gentleman, but only because they were next to the opposite sex.

Kaitlyn, who was sitting to my right, said, "OK, I think I had enough. Its time to go."

I heard her and Janet get out of their seats and leave, but I couldn't care less. Churchwomen act appalled by what took place, and then go home to have a long cold shower. The cousins hesitated, but followed them, trying to stay on their good side, of course.

The four seconds that Crystal exposed her beauties were the best four seconds of my life. As she walked towards the exit, she turned to her right and stared directly at me. No lie. Crystal wanted to make it look like I was just another guy, but I knew the real deal. How would she know exactly where I was if she wasn't thinking about me? I'd been with enough women to know when one was into me, and Crystal was no exception.

I concluded in my head that rain or shine, tornado or snowstorm, Saturday night was my night to be with Miss Quinn, and hopefully her friend as well. Bye, bye, Nivea.

The fashion show ended. The next step for the Phat Five was to go to the first-class executive suite at the casino hotel. Perfect, except for my scatterbrain best friend Q arranging a double date to go to a Saturday matinee shortly after. I had to come up with a good excuse to get out of the set-up. There were more important things at stake.

CHAPTER 66

Juanita and Shanice were well on their way towards Windsor, cruising on the 401 highway. Shanice was driving while Juanita had the passenger seat reclined to her comfort, looking relaxed yet slightly disturbed.

Shanice asked, "Why so quiet? Say what's on your mind, girl."

Juanita said nothing. Shanice asked if she was thinking about Eros.

"Little bit," answered Juanita. "I'm just wondering if our relationship is going to get better or worse."

"Have you seen signs that it may get worse?"

"Yeah, I think."

Juanita did not want to go into details because of Shanice's loathe for Eros, but she felt that her friend would bring it out of her.

"You think?" asked Shanice. "What you mean? I need details."

"Well, Eros seemed really excited to go to Jam Fest. Of course, it is the biggest party of the spring, but he turned off his cell and hasn't returned my call. Should I be suspicious?"

"Nita, you might be asking the wrong person, but I'm a keep it real with you. You know that I don't care for Eros and I think he's a player. Yet, you're my girl and I love you, so I'll respect your relationship with him, despite my thoughts. Hell yes, you should be suspicious, and this weekend could bring answers as to where you and him are headed."

"But I haven't heard from him."

"Exactly, so your man will be surprised to see you if you run into him. You'll know based on his reaction whether Eros is committed and faithful to the relationship. If he shows excitement and gives you a good explanation as to why he never called you, then you may have nothing to worry about, but if Eros looks worried or like you caught him taking a diarrhea dump, the brother's up to no good."

Juanita nodded her head. Her roommate was right, but she was not going to stop being optimistic, as long as he called her before the weekend was over.

"So Shanice, you really respect me and Eros as a couple?"

She sighed and smiled. "Yeah . . . you're a smart woman but I'm always watching him. I got your back if he messes with you."

"I know."

"He knows about what you did to your ex-NHL boyfriend with the dog food lasagna and Ex-lax cake?"

"Oh yeah! That's why Eros would be stupid to play me. Lord knows I can do worse than that!"

CHAPTER 67

Rancel Deverow tried his best not to look worried. He thought that Ajani Bethel would have been dead already.

The arrest at the U.S. border failed, and the hit man couldn't kill Ajani, according to Machete. Rancel realized that he should have hired his own hit man to kill him in Toronto instead of leaving it to his cousin. Now, the situation was out of his control.

The cousins left Toronto at four in the morning and arrived in Windsor at seven. They each ordered two exquisite rooms at the Hilton and slept for a few hours. Machete then called Martinez Estafan and arranged to meet them at the Real Feel in the early afternoon to complete the drug deal and organize a plan to assassinate Ajani. They easily crossed the U.S border into Detroit, thanks to re-arrangements with Kwame Moss.

The Real Feel was surprisingly busy for a Saturday afternoon. There was a large buffet of food, loud crunk music, lots of male customers, and at least twenty female strippers and waitresses collecting cash from doing what they do best. The Deverows entered the club through the front and made their way to the V.I.P lounge, where Martinez and Ricardo eagerly awaited them. They greeted with strong brotherly hugs.

"Whether its pleasure or emergency, it's always good to see you fellas," Martinez said without smiling. He looked very disturbed.

"Anytime, brother," said Machete. "The club looks more prosperous every time I come back here."

"It's all because we have the best food and women in Detroit. Combine topless skanks with a three-dollar seafood buffet, you destroy all competition. You guys want food,or booty? Anything you want, it's on me. Make yourself at home!"

Rancel nodded his head and smiled. "Just a Bacardi and some shrimp."

Machete said, "Nothing for me until we finish business."

"Alright," Martinez agreed. "Let's get started."

The men took only ten minutes to complete the paperwork and distribute the drugs in exchange for cash. Rancel and Ricardo took the briefcases of G.H through the back entrance to the basement while the other Estafan and Deverow remained in the lounge. Once that was completed and all four were sitting again in the lounge, the focus shifted towards Ajani Bethel.

"Big Cement just came back from Windsor two hours ago," said Ricardo. "Dude's stretched out on a bed with head injuries and body damage, yo. Nobody's ever taken out my cousin before!"

"How did Ajani do it?" asked Rancel. He had to know how Big Cement messed up.

"All Cement could remember was getting knocked out with a bat to his head and getting tied up and tortured by your boy in the middle of nowhere."

"Bethel's got luck on his side right now," Martinez said, "but it's about to end. First, the S.O.B comes in my club with fake crap and now he messed with my family. He's gone too far."

"Now I want to get a proper understanding of how all this crap started!" Ricardo snapped. "Why the hell did he come to us with fake pills?"

Rancel lied about how Ajani backstabbed the Deverow's by trying to take their clientele to start his own dealing empire. Machete then went further, describing how the plan to arrest Ajani failed at the border and added that he was surprised that the Jamaican received any money from the Estafans.

"Well, my brother messed that up, and the damage is already done," said Martinez.

Ricardo added, "He caught me off-guard, when I was high as hell but I'm ready to mess him up now! Where the hell is he?"

Machete said, "I don't know, but I have his cell number. He has no clue that we're here, and I have a plan to finish him off."

"Remember, this crap is personal for all of us!" said Rancel. "Bethel's messing up the family empire as we speak."

Martinez snapped, "Well, I'm tired of just talking! This B.S needs to be completed tonight. Machete, what's the plan?"

Machete described the set-up for murder. Martinez added input to enhance the plan, and everyone agreed to the script. Rancel smiled. He labeled himself as a genius for completely fooling his cousin in order to get what he deserved. More money, more power, and more respect.

CHAPTER 68

TEDDY

K.J, Q, Eros and I were waiting in the hotel lobby at Casino Windsor while Ajani was at the front desk getting the keys for the executive suite.

"See?" said Eros. "I told you I wasn't playing when I said that girl was the finest I've seen this year!"

Q said, "That girl looked sweet for real. I tried not to look too impressed with Whitney sitting next to me."

K.J said, "Eros, how could you not know what the girl's name was until she exposed her breasts? That's insane!"

"No kidding," Eros agreed. "I remembered so much about her once I saw those babies. Call it a gift or I'm just the shallowest guy ever."

"No argument there," I said. "Janet and Kaitlyn were so unimpressed by that display."

"That's because they're real women," K.J said. "Virtuous ladies that try to please God."

Eros said, "C'mon, guy! They may be good women, but deep down, they enjoyed what they saw. They just felt guilty about enjoying the scenery, so they walked out!"

I laughed. Eros couldn't have been more wrong.

"Eros, you're trippin'," I said. "Has it ever occurred to you that there are people that don't want to see indecent exposure?"

He said no. I decided not to argue with him. Eros wasn't trying to understand my logic. Yes, Crystal Quinn was very attractive, but surprisingly she didn't faze me, thanks to the grace of God. His presence was with me because I prayed for it before going to the fashion show. In addition, I was sitting next to my Jan-Jan, who was much more beautiful in my opinion. Was looking forward to what she would look like in a G-string outfit on our wedding night.

Changing the subject, I looked at my Italian friend.

"Q, Janet asked about your lady friend today."

Q said to me, "I figured she would. Did it look too obvious that I was into her?"

"What do you think?"

"You told her that Whitney's just a friend, right?"

"Yeah, but she knows that you and Trina's been having problems."

Oops. Said too much.

Q looked surprised. "Why'd you have to give her info about our marriage issues?"

"I didn't, Q. I just wanted her to keep y'all in prayer, that's all."

Eros said, "Q, why are you surprised? T-Henny tells Janet everything. She knows that Ajah's a dealer and that I'm unfaithful to women."

I had to defend myself. "Yo, I only told her you're a dog because you wanted to get with her sister two years ago and Janet wanted the 411 about you."

"Dude, you're whipped."

"No, I'm just open and honest with her, which brings up another issue: what's this about you coming to church with me tonight?"

Eros grinned. "Man, I'm tired of Nivea, so I used you and church as a reason not to be with her tonight. I want Crystal."

K.J said, "What you really want is God to strike you down with lightning."

"Oh, please, K.J, you're not all that honest yourself," Eros said. "Does your lady friend know that you smoked weed yesterday and rapped about sleeping with someone's mama?"

"Sorry to interrupt your smack, ladies," Ajani said as he approached us. "The suite is ready."

The executive suite was crazy ridiculous. Finest hotel room I had ever been in. It consisted of a kitchen, living room, a huge bedroom, and bathroom. The kitchen had marble counters, microwave, fridge, stove, and dishwasher. The living room had a green leather sofa and love seat, thirty-two inch TV with cable and DVD player. The bedroom had two queen-size beds with another big TV and DVD player, and the bathroom had double sinks, Jacuzzi, and a rainforest shower.

Everyone except Ajani was tripping as if we won the lottery. It felt good to have a friend who had lots of money. Yes, drug money paid for the suite and as a Christian, was I wrong to hang with Ajani knowing that he sold drugs? Perhaps, but I didn't smoke drugs or sell them, so I didn't feel conviction. In addition, I doubted that Pastor Jackson of Kingdom Workers Fellowship would refuse ten grand from someone who won it at the casino. Of course, that was only Theodore Henderson's blessed opinion.

"Yo, Ajah, how much did this cost?" asked K.J. "This joint has it all, man!"

Ajani said, "It cost enough, but don't worry about it. Just enjoy it 'cause this won't happen often."

Eros agreed. "You got that right! Ajah, you gotta let me use this if I get that chick tonight!"

"No!" snapped Ajani. "I may be anal for doing this, but I got this suite to relax. Any chick that comes here will ask questions and be suspicious, and I know you, Eros. You'll turn this joint into an orgy fest!"

"Trust me, guy, I won't—"

"*YES YOU WILL!*" we all said in a surprising unison.

"Whatever," Eros shook his head. "At least Crystal has money, I think."

Q, who used the phone immediately after dropping his travel bag in the living room, hung up and smiled.

"Eros, the girls are coming to get us in twenty minutes to go to the movies," he said.

Eros sighed. "Alright, fine. Just to let you know in advance, Q, I'm gonna fake a sickness and leave in the middle of the film."

"Why?"

"I told you, I've had enough of Nivea. I need to move on."

"You lied about me in order to get me involved with Whitney, and you're not sticking through the weekend?"

"Q, you'll be fine. Your game's on point."

Q sucked his teeth and went to the washroom. I wasn't surprised at Eros' intentions. He always thought about what *he* could get and who could help *him* get it. Eventually, I felt that he was gonna feel the consequences of his selfishness and greed.

I fell flat on one of the beds and got comfortable.

"Fellas, if y'all don't mind, I'm just gonna relax here for the rest of the afternoon," I said. "I likes my sleep."

"Guy, it's no biggie," Ajani said. "I got my kung fu flicks, and I'm chillin'. Later, I'll go downstairs to gamble, and then hit the jam tonight to watch K.J win the crown."

"Yeah, I ain't missing that!" said Q.

"No doubt, K.J," Eros said. "Whatever I'm into, I'll still represent."

"I hope so!" shouted K.J. "Y'all are my boys, and you bring the energy!"

I pretended to be asleep. As much as I wanted to support my cousin, I didn't want to go back to Jam Fest. K.J didn't know that yet, and I prayed that when I told him, he wouldn't hold a grudge against me.

CHAPTER 69

Q

It was almost two days since talking to Katrina; this was the longest stretch since being married. Yet, I was no longer worried. I didn't check her cell phone to see if she'd called, 'cause I was convinced that my wife was cheating on me, and I couldn't change the past. If another man was making her happy, then I needed another woman to make me happy, even if it was only for a weekend.

I had my arm around Whitney as we watched *How to Lose a Guy in 10 Days* at the cinema in downtown Windsor. Eros and Nivea were right next to us, and we were the only people in the room, so we could chat as loud as we wanted but I remained quiet because the roommates really seemed to be into the film.

Whitney was munching popcorn. I was sipping on Sprite. She smelled so good; I wanted to nibble on her neck right then. Couldn't care less about the plot of the movie 'cause I just wanted to make out. Yet, I was going to stay a gentleman. After the film, the plan was to go for dinner, hit the nightclub, and hopefully end with a night of passion. I hoped that the agenda would flow smoothly, even with Eros' idea of acting sick and leaving.

I moved my lips towards her cheek and gave her a light kiss. Whitney looked at me, smiled, and kissed me back on the lips. Then she continued to watch the film. She was smooth and sweet. Wished I had met her before I got married.

Suddenly Eros, who was very quiet from the movie's beginning, started to lean his head towards the ground, moaning in pain. The performance had begun.

"You alright, man?" I asked as Whitney and I both looked in concern.

"What's wrong, baby?" asked Nivea.

"Don't know," he grumbled. "That food from Burger King I had earlier isn't agreeing with me. I feel like crap."

Five minutes earlier, Eros came back from the washroom. Betcha a million dollars he put his forehead in front of the electric hand dryer, 'cause Nivea felt his head, and she was convinced.

"Dang, sweetie, you are warm!" she cried. "You want me to take you to the hospital? You might have food poisoning!"

He said, "No, baby, its not food poisoning. I just need to lie down."

"Well, lemme take you back to the hotel and take care of—"

"Nivea sweetie, I'll be fine. Don't miss the movie because of me. I'll just call a cab and we'll hook up when I feel better."

Nivea looked disappointed and helpless. Eros grabbed her hand.

He said, "You can wait with me outside till the cab gets here."

She agreed as they got up from their seats. Eros waved good-bye to us and left.

"Get well, guy," I said.

He was an excellent actor, a player who strived for lying perfection.

After they left the theatre, Whitney said, "I've never seen Nivea so into a guy like she is with Eros. I hope he's good to her."

I avoided that reply and said, "They look good together."

"Is he a player?"

Do dogs have four legs?

I lied and said that he wasn't.

"Good," she said, "'cause she'd be an excellent wife one day."

However, it would not be for Eros.

"As for me," Whitney continued, "I have no time for a serious relationship. School is too important to me right now. A weekend fling for me is just fine. No strings attached or any calls during the week. Just a little fun on Friday and Saturday's good enough for me."

In other words, the perfect woman for an affair.

"Yet, Q, I'm still very picky. I just don't want a man who looks good and has crazy game in the bedroom. I have to like a guy that is easy to talk to, not shallow, and of course fine-looking before I even think about sexing him."

"So, Whitney, where do I fit in?"

She looked in my eyes. "Why don't you hang out with me for the rest of the day and find out for yourself?"

Nuff said. We remained quiet until the end of the movie.

CHAPTER 70

EROS

Free at last, free at last!

The cab came to the cinema and I kissed Nivea good-bye. I told her that I would call later and I played real sick until the cab turned the corner. Always wondered why I never pursued an acting career.

I was so glad to get away from Nivea. After watching that dumb movie, she wanted me to meet her friend who was driving down from Toronto, her and some friend that was joining her. That's why I couldn't be a one-woman man. I hated to be introduced as somebody's man. Juanita did it enough times to confirm my desire to be polygamous forever. Unfortunately, I had to make one more stop at Nivea's because I foolishly left my clothes there. An absolute no-no for a player, but it slipped my mind when we rushed out of her apartment to get to the fashion show.

My quest to get the beautiful Crystal Quinn and her lady friend had begun. When I arrived at the casino hotel, I went straight to the front desk instead of the executive suite. Since I knew her name, I had to use it to get as much info as possible. The clerk was the same dude that wanted me to give him a hundred bucks for the floor of Crystal's room. Almost felt led to give it to him. That's how bad I wanted to get with her.

"Can I help you, sir?" the clerk asked.

"Yes, chief," I replied. "I need the hotel room number for a Miss Crystal Quinn."

"Sorry, sir, but I've been told not to give anyone that information."

Understood. But I wasn't done.

"Well, remember when I talked to you yesterday about you telling me the floor she's on? Well, I can get a hundred for you if you're willing to share what you know."

"Two hundred."

"Say what? Man, you're trippin!" I snapped. "I asked you for the floor, not her phone number!"

"So?" he said in a snotty tone. "That's info's confidential. Plus, you're not the only guy who wants her information."

Did I care? The cat was hating on me because I looked better than him. Well, I didn't know that for sure, but he was still an anal jerk.

"Look, chief, I know what you can do. Call Miss Quinn's hotel room and tell her that the guy she bumped into on Friday in the game room wants to speak to her."

"Ooooh, that's so specific. I need a name, sir."

What he needed was a slap in the face for his sarcasm. Crystal didn't know my name, but there was a chance that hearing my name would make her think of my dad, who was a regular photographer for the magazine that she featured in. Slim chance, but it was worth a shot.

"It's Eros Alexander."

He wrote "Arrows" on a piece of paper, but it didn't matter 'cause it sounded the same. Then he dialed the number to her room.

"Good afternoon, Miss Quinn. Sorry to bother you, but there's a guy here at the lobby that wants to see you. Says his name is Eros Alexander. What would you like me to say to him?"

The clerk said nothing for about twenty seconds. He looked disappointed.

"Alright," he said. "I'll tell him. You're welcome. Goodbye."

"Well?" I asked.

Looking ticked, he replied, "She'll be down in ten minutes."

Joy!

Thirty minutes had passed and I was still waiting. Was she coming down or did she stand me up? Did Crystal do this to all guys that she didn't know?

"Wouldn't hold your breath if I were you," the clerk said.

I said, "I'm breathing fine, boss, and you're not me, so you should do what you're paid to do, which is serve."

As soon as I gave him the wisecrack, Crystal and her friend came out of the elevator.

Oh my goodness, they were so sexy. Once again, everything seemed to move in slow motion. The girls walked through the lobby as if they were Cover Girl models on a runway; confident, smooth, crazy-sexy-cool. Made me want to munch them like cookies.

I stood up and walked towards them. As expected, Crystal gave me a surprised expression.

"You're the guy I bumped into yesterday," she said.

"And the man you were looking at during your catwalk at the fashion show," I reminded her. "My name is Eros."

"Wow. Never thought I'd meet two guys in my lifetime with that name. I'm Crystal, and this is my girl Kendra."

I shook their hands like a gentleman. Crystal's hand was soft while Kendra's was firm. If they were dating, Kendra must have been the head. She reminded me of the actress Grace Jones, except much prettier and she was Asian. Kendra smiled at me, but it was obvious that she was suspect of my intentions. I said that it was nice to meet her, but she didn't respond.

Crystal said, "Sorry if we look kinda surprised, but we thought that you might've been another Eros that we know."

I asked them if he was a pretty Black man in his late forties who was a video producer and photographer in Los Angeles. They looked more surprised.

Kendra finally spoke and asked, "Do you know him?"

"Better than anyone," I replied. "He's my father."

"Shut up!" Crystal screamed. "Are you serious?"

"He's the producer of over a hundred adult movies and photographer for *Hot Tub* and *Men's Fantasy* Magazine. I could name every film of his if you want."

"No, that's OK."

Crystal and Kendra looked at each other and started giggling.

"What's so funny?" I asked.

"We're going to get some lunch," said Crystal, ignoring the question. "Wanna join us?"

"Of course."

I followed them to the casino buffet. Walked past the clerk and stuck my tongue at him. He was covered with envy and anger.

As broke as I was, I paid for the ladies' lunch with my MasterCard. They were probably making seven times my annual income, but I had to have my A game on. I wanted my first menage et trois, and I didn't want to mess up.

Sitting at the table, I asked again why they were giggling about my pops. A son had the right to know.

"Your dad invited us to his condo in L.A last year," Crystal answered. "Your dad is an incredible man."

I felt a knot in my throat, I had a strong feeling that the models slept with my father. I always wondered if I would hook-up with chicks who gave up their goods to my dad, and at the present time, I didn't know how to react. Eros, Sr. was my role model, but I didn't want to share women with him. Yet, I was assuming, and I needed to know the truth.

"Did you . . . I mean . . . keep it real now, did you give him some?"

There. I asked.

"We almost did," Kendra said without hesitation.

"Almost?" I didn't believe her.

"Your dad took us out for dinner before going to his place, but later towards the evening, Crystal had food poisoning and we took her to the hospital."

Crystal added, "It was real close, but it never happened."

I decided to believe them. Either they kept it real or they were great liars like me. Either way, it was the answer that I wanted to hear.

I mentioned that I saw them at Club V dancing with each other and asked if they were a couple. Crystal admitted that they were, but they also liked men, which was obvious based on their meeting with my dad. However, I wanted to know which sex they preferred. Kendra said it was women, only if the man couldn't satisfy them. In other words, they weren't talking about me. When she said that, I got aroused. Crystal was the most beautiful and friendliest of the two, but Kendra presented a sense of challenge and adventure. I wanted them both equally.

"Your father has a serious fit body for his age," said Kendra, "and the women who I know got with him say that he's all game where it really matters."

"Yet," added Crystal, "I look at you and you're finer. Are you Latino?"

I said, "I'm half Puerto-Rican."

"I knew it when I first saw you. I love Latino men."

There was no doubt in my mind that these girls were freaks. Although they were a couple, I imagined they were adventurous with their sexuality. Juanita Velez times two with a bag of chips. The anticipation inside of me wanted to explode like dynamite, but I stayed cool.

I said, "Well, if you like Eros Alexander, Sr., you'll love Eros the second. I'm a younger version of him, with more stamina."

Kendra smiled. Crystal blushed as if she was surprised that I was so cocky.

"Confident," she said, "just like your dad. Are you a photographer or in adult films too?"

"No. I'm strongly thinking about it, though. The money in that industry is real good. What about you two, done any films?"

"No, we're just models. Don't do freaky stuff in front of cameras. But I love and respect the industry."

I'm glad you do, sweetie. Let us all love and respect it together.

We continued to eat while sharing stories about my pops, modeling, and the entertainment industry. They wanted to know why I didn't live in L.A, and I told them that my dad lives in Toronto and L.A throughout the year. Since I was eighteen, Dad lived in L.A more and preferred for me to stay in Canada for three reasons: one, to stay in his Brampton condo for free, two, free health care, and three, he wanted me to get a Canadian university degree because the tuition was much cheaper than the U.S. I promised them an excellent time if they ever came to Toronto for a visit.

There was chemistry in the atmosphere because we all wanted the same thing. I was so thankful for my pops, because if they didn't know or liked him, it would've been a greater challenge to get them interested in me. Looked forward to giving him a call after breaking them off, and rubbing it in that I scored with them and he didn't.

As we left the restaurant and entered the hotel lobby, I asked them if they were attending the Showcase Final at Club V.

"No," replied Crystal. "We'll be at a private pajama party at the Tropical Club tonight. It starts at nine. We have an extra ticket if you wanna come."

Of course, I wanted to go, without a doubt, but I didn't want to miss K.J's performance. However, if I went to see my boy, the chance for a threesome would be slim. I had to choose between loyalties and double the booty.

"This ticket is worth at least eighty bucks at the door if you don't take up our offer."

Loyalty or double the booty?

"I'll be there," I replied.

Crystal gave me the ticket from her purse and said, "I'll be looking out for you."

Sorry, K.J. I really, really owe you one.

CHAPTER 71

Nivea called the Casino Windsor hotel to find out how Eros was feeling, but she had no answer. She knew that the executive suite was under one of his friends' name, but she didn't know which one. Eros should have told her the room number, but Nivea could have asked for it. The most she could do was wait for him to call. Until then, the apartment needed preparation for more houseguests.

After the movie, Nivea dropped Whitney and Q at an exquisite Italian restaurant before reaching her crib. They were doing the things that she wanted to do with Eros, which was going out to dinner and getting a chance to really talk. As much as Nivea enjoyed the sex, she needed to know if Eros was the right man for her. She wanted to hear Eros say that he was in the relationship for the long haul and not for a weekend of passion. A long-distance relationship was a challenge, but Nivea was willing to go through it. Was he?

The buzzer on the intercom made noise. Nivea answered. It was time for a good time with her girlfriend and guest.

"Wow, I know people said Windsor was close to Detroit, but I didn't think it was separated by just a river," said Juanita as she and Shanice approached the apartment entrance. "We gotta go shopping there before we go back to T.O."

"I told you it was really close," Shanice answered. "That's why there's so much Michigan dudes honking at us. They love Canadian women 'cause they think we're sexy and will do anything to get with them."

"Sorry, that doesn't count me. I don't need an American man 'cause I already have one."

Shanice knocked on the door. A short and pretty Black woman opened it with a large grin.

"Niecey!" she yelled.

"Nivea!" Shanice yelled back as they hugged each other. "I want you to meet my friend Juanita. Juanita, this is Nivea."

Nivea greeted her with a hug. Juanita liked her immediately. She seemed like a warm person with a bubbly personality.

"Nita's never been to Jam Fest before," said Shanice.

"What? Girlfriend, you're in for a real party!" said Nivea. "Y'all come in and relax, 'cause you'll need the rest for tonight!"

The ladies entered with their small luggage and took off their shoes. Shanice asked Nivea where they could place their bags.

Nivea replied, "Y'all will be sleeping on the pull-out sofas tonight, but for now you can put you stuff in my room. Let me take it for you."

"Whatever, girl, we got it. Y'know how I am, I make myself right at home here."

Nivea laughed. "Alright, just don't mind the mess. My man left some of his clothes on the floor."

Juanita followed Shanice into Nivea's bedroom. Shanice quickly dropped her stuff on the floor and headed towards the washroom. As Juanita placed her belongings next to her roommate's, she could not help noticing the outfit that was next to the queen-size bed. A navy blue Sean John jogging suit looked exactly like the one she got Eros for his birthday. Surprisingly, it was next to a large baby blue Nike sports bag that resembled the bag Eros had in his condominium. It seemed strange, but Juanita did not want to get paranoid.

It's amazing how men think and dress alike sometimes, she thought, *but this is freaky. No, Juanita, you're just being pessimistic. That's not your man's stuff!*

She left the bedroom and closed the door behind her. Juanita decided to forget about the clothes and say nothing to Shanice about it.

CHAPTER 72

AJANI

After enjoying a kung fu movie with excellent fighting and terrible English dubbing, I ordered room service for the cousins and me. Smoked a couple of joints, which made me crazy hungry, and it seemed different because Teddy and K.J wouldn't join me. That had never happened before. Yet, we munched on perhaps the best New York steaks I've ever had in my life.

Despite a full stomach, I couldn't and didn't want to sleep. The nightmare of my son still freaked the hell outta me and I didn't want a sequel. I needed some inspiration, and I truly believed that winning some more money downstairs would be my answer. Thus, I refreshed my face, left the guys playing X-Box, and headed to the gaming room.

Just when I thought that my day would get slightly better, it got worse. Took out five hundred from the ATM and started with playing Caribbean Stud. I lost eight out of ten games and fled from the table as if it was infected with SARS.

Since it was the game that I knew best, I played Blackjack to increase my luck. I felt great when I won my first four games, but then I lost the next nine. It was wonderful to be Ajani Bethel.

Within forty minutes, I was down to a hundred and ten bucks. I figured that I couldn't do any worse playing Baccarat, my second favorite game. Well, I won the first two, lost the next four, won one, then lost four again. I was done like the *Arsenio Hall Show*, and responsible gamblers do not take any more cash out of the bank machine.

It was barely nighttime and I was high, angry, a loser, fatigued, and wanted dead or alive. Therefore, I needed to add alcohol to the mix. Dr. Phil probably had a better answer to my issues, but I never watched his program. I went to the bar and ordered a couple of Guinness.

While drinking, I wondered if the brew would be my last. Needed to think of optimistic thoughts, but it was hard. Hard to believe that two days ago, I had control in the drug game and now it was controlling me. I felt like Jason in *The Bourne Identity*, except that I did not have amnesia. I just didn't know how I got on a hit list when I tried to play fair game.

The Guinness was going down strong. Add that with a good NCAA B-ball tournament game and I felt a little less stressed. Some kid named Carmelo Anthony was balling for Syracuse.

Suddenly, a tap on my left shoulder disturbed me.

"W'zup, Ajah?"

I heard a strong Jamaican accent and I knew who it was before I turned around, Richie Ranks, a cat in his mid-thirties and one of my favorite customers. I hadn't seen him in a long minute. He was decked out in leather and sported a small afro that made him look too much like the comedian Bernie Mac. I had to give my boy a hug.

"Richie!" I said. "Where you been, star? Thought you was dead."

"You thought I was dead?" he asked with surprise. "Guy, I thought you was dead! I've been trying to call you for days."

Whatever.

"My number ain't changed, man. You never called me."

"What you mean? I've been calling the number on the card that Rancel gave me last week."

Finally I ran into a cat that obtained my private number from that punk.

I got serious. "Rancel wasn't supposed to give out that number. That's why I never answer it when it rings."

Richie looked at me as if I was speaking Mandarin.

"How you expect to have a successful business if you don't return calls?" he asked.

I looked at him as if he was speaking German.

"What business?" I asked. "I'm not in this crap to take over like Machete. It's too much stress!"

He took out his wallet and pulled out a card.

"Then what the hell is this?"

I took the card and read it.

BETHEL SYSTEMS INC.
Ajani Bethel
Founder, Independant Business Consultant
(416)555-9447

I was in shock. I had never seen the card before. Bethel Systems? Sounded like an information technology company. I asked Richie who gave him the card.

"Rancel," he replied. "He told me that you started your own thing with ecstacy pills, and you're an affiliate with Machete. I was happy when I found out 'cause I'm always looking for a deal on ecstacy."

"Who . . . what the . . . I ain't made this card. I don't have a Bethel Systems whatever."

"Then what's this card—"

"I don't know! It's a bunch of crap! Bethel Systems does not exist, and I am not selling any date rape pills! Who else knows about this?"

"I dunno, guy. All I know is that Rancel promoted you like a big chief when I ran into him and you know me, Ajah. When I want the stuff, I come to you, 'cause I'm down with any business you running, man. You've always been legit about your work."

We shook hands. I appreciated the support, but more importantly the info.

"Thanks, man," I said. "Just call me by the number I gave you before. Pretend you never saw this card."

"No doubt," said Richie Ranks.

He concluded by saying that he had to bounce because two French strippers wanted to get with him cause they thought he was Bernie Mac. Richie was describing them to me while practicing his African-American accent, but I wasn't paying attention. Everything started to turn red. I was mad as hell.

"Later, dog," he said. "I'll holla."

I waved my hand as he left.

I looked at the card again. All the crap that took place so far began to make sense. Rancel made the card and told cats that I was starting my own cartel, making it seem like everything was cool but I knew that Rancel envied and hated me. He always wanted me to fail an operation or a task, but it never went his way. Thus, Rancel had to find another method to take me down.

Being the punk that Rancel was, he wanted someone else to kill me, someone ruthless like his cousin Machete. Rancel must have told him that I was doing crap behind his back, like starting my own business and taking Machete's clients by using the tricks of the game that he had taught me. That's why Machete looked pissed off at me on Thursday. Pissed off, hurt, and disappointed, as if I stabbed him in the back.

Obviously, Machete had a difficult time digesting whatever Rancel told him because I was more loyal to him than anyone had been over the last three years. He didn't want to kill me, but probably felt that it was a necessity. Kwame Moss was paid to arrest me instead of letting me into the U.S. I was mad lucky to avoid it, and it was quite clear now that the G.H was indeed fake. If I made it across, which I did, the Estafans would take me out for delivering counterfeit material. That almost happened, courtesy of Big Cement. I really should've been dead, but I wasn't, and still far from being off the hook.

Thanks to Rancel, my weekend was a living hell. However, I was still alive, and I was ready for revenge. My blood was raging hot. My heart was trying to beat out of my chest. I wanted to kill Rancel by beating him to death and the more I drank the Guinness, the greater the rage became.

The phone that I ignored all weekend started to ring. Now I wanted to answer it. Lo and behold, the number on the ID belonged to Chief Deverow.

"What?" I snapped.

"Bethel!" said Machete. "What's with the tone? Who pissed you off?"

Was he for real?

"Don't act like you don't know nothing, Chete! Martinez's cousin tried to kill me yesterday!"

Realizing that my voice was rather loud, I walked out of the bar to avoid the suspicious looks.

"There was a misunderstanding. Meet me at the Hilton hotel around nine so I can explain what happened."

"Why can't you just tell me right now on the . . . hold up! You're in Windsor?"

"Me and Rancel arrived this morning."

They were in Windsor. Machete had no intentions on arriving before Monday. Because things weren't going their way, they had to make a move but I couldn't afford to give into their agenda.

"Why the hell should I trust you? You're supposed to be in Toronto!"

"Have you done anything wrong for me to kill you?"

"It depends on who you ask."

"You've been nothing but an asset to me, Bethel. You coming or what?"

I said nothing as I went to the hotel lobby and waited for the elevator. He called my name and repeated the question.

"Seen," I answered. "Nine o' clock."

I hung up the phone as I entered the elevator. My plan was to go to the executive suite and change into all black clothing. Then head to my Escalade. That's where I had to get my bulletproof vest. It was time for war.

CHAPTER 73

K.J

Ajani stormed past me like a madman.

Teddy and I were about to leave the executive suite and Ajani came in the crib angry as hell; it looked as if he was ready to kill someone. My cousin asked him what was wrong.

"Don't worry about it," Ajani answered as he changed into some black clothing. "I got business to finalize."

I said, "Hope to see you in the crowd tonight."

"Hope so too," he said quietly as he grabbed his coat and left.

Teddy asked me, "You ever wonder just how deep Ajah's in the game?"

"Wonder?" I responded. "His attitude shows it everyday."

"You think he'll ever get out before it's too late?"

"Ted, that's like asking the exact date of the apocalypse. I have no idea."

I couldn't help but feel helpless. Ajani was my best friend next to Teddy, but he was mad stubborn, and refused to let us know much about his drug dealing tribulations. It was good and bad at the same time.

We were on our way to the church for the Bless Fest concert. Butterflies were going psycho in my stomach. The Showcase Final was over four hours away, and I was trying to keep a low profile. Most finalists stayed around the hype of the Jam Festivities and used their popularity to get favor with media exposure, food, and women's phone numbers. As for me, I was going to church with another opportunity to see Kaitlyn Fuentes. She kept my mind off the hate I had for my ex-girlfriend and former sidekick. In addition, I had to stay focused, which meant staying away from Verbal Pain lovers and K.J haters.

Teddy was surprisingly quiet while driving, as if he didn't want to reveal something. Thus, I asked him what was up.

"Man, as much as I want to see you perform, I can't go to Club V tonight," he admitted.

I didn't expect that news, not from my cousin and best friend.

"You're not coming?" I snapped. "Stop lying, guy."

"I'm not, man. I don't feel good in that atmosphere any—"

"I come to your events at your church! At least you could support your cousin, who'll be on national television!"

"That's why I feel bad about doing it, K.J! I mean, before I went inside the club yesterday, I thought I'd be OK but it wasn't the same anymore. I wish I could explain how I felt, but it was just strange. It was like I wasn't supposed to be in that midst."

Teddy couldn't go into detail, so I couldn't understand fully where he was coming from. There was no doubt that my cousin was a changed man spiritually, but how bad was a few hours in a nightclub, especially when I was part of the biggest attraction?

"Ted, it's not like I'm asking you to help me rob a bank. It is the Jam Fest Freestyle Showcase Final! It's my long-awaited and highly anticipated moment and you're backing out?"

He looked like he wished he didn't say anything.

"Guy," said Teddy, "I couldn't be happier for you than I am right now. I'm your biggest fan! However, nightclubs are my weakness: the music, liquor, the booties, and the whole atmosphere. If I go tonight, I may want to start clubbing again, which'll mess me up as a Christian."

I still didn't get it. Didn't he know about having self-control? Personally, I thought Teddy didn't want to go for a reason unknown.

"So what?" I asked. "It's all about you now?"

"What the—?" Teddy snapped. "Look who's talking! This whole thing has been about you! Just remember who pushed hard to get your demo to the right cats so that you can be in this position right now!"

Ouch. I felt that brick to the head but I was stubborn, and I hated to lose arguments.

"Look, let's forget about it," I concluded. "You do what you gotta do, aight? Just do me a favor and drop me at the club at nine."

We stopped talking and went inside the church.

I felt weird when I entered the sanctuary. It was a good weird feeling, if there was such a thing. Right away, I forgot about how I was gonna defeat Roderick on the stage. I didn't think about the argument with Teddy. I didn't think about any of the crazy drama that took place thus far. The atmosphere was peaceful. I sat down in the front pew while Teddy made himself useful in the church basement.

Although the setting was peaceful, I began to feel slightly uncomfortable. I thought it was a feeling of conviction, but I didn't know why. Felt as if I had things under control. Felt as if I had done nothing wrong recently. Yet the feeling existed, and I wanted it to leave. Hence, I decided to close my eyes and meditate on the gospel music that was playing through the speakers.

I felt a tap on my left shoulder. I opened my eyes and saw Kaitlyn smiling and sitting next to me. Hallelujah. I said hello to her with a sexy grin.

"Hey, K.J.," she answered. "I'm glad to see you back."

"Well, I needed some inspiration before tonight's battle."

"You're in the right place. By the way, you sounded really good today. I don't listen to much hip-hop because of the profanity, but you got my respect 'cause you kept it swear-free."

"Thanks. I do my best 'cause my mother hates a potty-mouth. You sang wonderful today. I know I told you that already, but I was greatly blessed."

Kaitlyn grinned. "All thanks are to God. I'm nothing, but He is everything."

All I could do was smile. Kaitlyn was so humble. As beautiful and talented as she was, I wouldn't be mad if she had a big head, but she gave all of the credit to God. That made me even more attracted to her.

She asked me if I was staying for the whole concert or if I was leaving early again.

I said, "I'll be leaving at nine. Will I be able to see X-Secula perform?"

"Well, he's coming on in the second half of the program, but I may be able to get him up in the first half so you can see him." Then she winked at me. "I'll see what I can do."

"If it'll be a problem, don't worry about it. I'll . . ."

"You wanna hear him or not?"

"Of course!"

"Alright then." She got up from the pew. "I gotta get ready so, all the best tonight, K.J. Hope you win, 'cause that other rapper's too cocky and dirty-minded."

I grinned again. "Hope so too. You gonna pray for me?"

"Of course, are you gonna pray for yourself?"

"After I pray that God abundantly blesses you."

Kaitlyn smiled and walked away. If there was such a thing as spiritual flirting that must've been it, but I was going to pray for her and let my actions speak louder than words.

The concert started promptly at seven-thirty. They began with praise and worship music, but I didn't sing with the rest of the audience. I wasn't a singer, and I was saving my vocal cords for the showcase. Teddy and Janet were standing next to me and they had their eyes closed, vocals raised, and hands in full altitude. They were changed individuals indeed.

After the praise and worship, I was introduced to the most versatile gospel music I'd ever seen. The first act was some dude named Nigel Soyer from

Toronto. He had a smooth voice and a musical style that was comparable to none yet tight enough to be in any Christian or non-Christian's car stereo. I was very impressed. Next, was a dancehall cat named Jah Way from New York. He had long dreadlocks and had a rapid-fire chat like the artist Elephant Man. In addition, the lyrics seemed like it was strictly biblical. The crowd was blown away from his performance. After my shock, I couldn't help but jump on the gospel reggae bandwagon.

The third act was none other than X-Secula, the gospel rapper from New Jersey. Kaitlyn was a true sweetheart for re-arranging the program schedule. As soon as he spit the first bar in his introduction, I felt a powerful presence that carried him. I was immediately mesmerized, which said a lot because most rappers didn't get my full attention.

X-Secula did three songs. The first was *His Jam*, which described how Christian people should party. The lyrics and beat were solid. He was a real crowd-pleaser. The second selection was the track that was on Teddy's mix CD, and it sounded way better live. I had so much respect for his talent and the fact that he devoted it entirely to God. Moreover, he was honest and straightforward. Someone I could listen to anytime.

However, it was the third song that really blew me away. It wasn't a party jam or hardcore like the first two, but *Forgiveness* hit me like a sack from middle linebacker Ray Lewis. I remembered the third verse of the song so vividly:

"I still had mad hate for this person weeks and months later
Issues and drama in my life was much worse than greater
I never was one to have much physical pain
But my chest was always bugging and I had constant migraines
Laid off from my job and to add to my strife
Stress led to fights and separation from my wife
The church used to be my most favorite place
But I stopped going 'cause I didn't wanna see the man's face
But I went on Good Friday, a special occasion
Couldn't get with the worship, couldn't get with the praisin'
That really sucked because my soul was yearning
For a breakthrough, but then I heard an awesome sermon
It was more than a reminder of Christ's crucifixion
It was so powerful that it gave me conviction
Christ forgave everybody, including all his haters
By dying on the cross, can't think of anything more greater
Because of Him is the reason I have life today
But I couldn't forgive, so eternal death was heading my way
My mind was crazy thinking that I could out live this
Went up to the person and I asked for forgiveness

> For being unforgiving, we both shed the tears
> Suddenly all my physical pain disappeared
> Prosperity came my way, God did a one-eighty
> Now my life has more worth than a hundred Mercedes' because of
> *Forgiveness!*"

The chorus was so simple, yet very effective. Some lady was singing *forgiveness* continuously while X-Secula ministered over the melody. He said that if we can't forgive others, God wouldn't forgive us for our sins. Ouch. Therefore, his conclusion was that we had to forgive others even if we never receive an apology. Ouch, again.

Forgiveness. The word never left my mind after the song ended and X-Secula left the stage. The song was so powerful some people began to weep. To be honest, that was the last message I wanted to hear before the biggest moment of my life.

Since I heard about Bianca cheating on me with Roderick and afterwards breaking his jaw at Club Oasis, I said to myself that I'd never forgive them. Shoot, if I couldn't forgive my father for leaving my mom and me, why forgive two people that didn't bring me into the world? My unforgiving spirit increased my hate for them and before the concert, I depended on my hate and my raw talent to defeat Verbal Pain and shame Bianca. However, God used X-Secula to give me a convicting message. The big question was whether I would take the message outside the church building.

The time flew very quickly. Teddy told me that it was time to go. Never thought that he would have to remind me, but that's how blown away I was from the performance. God had me at the church for a reason, and it wasn't to get Kaitlyn's phone number.

During the next selection, Ted and I said good-bye to Janet and walked out of the sanctuary. As soon as we entered the hallway, X-Secula and Kaitlyn were talking. This was the perfect time to give the man his props.

Kaitlyn introduced him to us by his real name, which was Isaiah Kelly. We shook his hand.

"Man, you are incredible," I admitted. "I'm real glad I got to hear you."

Isaiah replied, "Kaitlyn told me why she wanted me to go in the first half, and I was more than happy to. My goal is to reach the cats who don't know or want to know more about God. Plus, she told me that you have crazy skills!"

Teddy said, "You and my cousin are the best rappers I've heard anywhere!"

I smiled. Looked at Kaitlyn, and her smile was big. God, she was beautiful.

Isaiah concluded, "Well, my man, remember where your skills came from. I try to make sure that He's glorified in everything I do."

That quote stayed with me.

I gave them both a hug and followed Teddy out of the church.

CHAPTER 74

Juanita felt very comfortable in Nivea's home. Shanice acted as if it was her second home, and she could see why. Nivea was a very sweet girl, and very hospitable. She treated everyone in her apartment as if they were family.

The ox-tail dinner from Rude Boy's made Juanita sleepy. Nivea offered her bed for a nap, and she took full advantage. What was supposed to be a half-hour snooze turned into ninety minutes. It would have been longer if Juanita did not hear a knock on the door.

Shanice opened the door without waiting for her response. She looked disturbed and confused, an expression that came only when Shanice talked to Juanita about men. Juanita hoped that it was not anything serious.

"Nice nap?" asked Shanice with a small grin.

"Too nice," said Juanita after a big yawn. "I stayed up too late watching TV this morning. You all right? You look bugged."

For ten seconds, Shanice said nothing. Then she asked, "Have you ever met any other guy named Eros?"

It was Juanita's turn to look confused. "No. My man was the first. His dad has the same name, but I've never met him. Why?"

"While you were sleeping, Nivea and I were just catching up with each other and she kept bringing up her man who came down for the weekend. Unknowingly, she kept saying 'my man this' and 'my man that' without saying his name. So I asked her what his name was 'cause she made him sound so great—"

"And his name is Eros?"

"Uh huh."

Juanita wanted to believe that she was still dreaming. She squeezed her left hand with her right, and she felt the pain.

"Niecey, I would easily respond by saying that it's just a coincidence, but . . . oh Lord, say it ain't so."

"What?"

Juanita pointed to the right corner of the bedroom.

"See that Sean John jogging suit on top of the Nike sports bag? I bought Eros that same suit for his birthday and I've seen a bag like that in his apartment. When I first saw that here, I wanted to freak out but instead I ignored it. But now that you say Nivea's man's name is Eros . . ."

She sprung up from the bed as if she was on a trampoline. Placing her hands on her head, she closed her eyes. Juanita felt like choking Eros by the neck.

I'm gonna kill him, she thought. *If this is true, he's dead!*

"Girl," said Shanice, "we need to find out the truth."

Nivea was in the kitchen taking out three wine glasses from the shelf. She had an expensive bottle of red wine that she could not wait to open, yet she felt somewhat bad about drinking. Bad because Eros was not feeling well and if he felt better already, he was at a church concert and she was going to a club. However, they did have plenty of sex in two nights, which was very sinful according to Christians. A couple glasses of wine seemed very minor in comparison.

She still had not heard from Eros. At the least, Nivea wanted to know if he was feeling better. She tried to call his cell phone, but it was still off from Thursday night. Nivea hoped that Whitney and Q would show up soon, because maybe Q knew more about Eros' condition.

Shanice and Juanita came into the kitchen. Nivea smiled at them and noticed that they looked tired still or worried about something.

"Hey," she said.

Shanice asked her if she was able to contact Eros.

"No," replied Nivea. "But I'm not gonna worry about it. If he's feeling better, he'll be at church right now anyway."

Juanita asked, "Is your man a Christian?"

Nivea answered, "He never said he is, and it kind of surprised me today when he mentioned going to church. He loves to party and he's a . . . you know . . . I wish I had a better name for it . . ."

"A freak?"

"Yeah," giggled Nivea, yet very surprised at Juanita's answer. *She don't know my man! How dare she call him a freak?*

"My man in Brampton is a freak as well. It seems as if he wants to do it at any given opportunity."

"Hah! Eros acts like he's addicted to Viagra."

"Eros? That's your man's name?"

"Yeah. Unique, isn't it? He's the first guy I've ever met with that name."

"Well, mine will be the second guy you meet with that name once I get in touch with him."

Nivea showed great surprise and said, "Oh my God! Your man's name is Eros, too? Niecey, why didn't you mention that when I told you his name?"

Shanice said, "Cause I thought it'd be a greater surprise if you two found out at the same time!"

"Wow, that unbelievable," said Nivea as she placed the wine glasses on a tray. "So, Juanita, your man's in Windsor?"

"Yeah, he came to Windsor with his boys on Thursday night," Juanita answered. "Him and his three boys came down in an Escalade and stayed with a friend who lives here and goes to the university. Do you know Teddy Henderson?"

Teddy? That's who Eros is helping at the church!

"I've heard that name before," Nivea said. "He sounds familiar."

"Teddy's cousin is one of Eros' friends that also came down and he's participating in the freestyle showcase."

Suddenly, Nivea felt very warm.

His name better not be K.J.

"Oh!" she replied. "He's a friend of Verbal Pain?"

Juanita said, "Verbal who? Uh uh. His name's K.J."

Oh, hell no! This can't be happening to me. This woman better stop messin' around and admit that she's not seeing anyone named Eros!

Nivea didn't respond to Juanita. She grabbed the tray, walked past the ladies and entered the living room. Of course, they followed her direction. Juanita asked her if Eros was a Black man.

No, missy, he's half Black and half Latino! We're not seeing the same man!

Nivea lied. "Yes, he's Black."

"Oh, OK," Juanita said in an unconvincing tone. "My man's mixed: half Black, half Latino, Puerto-Rican to be exact."

She tried to hold back the tears. Nivea didn't want to show her weakness, so she faced the window instead of the women.

"What's Eros' last name, Nivey?" asked Shanice.

Nivea turned around and snapped, "Why? What more do you know about Eros Alexander?"

Juanita asked, "You slept with him, right? Are his birthmarks on his left thigh and left butt cheek?"

Nivea wanted to say that she had never seen his birthmarks because the setting was always dark when they were intimate but she definitely saw them. She told Eros that they were sexy.

It was official. Nivea was played. While a couple of tears rolled down her cheek, she said yes.

Shanice said, "Girlfriends, you only know one man named Eros, and he played you both."

Juanita yelled out something in Spanish and walked out towards the deck. Nivea saw her anger and realized that Eros Alexander, Jr. was too good to be true. Tears were flowing out as quickly as she was wiping them.

Shanice started pouring the wine in the glasses. She gave one to Nivea.

"Come," she said as she grabbed Nivea's hand and led her to the deck.

"Drink?" Shanice asked her roommate.

"Oh yeah," agreed Juanita, as she faced the ladies and eagerly grabbed her glass.

If looks could kill, Juanita was a terrorist. Nivea was not sure if she was angrier with Eros or her.

"I'm sorry, Juanita," cried Nivea. "If I knew he had a girlfriend, I wouldn't have—"

"Don't apologize," interrupted Juanita. "We're in the same situation. Niecey, I should've listened to you. That lying S.O.B!"

Shanice said, "Hey, you both were in love. I just knew that any man who collected porn and has a father who produces porn has a hard time being faithful."

Nivea almost choked while drinking.

"Hold up! His dad's a porn producer?"

Juanita nodded and said that Eros owned over a thousand videos. The things that one can discover in a long-distance relationship.

Nivea asked her how long she and Eros had been together.

"About seven months," replied Juanita. "What about you?"

"I met him last New Year's Eve when I was in Toronto for the holidays. It was at a house party."

"I was in Puerto Rico during that time!"

"We've had a phone relationship from then until this weekend."

"When would he call you?"

"Usually in the evening between five and nine."

"The same time I was working in the mall."

Nivea finished her wine and asked Shanice to get the rest in the bottle. It was going down really good.

"Y'know," added Nivea, "I tried to come up to Toronto a couple of times this year, and he always had an excuse that he was too busy to see me."

"Hah!" yelled Juanita. "That boy works during the week and has every weekend off. He has no expenses 'cause his pops pays the condo mortgage via Western Union from Los Angeles every two weeks. Eros wanted to come to Windsor this weekend without me. And now I know why."

"Does he know you're here now?"

"Not if he hasn't checked his voice mail."

Shanice returned to the deck and poured more wine in their glasses.

"So," asked Shanice, "what's the plan? What y'all gonna do about this?"

"I wanna beat him down!" Nivea grumbled as she drank half of the wine in a single gulp.

"That's understandable, girl," Juanita said, "but revenge is way better if you don't drive on emotion. I'm a strategist."

"Strategist? Why? What do you have in mind?"

"Don't know yet. Where is Eros? You said church, right?"

"If he's not sick, then again, he probably lied about that too!"

"Well, he better be in church, 'cause that's the safest place to be right now. Do you know where it is?"

"Oh yeah! I have the Bless Fest flyer in my purse. Let's go!"

As they headed to the exit, Shanice snapped, "Hold up! You just had two cups to drink, Nivey, and Juanita, you look like you're ready to do some evil! For the sake of the human race, I'll drive!"

"Good looking out, girl," said Juanita. "I almost forgot that I just woke up. Gotta make sure my hair looks good!"

Juanita rushed to the bedroom. Two minutes later, she came out with her purse and Eros' belongings.

"You got a plan of revenge already?" Shanice asked her.

"No," she answered. "But looking at the stuff this boy has, I'm sure to come up with something vicious!"

CHAPTER 75

TEDDY

As much as I was enjoying the concert, I realized that K.J was about to face the greatest moment of his life. He worked hard to get to the Finals, and he just wanted his cousin and best friend at the venue for support. Yes, it was in a nightclub, but my purpose wouldn't be to drink or pick up women. If Woody Rock of Dru Hill and Michelle Williams of Destiny's Child had no problems being a Christian in a secular setting, then why should I?

"But Mummy, you have to understand, I had to say something to blow him away. I don't know J-Thrill's mama, and I don't want to sleep with her!" K.J said to his mother, who called for him on my cell phone. "Yes, I promise to keep it tasteful tonight . . . Really? They're all going to Uncle Kingsley's to watch it on satellite? That's serious . . . I'll make you proud tonight, Mummy . . . Love you too."

As he hung up the phone, I said, "Yo, Aunt Brenda wasn't too happy that I turned the phone off during the concert. I can't believe you don't have a cell phone!"

K.J replied, "Cause I don't want family to bug me all the time, especially this weekend. Guy, your aunt was tripping about what I said to J-Thrill, yet she told the entire family that I'm gonna kick Roderick's ass tonight! I don't get it, it's like she loves and hates this freestyle showcase at the same time. You know that all our Trinidad family is watching this tonight?"

"Guy, its gonna be huge! I should just let you keep the cell, 'cause it will be ringing off the hook once the showcase is over, and the calls will all be for you."

"Didn't I just say, I didn't want a cell for that reason?"

He gave me back my phone. I sucked my teeth and threw it in the backseat of my car.

We were almost at the club when I told K.J that I changed my mind and was going to enter the club. Instead of being pleased, my cousin sucked his teeth.

"Guy, you'd be stupid not to go back to the concert," he told me. "I honestly didn't want to leave. If this showcase wasn't tonight, I wouldn't be in this car right now."

I was surprised at his response, but I couldn't have been more happy. God really moved K.J in a special way during Bless Fest.

"You sure, dog?" I asked.

"Of course. Besides, Ajah, Eros and Q will be there. In addition, my new fans and I'm mad pumped, 'cause I'm taking the throne tonight!"

"Please take down that punk again, K.J. You broke his jaw already. Now break Roderick's ego."

"Word, cuzin."

When we arrived at Club V, the line up to get in was incredible. There were twice as many people as Friday night, and the traffic to park vehicles was really slow. I was blessed not having to do either.

I said, "Good thing you have a backstage pass."

K.J replied, "No doubt. At least I could . . . Yo, there's a cat from Roderick's crew giving out free CDs."

I looked where my cousin was pointing. Sure enough, there was a man in a Pacific Records jacket that was trying to be Santa in March. It was probably just a Verbal Pain album sampler or a CD of his overplayed single because his debut album had yet to be released.

"Verbal Pain really wants to win, and he thinks free stuff will get more votes."

"For some, but all people aren't stupid," said K.J. "The best freestyler will win tonight."

"Yes, sir. Well, man, I pray that God'll be with you, guide you, and if it's His will, that a phat record deal will come your way tonight."

"It's all up to God's will, huh?"

"Pretty much."

We gave each other the Phat Five salute and he left the car. As I was driving away, I saw people in the line-up treating K.J like a celebrity. He was pounding fists, giving hugs, and waving to fans. Of course, I couldn't stare too long because I was dealing with stupid drivers on the road, and I couldn't wait to return to Bless Fest.

On the way back, I started to talk to God aloud. It was my way of praying whenever I was alone. No tongue-speaking, no repetitive words, just talking and I made sure that the gospel AM station was playing softly in the background.

First, I asked God to help K.J win the showcase. I didn't know if He cared about cats dissing people through rhyme, but I guess that's why people ask for God's will to be done.

Next, I tried to pray for Ajani. I didn't really know what to ask except that he would quit the drug game before it killed him.

As for Q, he wasn't being Q. Thus, I prayed that he would get his act together and be a good husband to Katrina.

Finally, I asked God to use me as a shining light for Him and show integrity through my words and actions.

When I got to the church, I realized that I didn't pray for Eros. However, I was looking forward to getting in the building, so I got out of my car. It would've only taken an extra minute of my time, but I didn't feel like talking anymore. Wrong move. As soon as I opened the front door of the church, I realized that I should've followed the Holy Spirit. Janet was with two angry-looking women in the foyer.

Juanita Velez and Nivea Davis were together. That couldn't be good at all. Eros Alexander was in trouble, or about to get in trouble. Janet saw me as soon as I entered, so I had no choice but to approach her and the ticked-off duo.

"Hi Juanita," I said, "What's going on? I thought Eros said you were in New York."

"Teddy, where's Eros?" asked Juanita. "He told Nivea that he would be here."

Janet said, "Nivea approached me as I was about to go in the sanctuary. She told me what's going on."

Again, I asked them what was going on, even though I sorta knew.

"Your boy is playing both of these women, Bear!" cried Janet. "Don't act like you didn't know!"

My girlfriend did not have to say that. Juanita and Nivea looked at me in shock.

"Hey!" I said with my hands up. "This isn't about me, it's about Eros."

"Do you know where he is?" asked Nivea.

I shook my head, as I smelt the liquor in her breath.

"You're not lying, are you, Bear?" asked Janet. "Remember where you are."

I gave Janet an annoyed expression. She wasn't helping the situation at all.

"I don't know where Eros is, "I replied to Nivea. "Haven't seen him since this afternoon, when you picked him up at the casino."

Juanita asked me for our hotel room number. Why oh why did this have to take place in church? I so wanted one of the church leaders to interrupt the drama, but they were all being blessed in the sanctuary. How fortunate. I wanted to be drunk in the Holy Spirit, not talking to two drunken women.

I hesitated, but I showed Juanita my swipe card for the executive suite. I was in a no-win situation. If I told her the number, it would be the biggest sell-out move in Phat Five history. Being dishonest in the house of God was worse, but I didn't want to be in the middle of any future drama between Eros and the girls. If I decided to say or show nothing, it would look like I was defending a cheater, a wannabe porn star, a sexaholic, and a liar. However I had just prayed for integrity.

Most hotel cards don't have the room number on them for security reasons, but I put a post-it note on mine to remember where I was staying. They both looked at the card, and Nivea read the number aloud.

"Yes, that number is for an executive suite, "I added. "My friend Ajani booked it, and he specifically told us not to bring any guests, plus I don't think that Eros is there right now anyway. That's all the information you're getting from me. I don't like what he did to you both, but I don't like being a rat. However, I am saved now and I fear God, which is why I decided not to lie."

"We'll just wait in the lobby for him," said Juanita as she gave me my key. "It's an executive suite, so he'll show up sooner or later. Ted, I didn't want to put you on the spot, but a player's gotta pay for his actions."

Nivea added, "We won't let Eros know that you gave us this info."

That comment didn't cheer me up at all. I just wanted to get back to the concert.

"Thanks, Janet," they both said to my woman as they hugged her.

Nivea told her that she was fortunate to have a good man. Janet agreed. Afterward, my dancing queen approached me and grabbed my hand as Thelma and Louise left the building.

"I'm sorry that you had to be in that position, Bear," said Janet. "But you and I knew that Eros would get caught one day."

I sighed. "I know. But you don't know Juanita."

"What do you mean?"

"Let's just say revenge is her specialty."

We went back into the sanctuary and enjoyed the rest of the program. I tried my best to avoid thinking about Eros. If Juanita caught him alone or with another woman or two, he would pay for it tremendously. Then he would probably disown me as a friend once he found out how he was caught.

CHAPTER 76

Q

Whitney and I saw K.J walk into Club V with great confidence. Cats approached him for autographs just in case he was the next hip-hop superstar. Then a reporter called for his attention, and he went to the V.I.P lounge for an exclusive interview. It reminded me of my college B-ball glory days and I felt slightly envied. However, I was proud of Kellen Jamal Brar, and at the present moment, I was on the best date I ever had.

My date and I got into the club before it got really packed and were able to get a table around the game area. It was the third quarter of the Affair Bowl and it was going wonderful. The first quarter was the movie, which was nonsense, but being close to Whitney was sweet indeed. The second quarter was dinner at a fine Italian restaurant. The type where the menu was written in Italian and one could impress their date by speaking the language. We ate crazy good food, had good conversation about family and careers, and avoided talks about relationships and commitment. Footsie under the table was pretty fun as well.

I couldn't complain about the third quarter. Whitney was looking sexier by the minute, but I kept my composure. The goal was to keep conversation to a minimum, have a few drinks, dance hard, and watch K.J battle in the showcase. If I stayed in the game, the fourth quarter would consist of the physical finale that men craved. Time couldn't have moved any slower.

It seemed weird that the rest of the Phat Five were absent. If Eros were to show, he would be on the down low to avoid being seen by Nivea or Whitney. I wondered if he was able to connect with Crystal Quinn. A part of me wanted him to fail, 'cause the boy was too cocky for his own good.

I felt confident that Teddy would reach. Although he was born-again, the cat smoked weed the day before. What was a couple of hours in a club in comparison?

As for Ajani, he was unpredictable of late. It seemed that he couldn't get away from the drug game and it was keeping him occupied. Yet, he was a faithful and supportive friend that would arrive just in time for the action.

Whether they showed up or not, I was in the house, and couldn't wait for K.J to wreck shop. Until that moment, I had somebody to get my groove on with.

Old-school house music began to play through the powerful speakers. Whitney grabbed my arm like tug-o-war, pulling me towards the dance floor. I found out during dinner that she grew up in Chicago, so her reaction to the music didn't surprise me.

"Good ol' Chicago house!" she yelled. "Club music don't get better than this!"

Whitney shook her booty to the music as if she invented the genre. Being a traditional White boy who loved hip-hop, I tried to move like P.Diddy, but it wasn't working. I couldn't keep up, and it was looking embarrassing. Thankfully, I noticed a guy next to me who dressed like a young Don Juan. A typical wannabe pimp from Detroit, the dude was grabbing his woman by the waist and taking control with his footwork. I copied his moves as best as possible and by the end of the second song, Whitney was feeling me a little bit better. Either that or she just really liked me and tried to be a good sport.

The more we danced, the greater the chemistry became. I tried really hard not to get happy in the pants as her butt was pressed on me, but I failed. Whitney felt the difference immediately.

"Watch it, guy," she grinned. "When's your boy coming on stage?"

"Eleven," I answered, staring at my watch.

"Dang, that's more than an hour from now. If it wasn't for the showcase, I'd be ready to leave now. It's your fault!"

"My fault?" I asked in shock, worried that my dancing was leading to a fourth quarter meltdown.

"Yes, your fault. What cologne are you wearing?"

I told her it was *Cool Water* by Davidoff.

"That is a sexy, sexy scent, and I have a weakness for quality men's fragrances. You don't know what its doing to me."

Eleven p.m. could not arrive any slower.

CHAPTER 77

AJANI

It was half past nine, thirty minutes late for the meeting with the Deverows. At that point, I didn't care about pleasing them anymore. Rancel framed me, and I could've easily been dead or behind bars at the present. He was gonna severely pay for his intentions. Severely.

I sat in my Escalade parked in the underground lot of the Hilton hotel. Just finished smoking another blunt and it complemented my rage. I put on my bulletproof vest, followed by my leather jacket, came out of the vehicle and locked it. It was time for some action.

When I entered the lobby, I asked the White lady at the desk to direct me to the penthouse. She hesitated, seeing that I was an angry-looking Black man. Understandable I suppose but once she called Mr. Deverow and got his approval, everything was cool. I could've been nicer and spoke in plain English instead of patois, but like I said, I just didn't care.

I arrived at the penthouse and knocked on the door. Machete opened it, looking more laid back than ever with a cashmere bathrobe, silk pants, and platinum jewelry.

"What the hell took you so long?" he asked.

"What does it matter?" I asked back. "I'm here now."

Machete raised an eyebrow and allowed me to enter. The penthouse was fully loaded like my executive suite at the casino. The only main thing that was different was the entertainment room, which had a massive hot tub with three hot women soaking in bubbles. They must've came from the Real Feel.

"I thought this was a meeting," I said, acting as if the girls weren't even in the place.

"It is," said Machete, "but what's wrong with mixing pleasure with business every once in a while?"

Plenty. When I started working for you, you said that mix was like oil and water.

He said that Martinez loaned him some of his strippers, who were available to fulfill any sexual desire. Looked at the girls and they waved, but I didn't return the gesture.

Machete continued, "The girl in the blue bikini is Jennifer, the one in the silver thong is Kiwi, and the lady in the gold is Treasure. But you can't have her, that's my favorite."

"That's alright," I said. "I already have a woman."

"Bethel, relax. You're out of town with hoe's already paid for."

"I said I'm good. Where's Rancel?"

"Getting it on with a girl in his room across the hall."

Nuff said. I left the penthouse and went to Rancel's. Of course, the door was locked, so I pounded on it like a cop at a crack house. There was no answer after three seconds so I pounded again. That's when I heard Rancel drop a few F-bombs before opening the door. Wearing only an open bathrobe and boxers, dude was mad, but not half as pissed off as me.

"What the . . . Bethel, what the hell do you want?"

"*PAYBACK!*" I yelled as I punched him in the nose.

Rancel's nose gushed out blood like a faucet. He stumbled backwards into the dresser and fell to the ground. The woman he was with, got her naked self up, and ran to the opposite side of the room in fear.

"You're dead!" said Rancel as he wiped his nose. Wasting no time, he got up and swung his fist towards my face, but I caught it with my left hand. While squeezing his fist, I dropped a roundhouse kick with my right foot landing his stomach, followed by a kick to the chest. I was way too quick for the thirty-eight year old.

Next, I pushed him to the ground. All I wanted to do was torture Rancel for the crap he put me through and I barely noticed that the other women and Machete came in the room to see what was going down. I stomped my Timberland on his bare chest and pressed hard. The cat was in real pain and I was loving it.

"*So, thought your plan was gonna work, huh?*" I yelled as I pressed harder.

During the process, I almost cracked one of his ribs. Was a good idea, but I decided to let Rancel loose. I wanted to mess him up longer.

"You don't know who the hell you're messing with!" I preached as he slowly got up. "You wanna take me out? Here I am, guy! Take me out, 'cause all I see is the punk in you! You're just a punk bred-drin!"

Rancel barely caught his breath when he landed a hard kick to my stomach. Felt no pain thanks to my vest. Then he grabbed a lamp from the end table and almost smashed it on my head. It managed to catch the right side of my face and it hurt. Felt a big cut on my ear, which gave me more encouragement to beat him down. I swung at his face and missed. Then the man hit me hard in the stomach, but thanks again to the vest, it didn't faze me. I tried a second time for his face and nailed him on the jaw, followed by another kick to the chest.

I quickly turned around and noticed Machete and the women staring. The chicks looked nervous, but Machete was emotionless. Couldn't figure him out at all.

Because Rancel wasn't a challenge without a gun, I decided to conclude the matter. I placed my left arm around his neck and choked hard. With my right hand, I grabbed his right arm and placed it in a fracturing position. It was time for some forced confessions.

"*AARGH!* Chete, what the hell? Shoot him!" Rancel said as best as possible through the pain.

Machete said and did nothing.

"I got you where I want you!" I snapped. "Why don't you tell your cousin who started this crap!"

"Chete, shoot—"

"I can kill you right now, Rancel! Tell your cousin who made those crappy business cards about a business that doesn't exist!"

"I ain't saying sh—"

I pulled his arm harder. Rancel yelled in agony, but his stubbornness wouldn't give into talking. Thus, I decided to be his unofficial spokesman.

"Machete," I began, "you've known from the get-go that your envious cousin hated me because my game has always been tighter than his."

Machete said nothing. My chokehold on Rancel was tighter than ever.

"This punk never had the balls to take me out himself, so he wanted you to do it for him," I continued. "So, this cat makes business cards about a fake *IT* gig, telling folks that I'm an affiliate of you selling date rape pills. Now, in the past I've told you that I wasn't in this crap for the long haul, yet this messed-up cousin of yours must've told you that I was trying to take you down. If I'm wrong, tell me now!"

The Detroit strippers went back to Machete's penthouse. The drug lord ignored them, yet he was still without words and expression. Thought I was talking to a cement wall.

"*AM I WRONG?*" I yelled.

"Continue," answered Machete.

"I saw your face when I entered your office on Thursday. You looked pissed off. Obviously, you accepted family lies over loyalty. You should've killed me then when I didn't have a clue! Even during the failed attempts yesterday, I was still clueless. But now I know what happened, and I can honestly say to you that I've been a loyal bred-drin for three years! Your cousin framed me. *ISN'T THAT RIGHT, RANCEL?*"

Rancel was almost dead. I let go of my chokehold on him, but I still had him hostage by his arm. He started coughing, gagging, spitting, but no answer. I became furious, so I pulled out a gun from my side and aimed it at his head.

"I SAID, ISN'T THAT RIGHT, RANCEL?"

While coughing, Rancel said, "Just kill me already. I'll see you in hell, 'cause you won't make it past tonight."

I wanted to pull the trigger. I really wanted to kill him, especially for the fact that Rancel wanted to die before admitting the truth in front of Machete. Machete was confusing the hell outta me 'cause he was just watching his cousin being tortured. Was that a good thing? Was it a good idea to pull the trigger?

At that point, I didn't know. So I swung the gun across Rancel's head and knocked him out cold.

After he fell, I looked at Machete. He had a cold expression, as if he was mad that I took down Rancel or mad that Rancel deceived him. Maybe it was both.

"You could believe me or try to kill me," I said, standing like a soldier ready to continue battle. "If you choose the latter, I ain't going down without a fight."

"I believe you," said Machete. "Come with me."

He headed towards the exit.

"Why?" I asked. "Where you going?"

Machete turned around and gave me a vicious stare.

"I listened to you, now you're gonna listen to me!" he snapped. "Let's settle this in the underground parking lot, now!"

I followed him out, not because he told me to, but because I was ready for a conclusion to the matter.

CHAPTER 78

EROS

I was still bugging that I left my luggage at Nivea's. It was a big time stupid move for a polygamous man. I should've taken my stuff with me to the executive suite 'cause it would've avoided me from having to see her again. Thank God I was going to a pajama party, and I was wearing my lucky platinum silk boxers.

After the dinner affair with Crystal and Kendra, I went for a brief downtown Windsor walk. Ended up in a coffee house talking to a six-foot tall half-White, half-Asian stripper who was visiting from Toronto.

Another chick, another phone number, I couldn't help it. I wanted more variety and options than Direct TV satellite.

By eight-thirty, I was back at the executive suite. The place was Phat Five-free and I badly wanted to have my own private party. However, I didn't want to piss off my drug dealer buddy and end up riding a Greyhound back to T.O. For a moment, I pictured myself living in a house just as tight and fully paid for, thanks to a successful career as a gigolo or an adult movie star. Couldn't wait for that time of my life to come.

I took a quick shower before putting on the same platinum boxers. Sniffed it to make sure it still was semi-clean. It was a move that I promised never to repeat. I didn't have my extra clothes with me, and it was way better than using another man's briefs.

The only piece of clothing that I had to borrow was a shirt from one of the Phat Five. I didn't like K.J's stuff 'cause it was too generic. Call me shallow, but I was a designer label guy. Ajani had tight gear, but he hadn't been in the greatest mood since Friday, so I didn't touch his wardrobe. Q had incredible-looking shirts. He dressed better than I sometimes did, which was hard to swallow but the cat's clothes were too long because of his height. Therefore, I had to borrow something from Teddy. He had good taste, and we were built the same. Took his black Roc-a-Wear shirt, which smelled fresh 'cause Teddy didn't smoke. Sprayed some of Q's Cool Water cologne on my neck and wrists and bounced.

Upon arrival at the Tropical Club, I gave the cab driver twenty dollars for the lengthy ride. I was officially out of paper, so my only financial source was a MasterCard that I didn't want to use. However, I was a mack, so I had no choice. It was a surprise for me not seeing a line-up to get in, but I remembered that the admission was a hundred bucks. Only the exquisite cats would be in the house, like yours truly, thanks to a free ticket from Miss Quinn. I gave the ticket to some man at the door, and he gave directions to get to the V.I.P lounge. Sweet.

The club wasn't large, but it displayed elegance. It was located along Riverside Drive, facing the Detroit River. The outside looked like a mini-mansion, and the inside was decorated like a wedding reception. Guys were in boxer shorts or pajamas. Women were in sexy launderee or bra and panties, courtesy of La Senza and Victoria's Secret but it didn't feel like a hundred-dollar party. People looked upset, frustrated and bored. Definitely, a negative vibe was in the midst.

As I walked upstairs to the V.I.P lounge, the vibe got worse. Men and women were getting high from weed and cocaine. The music sounded wack. People looked like they were ready to get a refund and bounce. In addition, Crystal and Kendra were in nightgowns arguing with a dude in a business suit.

I could've went to the change room to get pajama like everyone else, but I wanted to make sure that everything was cool with the ladies first. Plus, I sat in the sofa nearest to them, and some guy at the opposite end was staring at me hard, and I didn't want any gay man lusting after my chest. I ignored his flirtations and tried to be nosy with the confrontation.

The models were cussing up a storm at the man in the suit; he must have been their agent. It sounded like they were upset about the lack of cash they received for the event. Crystal complained about the party lameness and Kendra was vexed about some jerk who said something offensive. Guess I missed some crazy drama earlier.

Kendra noticed me, and then tapped Crystal to let her know I was in the house. Crystal gave me a quick smile and concluded her argument.

"Well, we're out of this B.S party," she said to the man. "I'm warning you Jack, step up your game and get us better gigs, or we're finding a new agent!"

The ladies approached me, looking vexed. I said hello. They didn't return the greeting.

Instead, Crystal said, "We're outta here, you coming or what?"

Normally, I wouldn't respond nicely to a woman with a bad attitude, but she was the exception. I got up quicker than a teacher sitting on a whoopee cushion.

We took a cab back to the casino. Suddenly my idea for Saturday night changed because it was shortly after eleven and I expected to leave the party around two in the morning. That meant that there was a good opportunity to take the models back to Ajani's executive suite. Yes, I knew that Ajah shunned my request, but it would take place while the boys were at the showcase. I didn't expect them back before three, which was more than enough time to get my Luther Campbell on with the chicks and get room service to change the bed sheets if needed. I was going to be on bad terms with the Phat Five for missing K.J's big moment, so I had to make the most of the situation.

I sat between the models, acting like a gentleman. Crystal apologized for her attitude, than they explained what took place at the Tropical Club. They vented about how their agent told them that they were paid to make a guest appearance at the pajama party, but upon arrival were asked to model and strip. Both women weren't having it, and the club owner didn't want to pay them as a result. Kendra got loud and the man called her a bitch. The owner quickly apologized, but Crystal threatened legal action if they didn't get paid and so on and so on.

I understood their frustration, but their attitudes were stinking. It was so obvious that they thought they were the shiznit 'cause they were models from California. Personality-wise, I would choose Juanita or Nivea over Crystal and Kendra any day, but my goal was to get the double booty, so I stayed focused and concentrated on being a great listener.

"Ladies, you did the right thing," I said. "You were being aggressive, and you didn't give into your agent and the owner's crap. Business is business."

"Exactly!" agreed Crystal. "Eros, if there's one thing that I hate with a passion, its men who lie to get what they want. It pisses me off!"

Kendra added, "Men just need to keep it real with us, whether they're a player, gay, married, agent, whatever."

"At least you don't have to deal with that for the rest of the night," I lied.

I wasn't held at gunpoint, so despite their feelings, I didn't feel obligated to be truthful.

By the time we reached the casino hotel lobby, the ladies were in a better mood. They asked me more questions about my dad and we ended up laughing about the worst adult films ever produced. Women talking about porn was a major turn-on for me. It was an excellent time to pop the question.

"Would you ladies like to come to my suite?" I asked them as we stepped into the elevator. "My boys will be gone till at least three, so I got the place to myself."

"Sure, why not?" replied Crystal as she looked at Kendra with a grin. "Your suite is only across the hallway from ours, so we'll go to our crib first to freshen up."

I tidied up the suite quickly. Gathered the Phat Five's belongings and put them in the corner of the living room. To my surprise, I noticed an unopened pack of boxer briefs in Ajah's bag. Took a pair and gave myself a quick two-minute shower. Creamed myself with scented lotion, wore a silk bathrobe courtesy of the casino, and sprayed some more Cool Water on my neck. I was ready to go, soaking in the pool of anticipation. It was going to be the wildest night of my young life as a player. The first of hopefully many menage et trois' to come.

I heard a knock on the door after I put on some freaky R and B music in the stereo. Looked at my watch and it was exactly a half hour like the models told me before we stepped out of the elevator. Talk about Ajani Bethelian punctuality. The night was going so perfect. I made sure to knock on some wood before opening the door.

CHAPTER 79

Nivea was amazed at Juanita's calmness. After they left the church, the girls went to the casino hotel and went to the executive suite, despite Teddy's warning. As expected, no one answered the door when she knocked. They stuck to the original idea of waiting in the lobby until Eros arrived, but Juanita wanted another drink. Thus, they spent the last half hour in the casino bar.

Juanita handled her liquor as if she was drinking Kool-Aid. She was on her second Long Island iced tea, and she did not get too loud or emotional. Shanice was not drinking because of her driving duties, and that was good because her rage about the drama was increasing. Nivea knew that she got very emotional when she was drunk, and Shanice made sure that she did not get too tipsy.

Shanice looked at Juanita and said, "Girl, you're real quiet right now. You must have a plan in the works."

Nivea stared at her as well. She had just found out what Juanita did to her ex-boyfriend who was an NHL player. Feeding him dog food lasagna and Ex-lax chocolate cake moments before an important playoff game was bold. Who knew what she was thinking about doing to Eros?

"You know what? I still don't have a clue," replied Juanita. "When I did the dog food lasagna thing, I had time to prepare. Plus, I need to know who else he's been with."

Nivea asked, "Will that determine how bad the revenge will be?"

"Oh yeah! You still down with this, right?"

"No doubt, girl, as long as I ain't going to jail for it."

The ladies went back to the lobby and sat down in the sofas. No one was talking. Juanita started staring at the window, and Nivea had her face lowered. However, Shanice could not keep still. She started snapping her fingers and singing the lyrics to Janet Jackson's *I Bet You Think This Song Is About You (Son of a Gun)*.

Nivea raised her head and started humming the chorus. She had just seen the video a few days earlier. Then, it was funny to watch. Presently, she could feel every word to the song. Nivea was angry with Eros and herself. He only wanted to get between her legs and she was more than willing. Yes, she wanted him just as badly, but before the weekend, she promised herself that she would not sleep with Eros on the first night. First date sex was the case with five different guys in two years, and none of them lasted for more than two months. Eros was the sixth and lasted for almost three, which led her to believe that he was husband material. After all, they spoke for three months on the phone getting to know each other before sex, which is highly important for a successful relationship, right? Not if the man was a liar, cheater, and addicted to porn. Nivea fell for the lies, and Eros broke her heart. She jumped up from her seat.

"All right, I can't wait any more!" she screamed. "Where's he at? Let's hunt him down and kill him!"

Everyone in the lobby stared at her as if she was crazy.

Juanita said, "Nivea, relax, in due time, in due time!"

Lowering her voice, Nivea said, "It's that Janet song Niecey started singing! Remember that video? She got back at her man by doing some voodoo junk with the pin doll and making spiders come out of his mouth! Thinking about that got me fired up! You got a plan yet?"

"Not yet. I'm got something in the works, so . . ."

"Can I help you ladies with anything?"

That was the voice of the hotel desk clerk. He looked concerned yet intrigued by the drama that was taking place.

Nivea replied, "No, that's okay, sir. I'm sorry for the noise, I'll quiet down."

"Actually sir, maybe you can help us," said Juanita as she walked towards the desk. "Have you seen a Black-Puerto Rican man come through here in the last hour or two? He's about six feet, sexy face, short fade, metro sexual?"

The clerk started to type on his keyboard as if he was retrieving some important information. He asked her for his name.

"His name is Eros Alexander. We really need to see him."

He raised an eyebrow and gave a half-grin. "Arrows Alexander?"

"Yes, its spelled E-R-O-S A-L-E-X-A—"

"What do you want to know?"

Nivea and Shanice ran to the desk.

"What can you tell us?" asked a rejuvenated Juanita, taking a twenty out of her purse and placing it on the desk.

"Ladies, this info's on the house. He just came in here about a half-hour ago with his companions."

Nivea's jaw dropped. "Sir, did you say 'companions?'"

"Yes, two ladies from California," he answered in a surprisingly calm manner.

"That freaking boy is playing us with two women?" Juanita snapped. "That nasty, no-good . . . I can't believe this crap I'm hearing! Juanita, calm down, Juanita, calm down!"

"Calm down?" asked Shanice. "What for? You girls need to go all out ghetto now!"

"Sir, where is he now?" asked Nivea.

"I believe that they went to Crystal Quinn's executive suite," he answered. "Either that, or the other suite he's staying in."

Nivea's eyes were larger than ever as she yelled, "Crystal Quinn? Oh my God! Ladies, that is the woman I told you about that showed off her rack at the fashion show today! She was also making out with some chick on the dance floor last night! Oh, shoot, it's over now!"

She stormed towards the elevator with Shanice, as they cursed and acted as if they were guests on Jerry Springer. As Nivea pressed the elevator button, she noticed that Juanita was still at the front desk, looking at them in anger.

"Y'all come back here!" yelled Juanita.

"For what?" Nivea yelled back. "You have nothing planned, so I'm going ghetto on his ass!"

"Me too!" agreed Shanice.

"Sez who? I have a plan now!" Juanita said. "But it won't work if you act like you ain't ever left the hood before! Come back, both of you."

Shanice grabbed Nivea by the arm and they walked back to the desk. Nivea looked at the ceiling as tears flowed down her cheeks once again.

"Juanita," she cried, "I don't know how to stay calm. Nobody's ever cheated on me before!"

The girls gave a group hug. Nivea could not stop crying, and Juanita dropped a few tears as well. The clerk asked them if Eros played them all.

Juanita answered, "No. That's why you have to stay here, Niecey."

"No!" cried Shanice. "I gotta back y'all up! What if those chicks wanna fight?"

"OK, I see your point but remember, this is mine and Nivea's drama and not yours. As much as you don't like Eros, you'll need to keep your hands off him!"

Shanice nodded in agreement. Nivea looked at her high-strung girlfriend and knew that Juanita's request was easier said than done.

"Check this out," said Juanita. "Y'all ready for the plan?"

"Spit it, girl!" Nivea said with eagerness.

"Nivey, I need you to go to your car and get Eros' stuff, Niecey, see if you can get a good amount of ketchup from one of the restaurants. I'm gonna try to get some AA batteries for my digital camera at the gift shop."

Looking confused, Shanice asked, "Anything else?"

Juanita replied, "Yes, but we all have some in our purses, which is makeup. Now, here's the idea!"

CHAPTER 80

EROS

When I opened the door, I knew that I was in for an adventure.

Crystal and Kendra entered the suite wearing gray and white camouflage nightgowns. Kendra's was open so I saw her camouflage bikini outfit. Crazy hot. Crystal's was closed, but she came in with a camouflaged handbag. These models were serious about getting their freak on.

"Heyyyy," they said in unison as if they were the Doublemint twins.

"Welcome, ladies," I said with a grin. "If you're trying to enroll me for the army, I'll go to Iraq tomorrow!"

Kendra laughed. "That's alright, sexy. We're bringing the ruckus in here tonight!"

"Good, 'cause you best believe that I'm armed and dangerous! What's in the bag?"

"That's for us to know and you to find out," said Crystal as she caressed my chest. "Do you want to have an amazing night that you'll remember for the rest of your life?"

"No doubt," I answered. "I was going ask y'all the same thing."

"Oh, we have high expectations for tonight," said Kendra, "but we have some conditions."

"Conditions?"

"Yes, conditions," she said again as she began to massage my shoulders. "The only way this night is going to be satisfying for all of us, is if you let Crystal and I take control, nothing more, nothing less. Is that cool with you?"

I said yes. As if I was going to actually say no. Yes, they were in my territory and I'd known them for less than twelve hours, but an opportunity was an opportunity. I was about to experience what many men would never experience in a lifetime. In addition, I was confident in my skills. Sure, the models would start the night in control, but by the end, they would be submitting to me, buying me a round trip ticket to Los Angeles just for a re-encounter!

"Awesome," said Crystal as she opened her bag and pulled out a bottle of *Alize*. "Trust us, you won't regret it. Before we came, we asked room service to bring us some goodies like chocolate syrup, honey, whipped cream, and strawberries. Hope you're ready for dessert."

Like a kid ready to open up Christmas gifts!

We sat in the leather sofa and got tipsy while waiting for room service to arrive. Of course, they wanted to know what Ajani did for a living to afford such a place. I said that he was in real estate, having clients like Vince Carter of the Raptors and Carlos Delgado of the Blue Jays. Hey, I was on a role with not telling the truth, and they weren't going to meet Ajani anyway. Flirtations were heading to the next level. A tea bag and hot water couldn't create better chemistry. Suddenly I was down for whatever the models wanted to do with me. The bliss was that amazing.

Heard a solid knock on the door. The feature presentation was about to begin.

"Yes!" shouted Crystal. "I'll answer the door. Kendra, take him to the bedroom!"

I wanted to see who was at the door, but Kendra pulled me like a dog on a leash. She had the bag with her as well.

"Take off the robe and leave your boxers on," she commanded.

"Yes, ma'am," I replied, obeying Kendra without hesitation.

Sergeant Kendra caressed my biceps, chest, and thighs, saying that she was very impressed with my physique. Then she pushed me on the bed and sat on top of me. Very arousing indeed. Kendra reached inside the bag and pulled out four silk neckties.

"You tying me up?" I asked.

"Problem?" she asked back.

"Nnnnno, do your thang."

Kendra tied my wrists and ankles to the bedposts. It felt tight, but I didn't say anything. I was tied up once before by Juanita, but that was after seeing her for three months. Didn't really think it was that good when it happened. Suddenly I feared that the models could very well leave me in a hostage position and bounce without giving me some but I stayed calm and focused. Worse came to worse, my dad knew Crystal and Kendra, so if they pulled such a stunt, he had enough connects in L.A to mess up their careers for a long time.

After she completed her task, Kendra lied on me, as if I was a Serta mattress.

Looking directly into my eyes, she said, "Your eyes glow with confidence. I hope your game's on point."

"You have no idea," I said.

"No, you have no idea. Crystal and I can handle more than those chicks your dad works with."

"Speaking of, where is Crystal? Is she still here?"

"Good question . . . it don't take that long to—"

"*KENDRA, COME HERE*!" yelled Crystal from the door.

"*WHAT?*" yelled Kendra.

Crystal repeated herself. Kendra got off me, closed her nightgown, and went to the door.

Five minutes had passed. Because we were in an executive suite, walls separated the hallway entrance and the bedroom. Thus, I had no idea what they were up to. Being tied up to a bed, I started to get angry. Plus, it seemed as if the girls had left, 'cause I heard no conversation over the R.Kelly music. The worst thoughts came into my mind. What if they were setting me up for a sick and twisted practical joke that involved cameras and other crap? I immediately tried to remember the phone number of my dad's lawyer just in case I was about to be assaulted.

"*LADIES?*" I yelled.

"In a minute!" one of them sang back.

Ten minutes went. It was obvious that something was going on. It was confirmation after the lights suddenly went off and the music turned down. Not funny at all.

"Eros?"

"What the hell is going on?" I said with a frustrated look.

"We're sorry," Crystal said. "We went down the hall to get some ice after talking to the room service guy."

"About what?"

"Ways of getting the goodies without paying for it," Kendra said with a laugh.

They were lying in my opinion. The models couldn't be trusted but they crawled on the bed next to me, and all I could smell and feel were two incredibly sexy women. I couldn't see their faces, but their presence was felt big time. As long as the girls stayed true to their word, Eros was a happy man.

"Get ready for the unbelievable," said Crystal as she took off her nightgown. I couldn't see much in the dark, but I could tell that she was wearing the same bikini as Kendra and because I thought Crystal was more attractive, seeing her made me forget about everything that was negative.

"Close your eyes," she whispered as she kissed me on the lips. "And keep them shut until we say you can open them."

I obeyed. Crystal and Kendra then proceeded to rub their hands all over my chest. A minute later, I felt two hands massaging my thighs. Then I felt two hands fondling my feet. It had to be the most amazing sensation I'd ever felt in my entire life.

Maybe its the Alize that I just drank, but these chicks give a massage so mind-blowing, its ridiculous! Feels like there's four women rubbing me down! Wait a minute . . . FOUR WOMEN!

"Do we have company?" I asked, trying not to sound excited, but failed miserably.

"Yeah, baby," replied Kendra. "We invited some ladies to this party."

I was absolutely speechless. There was no way I could've been awake. I had to have been in the Playboy Mansion playing the role of Hugh Hefner, 'cause it was way too surreal. I really wanted to open my eyes, but if I was really dreaming, I didn't want to wake up. In my mind, I was celebrating as if I'd just won a hundred million bucks.

I'm about to have a menage et cinq! A MENAGE ET CINQ!

Crystal said, "I told you that this would be a night you'll remember for the rest of your life! Say hello to the ladies that will make it happen!"

In my sexiest voice, I said hello.

"Hello, Eros," replied a very high voice.

I said nothing. Her voice sounded so much like Nivea's. Why was I dreaming about her?

"Ola, my Puerto Rican stallion," said the fourth lady.

I said nothing again. Only Juanita called me that, and she was in New York. That was my confirmation that I was dreaming, 'cause there was no way in hell she was in Windsor.

Somebody turned on the lights.

"OK, open your eyes!" Kendra said.

I opened them, but I should've kept them closed. I went from having the greatest sensation to greatest shock of my life. Four angry women were staring at me. To my left standing next to Crystal was my weekend fling Nivea Davis. To my right standing next to Kendra was my amazingly unpredictable girlfriend Juanita Velez. I used to rock their world, and now they wanted to take me out of it. Both gave me a hard slap to the face to assure me that I was well awake.

Before I could react, I heard an annoying laugh near the living room. I looked, and there was Juanita's roommate and my number one nemesis Shanice Tucker. Of all the people in the planet Earth, why was she in the room? I turned back to my soon to be ex's. Why was Juanita in Windsor and not in New York? How did Nivea find me? When did she meet Nivea? How long have they known each other? How did they know the models? Who told Nivea and Juanita that I was here? What were these mad women going to do to me? These questions sped through my mind, as I was held captive. A living nightmare. Like the late Notorious B.I.G, I was ready to die.

"Nita, baby . . . Nivea sweetie . . . hi."

For a player who could talk his way out of any situation, I didn't know what to say. What could I say?

"Don't baby or sweetie us, you four-timing, lying, sonuva-ooooh!" snapped Nivea. "This is what you call being sick? This is what you call church? Boy, you'll wish that you were in the house of God after we're done with you!"

"Eros, baby," said Juanita, "of all the times I warned you about being unfaithful, you still went ahead with it. Not only with one woman, but three! Three, Eros? *THREE!* You really messed with the wrong women, boy!"

"Sweetie," I said to her, "I thought you were in New York. What happened?"

Juanita answered, "You would know if you listened to my message. But I see that you were quite occupied."

Snap. I knew I should've kept my phone on or at least check my voice mail.

I was in a no-win situation. Hell was about to break loose because Juanita, the queen of revenge was in the room. Her entire demeanor was frightening because she looked like a descendant of Queen Jezebel.

The story about her ex-boyfriend eating the dog food lasagna and Ex-Lax cake before an NHL playoff game made national headlines according to Teddy. I checked Google the day after he told me, and I read every article. The popular left-winger supposedly cheated on her just once. What was Juanita planning to do to me? Whatever it was, I needed a miracle to escape the inevitable. My conscience told me months ago to break up with Juanita, but the booty was too good. It was rare to find a woman who liked sex as much as yours truly. I thought that I could never be caught. Thought I was invincible. Now I was like Superman in a room full of Kryptonite.

"Y'know Eros, this probably looks totally planned out, but we just meet these ladies a moment ago," explained Crystal. "They came the same time room service arrived. At first, I was gonna prevent them from coming in, but I decided to listen to what they had to say. I told you earlier that Kendra and I deal with men who keep it real."

Kendra added, "And that's where you screwed up. Too bad, dog, it was going to be really, really, really good."

I gave the biggest pissed off sigh. I wasn't getting any, and I couldn't escape.

"Ladies, we're done with him," Crystal said to the party crashers. "He's all yours. So are the goodies if you want them."

"Sure, that would go great with our agenda," agreed Juanita. "And tying him up was a bonus! Thank you!"

Nivea said, "This is gonna be extra fun now!"

The models sat in the next king size bed; glowing in curiosity. Shanice approached my face with a grin bigger than Jimmy Walker's.

"*HAH!*" she yelled. "I knew you were skanky all along, Alexander! You were wrong to mess with close friends of Shanice Tucker!"

She started laughing in my face. Lord knows I hated her as much as Martin hated Pam in the TV show *Martin*.

"Get your foul-breath, hoochie drama self outta my face before I bite your ugly nose off!" I growled.

As a result, Shanice blew her breath into my face and moved away. I called her a you-know-what. She called me a piece of you-know-what. I'd never hit a female in my lifetime and if it wasn't for being tied up, I might've done something crazy. Shanice's presence made the situation twice as worse.

"Alright, that's enough!" Juanita snapped. "Eros, need I remind you that you're the one in bondage? Don't say anything negative about my girls or you'll suffer the consequences. Consider what you just said a strike one."

Whatever. Like I actually had a way of escape with the ghetto version of Thelma and Louise.

"We brought your clothes, Eros," Nivea sang as she brought my Nike sports bag from the living room. "I took back the Docker pants I got you yesterday. Good thing it wasn't worn, 'cause I'm getting my money back. I actually sacrificed buying groceries to buy the pants 'cause I thought you were worth it. Dang, was I ever wrong."

"And I took back the stuff I got you, which is quite a bit," added Juanita. "I had you looking real good for someone who always talked about being broke."

The models snickered at Juanita's remark. I didn't care, 'cause I was way past being embarrassed. Yes, I often told Juanita that I was low on funds after taking her out to a movie or dinner on the weekends. As a result, she would surprise me with some clothing from the retail store where she worked. In seven months, I received a Sean John jogging suit, three Tommy Hilfiger long-sleeve shirts, two pairs of Levi jeans, a pair of Timberlands, and a bottle of *Drakkar Noir* cologne, and my idiotic move was bringing it all to Windsor.

Juanita continued, "So that leaves whatever remains in the bag. There's some freaking expensive stuff in here, guy. Hope you have home insurance."

"Why?" I asked.

"Need you ask?" said Nivea. "Nita, want the underwear first?"

Juanita said yes, as she pulled out a pocketknife from her purse. Nivea gave her my six pairs of boxers and she start to cut. She shredded them all and they weren't the cheap Wal-Mart boxers either. However, I said nothing and just watched their joy as she cut the silk to pieces.

"Alright, what's next?" asked Juanita.

Nivea pulled out some of my socks, but Juanita said that losing them wouldn't be a big deal. Therefore, Nivea pulled out my Phat Farm sweater; it was a definite favorite, given to me from a woman I tutored at university.

"Ahhhh, nice sweater!" Juanita said. "Now ladies, if I was giving this boy clothes, and Nivea was giving him clothes, what are the chances that the rest of his wardrobe was purchased by other women he's slept with?"

Nivea answered, "Pretty high."

The others hummed in agreement.

"Wrong!" I lied. "For your information, that sweater is a Christmas gift from my dad. And who has proof that I've been with other women besides . . . forget it."

There was no use defending myself about not being a player. When I thought that I couldn't be caught, I did. Unless one of my boys suddenly entered the suite and ordered the women to leave, there was no means of escape. For the first time in my life, talking my way out of a situation was working against me.

"Yeah, you should quit while you're ahead," said Juanita. "Nobody knows when you're telling the truth or not. The amount of times I've called your crib at two a.m. and there was no answer tells me that you were doing more than just tutoring students. Sweater, please."

Nivea gave her the sweater.

"What, you're gonna cut that up, too?" I asked.

Juanita replied, "Nah. Too much work."

"Plus, this is much more fun!" smiled Nivea as she showed me a bottle of ketchup.

Juanita held up my white sweater and Nivea squeezed the red sauce all over it! I was so furious; I bit my tongue to prevent myself from cussing. The models grinned in amazement, and Shanice was laughing so obnoxiously I wanted to throw her out the window.

"You mind putting a muzzle on that bulldog you call Shanice?" I snapped. "There no pets allowed in this suite anyway! Matter of fact, just give her a shot and put her to sleep!"

"I warned you, boy, don't dis any of my girls in here!" Juanita said. "That's strike two."

I was pissing off the queen of revenge, which wasn't good but whenever Shanice opened her mouth, my blood boiled. Had to try to ignore her, but that was like me trying not to look at a nude woman.

"Wanna do the next article of clothing?" Nivea asked Juanita as she passed her the ketchup and held up a pair of jeans that I got from a former Raptors cheerleader.

"With pleasure," she answered.

The jeans were drenched with Heinz. The ex's took turns squirting ketchup on my blue Nautica shirt, black Roc-a-Wear sweater, two Nike fitted caps, three beaters, and two Ralph Lauren shirts, all given to me from former bed buddies. I had more clothes at home, but as for this weekend, I was officially out of clothes except for socks and the boxers I was wearing and, to top it off, I'd brought my favorite clothes too! Being a materialistic freak, I was horrifically furious! However, I kept my mouth on mute, even though I thought of every wicked thing I could call Nivea and Juanita but I wanted to make it through the night in one piece.

"Done?" I asked while glaring at them.

"Actually no," Nivea answered, showing me a bottle of Michael Jordan cologne. "Nita, did you buy him this?"

"No," said Juanita, "but man, Eros be smelling real sexy when he puts that on! Let's finish it off!"

I thought that they were gonna empty the two-thirds full bottle in the bathroom sink, but I was way wrong. Starting from my feet, Nivea sprayed the cologne and worked her way up. Every part of my body was soaked except the back. The smell was so powerful that I started sneezing and I told myself that I would never wear cologne again. When Nivea got to my head, she drenched my hair, sprayed it through my ears, then the cheeks, and caught me off-guard and sprayed it directly in my eyes. That is when I lost it!

For the next ten seconds, I called Nivea and Juanita every profane word that I could think of. I couldn't hold it anymore, and I knew that I was gonna pay for it but my eyes were burning like mad. Nivea looked like she wanted to kick the crap outta me, but Shanice pulled her back. Juanita just shook her head.

"Strike three," she said quietly as she pulled out her digital camera from her purse.

Juanita walked around the bed and took pictures of me from every angle. I had to ask her what she was trying to do.

"Creating a portfolio for megastud.com!" Nivea answered.

"Megastud.com?" I snapped, still squinting my eyes to look at her.

Juanita said, "It's a website full of men . . . seen by men."

"YOU WOULDN'T!"

"Try me. Smile for the camera!"

Juanita continued snapping. Crystal and Kendra were lying on the other bed laughing hard. The queen of revenge was about to send pictures of me to a gay website, and I got scared. I could take pain, get embarrassed, go without food for a week, and even give up sex for a few days but the last thing I wanted in this world was for people to think that Eros Alexander, Jr. was a homosexual. I had to get Juanita to reconsider, even if it meant begging.

"Oh my, this is too hilarious!" said Kendra, still laughing. "But this stench is too strong, I need some fresh air."

"Me too," grinned Crystal. "Take it easy, ladies. Stay strong. Eros, have a nice life."

They exchanged farewells with the women of payback and bounced. I ignored the models 'cause they were worthless to me at that point, and they were the reason why I was held hostage. Hasta la vista. My focus was on Juanita Velez.

"Juanita baby, Nivea sweetheart," I began. "If you want an apology from me, here it is: I'm sorry! I'm sorry for playing you both. If you feel that torturing me is the way to get back at me, I can live with that. Just please, please, please, please don't put my pictures on a gay website! Don't do me like that, yo!"

Shanice said, "Don't give in to him, girls!"

Juanita and Nivea said nothing.

"Give in? I'm already going back to Toronto with no clothes!" I continued. "I'm not even begging you to forgive me. If y'all wanna a faithful man, I'm obviously not the guy. I'm just asking you not to send those pictures. If you don't send them, I'll be a good sport and let y'all do whatever to me, meaning that after tonight I'll keep it confidential. If you send them, there will be hell to pay. I'll sue all three of you for psychological damage, assault and bodily harm! You wouldn't want that drama, right?"

"We can plead insanity and get away with it!" said Nivea. "You gave us emotional damage and stress!"

"Wouldn't work against Allen Dennis."

Allen Dennis was the best criminal lawyer in Toronto, top five in the country. Far as I knew, he hadn't lost a case in court in more than a decade. Moreover, I knew him.

"Allen Dennis?" snapped Shanice. "Cut the crap! You can't afford Allen Dennis!"

I said, "No, but he and my dad talk frequently. They've been close friends since high school. I got his number on my cell phone. Trust me, Nita, you don't need more bad publicity. That hockey player gave you grace. I won't!"

The girls were silent. Even Shanice the Beast sucked her teeth as if they lost the battle. Juanita started pressing buttons on the back of her digicam.

"Alright, I won't send the pictures," she grumbled. "But that doesn't mean we're done with you. We're gonna finish up and leave. Just remember this, Eros: whatever happens to you tonight is nothing compared to the pain of being used and betrayed."

Boo hoo. I honestly didn't feel bad for cheating on them.

Twenty minutes later, duct tape was over my mouth. From head to toe, I was smothered in chocolate syrup, strawberries, honey, and ketchup. That was after the women powdered my face with mascara, puckered my lips with Cover Girl lipstick, and painted my finger and toenails with polish. They laughed as if Chris Tucker was in the room making jokes. In addition, to add to the misery, they turned up the thermostat to the highest degree. It was about to get more funky than a George Clinton concert.

I looked at the women as they prepared to leave. If my stares could kill, I would be executed in a place where the death penalty is prohibited. Juanita and Nivea gave me their last curses and disses. Shanice the Beast slapped her booty and told me to kiss it. Then they left the suite and out of my life.

The torture was over, but the misery continued. I could not scream for help, couldn't break free, couldn't go to the bathroom and I had to do number one and two. I was hot, itchy, sticky, and smelly, feeling like an Oh Henry bar being hit by the sun and the CD in the stereo was skipping like crazy.

My only hope was the Phat Five. Sooner, later, or much later they would enter the suite to untie me. Then they would beat me down for not showing up to the showcase, messing up the bed, and trying to make the crib like a Playboy Mansion.

CHAPTER 81

Q

We danced for an hour without rest. Felt as I had burnt more calories in that span than the entire month of March. Whitney and I couldn't resist it because the chemistry was getting stronger but after the thirteenth straight song, we decided to get a drink.

The line-up at the bar was long, and there weren't enough bartenders to cater to everyone in good speed. I was waiting patiently for service while observing the crowd for Ajani, Eros, and Teddy. All three were M.I.A less than a half hour from the showcase. Surprisingly, I was concerned but not shocked.

Whitney was next to me, resting her head on my left upper arm. Then she pushed her nose to my shirt, trying to inhale my cologne. That led to her caressing my hand and massaging my lower arm, which felt really nice. Either she was really tipsy, horny, or both.

"Wow, I haven't danced like that in a while," admitted Whitney. "And you kept up pretty good for a White boy."

I grinned. "I did watch a lot of *Soul Train* growing up."

"That or you've grooved with a lot of Black women."

To say the least.

I asked her if she had seen her girls come in the club yet.

"No," she answered. "Nivea and her girls shoulda been here by now. Where's your crew?"

"Dunno. Could be on the line or mixed up in some drama. I haven't heard from them at all."

There was an awkward silence. Suddenly, Whitney's hand caress became more stimulating.

She asked, "Did I tell you that I love the cologne you're wearing?"

"Yeah, but I love repetition."

For fun, she asked me again in a sexier voice. Said the scent was like an aphrodisiac.

"Thanks," I answered. "It's done its purpose."

"Is it eleven o' clock yet?"

"In twenty minutes."

"That long? Got cash or a credit card on you?"

If I didn't have cash, I wouldn't be buying drinks. I asked her why.

"Let's go to the hotel across the street."

I thought I was daydreaming. Had to ask her to repeat what she said to make sure I wasn't tripping.

"Yeah, hotel," Whitney confirmed. "I want it now, and I don't like it in public places. I know the timing is bad, but I'm ready to go."

"Right now?"

"Right now."

Whitney was serious. She was ready, and suddenly I wasn't sure what to do. K.J was performing in minutes, and I was the only Phat Fiver present. I had to choose between supporting a friend in his finest hour or the weekend affair of a lifetime.

"It's up to you," she said. "But right now, I'll please you like a buffet to an empty stomach."

The chances of me never seeing K.J perform again were close to none. The chances of me getting with Whitney after Saturday was close to none. I had to make a very wise decision.

As soon as I closed the door of the hotel room, the passion began. Lust took full control as we locked lips and undressed at the same time. It was exactly like my single days in college, when girls dropped the silk as soon as they knew my income potential. This time however, I was married and actually feeling Whitney. However, I was too caught up in the moment to think about the former. Things were moving so quickly and I felt unprepared. I had to pee real bad because of the three rum and cokes I drank earlier. I didn't want to let loose of her, but I had no choice.

"Alright, hurry up," Whitney said after I told her that nature called. "You got protection?"

"No doubt," I said with the smoothest voice possible. "Be right back."

After emptying my bladder, I opened my wallet to find the five-star condom that I kept just in case Katrina didn't take her daily birth control pill. Been a long time since I had to use one, which explained why it was covered by a bunch of old receipts. When I quickly pulled it out, a bunch of paper and plastic fell to the floor. Perfect timing. I felt like leaving them on the floor because a horny woman was waiting for me, but I decided to pick them up. More than likely Whitney was gonna use the bathroom and I didn't want her going through my stuff. It was a good idea 'cause in the midst of the stuff was my wallet-sized wedding photo. The last thing I wanted to see.

I wanted to put it away quickly, but I gave it a good look. Katrina was drop dead gorgeous on our wedding day. Never saw anyone more beautiful in my life. When I saw her walking down the aisle, I believed that I hit jackpot that was worth more than any NBA multi-million dollar contract.

I laughed when I thought about the drama that took place that day. My family couldn't get over the fact that none of my four groomsmen were White. My parents tried to persuade me in changing the party, but I said no way. The Phat Five played second fiddle to nobody, and they represented like true bred-drin. Well, most of them did. Eros was the best man, and he threatened to stop the wedding from going forth. He was drunk well before the ceremony and mad that I didn't reconsider single hood. I almost went ballistic on my best friend, but Ajani and the cousins took control of the matter. They promised to give Eros an old school beat down if he messed up the wedding. He sobered and behaved real quickly. Even gave a half-decent speech at the reception.

Conviction really hit me when I thought about the ceremony. Katrina and I wrote our own vows. I remember her saying that she would stick with me through thick and thin, which meant so much because my NBA dream was shattered. Other than the suspect voice message on her cell, Katrina was an A-plus wife, putting up with nine months of my foolishness. One of the main things I stressed in my vow was to remain faithful to Katrina as long as we were together, and I was a minute away from breaking it.

My erection was gone. I no longer cared what Eros thought: my wife was innocent of adultery until proven guilty. As for me, I couldn't let my marriage get any worse.

I came out the bathroom to see Whitney naked under a blanket that covered her from the waist down. My erection came back. I was in a mega tough position.

"It's about time!" she cried. "Are you covered?"

I was wearing only boxers, which wasn't a good idea. I sat next to where she was lying.

"Whitney, I'm married," I confessed without looking at her.

"Oh, Lord," she said as if she'd been in the same position before. "So does this mean were not gonna do it?"

I looked at her as if she just turned purple.

"Huh?" I asked in shock.

Whitney sat up and placed her hands on my chest, giving it a nice caress.

"Normally, I'd slap you in the face and leave, but I want you and like I said before, I'm not looking for a relationship while I'm in school. I've had one-night stands with married men, so it's not a big deal."

Then she kissed me from my chest to my bellybutton.

"It's . . . all . . . up . . . to you."

Why couldn't she slap my face and leave? My flesh wanted to become the male slut from college again, but my mind was anti-Eros. It was hard, but I got up from the bed as she moved towards you-know-where.

"Too many consequences." I said. "Sorry."

Whitney sighed with frustration and disappointment. She reached for her bra on the floor to put it back on.

"Don't be sorry," said Whitney, "except for not telling me the truth from the beginning! How many lies have you told me this weekend?"

I told her that the stuff we talked about on Friday evening and at dinner was all truth except for me being single. Also added that Eros made up the story about the SARS incident because he wanted me to have an affair, and that I was dumb enough to roll with it.

"Well, I did find you attractive," she said. "Still do. It takes men lots of will power to resist sex, and you did it. You missed out."

I did not want to think about it.

"I don't know why you men put yourselves in these situations," Whitney continued. "It must be the single friends y'all hang with. Dang, now I don't want Eros getting involved with Nivea. Dude's gotta be a player."

I replied, "No comment. Looks like I wasted cash on this room, and I am missing my boy's performance. There's no way we'll get back in that club."

"We can watch the showcase here. It should be starting just now."

"Good. In the meantime, I'm gonna go to the lobby and have a smoke."

"All right. Man, Q, you got that Cool Water scent all up in this room! While you're gone, I'm gonna see what's on pay-per-view to help satisfy me."

She was definitely a freak.

I left the room after getting dressed. Pulled out Katrina's cell phone and slipped my wedding ring back on my finger. Hoped she had my phone 'cause I was ready to call her.

CHAPTER 82

AJANI

Machete and I said nothing from the penthouse to the parking lot.
Wondered what he had to say.
Wondered if I beat enough crap outta Rancel.
Wondered if the drama was about to end or start a next chapter.
Once we got to the lot, Machete lit up a cigarette and broke the silence.
"I always knew Rancel envied you," he began, "but I wanted to see how far he'd take it. When you were more productive in getting stuff done, I hoped that he would improve his game but Rancel just complained about how much time he put in getting my empire established and how he's too old to do the stuff you be doing. I only let him run on about it 'cause he's been with me from the beginning. Seen?"
I didn't respond. Just looked and listened.
"Rancel believes that he should have half the empire when I was the mastermind all along," Machete continued. "Yes, my cousin's been doing this with me from Kingston to New York to Toronto, been through the drama, the tough times, the good times, but that don't make a man fully eligible to run a function! Rancel's blood and I love him, but I ain't stupid enough to let anybody run my business. Yet, he is telling family that I treat him like crap and not giving him a fair share. He hasn't earned it yet! Ridiculous!"
I said, "Blood is thicker than water, but that doesn't mean it's more pure."
"Seen . . . Rancel threw me off with the business card. I usually know when something is a scam, but it actually looked legit. And by the way you were progressing, what'd you expect me to think?"
"You could've confronted me first!"
"Perhaps, but I don't trust anyone, Bethel. Nobody. The only people I ever trusted were my parents. I was a hot-blooded twelve year old who respected my daddy to the fullest and loved my mummy dearly. One day, my daddy came home

drunk as hell, argued with my mummy and beat the hell outta her. I was so mad at my father, I got a machete from the backyard and chopped off the same hand he used to beat her, which explains my nickname . . . My mother died two days later from too much body damage . . . I don't trust no one, Bethel!"

I was speechless. Machete never talked about his past other than dealing. My past wasn't that disturbing.

Machete's phone rang.

"Martinez," he said before speaking to him in Spanish.

I never heard him speak Spanish before; he was fluent at it too. There was a lot I didn't know about Mr. Deverow and at that point I stopped caring. It was all about my survival.

Machete hung up the phone.

He said, "Martinez said that whatever happened at his club yesterday will be forgiven if you give the money back. He just arrived in Windsor from the tunnel."

That was the best news I heard all day.

"That's it?" I asked. "The cash's in my trunk."

Didn't take me long to open the lift gate of the Escalade and grab the briefcase. It was a good thing I didn't take any cash from it. I handed the case to Machete as he quickly opened it to make sure all was legit.

"Good," said Machete. "Now, back to our discussion, I know you and Rancel have a mutual hate relationship, but there must be some truth to what he presented."

I snapped, "Chete, there's no truth to his s—"

"Everybody's got goals and intentions, Bethel! What are yours?"

I asked him if he wanted to hear my long or short term.

"Whatever," Machete replied.

"Well, it's definitely not to run my own G.H thing, 'cause I'm sick of this crap!"

There. I got it off my chest.

"It was a thrill when I started it," I continued, "but now, I'm so close to leaving it all. The money's too good to leave it completely, but man, I think about it every freaking day and it's not because we're criminals who could be behind bars or dead, but I want to see my son grow up and become a man, an honest man who goes for success the right way. Obviously if it was up to you, I wouldn't be here telling you this right now. Its one thing to have enemies, but with cats that you work with, for me, that's a lose-lose situation!"

"No doubt."

No apologies from Machete. Didn't expect any.

"Well, I gotta meet with Martinez, then its back to Toronto tonight," he said as he looked at his Rolex. "We needed to clear this out in the open. Now I can move on."

Was it intentional that Machete said "I" instead of "we?"

"Taking your cousin with you?" I asked.

"Perhaps," he replied. "If he's still alive."

I don't know why I asked him that. Maybe I wanted to beat him up again.

The drug lord went back to the hotel. I made my way to my ride, feeling fortunate that I survived Saturday. Yet, the night was not over, so I kept my guard up.

Opened the hood of the truck to make sure that a bomb wasn't planted in my engine, ready to explode when I started it. There was no bomb under the hood so I checked the interior for the same thing and found nothing. It was now time to bounce.

As I started the vehicle, I realized that it would be a miracle for me to catch the showcase at Club V. I didn't plan to miss the event so I had to quickly freshen up at the hotel and hopefully catch the final minutes. It was a long shot, but I had to make the effort.

When I drove in reverse, I noticed that something was freaked up in the front of the ride. I knew right away that it was a flat tire. Drama continued. I stepped out to discover it was the front right tire, flat as an airplane runway. It wasn't stripped, but the cap was unscrewed and left on the ground. Machete set me up again!

Next thing I knew, I fell to the cement, thanks to a piece of wood smashed across my head.

CHAPTER 83

Katrina Quintino was startled when she heard the cell phone rang. The ring tone sounded like Missy Elliott's *Get Ya Freak On*, and it was the first time she heard it all weekend. It took away the suspicion that her husband had women calling him and that Q really did work plenty of overtime hours. The caller ID showed the number of her cell that Q accidentally took to Windsor. Katrina wanted to talk to him, but his timing was off. Nevertheless, she answered the phone.

"Hello?" asked Katrina in a tone that intended to sound like she was still angry.

"Hey, baby. Whazzup?"

"Nuttin."

"Where you at? Sounds like Luther singing in the background."

"Oh, I'm on the 401, coming from a *waiting to exhale* evening with the girls," Katrina lied.

"OK."

She asked him if he was having fun at Jam Fest. Q said no, and she wanted to know the reason.

"Cause I upset you, plus I've been a terrible husband. Trina, if I would've spent some quality time with you before this weekend, my going to Windsor wouldn't have been an issue."

Katrina hummed in agreement.

"So, starting next week, I'm gonna do less overtime. In addition, I'll book next weekend off to spend time with you. I promise."

"I'll hold you to that."

"Do it. I'm for real this time, 'cause I'm really, really sorry for all of my actions this week. Will you forgive me?"

"Q . . . of course I forgive you . . . I have to—"

"And I gotta ask . . . oh, my bad, I cut you off."

She was so used to her husband interrupting her speech. Katrina told him to go ahead with his statement, but he insisted that she spoke first.

"I have to apologize for not telling you that Leron was coming to T.O this weekend."

"*What?*" shouted Q, "This weekend? Why you ain't said nothing?"

"Cause I just found out on Thursday morning and I wanted to surprise you. But you made me so mad, I didn't wanna say jack to you that day."

"Understood, but if you told me, I would've changed my mind and stayed home! I've yet to meet Leron."

"You would've stayed and missed Jam Fest?"

There was a long pause before Q said, "Probably not."

"Exactly."

"So that's the dude who left a message on your phone! You never told me Leron sounded like Barry White!"

She laughed. "His voice is pretty deep."

"That's not funny, Trina! He had me thinking that you were cheating on me! I was tripping!"

Katrina stopped laughing and began to cough. Q asked if she was all right.

"Yeah," she answered. "Yes, sweetie, that was Leron on the voice mail. He stayed at the apartment on Thursday night."

"When's he leaving?"

"Sunday, but he'll be back in Syracuse by the time you come back."

"Dang . . . But yo, how about this idea, baby?"

Q suggested that they go to Syracuse for the upcoming weekend to visit her cousin. Of course, Katrina had a large grin on her face. Her husband was being sensitive to her needs and interested in their marriage again. Just like the Damon Quintino of old.

"That's a great idea, Damon!" she exclaimed. "I really forgive you now."

"Oh . . . thanks. All right, baby luv, K.J's about to perform, so I'll call you later. I miss you lots. Love you."

"I miss and love you too," said Katrina softly as a tear fell down her cheek.

She hung up the phone and put it in her purse. Katrina no longer wanted to drink the glass of white wine she was holding. Conviction made its entrance, and suddenly she felt nauseous. All Katrina wanted to do was go home.

A dark-skinned man wearing shoulder-length dreadlocks and a goatee entered the living room and sat right next to Katrina in the sofa. He gave her a big smile. Katrina barely smiled back.

"Everything alright?" he asked.

"I just spoke to Damon," she replied.

"Your husband? What, he took two minutes out of his life to give you attention?"

Katrina did not answer. Instead, she got up from the sofa.

Shocked by her move, he asked, "What? Where are you going?"

She answered, "I can't do this again. I'm going home."

"You can't drive home."

"Yes I can. I only had a glass, I'm fine."

"So what's up? He apologized and now everything is cool? That White man doesn't know how to take care of you. Otherwise you wouldn't be here with me!"

"Look, last night was a mistake, a big mistake."

"Like I just said, you are here with me, Trina. If yesterday was a big mistake . . . I can't stop you if you wanna go. If neglect, miscommunication, and dissatisfaction are what you want, then go ahead."

Upset at his remark, Katrina marched towards the closet to put on her jacket. The man got up and followed her.

"Look, I'm sorry," he said as he held her hand. "That came out wrong. I just don't want you to leave."

Katrina released herself from his grip.

"Hey, just because your marriage didn't work doesn't mean I'm gonna head the same route, all right?" she snapped. "Everybody makes mistakes. It's all about how you fix them. Good night!"

Then she left.

CHAPTER 84

AJANI

Somebody slapped me hard in the face. Twice. That's how I woke up.

My arms were behind my back and my hands were in metal cuffs. I was sitting forcefully in a chair with my chest and legs strapped to it by chains. The bulletproof vest was not on me. The back of my head was bleeding and I had a serious migraine.

The person who slapped me was Ricardo Estafan. Next to him was his big brother Martinez and cousin Big Cement. It was a freaked up situation indeed.

"So, how does it feel to be in a hostage position, Ajah?" Ricardo shouted.

I ignored him and looked at Martinez.

I asked him, "So this is what you call forgiveness?"

"This has nothing to do with forgiveness, Mr. Bethel," Martinez answered as he lit up a Cuban cigar. "I forgave you for what happened at the club, like the miscommunication that led to a foolish deal. But outside the club, like what you did to my cousin and not returning the cash when asked, that calls for punishment."

Looking at Big Cement, I saw a bruised up giant who was ready to crucify me. Payback to him was looking real sweet.

"As for punishment, I'll leave it to my association," Martinez concluded. "I'm taking my hoes and going back to Detroit."

His strippers were waiting by the exit, which was about twenty feet away. So was Machete Deverow. The guy couldn't even look at me. Deep down inside, I felt that he knew that I wasn't a backstabber. Obviously, Machete was, and he didn't care because he trusted nobody. I wanted him to burn in hell.

I said, "Tell that punk you call a brother that whatever goes around comes around."

He knew that I was talking about Machete. Martinez grinned and told his family to make the torture twice as painful. Then he left with his tricks and Judas Deverow.

"Now the fun begins!" Ricardo yelled as he turned the chair and I around to face the opposite direction.

I saw the Detroit River and its skyline and realized that I was on the roof of the Hilton. The only thing I feared in life was heights, and I tried hard not to show it.

There were also three more people on the roof. Two guys and a woman. They were quiet, looked like Estafans, and strapped with guns. I figured they were spectators, 'cause cats like Ricardo and Big Cement needed no bodyguards. The woman looked very familiar, but I could not remember who she was, like I actually had quality time to think about it.

"You're in a no-win situation now!" Ricardo laughed. "When you mess with family, there's no escaping death. Not this time and never again!"

Big Cement held up the vest that they ripped off my chest.

"This crap can't help you here!" he roared.

Then they all started laughing, except for the lady gangsta who gave a small grin.

Ricardo delivered a sharp punch across my left jaw. He laughed again as if he was watching a George Lopez comedy special, and then punched me in the right jaw. The pain was agonizing, more than usual because I couldn't fight back. He said he was just giving me the warm-up licks before Big Cement took over. Wonderful. His next move was hard kick to my chest, which made me fall backwards with the chair. Then he kicked me twice on my side, and added three more punches to my nose, jaw, and stomach. I knew then why people preferred a bullet to the head over torture. If they were going to kill me, just fire a bullet already.

"I just had to give you a taste of what you did to my cousin," said Ricardo. "I'm done."

Not before dropping a big glob of saliva in my eye. I never felt anything so nasty in my life.

It was Big Cement's turn. This was a one-sided tag team event. He pulled up the chair and looked at me straight in the eyes.

"It would be so easy just to shoot you, but that's no fun," he said. "Now you're gonna find out why they call me Big Cement."

How fortunate. The mammoth lifted the metal chair and yours truly over his head. For three seconds I saw a magnificent view of Detroit. Then he threw me down on my side like an Olympic bodybuilder throws barbells. If the chair was wood, then I might've broken loose due to the impact. Unfortunately, it was metal. Wished my ribs were metal, 'cause I heard and felt them crack and all I could do was take the pain.

My misery was providing great entertainment for the Estafan family. Big Cement wanted to hype them up some more so he picked me up again, this time by my wounded side. I groaned like Serena Williams in a tennis match, and I rarely expressed pain. Then he threw me forward several feet, and the way I landed caused an injury to my back and neck. The throwing game continued at least four more times. The chair never loosened for me to break free and I was more and more convinced that Saturday, March 17th, 2003 was my last day on earth.

During the ruckus, I allowed my mind to wonder because it helped me think less about the pain, I wondered if K.J, Teddy, Eros, and Q would be the pallbearers at my funeral. I thought about never being able to have Savannah Shaw as my wife and I thought about not seeing A.J grow through childhood. That made me shed a tear. If I survived the beat down, which was pretty much impossible, I promised God that I would leave the drug game forever but how many times could I escape prison or death in a lifetime, let alone a weekend?

Apparently, I wasn't the only tearful one. The female Estafan started crying for unknown reasons. All I could barely see or hear was Ricardo yelling at her in Spanish. If it was Savannah sobbing, I would understand, but the woman didn't know me. It was quite annoying, but she managed to be less dramatic after Ricardo said whatever to her.

Finally, the tossing had stopped, but the torture continued. Big Cement gave me his contribution of punches and kicks. By the time he finished, I felt like a puppy ran over by a car but not fully dead. I couldn't imagine what I looked like. I had never been beaten up so badly. After Ricardo loosened me from the chair, I had zero strength to fight back. Not like I would in a five-to-one situation, with the five owning arsenal. I could fight, but I wasn't Jet Li. My hands and feet were still tied anyway. Big Cement grabbed my feet and Ricardo had my wrists. What I feared greatly was about to become reality.

"Now we're gonna show you why we came to the roof!" Ricardo shouted.

They carried me to the edge. I was so scared I almost pissed my pants.

"Shoot me!" I pleaded. "Shoot me before you throw me!"

"Why?" asked Big Cement. "So it could look like a murder?"

One of their spectators unlocked the cuffs. Then they held my body over the edge of the roof. If I wasn't afraid of heights, I would've taken the crap like a man but I had a hard time breathing, and I didn't have asthma.

Traffic was heavy on Riverside Drive. Judging from the height of the hotel, I would die before hitting the concrete. At least I hoped.

"Estafan family," Ricardo said, "get ready to bounce as soon as we start swinging him. Traffic is busy right now, but once it dies down a bit, we are throwing him in front of a car to make it look like an accident. Get ready!"

It was over for me, just seconds away from hell.

CHAPTER 85

Another dynamic sermon was finished and an invitation to the altar was extended at Greater Faith Temple in Mississauga. Savannah Shaw went to the altar on Friday night to receive salvation. Saturday was the opportunity to receive prayer on an unsettling issue.

Many people arrived there before Savannah, so she had to wait her turn. She didn't have to worry about A.J because her sister was supervising him. In addition, he had been sleeping on the pew since nine p.m.

After talking to Ajani late Friday night on the phone, Savannah had trouble sleeping for bittersweet reasons. Sweet for the overwhelming joy she was feeling from her spiritual transformation and bitter because she felt that something was not right with her man. Yet, she had no clear idea of what it was. Was Ajani in trouble with someone or the law? Was he feeling ill? Was he being unfaithful? Those were the three biggest questions that bothered her for so long. That is why she needed to pray with someone about her concerns. Savannah stood on the spoken word, which stated that when two agree on earth concerning anything asked it would be done by the Lord above.

"How can I help you, my sister?"

Savannah opened her eyes in surprise. She was so caught up in prayer that she didn't realize that the evangelist was standing in front of her.

"Oh," she said to her, "I need prayer for someone . . . my son's father."

"Okay," the evangelist replied. "Anything in particular?"

"Well . . . not really, but . . . well, yes. He and I have been together for a long time. He's a great man and an excellent father, but . . ."

Tears started flowing down Savannah's cheeks.

She continued, "I just feel that something's not right with him. Not mentally, but . . . I do not know, like he's in trouble or in danger. I can't explain it because I don't know what it is."

"Well," said the evangelist, "we can pray that God will protect him from whatever situation he's facing. Nothing is impossible for God."

Savannah nodded.

"What's his name? Is he saved?"

"Ajani . . . and no, he's not saved. I can't get him to come anywhere near church."

The evangelist smiled and said, "Remember, you can only do so much. Leave the rest to the Lord."

The two held hands and bowed their heads. The prayer was powerful. Savannah felt her faith increase tremendously as they agreed about God having his way in Ajani's life.

CHAPTER 86

AJANI

They started swinging me towards the street. Although I'd given up already, I was still terrified because there were no more answers of escape. I was going to be squashed like road kill in a matter of seconds.

Ricardo told everyone to head out. Guess it was time for my fate but after I heard the door slam the men started swinging slower. Apparently, someone didn't go downstairs. The lady Estafan remained. Ricardo yelled at her in Spanish. She yelled back at him with tears streaming down her face. Then Big Cement roared something to her, and she lashed back at him. Cement got angry and looked like he wanted to smack her.

Lord knows I wanted to understand what they were saying. Hoped it was about sparing me, but who was I fooling? The woman didn't know me, and I didn't know her. Whatever they were venting about, it prolonged my death. Didn't know if that was a good or bad thing.

The shouting match continued without a word of English. They still were swinging me. Through my pain and sudden nausea, I noticed that Lady Estafan was looking at me constantly. So was Ricardo, but it was an expression of strong disbelief. Cement had his usual look of hate. I was very confused to the point where I had to force myself to take a good look at the woman.

She definitely looked familiar, as if I was supposed to know her. Especially when I saw her slim light-skinned face and nose ring. Even the way she screamed sounded familiar but her blonde hair threw me off, and it shouldn't have because any woman could wear a blonde wig. I did know one thing for sure: in a positive or negative way, I did something to Lady Estafan because she didn't look at me like a stranger.

Suddenly in the midst of the quarrel, Big Cement gave me a harsh look and said, "This punk wouldn't save his own mama."

Finally the dialogue was switched back to English.

"What the hell do you know?" yelled Lady Estafan. "This guy saved Manuel's life! Yes, your son, Ricardo, and your god son, Cortez!"

I thought I was tripping from the beat down. Manuel?

I looked at the woman again. I couldn't believe my eyes, it was Carla, the mother of the kid I saved on Friday night! Manuel was Ricardo's son and Big Cement's godson!

I'd been through many crazy experiences in my young life, but absolutely nothing could compare to this. I was in the midst of an actual miracle.

"What time did this happen yesterday?" asked Ricardo.

Carla looked very annoyed at her baby father's question.

"What, were you high again when I was talking to you?" she snapped. "It was late yesterday afternoon when it happened. My God, Ricardo, I'm talking about your son, not a freaking stranger! Why would I lie about this?"

I could've said that Ricardo was high as a kite and screwing a stripper yesterday, but I wasn't stupid. I wanted my freedom. The way Carla spoke to him, it sounded like he hadn't been a very good father. Ricardo calmed down tremendously, looking slightly embarrassed.

To confirm Carla's story, he asked me to describe his son Manuel and the entire situation at the mall. I felt the extreme pain of my jaws with every word I said to describe him and the drama but it was well worth the pain.

"Put him down," Ricardo said to his cousin. "Call the family; tell them to wait for us."

They placed me down and sat me up against the ledge that I almost went over. Ricardo stared me in the eye while Cement made the phone call.

He said, "You are the luckiest man ever and I'm very lucky to have a living son today. Thank you."

I nodded my head without smiling. Mind was still in shock about what took place.

"Machete paid us big money to kill you," he continued. "If I were you, I wouldn't go back to Toronto. If you do, stay on the D.L 'cause they can't know that you are alive. Change your name, look, whatever. Long as they never find out. You hear me?"

Nodded my head again, he didn't have to tell me twice. I was officially done with dealing. Forever.

I looked at Big Cement. Not one to express emotions, he nodded his gigantic head at me as an expression of gratitude. I didn't return the gesture.

Carla stood next to her baby daddy. I looked at her and said thank you.

"No, thank you," she said. "Please forgive me for not acting sooner."

"At least you weren't too late, which is more than enough," I replied.

"Wow, we jacked you up," said Ricardo. "Let's get you some help."

Big Cement carried me over his shoulder as they rushed me to the hospital.

CHAPTER 87

K.J.

Forgiveness.
 I couldn't get X-Secula's song out of my head. That was good for the fact that the lyrics were positive and the delivery was outstanding but bad because I wanted to be angry-minded for the showcase. Yet, I couldn't resist the optimism.
 I was sitting in a soundproof private room exclusively for me while showtime was only minutes away. I had an actual hostess that catered to my material needs: food, liquor if I wanted it, water, batteries for the Discman. Being a celebrity definitely had its privileges. Of course, a celebrity had to give and take as well. Since I entered the club at nine, I had interviews with The Source, XXL, MTV, and Much Music. I gave and took more pounds than a British currency exchange. Signed autographs for women who saw me on TV Friday night. It was a good thing I didn't own a cell phone, otherwise it would ring non-stop but the experience was worth it, especially if I took the title from Roderick Bailey.
 I turned the Discman on and began free styling to a beat. Then I turned it off after a minute cause I couldn't concentrate. I thought about whether there were cameras hidden in the room. Thought about letting Eros, Q, and Ajani come backstage, but it wasn't a good idea 'cause I was already being distracted. Moreover, I thought about Kaitlyn, wishing that she were my woman. The hate that I was feeling for Roderick and Bianca had temporarily disappeared.
 Just when I decided to close my eyes and try praying, I heard a soft knock on the door. Looked at my watch and it was three minutes to eleven. Stage time wasn't until eleven-fifteen. Maybe it was my video girl wannabe hostess wondering if I needed anything.
 "Come in," I said.
 The door opened and I saw a video girl wannabe, but it wasn't my hostess. It was Bianca James.

Happiness aborted. The hate was back.

The way that she was dressed, Bianca looked like she was competing with Melissa Ford for Canada's favorite Ebony eye candy. A year ago, wearing a mini-skirt half way up the booty made me a happy guy with plenty of good times to follow in the bedroom. Instead, I glared at her like a mad pit bull.

"Hi," Bianca said softly.

I replied, "Roderick's room is down the hall."

"I'm here to talk to you."

"Really? The lady of hip-hop superstar Verbal Pain wants to talk to little ol' me? My God, I'm nothing compared to him. He's so bling, so handsome, so talented, and you're talking to me? Man, I'm blessed!"

I glared at her again, sucked my teeth, and sat in the sofa.

Bianca said, "I deserved that."

"What the hell do you want?" I snapped. "I'm busy."

"I know, Kellen. I'm sorry, but I don't know when I'll see you again after tonight, and this couldn't wait any longer . . ."

She paused. Then she started crying. Perfect.

"Sleeping with Roderick was a big mistake," sobbed Bianca. "I thought that it was the right thing for me, but I was wrong. It took me seven months to admit it. Oh Kellen, when we were together you were so right when you said that your friend was changing, but I refused to believe you. Roderick is a totally different guy since he hit the jackpot."

Tell me something I don't know, chicken head.

That's what I wanted to say to Bianca, but I stayed on mute. Tears were making her look hideous, messing up her thick mascara.

She continued, "Having money and fame is great and all, but to give it up for someone who loves you, supports you, and treats you like royalty? That is hard to replace after losing it. That someone was you, Kellen Jamal."

My, Bianca had oodles of revelation for me.

"Um hmmm," I agreed without looking at her.

"If I could turn back time, I would've never gone for Roderick and instead I would've treated you like a king. I'm not asking you to take me back . . . I'm just really, really sorry that I hurt you."

I never had seen Bianca cry so much before now. Either she was really sorry or she was giving a Halle Berry-like performance for the camera that I recently found behind the fake plant next to my chair. Whatever it was, the thought of her and my former friend sexing each other still bothered me greatly. I was still hurting eight months after the incident when I thought I'd get over it. I wanted to tell her off, but not in front of an unknown audience and especially if Kaitlyn watched the show later on.

"Well, I gotta get ready," I said as cold as possible. "Close the door when you leave."

Bianca looked shocked. I put on my headphones to show her that I was serious. Selected the beat for Eminem's *Cleaning Out My Closet* and cranked the volume. Then I closed my eyes to prevent myself from feeling sorry for her.

About a minute later, I opened my eyes because I heard the door shut.

I thought I could concentrate after Bianca bounced, but I was wrong. I clenched my left fist, wanting to break something. Squeezed my eyes real tight 'cause I felt a tear approaching. When it rolled down my cheek, it felt like boiling water. That is how angry I was.

I wanted to call Bianca a no-good, mega-materialistic, fake platinum-wearing, celebrity-stalking, fake U.S accent talking, 106 and Park-watching, ethic-illiterate, backstabbing, video girl wannabe you-know-what. Then that dude's song reappeared in my head.

Forgiveness.

"Why, Lord?" I asked.

I started free styling about the drama that was taking place, but I couldn't get past eight bars, and I wasn't in a flow.

Forgiveness.

I asked God if Bianca was just putting on a show for the camera. What if she wasn't sorry for hurting me?

Forgiveness.

Fine.

I stopped the music 'cause someone was knocking again. This time I was less optimistic and asked who it was.

"Your hostess," she sang.

I told her to come in. She asked me if I needed anything else before show time.

I answered, "Just a bottle of Dasani, and . . . Can you tell Bianca James that K.J wants to speak to her?"

The girl raised an eyebrow, knowing who Bianca was with, but she said okay to the request.

I stood up when Bianca returned a few minutes later. She looked afraid, not knowing what I was going to say to her.

"Hey," said Bianca.

"What you and Roderick did was foul," I said, getting right to the point. "I never got the chance to verbally make you feel like crap, and I could very well do it right now in front of the cameras! But I'd be a better man if I forgave you and moved on."

The woman started crying again.

"Come," I said, stretching my arms.

Bianca hugged me as if I was lost at sea. She really wanted me back, and judging by the length of the hug, she wanted me to seduce her but my heart already belonged to a Miss Kaitlyn Fuentes.

In a sexy voice, I asked, "Girl, remember when I was down and you'd give me one of those sensual, erotic massages?"

"Oh yeah," she replied while caressing my back. "Why, you want me to give you one?"

"Yeah, right. Give it to your man, 'cause he's gonna need it after I beat him down tonight!"

The intro for the showcase final had already begun. I had to wait backstage on the left side while Roderick and his crew were on the right and out of my sight.

Roderick always wanted cats around him, especially after I broke his jaw. They probably provided him with words that he yearned to hear, like he is the dopest MC and the next Jay-Z. I didn't need anyone around me to pump me up 'cause I knew I was the better lyricist, plus I helped make who Verbal Pain was in the spotlight. At least I had my boys called The Phat Five ready to cheer me on in the crowd.

"The challenger for the title has helped make this freestyle showcase the best in Jam Fest history!" the host Sho'nuff said to the audience. "Since last night, this cat has gotten nothing but the tightest reviews from the best execs in the industry! I'm a mention just a few:

'. . . one of the best free stylists I've ever heard, and I've been listening to freestyles my whole life!'

'Refreshing! Hip-Hop needs this MC more than ever!'

'His delivery and choice of vocabulary leaves you in awe and craving for more!'

'If the stage was a high school basketball court, he would be Lebron James!' WHOA!"

I heard the crowd cheer after the last testimonial. I was speechless; I could feel my head wanting to swell up.

"REPRESENTING THE T-DOT, O-DOT, CANADA, GIVE IT UP FOR KAYYYY-JAYYYY!"

I walked out to the platform, raising my hands like a champ. I saw twelve hundred tipsy folk making noise as if they were on BET's Comic View. I gave Sho'nuff a quick hug before facing the crowd.

I couldn't find or hear my boys in the audience. I knew it was a big crowd and the lights were dim, but on Friday night, the Phat Five was in the front row making crazy noise. I didn't even see the girls that were with Eros and Q. It was very strange and surprising.

Sho'nuff continued, "And now, introducing to some and presenting to others, the 2002 Jam Fest Freestyle Champion! Without a doubt, this cat has proven to us why he won last year, and this is what people had to say about him now . . ."

While the host shared the testimonials that I didn't care about, my focus remained on the audience. Q, Ajani, and Eros weren't visible and it didn't make sense. Nobody was more punctual than Ajani was, so I knew he wasn't in the club. I didn't think that Q and Eros would be so caught up with their flings that the night I anticipated for months would become secondary. I was so disappointed and angry. Selfish punks! Where was the Phat Five loyalty?

Forgiveness, forgiveness . . .

Chorus refused to leave my mind. Wished it would, but I really didn't want God to be angry with me. I had to close my eyes and concentrate on the battle that was only seconds away.

"*. . . ALSO FROM THE T-DOT, O-DOT, HERE HE IS! GIVE IT UP FOR PACIFIC RECORDING ARTIST VERRRR-BAL P-P-PAIN!*"

As the crowd made noise, Roderick came on stage acting buck wild. Hyper as if he finished of a gallon of sweet red Kool-Aid. Homey was acting more crunk than Lil Jon and the Eastside Boyz. The once mild-mannered cat from Scarborough done changed for the fame and fortune, and was looking very stupid. I had to grin in disgust.

Once his intro was completed, Roderick calmed down as we got into our battle positions. I looked at him with a real serious tone. He wasn't smiling, and I didn't know if he was looking at me 'cause the idiot was wearing sunglasses. That told me two things. One, Roderick was high and didn't want to show it, and two, looking at me was like O.J Simpson looking at Fred Goldman. We both knew who was the bad guy.

"What makes this battle highly anticipated is not only the talent of K.J and Verbal Pain, but their history," said Sho'nuff. "These guys not only grew up together, but they used to be a hip-hop duo! Called themselves Phenomenal!"

Mixed reactions came from the crowd. A few cheered. Some laughed. Many gasped in shock.

Un-expectantly, the host told the DJ to play a track.

> Tell them cats in the boroughs that we don't play
> Don't mess with Verbal Pain
> And don't mess with K.J
> We're not your average cats from around the way
> Cause if you listen to our rhymes, we got something to say

That was the chorus of *Don't Mess*, one of Phenomenal's first songs. It was so wack, we refused to release it to the public, with good reason too, because the audience got a good chuckle from it. I didn't know how Jam Fest got a hold of that track. I lowered my head and anxiously waited for the DJ to come back to 2003. He turned it off after a very long thirty seconds.

"My, my, how they've grown," laughed Sho'nuff. "Since Phenomenal, the duo went their separate ways, got involved with some crazy drama, and now they are here, battling to see who is the real *Phenom* and the Jam Fest freestyle champion! So let's do the coin flip to see who battles first!"

Sho'nuff flipped a penny and asked Roderick to call the face. He said heads. The result was tails. Joy.

"K.J wins the toss," said the host. "K.J, you wanna go first or second?"

I said second. It wouldn't have hurt me to go first, but I wanted him to challenge me.

The host explained the rules of the finals. It was two battle rounds, with each rapper having forty-five seconds per round. After the second round, the audience would vote for the best freestyler. Whoever got the most votes would be crowned the champion.

"*DJ, RUN THE TRACK!*" yelled Sho'nuff.

A bass-heavy East Coast beat started playing. I couldn't recognize the production but it didn't matter 'cause it was definitely flow-worthy. Roderick felt the need to hype the crowd with a chorus before free styling.

"Yeah, yeah!" he shouted. "Everybody say *VERBAL PAIN!*"

"*VERBAL PAIN!*" said half the crowd before Roderick asked them to repeat it three more times. To each its own, I guess.

He said, "Alright,

> K.J, I guess your moment of fame has just begun
> But its gonna be over by the time this battle's done
> You're just a hating S.O.B who's afraid of being a hit
> So you tell yourself you're the best when it's all a bunch of bull—
> Hah! Thought I was gonna cuss but my game is on lock like pad
> But you're mad because my career's more straight than six o' clock
> And your job is at a barbershop trying to cut some hair
> But you can't even buy a vowel 'cause you have an empty chair
> All the time, 'cause people know you're cutting is wack
> Just like your rhyming, you sound like DMX on crack
> That's why I had to leave your butt and go solo
> And take your girl and make her more wet than water polo
> I know what I did makes me look like a sinner
> But the woman could differ between a loser and a winner
> And the people know the deal between a vet and a beginner
> And who's the best, especially when I repeat in Jam Fest, YES!"

Roderick came strong, but not incredible. Dude was smooth, but not mind-blowing. He was definitely ready for a battle. Two of the five judges were on their feet, giving "you-struck-a-nerve" expressions after the "DMX on crack" blast. Roderick hit big with that line, but he struck a nerve with the "wet like water polo" remark. The crowd showed their love after hearing his ear candy, but I was ready to open a can of worms and blow everyone's mind.

The beat was on again. Forget pumping a crowd, I was ready to spit!

"Yo,
'DMX on crack?' This coming from a backbiter?
Maybe I should tell the people that I was your ghostwriter
They could've found out from E! True Hollywood Story
But tonight is when I wanna see your fall from glory
So what's up with you tonight? Actin' like you're Lil' Jon
But you can't even get crunk 'cause you have nutting going on
If I want, I can tell everyone about your flaws
How about the time I decked you and broke your jaw?
I'm the man in Phenomenal that gave it to the people raw
I used to give you more advice than Dr. Phil McGraw
Now you've reached success without cutting any slack
With your wisdom, but you used it to stab me in the back
How bout stabbing me in the front?
I could be tied up, high on coke and you still can't get what you want
So if you want, I could inform the host and the sound crew
That you're disqualified and backing out of round two
WHAT!"

The people at Club V were making crazy noise. The five judges reacted as if I was Vince Carter dunking over the seven-foot Frenchman in the 2000 Olympics. The rhyme came through tough, even though I had so much more to say. Adrenaline was flowing through me like water through a fire hose. Looking at Roderick's dumbfounded response to my rhymes made me eager to destroy him but I had to calm down. Drink some Dasani. Breathe in and breathe out like a normal man.

"*ARE YOU HEARING THIS?*" screamed Sho'nuff. "*IS THIS A BATTLE OR WHAT?*"

People screamed "Verbal Pain." People screamed my name. Yet I couldn't see or hear my crew. Screw them was my thought towards my boys, with the exception of Teddy.

The host added, "Looks like some skeletons are coming out tonight! Y'all cats ready for round two?"

"I'm ready!" Roderick said. "Let's go!"

"Bring it on!" I agreed.

Sho'nuff gave the DJ the cue to begin. I looked at Roderick and saw a more ticked off cat than two minutes prior. The tension between us was thick with no signs of clearing up.

The beat for round two was very plain. It was more simple than a human beat box, straight up old school. It was perfect for the competition because we had to have tight lyrics without much support of the music. The audience would hear every syllable so it was excellence or death on the microphone.

Roderick didn't waste time with an intro. He took off his sunglasses and stood about half a foot away from my face.

He said,

"Back out of round two? Guy, you must be crazy
Think a couple of good rhymes from your mouth is gonna faze me?
Child, please! I never back down from wannabe rookies
I chew steak while you're still sucking arrowroot cookies
But Yo, we wouldn't have all this crazy drama
If we weren't broken up by your ignorant mama
Who thought that this hip-hop won't take us far
But she was talking about you, Mr. Kellen Jamal Brar
But I give you some credit for getting the crowd buzzin'
Thanks to the tape submitted by your hypocrite cousin
I guess Mr. Christian couldn't make it tonight
And I don't see your friends who took part in our fight
I guess the Wack Five didn't wanna see the fuss
Of Verbal Pain kicking your gluteus maxim us
Cause yes, I bring the homers and hits like Sammy Sosa
And my rhymes are hotter than your father's samosas
Oh wait, I forgot! You don't know your dad
I guess that's good 'cause I'm hurting you real bad
But I wanna meet him when the timing is good
Cause I heard he's a film director in Bollywood
Then I'll be large in North America and in India
And I'll know for sure that my race and your race won't be into ya
HAH HAH!"

Ouch. Never in my life have I heard Roderick spit like that. Tightest rhyme he ever delivered. Not only did he open a can of worms, but an entire case, and they were scattered all over the stage. Verbal Pain gave the people what they wanted, and the crowd went completely bananas.

Suddenly, everything was looking red and black, it must have been the increased rage in me. I was ready for my comeback, and it had nothing to do with lyrics. While Roderick was still looking at me, I revisited the night at Club

Oasis. I squeezed my fist and punched him so hard on his healed jaw; he fell off the stage towards the audience! Bodyguards rushed me, as well as Verbal Pain's crew. The crowd was uncontrollable. Chaos had taken over.

My left hand was into a tight fist, but I didn't swing it. Not only did I want to hit him in the jaw I broke, but also I wanted to pulverize him. Roderick called my mom ignorant. He made fun of me for not knowing my dad, who was supposedly rich and famous in India for his Bollywood films. Two sensitive issues that called for a beat down.

Although I was mad at my boys for not attending, I was pissed that Roderick dissed them. I was mad that he called Teddy a hypocrite because he was in the club on Friday night. Words only a true punk could express when my crew wasn't in the house to have my back and with no Phat Five in the house, I wasn't going to throw another punch and forfeit my chance to win the championship.

I only had seconds to prepare my revenge. The audience was louder than ever, and Sho'nuff was trying to tell them that I still had to spit. The judges were on their feet as if they already decided on the winner. Some were shouting for me to rip Verbal Pain's head off and other explicit advice. Suddenly I was a huge underdog to win. Excellent.

Back came the beat. I looked at Roderick and pretended to break the microphone's head as if it was his. I needed to deliver the verse of a lifetime, and I needed creativity to do it. Bringing up Roderick's past wouldn't do it, although I knew more about him than anyone in the entire club. Everyone expected me to go that route, and I wanted to badly. However, I had to use the assets that he lacked big time during our Phenomenal days and present. It was knowledge and intelligence. After all, I didn't study a page in the dictionary daily as a kid for nothing.

"Prepare to be schooled," I began.

> "Yo,
> Everybody here is expecting me to stoop down to your level
> But your mind is like the pit of Hades, too many devils
> I could bring up issues that'll bring your decimation
> But I'd rather spit the lyrics that bring commemoration
> Like instead of crap, I say that your whole style is septic
> And instead of dead, I say that you're lyrics are uncryptic
> And if you dis my family and friends again,
> I'll make sure that you'll be trippin like an epileptic
> So I'm a ask you something Mr. Roderick Bailey
> How many freestyles do you write on the daily?
> I had to ask 'cause your mind is still primitive
> You can never touch K.J 'cause I'm the definitive

On this stage, excuse the self-exhortation
Because I'm the president of this freestyle nation
But to know that it doesn't take rocket science
Then again, you can't operate a kitchen appliance
The fact is, you're not hardcore 'cause you're too synthetic
Extroverted and insecure, man you're so pathetic
As a matter of fact, after I release this
You should be like my cousin and give your life to Jesus
Cause He's the only one that will take you as you are
As for me, I'm the new champion and superstar!"

Wow.

I surprised myself, but I refused to show it. All of the responses that Roderick received were matched after my performance. The only exception was a surprise appearance by the host of BET's *Rapcity* and the star player of Detroit's NBA team. They came from backstage just to show me some love. Caught me off-guard, but it was worth it just to see the envious expression on Roderick's face.

After the crowd calmed down, Sho'nuff reminded them that it was time for their votes. All of them received a ballot and a pencil as he introduced R & B artist Mya to perform during the intermission.

I gulped down my Dasani. Felt so good down my throat. So would a glass of champagne after an outstanding victory.

CHAPTER 88

K.J.

Twenty-five minutes finally came. It felt like an hour. I received the cue to re-appear on the stage. I had to stand next to Roderick as Sho'nuff came forth with an unopened envelope in his hand.

I'd never been so nervous. Winning the showcase and landing a record deal was so important to me that anything less would be an insult, unless I was rapping against Rakim or the Notorious B.I.G. As a former ghostwriter for Roderick, I truly believed that he lacked the creativity skills to write or freestyle quality rhymes. There was no doubt in my mind that he had insiders giving him info about my boys and telling him what to say. If he didn't know me so well, Roderick would've came through weak. I would never accept losing to a phony M.C.

"W'zup, y'all? The results are in!" The host said. "I don't know about y'all, but this is the best battle I've seen in years! Verbal Pain and K.J, y'all are both winners in my opinion."

The crowd cheered. I was glad Sho'nuff wasn't the deciding vote.

"But before we find out who's the freestyle champ," he continued, "let's hear what the pros have to say. Give it up for the judges!"

Yay. Drag it on for TV ratings.

I shouldn't have complained in my mind, but anxiety was killing me. The first judge, an executive of Source Magazine, was grinning hard. He said that he loved every second of the battle and that both Roderick and I had a bright future in hip-hop. Yet in my favor, he gave me a perfect ten compared to a nine score for Roderick, concluding that my commanding voice and vocabulary was the deciding factor. I nodded at him and smiled.

The second judge was a pretty Black woman who resembled Sanaa Lathan's character in the Brown Sugar film. She was an executive for one of the top talent agencies in North America, and she also gave me a ten. Roderick got an eight out of ten from her. The only thing she said was that listening to me was refreshing because I delivered with a passion for the culture rather than the industry. It was a true complement from a true Hip-Hop fan.

Judge number three, a top-notch producer for many big names in Hip-Hop, said both of us were excellent and gave us perfect scores.

Judge number four seemed to be everything that the second judge wasn't. The only CEO of the five judges said that I was great but Verbal Pain is a name that people will see on MTV and BET for years to come. Thus, she gave me an eight and Roderick a ten. She probably thinks that Nelly's the greatest lyricist of all time.

However, the best complement came from Daddy J, the fifth and final judge. Old school MC and one of the greatest freestylers ever, he was an underground legend but industry-wise cats never got with his vibe. Daddy J stood up from his chair and stared at Roderick and me.

"Verbal Pain, you the man," he said. "Last year, I said your futures tight, and that ain't changed. But K.J, you are a freak of nature! You use big words, but it doesn't sound written, which proves that you got crazy knowledge. You are a natural, dog, just like me when I was your age. If you play your cards right, you will be a hip-hop icon. Everybody heard that from Daddy J first! I give Verbal a nine and K.J a perfect score. K.J, this is your time! *THIS IS YOUR TIME!*"

Before Daddy J finished, a large group of people cheered and screamed my name repeatedly. Four of five judges thought I was the better MC, giving me a forty-eight to forty-six edge over Roderick. It was enough to confirm in my mind that I was the new champion but it was still up to the votes of the clubbers.

I raised my fist like a champ. Roderick lowered his head to avoid glancing at the crowd. He couldn't stand the attention directed at me. Too bad, so sad.

"OK, so the judges favor K.J, and the crowd's feeling K.J, but it's all up to the votes!" Sho'nuff said. "Only the party people voted tonight, not employees of Club V or the Jam Fest staff and volunteers, just to let you know. On that note, its time for the moment of truth!"

The host opened the envelope. I bowed my head and closed my eyes.

"The winner . . . only received fifty-one percent of the votes, which makes this the closest battle in Jam Fest history. The 2003 Jam Fest Freestyle Showcase Champion is . . ."

I squeezed my fists as if I was trying to crush diamonds.

" . . . *VERBAL PAIN, ONCE AGAIN!*"

It felt like my heart stopped beating.

I couldn't believe what my ears had heard, and I wasn't the only one. Roderick jumped in surprise as if he just won the lottery. Seconds earlier, his ego was crushed and the votes built it right back.

"YEAH!" he screamed. *"THE FANS KNOW WHO'S THE MAN! THE FANS KNOW WHO'S THE FREAKING MAN!"*

So he thought. The way a good bunch of people started cursing and booing, you'd thought that the results were a huge mistake. The judges were speechless, except for Daddy J, who shouted, "recount" as if it was the 2000 U.S election. Maybe it was a mistake, but who knew? If the judges expressed their opinions before the voting, I knew I would've won. Half of the crowd were under twenty-one years old and probably couldn't care less if a freestyle sounded phony or not. Perhaps they were more impressed with lyrical drama than strong diction. Maybe most of the females were pop music fans and voted for Verbal Pain because he was more commercial. Maybe I wasn't supposed to win because Verbal Pain's album release was weeks away and a loss would greatly affect his sales.

Maybe God had me lose because I said that Roderick needed Jesus and I acted as if I didn't need him. Whatever it was, I was too shocked and angry to do or say anything. I just wanted to escape the spotlight, play X-Box, and eat a big fat curry goat roti alone, but that wasn't going to happen.

I gave Roderick a quick hug. Don't know why I did it because I hated him. I didn't want to like him or forgive him. It was painful for me to stand through his acceptance speech. Couldn't accept losing to a backstabber and a phony.

Forgiveness.

Told God that I wasn't ready to do it. Yet, I was crazy enough to ask Him why it was His will for me to lose the battle.

CHAPTER 89

Rancel had never been more beaten and embarrassed in his adult life. Ajani made him look weak and pathetic in front of his kingpin cousin. He had to accept that Ajani beat him at his own game, at the present moment. The main problem was that Machete discovered the truth and any small ounce of trust that Machete had for Rancel was probably diminished.

His body felt broken, his head was pounding, and he was breathing heavily. Once occupied by guests, the penthouse was vacant and quiet. Rancel wondered what went down as he searched the place for dead or alive bodies. When he noticed that the place was people-less, he proceeded to the washroom to deal with his wounds. Machete arrived seconds afterward.

Rancel stared at his cousin through the mirror. Machete had a small grin, which slightly puzzled him.

"That boy messed you up," said Machete. "And all this time, I thought you had game."

Rancel continued to wash his face.

"Where is he?" he asked.

"Get your stuff if you're coming back with me to T.O." Machete said without answering the question. He headed towards the exit.

"Is Ajah dead or what?"

"Guy, I don't have to say crap to you!" snapped Machete. "I'm leaving now, with or without you in the car!"

He slammed the door as he left.

"Two extra large coffees, one black and two sugar, the other with three cream and four sugars."

Rancel went into a Tim Horton's restaurant while Machete pumped gas in preparation for the drive to Toronto. They had already driven for a half-hour without any word exchange. That meant his cousin was highly pissed at him.

After they left the gas station, there was still no oral communication between the two. Rancel had to know what happened to Ajani, so he decided to break the ice.

"Where's Bethel?" he asked again.

His cousin sucked his teeth.

"What the hell, Chete? Just answer the question!"

"Why?" snapped Machete. "Cause it's easier than trying to find out for yourself? That's your problem, Rancel! You always want to take the easy route to get what you want or need! It's been—"

"Look, all I—"

"Shut up! I am talking now! You had your chance to speak when you were being dealt with. Now it's my turn."

Rancel turned towards the passenger door window.

Machete continued, "It's been half a decade now from the time this empire exploded, and your ass hasn't changed yet. Three years ago, I brought Bethel in to see if you'd step up your game, but all you did was complain and grumble. And now, the best cat that ever worked for me is dead! Does that answer your question? Are you happy now?"

Rancel took a long sip of his coffee, preventing himself from expressing joy.

"Yeah, the boy you hate is dead," said Machete. "Instead of you killing him yourself in your own creative way, you left it up to me; you're always looking for the easy way out and you wonder why I don't let you have more control of the business. I cannot believe that I fell for your crap. You messed up, cuzin, you messed up. The little confidence I had in you to maybe do this one day is done. I am watching you like mad now, Rancel. Another wrong move and its over and you have no one to blame for this than yourself."

Machete opened the lid of his coffee and took a big sip. Rancel looked at him with conviction.

"You're right, I messed up," Rancel said. "I can't change what I did. When Ajani came aboard and you started showing him favor, I was mad. I always believed that this business should stay in the family. Not Jamaicans, but the Deverow's. The Estafans keep it in the family. Asian families do it; Italians do it, why should we be different?"

"Because I can love family, but I can't trust them," Machete said as he released a strong cough. "After what your uncle did to my mother, why should I think family is the best route to go? You're not proving me wrong."

He began to cough again, as if he was trying to spew something out.

"What's wrong?" asked Rancel.

"Something's in this coffee," Machete said. "It tastes foul!"

"Maybe the cream's rotten."

"IT'S NOT THE CREAM!"

Machete's arms and upper body suddenly began shaking. Rancel placed his right hand inside his leather jacket. The Cadillac began swerving off the highway.

"*YOU POISONED MY DRINK!*" yelled Machete.

He managed to keep his left hand on the wheel as he tried to get his gun from his belt.

BANG! BANG!

Rancel's left hand was controlling the steering wheel as he shot his cousin twice in the chest. The car was still pushing sixty miles an hour when he put his left leg over Machete's leg to reach the brakes. There was little traffic as Rancel maneuvered the car to the side of the road. He put it in park and turned off the outside lights.

Getting out of the car, Rancel walked around and opened the driver's door. He grabbed Machete and lightly slapped his face. Then he opened his jacket to make sure his cousin was not wearing a vest. Once he saw the blood, he knew the drug lord was dead.

A tear fell from Rancel's eye.

"You're right, cousin. Family can't be trusted," he said. "Too bad I had to kill you to get what I deserve."

With his wounded body, Rancel managed to lift his short, stocky relative over his right shoulder and take him down and up the ditch by the roadside. Once he reached the bushes, he dropped Machete and left him with his gun. Finally, Rancel took the cash and credit cards from his cousin's wallet and placed it back in his pant pocket before leaving towards Toronto.

It was shortly after three when Rancel arrived at the Irie Club. He was pleased to see a good number of cars in the parking lot, meaning liquor and food had to be selling well. Before exiting the Caddy, he tried to look as fresh as possible, which was almost impossible from a car mirror. Rancel got out of the car and entered the back door of the club, which was the kitchen.

Cleaning the stores was a fine Indian woman in her twenties. She worked when Rancel's long-time lady Debra was at home with their children. He grabbed her tiny waist from behind as she smiled.

"Hey!" she said after seeing Rancel's wounds. "What the hell happened to you?"

"Nothing major," he lied.

"Where's Machete?"

"He stayed in Detroit. Why? Everything alright here?"

"Everything's fine in here. The club has been very busy tonight. However, some guy named Rex Marcos wants to talk to him. He's in the dining area stuffing his face with ox-tail and Guinness."

Surprised, Rancel glanced in the dining room and saw the Filipino eating by himself. He also noticed a few other people socializing that were not regular customers. It was very strange for the Irie Club at three in the morning.

Rancel asked, "How long have these people been here?"

"A good while," she replied. "But we gotta close now, so they gots to go."

He hummed in agreement and went towards Rex.

"Rex, my man," Rancel said as he shook his hand. "Everything cool, how are things?"

"Rancel," said Rex as he wiped his hands and face. "I'm glad I caught you. Look, I need to make another order. It has been only a day and I already got more requests. Can you hook me up, or do I need to meet with Machete?"

Rancel grinned and said quietly, "Machete's not here, but I definitely can hook you up, no doubt. How bout we meet in the office when you're done eating."

"Excellent."

"How's the food?"

"Oh my God, this food is serious, guy," answered Rex with his mouth full of rice and peas. "Ox-tail is so tender, it slides off the bone. I'm telling you, food isn't half as good as this in the pen."

"Oh yeah, didn't get fed too well behind bars, huh?"

"Oh, no, I'm talking about you. Turn around."

Rancel slowly turned around in hesitation. Every new customer, which totaled nine people, dropped down their menus and pointed their guns directly at him. He knew immediately that they were cops. Rancel looked back at Rex in frustration and disbelief.

"Move one inch and you're done," Rex said in the midst of sucking a meat bone. "Don't know where your cousin is, but we got you. Name's Ike Trencio, Toronto Police, and you're under arrest."

CHAPTER 90

TEDDY

For seven months, I believed that the night the Phat Five and I got kicked out of Club Oasis would be untouchable in terms of our craziest night ever. However, having friends like K.J, Ajani, Q, and Eros makes the unexpected seem normal.

First, after meeting with Nivea and Juanita and fearing what they were gonna do to Eros, I experienced an awesome time at Kingdom Workers Fellowship. The concert was unbelievable. Deitrick Haddon and the Voices of Unity rocked the house and I praised God as if it was my last day on earth. Bishop Jackson surprised the congregation with the announcement that Sunday's afternoon service would be shown live on television throughout Southern Ontario. Nobody expected the news so soon, and everyone celebrated. In addition, most importantly, many people received salvation at the conclusion of the event. It was the best concert I'd ever attended.

Once the concert was over, Janet looked at me and knew right away that my mind was on K.J. Thus, we rushed to Rude Boy's to watch the showcase. Kaitlyn and Isaiah a.k.a X-Secula followed us shortly after.

If people weren't at Jam Fest or Bless Fest, there were at Rude Boy's. The restaurant was packed and the waiting time for a seat was thirty minutes, mainly because cats were glued to the TV screens watching the battle. It had already started when Janet and I arrived, so we decided to watch it in the bar area.

The battle was outstanding, but the outcome was ridiculous. Most of the people were highly upset that my cousin lost when he was the better M.C. Janet believed that the result was fixed, and I agreed. As much as Roderick dropped the most dissed-filled rhyme I ever heard, K.J responded with intellect. Isaiah couldn't stop talking about how tight he was. Kaitlyn said very little, but her expression said it all. She looked as upset and disappointed as K.J did on the big screen. It was so easy to see that chemistry was brewing between them.

As soon as the battle was over, my cell was ringing off the hook. Aunt Mavis was furious about the result and the way Roderick dissed the family. Good thing she was in Toronto 'cause K.J's mama was a fighter. Of course, she wanted to talk to her son, but I told her that I wasn't at the club and that I'd get him to call her ASAP. I was eager to get with him as well 'cause I knew that he was crushed by the outcome.

My nineteen-year-old sister Gabriella called to vent afterward, followed by my parents, my older sister Camille, and my cousin Dexter who watched the showcase from his home in Port of Spain, Trinidad. Unfortunately, I had to let him go two minutes into the call because K.J was on call waiting.

I vented right away about the result, but K.J wasn't in the mood to talk about it. There was no doubt in my mind that he was pissed off. I was curious to know why he was calling from a pay phone and not from one of the Phat Five's cell phones. K.J told me that they didn't show at Club V and he didn't know why. I was so shocked and mad that I almost dropped the F-bomb in front of my Christian friends. Told my cousin that I'd be at the club to pick him up in ten minutes. Then I explained what happened to Janet and asked her to order me a goat roti.

On the way to the club, I was angry and confused. Why weren't the guys at Club V to support K.J on the biggest night of his life? The fact that he lost the showcase made me more upset about it. I knew that it wasn't God's will for me to be there for the event, but at the same time I felt like I should've represented him. Especially, if I knew that the other three guys had other selfish priorities.

The cell phone rang again. Another number I didn't recognize. I answered and Q said hello. I went off on him, asking him what the hell was so important that the fellas missed K.J's performance. Q apologized immediately, saying that he was at Club V before the rest of the crew but left with Whitney to a nearby hotel. He said that it was a dumb and selfish move. I shook my head. Q took Eros' advice and cheated on his wife. I couldn't say that I wasn't disappointed in him. The guy wasn't even married for a year.

I told him that K.J lost the battle, not bothering to ask if he slept with Whitney 'cause I already made my assumption. He replied that he watched the entire showcase on TV. Q asked what the plans were for the rest of the night, as if I actually knew! I was going to pick up my cousin, Ajani was M.I.A, Eros was M.I.A, and I was mad hungry. I said I didn't know, sucked my teeth, and told him to meet us back at the executive suite when he was ready. At that point, I couldn't care less what my friend wanted to do. He cared more about getting some than staying loyal to his boys or his wife, so currently Q was a waste of my time. I didn't tell him that, but I ended the phone call as an indication.

The phone rang again. Caller ID showed the number of K.J's mom. Aunt Mavis had no patience. I let it ring out. After my cell stopped ringing, it started again less than a minute later. It was Aunt Mavis again. I could've answered it, but what was the point if she wanted to speak to her son who wasn't with me yet? It rang for a shorter time than the first. She probably hung up and called my mom to ask her why I was being so rude.

I arrived at Club V and rescued K.J from the many folk that were giving him props for his performance. I witnessed the beginning of his celebrity lifestyle. K.J was happy to see me and people were shocked to see him get inside of an old Honda Accord. I laughed. My cousin gave a short grin and said that he was so looking forward to crashing at the executive suite. I wanted more details of the battle but I told him to call his mother ASAP to avoid her from getting a heart attack from anxiety. As I reached for the cell, it started to blow up again.

Thought it was Aunt Mavis again, but I was wrong. It was another unrecognizable number. Must have been Q calling from the hotel again. While it was ringing, I passed the phone to K.J and told him to cuss Q out for not showing up. Obviously, I was not in a Christ-like mood.

K.J answered. Said that he wasn't Teddy, but he didn't give me the phone. Didn't sound like he was talking to any of the Phat Five, although I heard him say Ajani. In a serious tone, my cousin told me to turn down the music. I turned it down and asked K.J what was wrong, but he didn't respond. He told whomever he was talking to that we were on our way and hung up the phone. Then K.J informed me that he was speaking to a woman with a heavy-Spanish accent who told him that Ajani was badly wounded and was taken to the downtown hospital! That is all he knew from the conversation. Instantly my mind converted back to spiritual mode and I began to pray without speaking. I did not want to lose my longtime close friend without offering him the gift of salvation. I took every shortcut that I knew, and sped to the hospital.

K.J called Q's cell and told him the news. Then he called Eros' cell, but of course, he got the voice mail right away. K.J left a message, but we both knew that Eros wasn't gonna hear it 'cause he said it was going to be off all weekend. No one knew where the boy was, and at that present moment, we didn't care.

We arrived at the Hotel-Dieu Hospital. Immediately we went to the receptionist desk in the emergency area to find out where Ajani was located, but a Latina woman dressed in black approached us. She said her name was Carla. Didn't ring a bell as to who she was until K.J said that she was the mother of the kid that Ajani saved at the mall on Friday but I was still confused. What did Carla have to do with what happened to Ajani? That's when she asked us to sit down in the waiting room 'cause the medical staff was currently working on him. Carla wanted K.J and I to gather close so that nobody in the building could hear what she had to say. Her story was unbelievable. Her baby daddy was a leader of a small group of dealers that tried to kill Ajani, and Carla was among them! Because of what Ajani did for her son, Carla begged them not to kill him, which consisted of torture and throwing him off the twenty-four story Hilton Hotel! Once Carla's man knew why she was crying, he apologized to Ajani, rushed him to emergency, and insisted that Carla stay with him until he was fully taken care of. Incredible!

Q arrived after Carla finished explaining what happened, but she didn't mind telling it again. I didn't mind hearing it again. All K.J and I could do was shake our heads in awe. I thought of God's amazing goodness. He allowed me to get so hungry in the mall that Ajani and K.J had to wait for me to get some food. If I'd decided to get some food at a later time, Ajani wouldn't have been around to save Carla's son's life and he would be road kill on Riverside Drive. It was easily the most inspiring dramatic story I ever heard.

All four of us sat and waited for the doctor to give us a report. We said very little. I thought of Savannah and my godson A.J and prayed that God would give Ajani another chance to live a life free of the drug game. The Lord knew that I didn't want to be the one to deliver bad news to a family that didn't know about his lifestyle.

I was quickly comforted when the doctor finally approached us with a smile on her face. She said that Ajani wasn't in critical condition but had a cracked rib, broken right arm, neck and back pains, and many bruises. He would need plenty of rest and rehabilitation. The doctor asked Carla what happened and she said it was a disagreement between friends gone badly. If the doctor bought that story, it would be great 'cause the last person that Ajani wanted to talk to was a cop. She didn't ask any more questions, and gave us the okay to see our wounded friend.

Ajani was glad to see us, but he looked ashamed and embarrassed. We had never seen Ajani look so messed up physically. It seemed so surreal 'cause none of us had ever seen him in pain before. He didn't have to explain the situation and we didn't need one. Ajani was in too deep with the drug game and blessed to still be alive. He did tell us that he was done with drug dealing for good. After hearing what happened, I believed him. He loved Savannah and A.J too much to let it get the best of him and it almost did. Thank God for second chances. I asked him if he told Savannah what happened. He shook his head, saying that he wanted to reveal his secret to her face-to-face rather than over the phone. I respected his decision.

He apologized to K.J for missing the event and asked about the outcome. K.J said that he lost but would go into details the next morning. Obviously, the fact that a long time friend almost died was more important to K.J than a freestyle battle. Ajani also wanted to know why Eros wasn't with us. None of us could give him an answer. He looked like he wanted to comment about his behavior, but decided to just shake his head. Good thing, 'cause Ajani had enough issues to deal with. In addition, I had yet to tell the guys that Juanita was in town and ready to destroy him.

We had to leave the room because Ajani needed further treatment. He asked us to change the flat tire on his Escalade at the Hilton hotel and gave us his keys and a credit card to pay for the executive suite. We promised him that all those things would be taken care of in the morning. Carla needed a ride so we took her to her house in South Windsor.

After we dropped her off, Q apologized to K.J for missing the showcase. That's when I noticed a different side of my cousin. He didn't argue or vent and told him not to sweat it. Obviously, K.J was upset that his boys weren't there, but he was the most unforgiving cat I knew. X-Secula's song must have hit him like a ton of bricks.

Q then decided to give us the details of his night. At first, I didn't want to hear it, but I'm glad I did. Dude did not sleep with Whitney. Q wasn't known for lying, but it seemed shocking to me that he didn't give in. Conviction was a powerful thing. I told him that I was sorry for pre-judging his actions. Guess he really didn't let Eros make his important decisions after all.

The adult star wannabe was our next subject of discussion. I told the guys about my encounter with Juanita and Nivea at the church. Q and K.J were shocked to the point where they looked like they wanted to laugh their butts off. We came to the conclusion that Eros was hiding, if he wasn't already caught. Only time would tell.

When we arrived at the casino hotel, we had a debate about the wildest Phat Five weekend ever. Q's vote was Caribana Weekend 2001, when we hit ten nightclubs, Vince Carter's charity game, and the parade in three nights. I disagreed 'cause my wisdom teeth were taken out three days before the weekend and I was grumpy as hell. K.J couldn't decide between the Club Oasis fight weekend and the present one. My vote was the present, and while we went up the elevator, I defended my argument with a quick review of the events. Q suggested that we make the vote on Sunday night, 'cause the weekend wasn't over. I said fine, but I had made my decision.

I so looked forward to relaxing in perhaps the nicest hotel suites in the city. However, when I opened the door, immediately we felt the ridiculous heat. The suite had a funky stench of cologne and food. It smelt nasty, and I hoped that we entered the wrong crib. Yeah right. Then we heard some loud mumbling. We looked at each other with a clueless expression as we followed the scent and the noise.

I would never forget this sight as long as I live! Our boy Eros Alexander, Jr. was tied to the bed smothered with sticky food all over him! The bed was a mess! The carpet and his clothes were all over the floor and at first, it made me scream out loud because I thought it was stained with blood but it was ketchup, thank God! The room was a disaster, victimized by Hurricane Juanita.

Eros was flapping like a slice of bacon, yelling at us to set him free. I felt for my friend, but I couldn't move and I was speechless. K.J and Q looked dumbfounded and just stared at him. It was a MasterCard moment and none of us had a camera. Q was the first to agree that this was our wildest weekend ever. K.J wanted to know when the Phat Five became a far cry from being normal. Did we even know the definition of normal?

All I knew is that the night was far from over and I had to go to church on Sunday. My question for God was whether I would have guests with me.

PART 4

SUNDAY

CHAPTER 91

TEDDY

It was good that Bless Fest was concluding with a service at one in the afternoon. There was plenty to do before then. I woke up at nine with only four hours of sleep. Mad, mad tired, but I forced myself out of the most comfortable queen size bed I'd ever slept on.

It was the only bed of choice, so K.J, Q, and I put our names in a hat to see who got it. We weren't fans of sharing mattresses with the same sex, no matter the size. I won the bet of course. Eros was intentionally excluded, because if he didn't make the decision to knock boots with the models in the suite, his ex's wouldn't have trashed the room. We wouldn't have it any other way. K.J and Q slept in the two sofas, and Eros slept on the carpet without complaining.

Yes, I was a part of the reason why Eros was caught, but he had yet to find out. I needed the right opportunity to tell him, and the moment we rescued him wasn't the time. After our shock, we cut the ties from the post and pulled the duct tape from his mouth. That's when the boy went off! Dude was yelling and cursing about what Juanita and Nivea did to him. We backed away from Eros real quick, 'cause he was a mess! He looked like he was buried in crap, even though it was a bunch of sweet toppings and cologne and he smelt like urine 'cause he wet his boxers! Eros said that he was tied up for almost four hours and he couldn't hold it anymore. That was enough info for us. He wanted to give us details about the event, but we literally pushed him into the shower! Thank God, we didn't have a water bill, 'cause was in there at least an hour and a half.

While Eros was bathing, we made some moves with the suite. We turned the A/C on and called for emergency housekeeping. A lady came within twenty minutes from the call, and Lord knows she wasn't happy. She was mumbling and cussing while doing her job at four in the morning. She dumped the bed sheets, blankets, and pillows and replaced them with fresh material but none of us wanted to sleep on it, based on what fluids could have remained on the mattress. We told her to dump Eros' clothes in a garbage bag. I didn't know if he wanted them dry cleaned, but the way Heinz was stained on the clothes, it almost made more sense to buy a new wardrobe. The housekeeper did a tight job with the little time she had to clean. We were grateful, so Q went to the ATM to give her a real nice tip.

Eros came out the washroom wearing a hotel bathrobe. He went into Ajani's bag to grab a new pair of boxers. He obviously snooped through our stuff, 'cause I saw my black Roc-a-Wear shirt on the sofa. At least it wasn't sprayed with ketchup. We all sat in the sofas, Eros was ready to tell the crazy drama and he did it with explicit detail.

I didn't know how K.J and Q felt about the incident, but my emotions were mixed. Other than the fact that Eros had no clothes, I didn't feel bad for him. He was bound to be caught eventually. I was upset at Eros for missing K.J's event and using the suite for his attempted menage et trois. Ajani specifically told him not to bring any girls over, and if he wasn't in the hospital, Eros would've been dealt with big time. Eros kept telling us how sorry he was for what happened, and he was surprised and thankful that Ajani wasn't around to see the damage. That's when we told him what happened to Ajani. Then Eros felt more stupid about what he did. At first, he was speechless, but afterwards he begged us not to tell him what happened. We agreed, 'cause that was between him and Ajani.

I know that Eros was traumatized by the event, but he had no regrets for cheating on Juanita and Nivea. That didn't surprise me, 'cause Eros was a selfish cat. What did surprise me was the fact that he never asked K.J how he did in the showcase. I know that rubbed K.J the wrong way 'cause he wasn't trying to tell him anything if Eros didn't ask. If I were my cousin, I would have done the same thing.

Next, Eros wanted to know how he was caught so easily. That was an excellent time for me to ask the crew what they wanted to eat, 'cause we all were hungry. We agreed on pizza. I grabbed my car keys and drove to Ferrary's Restaurant, a twenty-four hour joint near the university. On the way, I called my baby to let her know what took place since I left her at Rude Boy's. Janet didn't answer the phone, so I left a message. When I came back to the suite forty minutes later, Eros was passed out on the carpet. Dude was physically and mentally exhausted. Q, K.J and I ate while watching TV and laughing at how Eros got punked. When I asked them what they said when Eros asked who ratted him out, the guys had my back. They explained that if Juanita and Nivea were destined to meet, then eventually Eros was destined to be caught. The answer couldn't have been better.

Not only was I surprised that I got up so soon, but I wasn't the first one awake. K.J was by the window of the suite ironing clothes in his bathrobe.

"Guy, did you even sleep?" I asked him while turning on the coffee maker in the kitchenette.

"Not really," answered my cousin. "I'm still overwhelmed by the events of last night."

"Me too, but I likes my sleep. So does Q and Eros. They're both knocked out."

"What time does church start?"

"One."

"For real?" K.J asked with surprise. "All this time I've been rushing to be ready for ten or eleven! No wonder you're chilling."

"Not really," I said. "We still gotta fix Ajah's ride and hopefully pick up Ajah as well."

K.J hummed in agreement, but we knew there was a big possibility that Ajani would have to stay another night or two in the hospital. He was beat pretty badly, and a three-hour drive to Toronto could be very uncomfortable for him. Then again, we knew that Ajani was hardheaded and would probably try his hardest to leave Windsor before the afternoon was done.

I turned on the TV and started flipping the channels with the remote. Found Bobby Jones Gospel on BET and kept it there. Asked K.J how he felt the day after the biggest night of his life.

"Different, guy," he replied. "When I found out the result, I was mad as hell. I hated Roderick even more, even though I was able to forgive Bianca."

I smiled. "Wow. X-Secula's song got to ya, huh?"

"Guy, you have no idea! She came in my change room crying yesterday. Ted, I honestly wanted to slap the hell outta her but I couldn't get his song outta my head. I was able to give her a nice hug and finally close that chapter of my life. Felt pretty good, too."

I told K.J that what he did was absolutely powerful. He was always a grudge-holder like his mom. Aunt Mavis never forgave Uncle Samuel for leaving her and K.J years ago. K.J inherited that unforgiving spirit which became his stronghold for years. It used to take him forever to forgive me for little stupid stuff I did to him back in the day, like the time my stereo ate his all four of his Eric B. and Rakim cassette tapes. Guy didn't speak to me for almost a month. Thus, K.J forgiving Bianca was entirely a move of God in my opinion.

"Yeah, it was powerful," he continued, "but that attitude disappeared once I stepped on stage. I was mad at the fellas for not showing up to support me. I was even mad at God for not allowing me to win after Roderick dissed my loved ones and me on international TV. Why He allowed that to happen didn't make sense to me at all."

"Especially when we know that Roderick ain't nothing without a ghostwriter," I said.

"Exactly! But you know what, cuzin? If I didn't go to church before the event and if you didn't give me words of wisdom, I would be a disturbed cat right now."

"What did I say to you?" I asked, forgetting the conversation that took place in my car on the way to the club the night before.

"Remember? You said that if it were God's will, I would get a record deal." K.J. said.

"Oh yeah," I nodded.

"Well, at first I took that as winning the showcase, because a win meant an automatic record deal. I lost the battle unfairly, and many cats saw that. The support I received after the event was unbelievable. Just as I was ready to seclude myself from everyone, a dude from Def Jam spoke to me about signing with their label."

My eyes grew bigger than that chick from the show Girlfriends.

"DEF JAM?" I shouted. "You didn't say nuttin' about Def Jam last night! That's the biggest label in hip-hop, yo!"

"I'm not done," K.J continued with a surprising calmness. "The dude from Def Jam asked for my phone number in Toronto, and he said that I should expect a call real soon."

At that point, I lost all of my dignity. I was jumping on the bed with excitement. K.J was gonna be rich and famous! I made so much noise, and Q still slept through it.

"Hold on, yo!" K.J added. "Another cat from Elektra Records and a guy from Columbia Records came right after, saying the same thing. There's gonna be a bidding war to sign me!"

I ran towards my cousin and hugged him. Then he backed up as if as if my name was Influenza.

"Sorry," I said. "Guess I should brush my teeth."

"Yeah! Brush good, and then gargle some Listerine. Matter of fact, drink some Listerine, 'cause that's some septic—"

"You know what? Quit while you're ahead, 'cause I ain't afraid to get ig'nant on ya! You may be a celebrity, but you're still my little cousin!"

I went to the washroom to eliminate the funk. That's when Q woke up.

"What's with the ruckus, yo?" he asked, still wrapped in a blanket.

K.J told him the news while I brushed. I couldn't believe that he kept that news to himself for so long. Gave him plenty of credit for putting his boys' needs before his last night, especially when we weren't there for him.

"Congrats, K.J, you did it!" said Q, who started yelling cheers. "I should have been there for you yesterday, 'cause now you probably won't give me a shout out in your album cover."

K.J said, "That was a stupid thing you did, but I don't wanna hold grudges anymore. It doesn't mean you're off the hook, though."

My stomach began to growl. It was time to make some moves.

Twenty-five minutes later, we left the executive suite without Eros 'cause he was still sleeping. Before going to the Hilton to fix Ajani's ride, we picked up breakfast from a McDonald's drive-thru. When we entered the underground parking lot, it was a relief to see the Escalade in good shape. A hot vehicle with a flat tire going untouched in downtown Windsor was a blessing.

Changing an SUV tire was tougher than a regular vehicle, but we had the muscle and expertise to get it done properly. Q was fully describing his Saturday night adventure again when suddenly my cell phone rang. I answered it without checking the caller ID 'cause I figured it was Janet, Eros, Ajani, or someone calling for K.J.

"Hello? Hi, Great-Granny!" I yelled, bringing out my Trini accent. "No, this isn't Kellen, its Theodore... This isn't Kellen, Great-Granny, its... Great-Granny, Great-Granny?"

I gave the phone to K.J.

"It's our great-grandmother," I said. "She's still talking 'cause she thinks I'm you. Her hearing aid must be off again."

K.J grinned and began chatting with her.

Q said to me, "You might as well let him keep the phone today 'cause all the calls will be for him."

"He needs his own phone," I said. "But anyways, back to your story. Man, I figured the man on Trina's voice mail was a relative you didn't know. Next time, trust your heart before Eros Alexander."

"I know, guy. I came so close to ruining a good thing. She might've never found out if I did sleep with Whitney, but conviction is the worst feeling in the world."

"True dat. I felt it in a different way when Janet caught me smoking weed on Friday."

"See, Ted? That is nothing compared to adultery. Isn't adultery one of the *don't dos* in the Ten Commandments?"

"Yeah, I believe so."

"So, does that mean all adulterers go to Hell?"

It was evangelism time.

"It's not the adulterer that goes to Hell, Q," I explained, "'cause an adulterer can repent from his old ways and become righteous. But those who don't give their lives to God are the ones who don't go to Heaven."

There was twenty seconds of silence between us. All I could hear was K.J's loud mouth.

"You going to Heaven?" asked Q.

I answered, "Hope so."

"Where in the Bible does it say people who do wrong aren't going to Heaven?"

"I didn't say people who do wrong. We all do wrong stuff. I said those who aren't Christians, or people who don't live according to God's word."

With a sad voice he said, "Man, I thought only wicked people go to Hell, like Hitler or dudes who molest children."

How soon did I forget that I used to think the same way? When R & B star Aaliyah died in the plane crash, I thought she was going to Heaven for sure. I thought the same thing for Tupac, Biggie, and Big Punisher. After I was saved, I realized that God was the only one who determined where their eternal home would be.

"The Bible explains what I'm talking about, but I'm new to the faith and I don't want to give you wrong information," I said. "So, how about coming with me to church this afternoon so my pastor can give you a better explanation?"

Q laughed. "That's alright, guy. I don't need to know that bad."

"It's a youth service. Plus, at this church, you get good music and an excellent godly message. You won't regret it, trust me."

"It's not that . . . I don't know, I'll think about it."

"Think about a nice American dinner that consists of BBQ chicken, collard greens, cornbread, biscuits, macaroni, and stuffing. That's what the church is serving afterward."

"Dang, Ted, why you had to bring food in this discussion? I'm a sucker for anything with BBQ sauce on it."

"Then you'll love the food they serve at my church, yo. The chickens smothered in a rich, homemade sauce that'll make you get crunk. You'll be licking your fingers and begging for more, plus, the desserts they serve is off-the-chain! Their cheesecake—"

"Alright, fine, I'll go with you. As long as I get some food and I don't have to wait too long for it."

Q was a guy who loved soul and West Indian food more than my own people, and it was a tool to get him to join me. K.J needed hip-hop and a beautiful woman of God. When I went to Kingdom Workers Fellowship for the first time, my reason was simply to make Janet happy. Of course, God had a different agenda and turned my life around for the better. My prayer was that God would do the same for K.J and Q before they left Windsor.

It didn't take long for Q and I to put on the spare tire and attach the Sprewell rim back in place. K.J wasn't helping because the calls kept coming for him. Just as we were putting away the equipment, my cousin approached me with the phone.

"Ted, it's Ajah," he said. "He hates the breakfast the nurse gave him and wants to know if we can get him some ackee, saltfish and dumplings from Rude Boy's."

I laughed, "Rude Boy's ain't open until noon. This ain't Toronto. Finding a place that sells a West Indian breakfast in Windsor is like finding people playing hockey in Jamaica."

K.J told him what I said. Then he said all right and hung up.

"He said bring him whatever, as long as its not cold oatmeal."

"Nuff respect, bred-drin," said Ajani to us as we arrived with a Burger King breakfast.

We gave our greetings and asked how he was feeling. He said that he felt like how he looked. Nuff said for now. At least he was able to sit up in the bed and eat. Ajani chewed very slowly and waited until he finished his first mouthful of food before speaking.

"Where's Alexander?" he asked. "Did he show up last night?"

I looked at K.J and Q, who were both smiling with me. Who was gonna break Eros' promise?

"Oh yeah, he was at the suite when we reached," admitted Q. "Guy, you won't believe what we saw when we showed up!"

"Try me."

We shared the drama. Ajani's jaw was in pain from the fight, but he laughed for a long time. You know we had to join in. It is a good thing Ajani had a private room 'cause we carried on as if we were watching The *Original Kings of Comedy*. If Eros knew that we were carrying on as so, we would probably be the Phat Four but a funny story was a funny story.

"That's so freaking funny," said Ajani as he coughed from over-laughing. "Serves him right for not listening to me."

I asked Ajani when he would be released.

"I wanna leave now," he said, "but they want to keep me here until tomorrow morning. If they see progress, I might be able to leave today. But that'll mean a visit to my family doctor, rehab, and sick leave from work."

"Good," I said, "'cause knowing you, you'd go back to work tomorrow."

"Of course."

K.J said, "Guy, forget about getting paid for once in your life! It is a miracle that you are alive today. Life is too short for us to keep messing with foolishness."

"The foolishness is done, K.J," Ajani replied. "I just can't stand being helpless like this. I'm ready to start my new life now."

"You can," I said as my cell phone rang. "And while you're resting, you can get your new life all planned out. Who is calling for you now, cuzin? Oh, it's your mom again."

K.J sighed as I gave him the phone. "I'll talk to her outside. It's the third time she's called already today."

Q's phone rang also. "It's Eros, he probably wants to know where we at."

They both left the room. There was an unusual silence between Ajani and me.

"Yo, this juice y'all brought is warm. Pass me the drink from the nurse."

I passed him the juice. As he was drinking in the bed, I noticed the many bruises and scars on his face and arms. I could tell homeboy was in pain. He probably had tons on his mind as well.

"I haven't looked in the mirror yet," he admitted. "How do I look? Keep it real."

"Like you got dealt with," I replied. "Need I go into detail?"

"Nah. Maybe you can answer this better: You talk to God much?"

Whoa, was this another evangelistic encounter? What Min-T said to me on Thursday was truly prophetic.

"I try to," I answered.

"Does He always listen?"

"I think so. But it doesn't mean He does everything I ask."

"Example?"

I grinned. "Like, this weekend I didn't want you guys to persuade me into doing stuff that I used to do, so I asked God to take away the temptations. He didn't do it. Everybody goes through temptation, even Jesus."

"Like when He was asked to turn stones to bread?"

"Exactly."

"So when was the first time you felt God?"

Deep question, it made me feel overwhelmed. Ajani never had questions for me. He was the street-smart, criminal-minded, prideful, tough guy that seemed to know a little of everything, except salvation. I wanted to give him the most dramatic example I could think of, but my lifestyle wasn't dramatic. I was an ordinary guy with extraordinary friends, trying to serve the Lord. Thus, I had to be Teddy Henderson and nobody else.

I told Ajani about the night before I was saved. I had planned to go with Janet to church on the upcoming Sunday, but I wasn't looking forward to it. Matter of fact, I was dreading it 'cause it meant a Saturday night at the club without getting drunk or tipsy. As I was getting ready to leave the crib around nine-thirty'ish, Janet and I had an argument about my decision to go clubbing. It only encouraged me to leave sooner than usual out of spite but I didn't want to leave before watching the final five minutes of the Raptors game against the Sixers.

During commercials, I switched channels and happened to notice Bishop T.D. Jakes preaching. Never heard him before, just recognized him from a *Time* magazine cover. He was speaking to an arena full of men. I never changed the channel back to the game. Men were crying, cheering, shouting, and dancing. It blew my mind 'cause I'd never seen men do that for anything other than sports, concerts, or strippers. Didn't understand the emotions until I heard the preacher speak. God used that man to make every listener think that Bishop Jakes could read minds. He explained how I felt about Janet being saved and the issues that I had to overcome. It was deep, so deep that I never left the apartment that night. After listening to that message, there was no doubt in my mind that God was real.

After I finished, Ajani said nothing for at least thirty seconds. Felt like five minutes. Whatever I said must have hit him hard. At least I hoped it did.

"You seen the movie *Final Destination*?" he asked.

I said, "*Final Destination*? Isn't that about a group of people who escape death and it ends up getting them back?"

"Yeah. Guy, I am not supposed to be here. Death should have taken me out a long time ago, especially last night. Now I'm really on its hit list."

"Ajah, there's a big difference between you and the movie. Yes, you and those characters escaped death, but those cats in the film didn't call on the Lord to save them. You did. That changes everything."

"Yo, star," Ajani said while shaking his head. "Did you hear what you just said? Say that again!"

I repeated my statement, shocked that what I said blew Ajani's mind. After hearing what I said the second time, it blew my mind.

"That's deep, guy," Ajani said. "I don't care what Eros thinks, you're a changed cat for real."

It pleased me to hear him say that.

We continued to talk, although I felt like Ajani needed to rest but the man had plenty to say about the events of the weekend. Then he gave me joy when he mentioned that Savannah was saved on Friday night. He didn't know how to feel about it, and I couldn't blame him. Two months prior, I was in the same situation. I just told him to enjoy the new Savannah Shaw, because their relationship was about to change for the better.

"Oh, its gonna change alright, but I don't know about it getting better," he admitted. "You wanna tell her what I've been up to for the last three years?"

The Spirit was telling me to pray for Ajani at that moment. He needed prayer, but I didn't want to organize it. I'd never prayed for anyone out loud before, and I didn't want to mess up and sound stupid. Intimidation was hitting me big time. That meant that I had better do it.

"Ajah . . . I hope you don't mind, but I wanna . . ."

"Yo, cuzin, take this phone from me and turn it off!" K.J said loudly as he entered the room. "I'm already tired of telling people about how I felt last night. Can't a man rest for a minute without someone wanting to know my business?"

Interrupted by K.J. That was my lame excuse to avoid praying for Ajani.

"Get used to it, boss," Ajani said to him. "You're a superstar now."

"Where's Q?" I asked.

"In the Escalade, talking to his wife," K.J answered. "Don't worry, Ajah, we'll take good care of your ride."

"You better," said Ajani. "Is it still in one piece?"

"The ride's fine," I said. "Nobody messed with it, which is a big blessing. Hey, man, we're gonna come back later after we check out of the suite and go to church. That cool?"

"Church? Who's going with you?"

"K.J and Q."

"What about Eros?"

Oh yeah! What about Eros?

"He can chill at the apartment," I suggested. "Don't think he wants to be near any people right now."

K.J said, "I don't even want to be near him right now. He's bitterer than Archie Bunker accidentally using Preparation H to brush his teeth."

We laughed. Then Ajani said that if he were well, he would actually go to church with us. That's when I remembered Saturday night's announcement at church.

"You can watch the whole service live on cable twelve," I said with excitement. "It'll be the first time Kingdom Workers Fellowship will be seen on TV. You can see Janet's team dance, singing, rapping and the word. Check it out."

Ajani raised his eyebrows but said nothing. Then the nurse came in to assist him with a bath, and that's when we left.

Eros was sitting in the sofa watching TV and eating cold pizza when we arrived at the executive suite. Like K.J said at the hospital, the guy looked bitter. Shoot, I would be too if all my clothes were ruined by ketchup. We all asked how he was feeling. He sucked his teeth.

"I'm bugged the hell out!" snapped Eros. "When I woke up, I thought yesterday was a dream. Then when I realize that I was without clothes and women to bang, I went into depression mode! Everything was going so freaking smooth until last night. Those chicks were wrapped around my finger, yo! And then I got beat at my own game."

"That's because you put too much on your plate, guy," said Q.

"No, it's because I didn't plan properly. Those chicks don't realize what they did to me! Now my game will be ten times as tight. No more multiple encounters with the same woman, I am getting ready for a sexual rampage, and nobody will be able to stop me. Nobody!"

Talk about being optimistic for all the wrong reasons. K.J, Q and I looked at Eros as if he was smoking lettuce.

"So, K.J, how was last night, guy?" asked Eros for the first time since we rescued him over eight hours ago.

My cousin raised his eyebrows. He was uninterested in being nice.

"Bro, I'm sorry for what happened to you," K.J said, "but your clothes would be stain-free if you weren't so stinking selfish. I looked for you in the crowd, guy. No Eros. You thought with your nuts and look, consequences kicked the crap outta you."

"Yo, don't just attack me!" yelled Eros with his hands up. "I wasn't the only person M.I.A for your event!"

"I know. Ted told me in advance that he wasn't coming. Q and Ajah missed it, but at least they apologized."

"Oh . . . I'm sorry, man. I should've been there for real," said Eros in an unconvincing fashion. "You still didn't answer my question. Did you win or . . . hold up! Q, you missed the performance too, how come? Did you bang Whitney?"

That was K.J's signal to end the conversation. He got up off the sofa and went to the washroom. Shaking his head, Q answered Eros with a no and that everything was good between him and Katrina. Eros sucked his teeth.

"Soft, man, you're soft," he said.

"No, I'm smart, Eros," responded Q. "At least I can have sex when I get home."

"Funny. Don't come to me when you find another man screwing your wife in your house."

"Speaking of, genius, the guy who left the message on Trina's phone was her cousin who plays college football for Syracuse."

"Oh, really, have you met him?"

"Not yet. I will when the wife and I go to New York this week."

"OK, whatever. Still wouldn't trust her if I were you. All women are evil."

I really wanted Eros to shut up, but I kept quiet and left the living room. K.J was sitting on one of the king size beds watching TV, so I took possession of the other one and took out my student Bible from my sports bag. Didn't have a particular Scripture that I wanted to look at so whatever page I opened, that's what I was gonna read.

The word presented me with the book of Mark, the eighth chapter. Tried to study it, but it was hard to concentrate with the TV on and Eros and Q talking loud. So many other things were on my mind as well but I did manage to meditate on a Scripture verse. Verse thirty-six quotes Jesus asking his disciples **'what will profit a man if he gains the whole world, and lose his own soul?'** Very thought provoking. I wanted to analyze the verse and the chapter but it would have to wait. Placed a bookmark on the page and closed the Good Book. Headed back to the living room because a heated argument was taking place.

"Then how did they find out, Q?" asked Eros.

"I told you, I don't know!" Q snapped. "I didn't say jack to Whitney or any of your girls as to what you were doing!"

"What's going on?" I interrupted.

"Henny," Eros began, "I'm trying to figure out how I got caught last night. I understand that it's a small world for the fact that Nivea and Juanita's roommate are longtime friends. It's also crazy that Juanita ended up coming to Windsor instead of going to New York. Crap happens; I'm living proof of that. But they shouldn't have found me unless somebody played the rat!"

"And it wasn't me!" Q yelled. "If I'm on an excellent date, why would I want to talk about you?"

It was easy to see that Q was pissed 'cause he started turning red. He was trying his best not to say it was my fault. Eros refused to believe him. Therefore, it was time for me to confess the truth and declare Q's innocence.

"Remember when you told Nivea that you were going to church with me?" I reminded Eros.

"Yeah, at the fashion show," he said. "Why, did she actually show up at your church?"

"Yep. With Juanita."

"Did you talk to them?"

I nodded and explained what happened in the lobby of Kingdom Workers Fellowship. I didn't leave out any information so he could fully understand that I didn't try to get him busted. However, I was talking to a bitter Eros Alexander, Jr. who just was screwed over by five women.

He glared at me. Dude went from pissed off to furious.

"I can't believe it!" Eros said. "You actually gave them our hotel info?"

"Eros, I'm really sorry, man! They totally caught me off-guard, and I didn't wanna lie in church! I told them that you wouldn't be there anyway! What was I—*AAARGH!*"

Unexpectedly, Eros punched me in the stomach! Pain was so sharp it got me on my knees. I never thought the dude was gonna hit me. I was so shocked; I didn't know what my next move would be.

Q yelled, "Eros, what the hell's wrong with you? Ted didn't mean what he did!"

K.J entered the living room.

"What the . . . you told him what happened, huh?" he asked me.

I said nothing I was still on my knees and coughing.

"I'm here accusing Q, and you're the real backstabber," said Eros. "What kind of an F-ing friend are you?"

That comment did it. Now I was furious. Eros questioned my integrity and friendship and dressed it with an F-bomb. Forget trying to be a witness and letting my lights shine. I was ready to let my flesh take full control. Letting Eros know how I felt about him was long overdue. However, before I spoke, I got up, looked him right in the eye, and kicked him hard in his favorite organ.

"*OHHHHHHHH!*" Eros hollered before cussing me out again.

But he didn't stay down long. Eros got up and tried to swing at my face, but Q grabbed his right arm and held him hostage. I told him to let Eros go so I could beat him down, but that dream was intercepted by my two-twenty plus pound cousin who squeezed me like a python.

"What kind of friend am I?" I snapped. "How soon did you forget that I was the one who warned you about Juanita seven months ago? You didn't listen! Now look at you! All depressed like you are a freaking victim who did nothing wrong! You lucky K.J's holding me 'cause I can give you plenty to cry about, punk!"

"Whatever, hypocrite! I—"

"Shut up, I ain't finished! The real question is what kind of friend are you, Eros? It is real nice when I tell you that I am a Christian and you judge me as a hypocrite. Then, when I practice integrity like telling the truth, you label me as a backstabber. Nice! But it's not just about me, how about Q? Real boys wouldn't encourage bred-drin to mess up their marriage! What, should everybody be a loose cannon like you? And who is fooling who about last night? Real cats apologize when they disappoint their boys! You didn't try to make K.J's event 'cause nothing was in it for Eros Alexander. That's why you followed two hoochies instead!

Finally, we know that you're a cat who has no clothes, and I hope that none of us will ever experience it. You went through some crazy crap and you were dealt with by five women. But, brah, it ain't all about you. Your boy Ajah is hurting all over in a hospital bed! You lost your women but so what? Ajah almost lost his life! Think about that! So, next time you wanna criticize one of us, look in the mirror, guy. That's not hard 'cause you do it every twenty seconds anyway. Q needs to let you go, 'cause if you really think that you're an innocent cat, then hit me again! I dare you!"

I also wanted to vent about Eros sweating my favorite shirt and pants without permission, but I left it alone 'cause I said a mouthful. Was I the same cat who was evangelizing less than two hours earlier?

Eros stared at me speechless, looking so ready to beat me down. Q had already let him go. K.J was still holding me, and it was a good thing. The Teddy of old was back and I didn't want to leave. I wanted him to hit me so I could have a great reason to fight but Eros did nothing and walked away.

"Not the best way to get ready for church, huh?" K.J said as he released me.

I didn't ask for a glass of conviction juice, but my cousin gave it to me and I drank it. Q, who looked at Eros and me in awe and shock, shook his head and grinned after K.J's comment. Perhaps I did overreact, but Eros struck a nerve and I didn't regret a single word I said to him.

My cell phone rang again.

"Tell whoever it is I'll call them when I get back to T.O!" K.J said in frustration.

The caller ID was the hospital. I told them it was Ajani as I answered the phone.

"Yo, star, y'all still at the hotel?" he asked me.

"We're gonna check out just now," I replied.

"I'm not calling about that! Turn to channel twenty-six! Quick, hurry up!"

It had to be serious because Ajani sounded excited. I turned on the TV in the living room and asked him what was going on. He told me to put his voice on speakerphone. I told the guys to watch the big screen.

Sure enough, there was a huge reason for Ajani to get excited. According to a Toronto news program, the city's police had made the biggest OxyContin drug bust in Canadian history. They showed scenes of the Irie Club, where a few guys including Rancel Deverow were locked in handcuffs. Cops also raided the warehouse in Scarborough that was manufacturing the drug. It seemed surreal because one of the main contributors of the fallen empire was our boy Ajani Bethel.

"Ha ha ha!" laughed Ajani. "What goes around comes around, Deverow!"

I believed that all of us knew and understood what went down, but we flooded Ajani with questions, wondering what really happened between him and the Deverows. Unhesitant, Ajani gave us the lowdown on his adventures from Thursday afternoon to the present moment. He was so right about the opinion that he should've been dead already. Instead, the man was a miracle.

Q asked, "Ajah, you have any clue where Machete is during all of this?"

"Who knows?" he answered. "He's probably hiding, or he could be dead."

"Obviously not by the cops, 'cause they don't even know what happened to him," K.J said.

"Yo, God kept me from getting killed here in Windsor and arrested in T.O," Ajani testified. "If I go back to dealing, that would be like slapping Him in the face!"

I hummed in agreement while looking at my watch, it was twelve forty-five.

"Hey, Ajah, we gotta roll out! See you soon." I said.

We all said our farewells before I hung up the phone. I saw Eros noticing us grabbing our luggage and putting on our jackets.

"So where are we going now?" he asked.

"Church!" I answered with pride. "Wanna come?"

Eros sucked his teeth. "Why do I want to go to church after a weekend like this? Hah, you're on your own, guy."

"Actually he's not," said Q. "We're all going to church."

"What?" he said in surprise. "Y'all forget about me? Where am I gonna go? I don't even have clean clothes to wear!"

"Well, someone here has an apartment to chill at, but you just punched him and called him a backstabber."

I acted as if I didn't hear what Q said. Pulled out a blue turtleneck sweater, white T-shirt, and a pair of black jeans. Never swallowed so much pride in my life. My flesh didn't want to be nice, but I had to shun it despite the fact that I was ready to disown Eros as a friend. I walked over to him and displayed the chosen outfit. He didn't want to take it.

"What's the point of lending me your clothes if I have to take them off before going back to T.O?" snapped Eros.

I threw the clothes on the bed he was sitting on.

"No, you can keep them," I answered. "It's just material stuff. Right now, I know your pride's keeping you from asking if you could chill at my crib until church is over. I understand you're upset at me. So lemme answer it for you: NO! You disrespected me, and I don't wanna be late for service!"

Eros said nothing. I grabbed Ajani's luggage and mine and left the suite. Didn't want to miss a second of what God had in store for the end of a crazy weekend.

CHAPTER 92

TEDDY

I drove my car to Kingdom Workers Fellowship. Q decided to roll with me while K.J drove the Escalade, accompanied with the bitter guy.

Q looked relieved to travel with me, even though the drive was only five minutes. Like me, he was tired of listening to Eros and was thankful for me telling him off. I just smiled without comment. Didn't want to talk about it 'cause I was still angry about the incident and I wanted to move on. My mind was plaguing me with questions. How would my boys, especially Q, react to the high-energy, charismatic service? Was Eros going to change his mind and join us? Was I wrong in hitting him in the nuts? Was Ajani really going to watch the service on TV? Would this make or break the friendship of the Phat Five? I really had to be less anxious and allow God to handle every question in His own way.

Q and I waited in front of the church entrance. After the Escalade was parked, only K.J came out of the ride. It didn't bother me that Eros was uninterested. I really didn't want to see his face at all. He knew where we were at if he really needed us.

We arrived shortly after the praise and worship music started. The sanctuary was packed with limited seating available. I enjoyed sitting close to the front, but that wasn't going to be a reality that day. The usher found three seats in the second last row and that's where we sat. Wasn't a bad thing, because Q was a tall cat anyway.

The guys had to have been shocked to see me sing the church songs. I barely quoted rap lyrics when I wasn't born-again. They didn't sing, but Q and K.J were standing and clapping their hands. It was good to see, considering the fact that it was K.J's third visit and Q's first time in a Pentecostal setting for something other than food.

After praise and worship was a brief meet-and-greet moment. Janet was very excited to see Q and K.J, especially after the adventures of Saturday night. Min-T was also glad to see my boys. Because there were so many people to greet, they didn't try to chat. Min-T winked at me and pointed to the sky, indicating that the word he gave me on Thursday was truly from the Lord. I nodded my head and grinned.

Following the fellowship was offering time, a great solo by Kaitlyn, an awesome dance number by my baby's dance crew, and a special Hip-Hop selection by X-Secula. Those who weren't at the Bless fest concert on Saturday received a small taste of how good the event was. Judging by the applause, the people weren't disappointed.

Finally, it was time for the sermon. Pastor Jackson approached the pulpit, and I highly anticipated a dynamic message from him, especially for the first TV broadcast in the church's history. However, to the surprise of many, Pastor said that the Lord told him to allow Tyrone Carter a.k.a Min-T to bring the word. I thought that was so ideal and a great idea because Min-T was young, zealous, and had a strong passion for God that many youth needed to see and hear.

Min-T was an incredible motivational speaker. He knew how to get people's attention and it was working for K.J and Q. I prayed that God would speak to their hearts in a powerful way. I also prayed that Eros would make his way inside the sanctuary before the service was over. When the Power Point presentation began for Min-T's sermon, I knew that my prayers would be answered. The title of the sermon was "The World's Approval" and the focused verse was Mark 8:36. I was reading the same verse that morning!

My boys must've thought that I was tripping 'cause I was grinning hard and tapping my feet while sitting. I didn't expect them to understand the revelation. God, I couldn't explain it anyway. All I knew in my heart was that something incredible was about to happen!

CHAPTER 93

K.J.

It felt strange when the fellas and I walked into the sanctuary. Some people stared at me hard, trying to figure out if I really was the guy on the Club V stage. Their expressions alone made it easy to observe who was clubbing at Jam Fest and who was praising at Bless Fest. A few faces recognized me from the showcase and nodded their heads. Two or three should've been wearing a robe and carrying a gavel, 'cause they did a terrible job not showing that they were judges. They viewed me from head to toe, probably wondering how I had the nerve to come into church after rapping ungodly stuff on international TV. My bad. If the church had a sign outside that read Saints Only, I'd leave immediately, dragging the judges and half the congregation behind me.

As the praise and worship music went forth, I started to clap but my mind was on Saturday night. It hadn't really hit me that despite losing the showcase, two of hip-hop's biggest labels wanted to sign me! Hundreds of thousands, possibly a million people saw me perform on TV! My days of being a broke college student and a part-time barber were almost over! Yet, at the present moment, nothing was more important to me than being in the house of God.

The atmosphere felt good. Must've been the anointing, according to church people. I didn't understand the word fully, but I knew that being in the place felt extraordinary. I was at peace. Something I wish I felt everyday.

During the brief fellowship session, Janet gave me a hug, expressing her joy to see me at church again. Teddy's friend Min-T did the same thing. Then suddenly a small group of teens came up to me asking for my autograph. Even church kids saw my performance! I signed a few small pieces of paper but refused to sign a young girl's Bible. It just didn't seem right.

Kaitlyn wasn't able to come to me during fellowship 'cause she was on stage with the praise and worship team. We did eye each other. She gave me the prettiest smile I'd ever seen in my life.

Offering followed fellowship. The pastor's wife said on the pulpit that guests were not required to do something called tithing, but everyone was encouraged to give an offering. I only had thirty bucks, which was going to be my lunch money for the rest of the week. Told myself that I had to spend wisely, but then I laughed. God was good to me, and I was going back to T.O as a celebrity. The chance of me sleeping for dinner was like the Toronto Raptors winning the NBA Finals. I dropped a twenty in the offering plate like it was on fire.

Kaitlyn sang a song called *Because of Who You Are*. She sang the worship song with incredible passion. I was mesmerized by her performance 'cause it was obvious that she was singing to God.

I so enjoyed getting to know Kaitlyn during the weekend. She was the total package inside and out. Yet, the more I fell for her, the more I felt that she wasn't into me. I thought Kaitlyn liked me as a person, but I concluded that she was going to be the wife of a pastor. Not a feisty, conscious rapper like me. Didn't mean I was gonna give up pursuing her.

Janet's dance troop was off the hook as expected. My man X-Secula rapped again, and he was ridiculous. Best MC I ever heard. Told myself that once I became a name in hip-hop, I was gonna get him much deserved recognition in the industry.

Then came the preached word of God by Min-T. Had no idea the dude could preach. His confidence on the pulpit reminded me of a guy named Creflo Dollar I saw on TV a few weeks prior. His zealous attitude immediately grabbed my attention. I didn't have a Bible, but everything was presented on a projector screen. The church did everything with excellence. When Min-T mentioned the key scripture verse, Teddy got giddy like a three year-old watching Dora the Explorer. Didn't know why, didn't ask. But I read it very carefully:

> "For what will it profit a man if he gains the whole world,
> and loses his own soul?"
>
> Mark 8:36 (NKJV)

Min-T gave a testimony about his early adult days as a saxophone musician. At the age of nineteen, he was playing in a band doing jazz concerts across the world. He was swimming in fame and fortune. Min-T said that at first it was a dream come true, yet every night before he went to sleep he felt emptiness. Trying to fill the void, he involved himself in orgies with women, marijuana, and cocaine. To make a long story short, his experiments led to a dramatic downfall in his career. The day before he was supposed to go to a rehab clinic in Detroit, Min-T saw and heard Pastor Jackson preach at an outdoor revival.

He received Christ as a result of the meeting in 1997, and has been on fire for him ever since. God was the solution to his emptiness.

That story hit me hard. It seemed as if the sermon was intended just for me, and I started to wonder if Teddy was telling Min-T my business but as I saw how others were reacting to the message, I knew that it was sent from God. Even Q looked like he was absorbing the Word like a sponge.

My goals for the weekend were to show the world that I was the next great MC. I believed that I did, contrary to the belief of fifty-one percent of Club V's drunk folk. The cats that counted, such as music executives and hip-hop personalities, knew that I was more of the real deal than Verbal Pain. My raw talent got me towards fulfilling my desire. It was what I wanted and I thought it was what I needed.

When I woke up on Sunday, I wasn't overjoyed like how most would feel in my position. X-Secula's *Forgiveness* song was in my head again. I didn't want to think about it because it brought back memories of my dad. Memories that led to my hate for him. Hate that escalated from un-forgiveness. Un-forgiveness that made me a bitter man every day, including the day after the greatest event of my life. I told myself that my bitterness had to go, especially if I wanted to sleep more than three hours a night on a consistent basis. My solution was the title of the song. I had to forgive my father and Roderick Bailey.

As I sat through the service, I wanted to believe that I didn't have to forgive those men. I wanted to believe that making hip-hop my lifestyle and surrounding myself around positive people would be enough to end my bitterness. I had to come to the realization that even if I was able to become a hip-hop superstar, marry Kaitlyn, start my own school, and buy my moms her dream home, I would still sleep only three hours a night. The world was mine for the taking, but my soul was decaying because I couldn't do what Jesus did for me on the cross years ago. *Ouch.*

The peaceful feeling that I had at the beginning of service turned into fear, which quickly led to conviction. It felt as if I heard a voice saying that if I didn't make God my number one passion, I would never be happy. I had to let Christ take control of my life because Kellen Jamal couldn't make Kellen Jamal happy.

A tear rolled down my cheek. It was time for a change to happen.

The sermon was concluded and Min-T offered the invitation of salvation. Before he fully explained to the audience why one should accept Christ as their Savior, I tapped Teddy on his shoulder and told him I was going to the front. My cousin smiled, got up from his seat, and went with me.

CHAPTER 94

Q

I was hoping that church wasn't going to be as long as Teddy predicted. Two and a half hours seemed very long, 'cause when I went to Catholic Church with my parents as a kid, forty-five minutes felt like eternity. My stomach was already growling for the soul food that Teddy promised we'd get following the service. I wasn't even in the church yet, so my situation wasn't good.

Furthermore, I wanted the day to fly quick 'cause I was ready to go home. If everything went well for Ajani in the hospital, we'd be on our way to the Greater Toronto Area around early evening. It was one of the craziest weekends I'd ever experienced, and the thought of my condominium made me crave relaxation. Plus, I was in crazy heat. Not sexing Whitney was like a starving man resisting a plate of his favorite food. Nah, it was like resisting an all-you-can-eat buffet! But, I'm glad I didn't give in, 'cause Katrina was a wonderful wife. Despite my mistakes as a husband, I believed that she was faithful to me. Hopefully faithful enough to re-greet me with the sexy lingerie she wore on Thursday.

So Eros decided not to join us for the service. I don't blame him, plus all of us were tired of hearing his voice. Eros' ego had grown ten times the size of his head recently, which is why he wouldn't admit that he screwed up. I was so glad Teddy told him off, 'cause I so wanted to tell him that he deserved what those girls did to him. Maybe that was mean for me to think that, but the cat almost convinced me to ruin my marriage. Thank God for common sense.

Man, the church was nice-looking. There were plenty of youth in attendance as well but what impressed me the most was the church's racial diversity. Everybody was a different shade of brown, and that made me feel more comfortable. It was so packed that we had no choice but to sit in the back. That was good for me because of my height and if I had to sneak out of the building for a smoke. I hoped that I didn't have to, because I was sick of giving into the nicotine and I needed to quit big time.

Even though I was hungry and horny, it didn't stop me from enjoying the program. The opening singing was pretty good and fellowship time was kinda funny. Three or four people had no idea who I was 'cause they asked me if I ever considered playing B-ball for a living. Two girls didn't know my name but asked for an autograph just in case I was somebody important and an elderly woman said that she enjoyed watching me play for the Detroit Pistons. Oh, how I wished she were right.

I had no cash for the church offering, so I charged twenty bucks from my Visa. I thought I could at least contribute to the highly anticipated dinner afterward. The dance, hip-hop, and solo by the girl K.J liked were impressive. It was just like the one Bobby Jones gospel show I glanced a few months ago on BET.

A minister nicknamed Min-T who barely looked over the age of thirty, presented the sermon, and he was a great speaker. This was way more enjoyable than the priests my parents pretended to like. Min-T seemed like a down-to-earth guy that could easily relate to the struggles we face today, which was refreshing to see from a church person. It was no wonder Teddy wanted us to come to Bless Fest.

Min-T gave a dynamic story of his life, although I couldn't remember a lot of details due to my thoughts of eating chicken with BBQ sauce. However, the main points that stuck with me were that Min-T had the great lifestyle and lost everything, but God restored him after wanting to commit suicide. It was very inspiring to hear, 'cause I so felt like giving up after the doctors said my basketball playing was done. There was little reason for optimism in my life, because basketball was my world. I loved it more than my wife, and it showed very quickly in my marriage.

I wasn't sure if I really needed to give my life to God. Mind you, my life wasn't great, but it wasn't terrible either. Yet, God's love seemed real as it showed through the Christians in the service. I think the atmosphere in the place made the message sound so alive and it was peaceful, even though the people weren't trying to be quiet. Seemed like an oxymoron, but it made perfect sense to me because the people were filled with joy. It looked like a constant joy that never went away. Something I hadn't experienced since college, and once it left it never came back on a regular basis and eventually, it left completely. Something needed to happen in my life in order for it to come back.

There were three things that I wanted to happen in the very near future. The first was a great marriage with Katrina, which was an uphill battle yet a great possibility. Second was to quit smoking. I regretted the day I resumed the habit, and I needed to be free of nicotine if I wanted the third thing to happen again, which was playing pro basketball. It was an extremely long shot, but it could happen with plenty of faith, determination, and discipline. I lacked those qualities for the last two years. Maybe I did need to give my life to God so he could restore me like Min-T, but there was one thing that was holding me back, and it was my wife.

Katrina was an atheist. She would shun at the thought of me going to church. She didn't want a reverend to conduct our wedding ceremony, but she gave in to prevent any conflict with our families. Katrina went hardcore with it after 9/11/2001, because she refused to believe that a God who's supposedly perfect would allow thousands of people to die through catastrophe. I never debated the issue because I wasn't one to discuss God-related material but that would change if I received salvation. What was more important to me, a relationship with God or a stress-free relationship with Katrina?

After the message, the speaker asked the audience if there was anybody who wanted to receive salvation. K.J was the first person to walk to the front, and Teddy went with him. Teddy was already saved, so I think he went up just to be supportive. That amazed me big time! K.J was days away from signing a record deal that would make him rich and famous. Wasn't he already on the right track? Then again, perhaps he wanted God to control his destiny to prevent big challenges from killing his dream. I became envious, I should've had God in my life while I was playing college ball. It might've prevented a whole lot of drama from occurring.

Lord knows I wanted to join the cousins at the alter and I wanted Christ in my life, but I thought of my wife. Katrina would be disappointed. Fear had set in my mind, and then I felt a tap on my right shoulder. It was the guy who did the gospel rap, asking me if I wanted to go up for prayer. I was about to shake my head, but then I realized that prayer wouldn't hurt my situation at all. Matter of fact, it would make it better. I smiled and said yes, hoping that a prayer would be the beginning of my happiness.

CHAPTER 95

EROS

It was getting real uncomfortable sitting in the SUV. Every move I made seemed to trigger groin pain. It was annoying and frustrating. I was tired of playing Playstation and watching DVDs 'cause I wanted a bed to sleep in. I just wanted to go home, drink something heavy, and watch porn until I fell asleep.

Never in my life have I been so mad at everything around me. I was angry that I had no clothes other than what was on my body. Mad at my boys spending over two hours in church, forgetting that I existed. Pissed off at Teddy for damaging my favorite organ and most importantly, I was mad at the opposite sex for being the opposite sex.

I'd known Teddy for about eight years, and he never hit me or told me off before Sunday morning. He did have a small point that I was being selfish over the weekend and maybe I shouldn't have hit him in the stomach, but the boy should've kept his mouth shut about where I was to those two witches. So, what if he'd have to lie about me? God would've forgiven him. Shoot, the boy claimed he was born-again, yet he gave into smoking weed and clubbing on Friday. I really believed Teddy showed the girls his hotel key so I'd be caught. Whether I deserved my punishment or not, he stabbed me in the back, and it would be hard for me to trust him again.

Nobody had my back about the incident, but I couldn't blame my boys. K.J deserved my support at the showcase. He still didn't tell me how the battle was and how he placed. Ajani almost died while I was trying to bang two chicks in his suite without his blessing and Q was sick of me trying to make him a player. So, I should've been a more supportive friend, I guess. As for what those girls did to me, I wasn't repentant what so ever.

I'm sure that a regular player would change his ways if they experienced what Juanita, Nivea, and those models did to me. I'm sure that a regular player would become a one-woman man and treat his woman like a queen forever more. However, I wasn't a regular player. I hated women more than ever. They brought the Incredible Hulk out of me.

Many people would disagree with my attitude, but I had a good reason for my anger. If I was a faithful guy who found out that my girl was cheating, would I try to get her back through physical humiliation and destroying clothes? Only if I was a man who enjoyed humiliating women. But, an average Joe wouldn't resort to that and ruining their wardrobe. That was considered psycho! Women would do it to men because they are evil and receive praises from their girls. Left Eye was applauded when she burned down her boyfriend Andre Rison's home. It was only luck that they got to do their evil intentions on me. Never again!

I promised myself that I would elevate my game once I returned to the GTA. No longer would I sleep with women looking for a relationship. My goal was to date, bang, and move to the next woman. Becoming a maintenance man or a porn star sounded more inviting by the minute. Plus getting paid for the art I did best was way past due.

The time was approaching three-thirty. Church didn't seem done and I had to pee but I didn't want to go in the building to use the washroom. It was the whole church setting and its people that I couldn't stand 'cause they couldn't stand cats like me who preyed on the fine sisters. However, my bladder wasn't a respecter of person, and it had holding issues since the torture. Hence, I got out of the Escalade and went inside the building.

The men's washroom wasn't hard to find 'cause it was in the lobby. I'm glad there was a toilet available 'cause I had to pee sitting down like a woman. Yes, Teddy hit me that hard! Minutes afterward, I left the washroom and headed towards the exit, but the noise and applause in the sanctuary made me curious. Don't know why, 'cause it wasn't like I'd never been to a Pentecostal church. One of the doors was open, so I took a quick peek. People were at the front of the stage lifting their hands and getting extra spiritual. Including three cats that looked like Teddy, Q, and K.J.

Now I was extra curious about what was taking place. I sat in the last row, trying to figure out what I was witnessing. It looked like Q and K.J got bit by the Born-Again bug just like Teddy. Their hands were in the air, doing the rituals like everybody else. Why would a hip-hop artist and a former basketball player want to become Christians? It's not like they were in dire straits or on their deathbed. Then again, neither was Teddy, but I didn't fully understand why he made that move. They looked serious up there too but were they for real? I wondered what was preached for them to make such a decision.

I know K.J liked the singer who resembled actress Eva Mendes, but why go the born-again route to pick her up when he could have groupie women as a celebrity rapper? Q must've gone up because he was too insecure and weak to solve his own problems. Whatever the reasons, I chose to blame Teddy. Why else would the Phat Five be in church during Jam Fest weekend?

I was upset and disappointed. If those guys received salvation for real, Ajani and I would be the last true partiers standing. Did that mean the end of the Phat Five going to clubs, smoking up, and getting tipsy? I definitely didn't want to hang around three Jesus freaks; that was almost as bad as being in a monogamous relationship.

A small part of me understood why anyone would want to give their life to God. The setting seemed emotional. People were crying, shouting, dancing, and praying. I actually kept my mind away from lustful thoughts for a brief moment. Yet, I would never surrender into Christianity. Sex was too good for me to give up until marriage, especially since I decided years ago that I was never getting married. God and I just didn't see eye-to-eye.

I went back to the Escalade before the guys were done at the front. Nobody was going to persuade me to become something I didn't want to be. If I needed God, I knew how to talk to him but I loved my lifestyle, and I wasn't going to change it for anyone.

CHAPTER 96

K.J

For a long time, I studied the Bible and the foundation of Christianity. I compared it with other religions and wondered why Christianity was the most popular. I discovered the answer while spending time at Bless Fest weekend. Being a Christian isn't religious, it's about having a personal relationship with God and striving to please Him and that's what I was ready to do.

After I went to the altar, about fifty people joined me to get salvation. Including Q, who was accompanied with Isaiah! Isaiah hugged me, Teddy hugged Q while trying to hold back tears, and I hugged Q. It was an emotional moment that I'd never forget. We, with the rest of the people at the front said what the pastor called "the sinner's prayer." From that point, we were considered Christians. It felt so right, yet it seemed so surreal. Dramatic events were happening at an extremely fast pace.

Before we went back to our seats, Q and I had to go to another room with the rest of the new converts. It wasn't for very long and basically one of the church's ministers asked me if I had any questions about what I'd just did. I said no. Then he asked me to fill a confidential short form that asked for my name, address, and three most important prayer requests. Without being specific, I wrote wisdom in making career choices, family restoration, and peace. He read the form and immediately prayed for my requests with me. Knowing that I didn't live in Windsor, he concluded by highly recommending that I find a church home in the GTA. I nodded. Then he said that he'd keep my requests in prayer throughout the week, and to expect a phone call from him just to see how I was doing. It was a thoughtful and encouraging five minutes.

Once church was over, people rushed towards me. Word spread to the church folk that I was a reality TV star who could rap very well. I shook many hands, gave some hugs, answered some questions about the experience, and signed a few more autographs. A few ladies were trying to eye-seduce me, not caring that I'd just been saved and we were in God's house. That's when I tried to look at Kaitlyn, who was talking with other people. One guy threw me off, asking me if I was going to do gospel rap because of my salvation.

"I don't know," I said to the man. "Haven't thought about it yet."

"You need to. Christians can't be doing what you were doing last night."

I stood there speechless as he left. Before him, everybody was speaking words of encouragement.

"Don't let him steal your joy," said Isaiah as he approached me from behind. "Enjoy what the Lord has done in your life."

As I gave him a hug, I asked, "Yo, is that supposed to be my next move? Become a gospel rapper? No offense, man, 'cause you're incredible at what you do."

"None taken. My advice for you is to seek God. Talk to Him like you talk to me. Give Him thanks every day for His grace and mercy, read his word and if you do all these things, He will direct every area of your life."

A pretty good answer for not answering my question. For a few moments we talked about everything that took place from the time I met him on Saturday night to the present moment. When we discussed hip-hop culture, it was like I was talking to a clone. Our passions were almost identical, and the way we shared our thoughts and feeling about the music, one would've thought we had known each other for years. I definitely had the highest respect for him as a Christian Hip-Hop artist.

"Yo, somehow someway, we gotta hook up soon," said an enthusiastic Isaiah. "I need to get you on my upcoming album, so make sure you don't bounce before giving me your address info."

"We aren't going before getting some food first. I'm mad hungry," I said.

"No doubt. I'll see you downstairs then."

"Cool."

As he left to talk to some of his fans, I noticed Kaitlyn in the front of the church finishing a conversation with another lady. This was my opportunity to talk to her one last time before leaving Windsor. I threw a mint in my mouth and hoped for the best. Kaitlyn saw me approaching and smiled big, leaving me no choice but to do the same. Her positive energy was addicting.

"Look at you," said Kaitlyn as our hands greeted. "You must be feeling like a billion dollars right now."

I replied, "Better than that, this feeling's priceless! There's so much things I'm feeling right now, I can't even describe it, Kaitlyn. God is so good!"

"All the time! Get ready, K.J, 'cause the Lord's gonna do something in your life that's bigger than any freestyle competition. I see you as a strong leader and someone that's gonna reach today's youth in a dynamic way. I saw how people came to the altar after you made the first move and I see how people are drawn to you, celebrity or non-celebrity. Trust me, its powerful!"

"Funny you say that, 'cause that's how I see you. Without having to be loud or flashy, you stand out in everything you do. If you were standing next to Halle Berry, J.Lo, Carmen Electra, and Beyonce, you'd still stand out. Not because you're equally beautiful and more, but because God's presence is shining all over you. People love you 'cause you're a diva of humility. Women like you absolutely blow my mind."

I made Kaitlyn blush again, except this time she kept eye contact with me. If she wasn't into me, I didn't know the definition of attraction.

"Wow," she said, "you got lyrics with or without a microphone. You are definitely a man who says what's on his mind. I thought you were giving me encouragement, but it sounds like you're trying to pick me up again."

"I'm doing both," I admitted. "But please don't think that I got saved just to get with you. If I never see you again, I'm still gonna serve the Lord."

"Good, 'cause I can't give you what you want in life."

"What about friendship and ten digits?"

"For you, I can say yes to that."

Friendship, the F-word that men hate to hear or say when they want to get with women but it was ideal for us because we barely knew each other. Also, we had busy lives and lived four hours away from each other. If Kaitlyn was going to be my future wife, friendship was important and because she was a seasoned Christian, sex was out of the question. But I had to stop myself from thinking too far ahead.

Politely changing the subject, Kaitlyn asked me if I had an idea of which church to attend once I returned to Toronto. I shook my head, asking her if she had any recommendations.

"I don't know any in Scarborough where you live," said Kaitlyn, "but there's one in Brampton that I really love called Harvest Worship Tabernacle. It's a multicultural, relationship-based, high-energy church that focuses largely on worship and God's word. I go there whenever I'm in the GTA and as a matter of fact, Min-T is preaching there in two weeks and a few of us are going up for the trip."

"Say no more. I'll check it out on Sunday," I said. "Word of mouth is the best advertising."

Suddenly, Teddy, Janet, Q and Min-T approached us. We all talked about the service, details of how Ajani and Eros were doing, and my record deal offers as we went downstairs for some food. It was a joyous moment, but most importantly, I had peace in my spirit. Having the Lord run things in my life was the greatest feeling in the world.

CHAPTER 97

TEDDY

"Ted, I thought about what we talked about this morning, and after I went to the altar, there was no way I couldn't give my life to God," Q said with an expression of joy. "I need Him to help me get my life back on track."

I said, "If you put Him first, God will do wonderful things for you but I'll keep it real with you, Q, good things don't happen overnight. The road may get rocky but if you keep trusting God, favor will head in your direction."

"Man, I hope so. I don't know how I'm gonna tell Trina what happened today. She's an atheist."

As we were on the line waiting for dinner, I felt the need to pray for Q. My faith was at an all-time high thanks to the salvation of Q and K.J. Without feeling the need to let him know what I was about to do, I turned around to face him and placed my hand on his shoulder.

"Father God," I prayed, "we touch and agree right now about the good things you're about to do in Q's life. But Lord, we know that Katrina does not believe that you exist. We pray that she will believe in you and want to know who you are based on your presence on Q's life. Bless their marriage and we pray for total prosperity in their lives. We ask all of this in the name of Jesus! Amen."

"Amen," said Q as he pulled out a pack of cigarettes from his pocket.

"Yo," I said in panic, "you can't smoke in here. You gotta do that outside!"

He looked at me with an *I-know-that-stupid* expression and threw the pack towards a garbage pail that was about twenty feet away. It was nothing but pail.

"When I had to fill out the info form, my three prayer requests was marriage restoration, getting to the NBA, and to quit smoking," said Q as a few people applauded the shot and what he threw away. "If I can pick up the habit, I can drop it again!"

"No doubt," I replied.

"You saw those two teenagers I spoke to after church? They both knew about my game, and one of them actually promised me that he'd pray every day that I get a chance to play professional basketball. Now, if those kids have faith in God like that, I have to equal it and then some. Sky's the limit, baby!"

I nodded my head in agreement. The food at the buffet seemed unlimited as well. For an optional love offering, we had a choice of BBQ chicken, BBQ ribs, rice and peas, fried rice, macaroni pie, tossed salad, coleslaw, pasta salad, croissants, spring rolls, and fruit punch. A deal you couldn't find anywhere in Windsor. I asked Janet to prepare a take-out container for me while I gathered food for Ajani and Eros.

I thought about both friends as Min-T delivered a powerful sermon. It was unfortunate that Eros didn't make his way in the service to hear the Word. I hoped that Ajani took the opportunity to watch the service on TV. Nevertheless, it was an awesome day as I witnessed Q and K.J give their lives to Christ. They had great challenges ahead, but Jesus was on their side now. God had certainly increased my expectations during Bless Fest weekend.

As the entire gang prepared to sit at a table, the cell in my pocket started to vibrate.

"K.J, are you still unavailable?" I asked my cousin as I opened the phone to see the caller ID.

"Yep," K.J quickly answered.

"Oh, never mind, it's the hospital. Hello . . . Don't worry, we'll be right there!"

I hung up the phone with a serious expression on my face. Janet noticed it right away.

"What is it?" she asked.

"It's about Ajani," I said. "We have to go to the hospital now!"

CHAPTER 98

AJANI

As crappy as my body felt, I felt like a dozen monkeys were off my back. I was a believer of what goes around comes around, and Rancel Deverow was the latest victim. I began to flip through the Toronto news channels with the hope of discovering more information on the drug bust. No chance. The story was too new, and the details I really wanted to know had to be obtained from insiders. I wasn't calling anyone 'cause I'm sure rumors were spreading about my death.

I was about to attempt eating my fat-free, salt-free, sugar-free lunch courtesy of the hospital when two cops entering my room interrupted me. Being a former criminal for less than a day, I hated cops and they were White, which made it worse in my opinion. Obviously, they were in my room to ask questions about what happened, but I kept my guard up. There was no such thing as a trustworthy cop.

I kept the story short and simple. Carla and I scripted the story before she left yesterday. A friend from Detroit and me got into a heated argument based on a misunderstanding. He thought I was sleeping with Carla, his fiancée and that led to a gruesome fight. Carla broke up the battle, telling her man that what he heard wasn't true 'cause people mistook her for her younger sister. Ricardo believed her, forgave me, and I forgave him. Then he went back to Detroit. I asked them not to press charges. The police took notes and asked clique questions. Then they told me to have a nice day and leave Windsor as soon as I got better. How courteous. I had no tolerance for cops so it was good that they didn't stay long.

Frustrated, I began searching for something else to watch. I needed to keep the positive energy I was feeling, 'cause I hated being restricted to a hospital bed. I had to be thankful to God for escaping death once again, but I questioned why. Was the Grim Reaper around the corner or in the hospital? Why was I still alive? I wanted answers. I told myself that if I was well enough, I'd follow Teddy to church. Immediately after I said that, I flipped to a channel that had a familiar looking lady singing gospel music, she looked like the pretty Latino woman that K.J was digging. It was Teddy's church live on TV, what perfect timing.

All I wanted to hear was a message about God, and that was very unusual for me because I hadn't been inside a church in over two decades and it hadn't been a nice experience. I was an energetic five-year old kid in a small chapel in Kingston, Jamaica. Seemed like the preacher was yelling at us as if we were evil. The thirteen people in attendance were running around like headless chickens, crying like babies, and singing loud and off-tune. I didn't understand the agenda whatsoever. My mother never went back and neither did I. Since then, church always left a bad taste in my mouth.

I didn't feel like watching the church sing, so I did some channel surfing. The Raptors game was in the first quarter and they were already being blown out. NCAA B-ball wasn't on yet. TBS was showing the *Rush Hour* movie again. It was back to the church program.

After more singing and a few church commercials, the program got interesting. The music and dance numbers were tight. The people were having fun in church, which was a nice surprise for me and it had Christian urban music. It seemed odd, but it actually worked. Kaitlyn's solo wasn't unexpected, but Janet's dance troop was tighter in the church than it was before she was saved. The hip-hop cat was tripping me out and they quickly took away my belief that all churches were out of touch with society.

I heard my cell phone ring. It was probably Savannah. I still wasn't ready to talk to her. Telling her that I was in the hospital would lead to extra drama that I wasn't ready for yet. She would probably arrive in Windsor before I had a chance to hang up the phone. There was no great explanation to give Savannah about my condition. Lies were out of the question, and so was avoiding her altogether and I still had a four-hour drive ahead of me to figure out a game plan.

Finally, the sermon was about to be presented. I thought the message would've been from the pastor, but he called on some guy named Tyrone. He took advice from Erykah Badu, I guess. Dry joke. I honestly didn't want a young cat telling me about God. After all, preachers were usually old men who knew the entire Bible better than own family, right?

Man, was I wrong. The man knew God, and it showed through his message. I couldn't remember the scripture verse that he based his sermon on, but it had something to do with men who tried to gain worldly possessions and lost their souls. At first I felt for sure that he wasn't talking about cats like me, 'cause I'd never lost my soul or sold it to the devil but the speaker used his life story as an example of what the verse was explaining.

The man went from rags to riches to rags as a jazz musician. Fame and fortune was his world and his desire but the speaker was moving quickly down the road to hell. What hit me like a ton of bricks was when he described how everything started to crumble after he got involved with drugs. His promiscuity with sex led him to impregnate two members of the band that he toured with and he begged them to have abortions, which didn't work so he had to give them fifty grand each to do it. The cocaine highs messed up his performances, resulting in unemployment and he lost his home due to lack of cash and owing the government tax money.

The weekend up until the present moment was my example of life falling apart as a criminal. My bodily wounds were the result of living dangerously, and I considered them as a reminder that I should've been dead. The preacher said that if it weren't for the grace of God, he would've committed suicide. Was it grace or luck that saved me from being thrown off a twenty-five story building?

If it was really grace, it has been riding my back for a long time. I got through the crazy drama of the weekend thanks to grace. Grace saved me from killing someone or being murdered when the opportunities were plentiful. The fact that Savannah was still my woman and A.J wasn't exposed to my lifestyle was a result of grace. The reality that my four friends still socialized with me even though I was a police target was grace kissing me on the cheek. I used to call all of it luck, but after the miracle on Saturday, I realized that luck was limited. Grace has staying power.

I made the decision not to deal anymore, but I knew the consequences weren't going to be pretty. I didn't want my lady and son to see me in a wounded, defeated condition. The truth would hurt Savannah big time and I could lose the love of my life for good. As for being paid, I would have to do it the honest way. It wasn't being law-abiding that I hated, but the monotony of driving a mail truck day in and day out. Quitting that job wasn't an option at the moment, but I would be off for a few weeks on sick leave. That would give me good time to weigh my life options.

My situation with the Deverows were still unresolved. Yes, Rancel was in jail, but where was Machete? Was the man who asked me for drugs in Toronto an undercover cop who did the drug bust? If so, was I next on his list, and last but not least, what would happen to me if the Deverow family knew that I was still alive? I knew the answer to the last question. The basement in my home was going to see plenty of me in the upcoming weeks.

My future wasn't looking good. If it wasn't for my family, I would move to the U.S or back to Jamaica and start fresh. There had to me more to life than what I was picturing. I began to fear the worst as I lay in the hospital bed. Pessimism wanted to take over and suddenly I desired to stay in the hospital just so I wouldn't have to go back to Toronto.

Shut up, Ajani! Don't be stupid.

I made myself listen to the rest of the message and thank God I did, because I was quickly realizing who God is. The preacher was broke, unemployed and homeless. When he gave his life to the Lord, a miraculous transformation took place. He was set free from drugs and alcohol, went to university, got a degree in music, got married, had two children and a full-time job as a youth pastor in the church. God gives people second chances to get their lives together.

The speaker added that for the first time after his salvation, he had a spirit of peace in his life.

PEACE?

Said the word so loud in my head, I thought I actually shouted. Peace? I almost forgot the meaning of the word. Dang, the last time I felt peace in my life was . . . I couldn't remember. Not since I moved to North America as a pre-teen. I forgot how peace felt. Never slept more than five hours a night with my eyes shut. I was always prepared for a life-or-death battle. Was peace an actual reality?

Soft music began to play. The speaker finished his message with an invitation for anyone who wanted to give their lives to God. He said that it was God's divine plan for me to listen to the message. In addition, he added that if the word spoke to me, then God wants to change my life for the better. While he was speaking, the camera focused on someone walking to the front of the church to be saved. It was K.J, and Teddy went with him! Obviously, I wasn't the only cat inspired by the message and it happened to be my two closest boys! Seconds later, several more followed K.J's footsteps. I just stared in amazement.

If there was anyone I knew that always kept it real, it was K.J. That's why when I saw him lift his hands and shed a tear, I knew he didn't go up to impress the lady vocalist that he talked about all weekend long. The camera focused on the crowd again, and suddenly I noticed a tall white boy with his head down and eyes closed. Q was among the crowd receiving salvation as well! Didn't see Eros, but that wasn't a surprise. That meant that in a span of four days, I discovered that Teddy, Janet, K.J, Q, and Savannah gave their lives to the Lord. Five people that were positive energy in my life, yet they wanted God to change their lives from good to great. What was I waiting for?

Once again, I thought of how I called on God when there was a ninety-nine point nine percent chance of me dying on Saturday night, and not being able to see my family again. He listened and that thought alone made me drop uncontrollable tears like a little boy who just was beaten with a stick. There was no doubt in my mind that I wanted to have Jesus in my life!

I turned off the TV, still crying. The warmth of the tears was stinging the cuts on my face. The nurse heard me and thought I was in pain, but I just shook my head. After she left the room, I realized my tears were representing happiness. I told myself that I was gonna ask Teddy to pray for my salvation when he arrived from church. It was time for a transformation!

However, when I spoke my thoughts aloud, the atmosphere changed in the room. Seemed as if the heat was turned up, 'cause I started to sweat. A headache was developing quickly and the pain of my bruises escalated. Didn't know what the hell was going on. Minutes passed, and the headache was turning into a migraine. It started to pound like a subwoofer speaker at a reggae concert! I put the pillow over my head to block any light, but it accomplished little. My body felt like it was on fire and I needed the nurses' help, but I was stubborn. Didn't want them to tell me I needed to stay another night. I told myself that if I tried to rest, the pain would decrease. Therefore, I closed my eyes and hoped for a physical breakthrough.

Minutes upon minutes passed, and the pain went nowhere. It was a physical attack unlike anything I'd ever felt in my life. It felt like it was more than a natural occurrence. It seemed like death was trying to take me while nobody was around. The room was starting to dim, but not in a good way. My body felt pressed to the mattress as if a heavy man was standing on me. I cried for help, but my voice was weak. Nobody was coming. Where was grace when I needed it?

Grace is gone, Ajani! You're mine now!

Sounded like the voice came from within the room, but nobody was around. Forget waiting for Teddy and the guys to show up. I needed God to save me right then, just in case I didn't make it out of the hospital. Somehow, I managed to grab the telephone to dial Teddy's cell phone number. Good thing I remembered the number, 'cause my cell phone with the contact list wasn't within arm's reach.

"Guy," I said to Teddy, "I need to be saved now!"

He said that he was on his way. I dropped the receiver without hanging it up. The migraine pain accelerated.

"God," I pleaded, "save me from this misery. Anything that you want me to do, I'll do it!"

Instantly the pounding in my head calmed down. It was enough for me to fall into a deep sleep.

"Ajah? Ajah!"

Hearing Teddy's voice, I opened my eyes from a power sleep that felt like it lasted a few hours. To my surprise, there were seven people in the room: Teddy, Janet, K.J, Q, K.J's lady friend, a dude who looked like the rapper at church, and the guy who preached! It definitely felt like I was dreaming.

"Brought you some food, dog," K.J. said, "and some company. You know Kaitlyn from the fashion show, and this is Isaiah a.k.a X-Secula, and Minister Tyrone Carter."

"But off the pulpit we call him Min-T," added Janet as she kissed me on the cheek. "How are you feeling?"

Good question. I felt the kiss and the pain in my body, so that confirmed I wasn't dreaming. As for the extreme headache, it was almost gone but I still needed a Tylenol.

"Up and down," I replied. "I saw all of you on TV today. The message was good."

"Glad you checked it out," said a happy Teddy. "So I guess you know what happened to your boys."

I nodded and said, "If I was there, I'd take the same route."

"That's why we brought the church with us. When you called me, I asked the whole crew to come so that we could do this right."

Q said, "Ted had us tripping though! The guy made us thought that you were dying."

I told them that Teddy was half-right as I explained what happened to me from the time the service ended to the present moment. Everybody listened in amazement and silence.

"What you experienced was an attack of the devil," said Min-T. "He wanted to kill you before you got a chance to accept Christ as your Savior but we can stop that right now if you're ready to make that commitment."

I nodded.

"Then repeat these words after me," he said. "Dear Jesus . . . please forgive me for everything I've done to displease you . . . you said in your word that if we confess our sins . . . you are faithful and just to forgive us . . . and cleanse us of all unrighteousness . . . Lord, I open my heart to you . . . I want you to be number one in my life . . . this day and forever more . . . Thank you Lord for saving me . . . In Jesus name . . . Amen!"

As I repeated after Min-T, so did everyone in the room, immediately I felt God's love. Tears fell down my face again. After the salvation prayer, I lifted my hands and thanked God for giving me another chance in life. The gang began to clap their hands and celebrate as if I'd just won the lottery. When that happened, I saw Eros enter the room. He stayed by the entrance, waved at me, and said nothing. I nodded my head and continued to praise God. Nobody was ever going to steal my joy and peace again.

Min-T placed his hand on my shoulder and said, "Lord, we also pray for Ajani's healing right now. You said that its because of the pain you endured on the cross, we are healed. So now, we ask in faith that you completely heal Ajani of his wounds, his bruises, and his headaches in the name of Jesus! We thank you in advance for the victory and give you praise! In Jesus' name, amen!"

Just when I thought that God did enough on Sunday to prove that he's awesome, another super blessing happened in the midst of those who visited me. The doctor came in the room to check how I was progressing. I told him that I was doing much better, despite my wounds. After giving me a check-up, he couldn't prove otherwise so he gave me the okay to be released at six p.m.! Of course, that meant I had to visit my family doctor in Toronto, stay away from work, and visit rehab regularly. That sucked, but it was way better than staying in a hospital. The challenges and victories of a new life was about to begin.

Everybody did their best to take care of my paperwork and help me walk out of the building. Never in my life had I needed assistance for such little things. Thank God for true bred-drin. As soon as they helped me get into the back seat of my Escalade, I took out my cell phone. It was time to give my lady a much-deserved call.

"Hey baby," I answered after Savannah said hello.

"You don't know how to call people back?" she snapped. "I've wanted to talk to you since last night! I worry about you, y'know!"

"I know, and I'm sorry. Yesterday was a rough night."

"Wild weekend?"

"Baby, you have no idea. How's Lil' Man?"

"A.J's sleeping. We're on our way back to Richmond Hill right now."

"Did you enjoy your weekend?"

"Oh, Ajah, it was incredible! Life changing, I can't wait to tell you about it when you get here."

"I got stuff to tell you as well."

"Really, like what?"

"Not now, Vannah. It has to wait till I come home."

"You have to confess something again?"

Savannah sounded like she had flashbacks of when I told her I was a big-time cheat, I couldn't blame her. I just wanted to tell her that I gave my life to Jesus, but I would have to add the fact that she'd been dating a criminal for three years. I couldn't say one without the other and I had to tell her face-to-face.

I laughed, "Baby, just think about the Victoria's Secret stuff I got you instead of worrying about what I have to tell you."

She sucked her teeth.

"K, fine," said Savannah. "Hey, did you hear about the big multi-million drug bust in Scarborough? It was right by your old neighborhood, too! Everybody's talking about it!"

"Yeah, I saw it on the news."

"I hope the cops catch everyone involved in that mess, the drug game in T.O's gone way outta hand."

"Yeah, no doubt. Hey, I'll see you in a few hours, alright?"

"OK, sweetie. Drive safe. Love you."

"Love you too."

As I hung up, I prayed that peace of God would remain in me, 'cause my home would need it more than ever on Sunday night.

CHAPTER 99

TEDDY

Because of an exhilarating weekend and a sunset already in the midst, we decided to do the farewells in the hospital parking lot. While Ajani was on the phone, I went towards Q and gave him a hug. I asked him who was driving the Escalade back to Toronto.

"I guess I'm driving the first half," answered Q. "At least it'll keep my hands busy if I crave a cigarette."

"You'll be alright," I said. "Just think about what you want for the future and stay focused. All y'all should call each other frequently uplift each other and go to the same church. Do whatever it takes for you to keep your mind on the Lord."

"I hear ya, bro. So when are you coming up to T.O again?"

"Hopefully soon, I just found out that Min-T's preaching in Brampton in a couple of weeks, so I might roll with him for the support. Plus, a financially challenged student like me needs a few groceries from his mama anyway."

"True. Well, if Min-T's preaching, I'll be there to listen."

I gave him a pound and went to K.J. He was hugging Janet and Kaitlyn when I approached him.

"Guy!" I shouted. "Check a calendar when you get home, realize that it's 2003 and get yourself a cell phone like tomorrow. I wanna know all your plans from this day forth. Just call me your bootleg manager from now on!"

"Whatever, punk," K.J smiled as we hugged each other.

"I'm serious, but on the real, cuzin, I'm really proud of you for everything you accomplished this weekend. Especially this morning."

"If it wasn't for you I wouldn't have gotten saved. Actually, I should thank Janet for getting you saved. No, I should thank Kaitlyn for getting Janet saved."

Kaitlyn said, "Keep this chain reaction going and we'll be here all night."

Janet said, "Nah, Kate, he was gonna end at you. He's single and really wants another hug from you, that's all."

The smack talk continued for a few minutes before I noticed Eros sitting in the SUV. He was acting as if he had no friends at all, the current black sheep of the gang. As much as I didn't want to talk to him, I thought I could at least say bye. So I went towards Eros and gave him a head nod. He did the same.

"Thanks for getting me some food after church," he mumbled. "I'll return your clothes by mail after I wash them."

I sucked my teeth and told him not to sweat it.

"Just worry about staying outta trouble," I concluded.

"You got that right."

We gave each other a handshake. As I left him, I realized that through good or bad times, our friendship wouldn't be the same after our heated confrontation.

As I faced Ajani, he was already off the phone and saying farewell to Min-T and Isaiah.

"Look what God did through you, Ted," said Min-T. "Prophecy fulfilled."

Isaiah said, "Three friends born-again, with three totally different lifestyles. Ajani, your testimony can be a movie, yo!"

Ajani grinned. "Don't finish the script yet. The drama's not over."

"But the outcome already is," Min-T confirmed. "You're an overcomer getting ready to live the victorious life!"

I smiled at my longtime friend and shook his hand. Ajani grinned back. We didn't have to say anything to each other. He knew that I was going to pray for him and his family. I felt confident that Ajani was going to be successful at anything he put his heart to. Moreover, he was born-again, and so was Savannah. I pictured nothing but great things in their lives.

It was almost six-thirty by the time the good-byes were completed. They drove away as I said good riddance to the wildest weekend of my life.

The Christian walk consisted of keeping on the narrow, unpopular road. During the weekend, I tried to make an exit to the widely used highway a couple of times. However, it was by the grace of God that allowed me to keep pressing on the road less taken. As a result, three people decided to join me on the journey. That was the confidence booster I needed to continue living in accordance to God's agenda.

I smiled at Janet, and gave her a kiss on the lips as the rest of us headed to our homes.

CHAPTER 100

The drive back to Toronto was extremely unusual. The guys went two and a half hours without speaking a word to each other.

Ajani sat in the back seat with his eyes wide open. The closer they got to the city, the more terrified he became. Saved or unsaved, he could not get away from the tasks that lied before him. Most importantly, he did not want to lose Savannah. Thus, Ajani's trust in the Lord would be put to the test very shortly.

Eros was at the other side of the back seat, pretending to be asleep. He was so angry at the fact that situations did not go his way. In his heart, Eros knew that his attitude towards women was harsh, but to change meant too many adjustments to his lifestyle and unlike his four friends, he was not going to change, even if it meant staying bitter.

Q was in the front passenger seat with a smile on his face. For the first time since his wedding, he felt joyful. He was ready for the journey towards restoration, feeling confident that the prayer agreed by him and Teddy would be answered. In addition, imagining Katrina in the lingerie she wore on Thursday made Q glee with optimism for what was waiting for him at home.

K.J was in deep thought while driving the Escalade. He had become a celebrity and a Christian in less than twenty-four hours. Two term papers were due at the end of the week, and K.J had to make public appearances, arrange meetings with record label executives, and work some hours at the barbershop so he would be able to pay his rent for April. Somehow, in the midst of his busy schedule, he would have to make time for going to church and talking on the phone with Kaitlyn. The challenge would be great, but he was determined to let God have full control of his life.

Finally breaking the silence, Q asked everyone if they had participated in their last Jam Fest.

"Speak for yourself," Eros said as he opened his eyes. "I'll be there next year, no question about it and with a stronger game plan, too!"

Ignoring Eros' answer, he asked, "Ajani, what about you?"

"Guy, that's too far for me think about now," answered Ajani. "After this weekend, I thank God for every minute of life He gives me. I'll be blessed to make it past this week."

"The drug bust issue is really bad, huh?"

"Q, you have no idea."

"Dang . . . K.J, what about you?"

K.J replied, "They might ask me to attend, now that I'm Jam Fest alumni, especially if the event blows up in the TV ratings."

Eros asked, "Would you go in the battle next year?"

"Nope," K.J admitted. "I'm so ready to move on from that phase. I don't wanna do freestyles like that anymore. I don't even wanna watch the replay on TV."

"I wanna see it. I at least owe you that," Ajani said.

"Forget about it," said K.J. "That stuff is petty to me now."

"Damn, yo!" Eros shouted. "Y'all attitudes have changed for real! What did that man preach about anyway?"

"Plenty," Ajani said. "The message is on CD. When Ted sends it to me next week, I'll let you borrow it."

"Take your time with that. If it's not visual with pictures of female skin, it'll just collect dust in my house."

K.J shook his head and said, "If anybody needs that word Eros, it's you."

"K.J, when I'm ready for God, I'll just ask for Him. If God's cool with me becoming a gigolo or porn star, then me and him can be real tight!"

Q, Ajani, and K.J all sighed in unison.

Q said, "Yo, K.J, take the Mavis road exit. That's a shortcut to my crib."

On the way to Q's apartment in Mississauga, they stopped at a major intersection.

"K.J, turn the heat down," said Ajani as he lowered the power window. "I need some serious fresh air."

"Ajah, I'm taking your advice about spoiling the wife," Q said. "I'm taking Trina to Syracuse tomorrow for a couple of days."

"That's nice," he said. "They got some nice hotels there."

"Any recommendations?"

Ajani did not answer. His eyes were on a person driving a black Lincoln Navigator on the right side of the Escalade. The driver was looking directly at Ajani as if he recognized him from somewhere. He looked like Rancel with dreadlocks. As soon as Ajani knew who he was, he rolled up his window. Not delivered from his cursing, Ajani dropped an S-bomb in anger.

"What's wrong, guy?" Eros asked.

Ajani said, "K.J, when the light turns green, drive slow enough to let this Navigator pass you."

K.J nodded, even though he had no idea what was going on. The light went green, and K.J drove about twenty kilometers an hour. The Navigator made a right turn.

"I didn't want him seeing my license plate. Dude was looking at me hard," Ajani said, breathing a sigh of relief.

"Why, who was that in the Lincoln?" asked K.J.

"It looked like Denzel Deverow, Rancel's younger brother. Dude lives in New York, but he must be up here to bail out Rancel."

"Does he know you?" Eros asked.

"Oh yeah," replied Ajani. "Dude's quiet, but he can't stand me just like Rancel. That was the last cat I needed to see. If Denzel thinks he saw me and tells Rancel that I'm alive, then . . ."

Q said, "Let's hope that he didn't recognize you looking all wounded."

"Hope not. Dang, now I know why I received Christ today, 'cause right now I need Him to lead me more than ever."

"Don't we all," K.J agreed. "Only He could make sense out of our crazy drama."

ACKNOWLEDGEMENTS

Congratulations and thank you for finishing this book. People have very busy lifestyles, so I don't take your time and dedication for granted. I hope that reading CRAZY DRAMA was worth your leisure time, and I pray that this won't be the last D.A. Bourne novel that you'll read. To be honest, I'm just getting started!!!

Other than my wedding day and the birth of my daughter, this has to be the greatest moment of my life. Having a published novel is a dream come true, because it was a struggle to get here. I told God years ago that I wanted to minister to people worldwide through the media. I thought that it would come through gospel hip-hop. Although I love the music, God had another open door for me, and I'm so glad that I went through it.

The idea for this story came to me almost seven years ago when I was living in Windsor. The University of Windsor has an annual event in March called Sports Weekend (Jam Fest without the Freestyle Showcase). Many students (including myself) had to deal with the peer pressures like Teddy, except that we weren't fortunate to have a Bless Fest as another option. Hence, I developed the characters and began to write and the story was called SAINTZWEEKEND (the original name for Bless Fest). That title didn't last long 'cause it didn't sound too appealing. So I changed it to 5-4-3-2-1 (5 friends, 4 days, 3 nights, 2 parties, and 1 God), but that would've been a title that wasn't self-explanatory. My third choice was THE VIBE OF NECESSITY (ch. 41). I thought it sounded okay, until one of my boys told me that the name alone would defer him from buying the book. And he was right. The title had to be catchy enough for those who don't know me to grab it from the shelf. So I kept it short and simple: CRAZY DRAMA.

I have multiple reasons why this took seven years to complete, and if I explained it fully, reading this may take a while. All I can say is that God's timing is perfect, and the trials that I endured gave me better knowledge and understanding of this profession.

However, I will answer questions that some of you may have, such as:
What genre is CRAZY DRAMA classified under?

A: Good question, I'm glad you asked (lol). This book is Christian fiction, but some religious folk and the CBA may strongly disagree. I call this Life Fiction. Many novels glorify the sins of the world, and according to Romans 8:36, the wages of sin is death. Even though my stories bring the drama, my goal is to glorify Christ, who is "the way, the truth, and the life." (John 14:6)

Is OxyContin a real drug?

A: Yes.

Is OxyContin a serious problem in Toronto as portrayed in the novel?

A: Not even close.

Is Ghetto Heroin real?

A: No.

Is Hillbilly Heroin real?

A: Yes.

Which Phat Five character best resembles D.A. Bourne?

A: None of them! I'm in this career for the long haul, so I can't afford to write stories that are only based on my life. That's what biographies and autobiographies are for.

Are the Phat Five based on actual friends?

A: No, and for a good reason. If you've seen the movie *The Best Man* starring Taye Diggs and Morris Chestnut, you'll understand why.

What do the initials D.A. stand for?

A: Not telling. But I'll give you a hint: Both of my names are in the book of 2 Samuel.

And finally, the question everyone wants to know:
WILL THERE BE A SEQUEL??????

A: I'll think about it. Just playing. Presently its in the works. How will Savannah react to Ajani's news? Is Mr. Bethel wanted for dead? Will Eros change his ways? Will Q's marriage survive? Will K.J walk in integrity as a hip-hop star? What new trials wait for Teddy in Windsor? I have the plot ready to be written, but it won't be my second novel. UN-SHAKEN is the next book, which has nothing to do with the Phat Five.

Now, let's get to the real purpose of acknowledgements.

All of the praise, honor, and glory are due to my Lord and Savior Jesus Christ. My love for you is more than just an award show shout-out. You have been my father and provider through everything. Thank you for your grace and being patient with me when I didn't have enough faith in you. Thank you for showing me the importance of having a personal relationship with you, and may I forever trust in you for *everything*. And Lord, give me immediate conviction if I do anything outside of your will.

To my wife Julia, my best friend and the greatest woman in the world. Thank you for your continued love and support for me. Thank you for pushing me when I was procrastinating, and most importantly, thank you for being a true woman of God. I love you so much, and always remember that my success is your success, 'cause were in this together.

To Jada Makayla, my daughter. You bring me so much joy, and the more I see you grow, the more I want to be the best father in the world for you. I love you, Spunky. Sorry that my book has no pictures in it.

To my parents, Godfrey and Eula Bourne, for showing me the importance of being a Christian seven days a week. It was so good to see you living the same life inside and outside of church. Love you both. Much love also goes to my mother-in-law, Esther Anthony, for her never-ending love and support. Thank you. To my little brothers Dwayne and Dale Bourne. Enter every door that God opens for you. Stay focused, and pray for some wives, 'cause I want to be an uncle. Stop laughing, I'm serious.

To my pastors, Kevin and Pamela Begley, two of the greatest people on the planet. Words can't describe how thankful I am for you. You have poured so much spiritual insight into me, and continue to stretch me towards reaching greater heights. Because you're always pursuing godliness and excellence, it has now become contagious. I love you both, and I pray for great abundance of prosperity for you and your family. To my HWC family, thank you for making Harvest Worship Centre the greatest church in the world. God has so much in store for us; we won't be able to contain it! 2007 is going to be an incredible year!

To my former pastor, Bishop C.L. Morton, Jr., for opening the first door for ministry. When other churches in Windsor would've shunned gospel rap, you accepted it as a tool to reach the lost. Your teachings also introduced me to the Holy Spirit, and for these things I will always be grateful. To my "Momma", Lady Yvonne Morton, thanks for always keeping it real and treating me like a son. Love you both.

To my grandmother, Hyacinth Bourne, who is an inspiration to many and a tremendous blessing in my life. Ninety years young and still standing strong! Love you, Granny.

Thank you, Xlibris Publishing for doing a magnificent job with this book. I didn't have to face rejection letters and I maintained creative control, which is very important to me. Keep up the excellent work!

I have a list of many close friends and family who've supported me with encouraging words and prayers, but if I included them individually on this, I'm bound to forget somebody important. So to play it safe, much love goes out to my family and friends in Toronto, Windsor, New York, New Jersey, Detroit, Atlanta, The Bahamas, St. Vincent, and my Daimler Chrysler co-workers in Brampton. Thank you, thank you, thank you!

If you've enjoyed this book, feel free to let your favorite online bookstore know about it. Word of mouth is always the best advertisement! My e-mail is *da.bourne@hotmail.com*. I love you all, and remember that through Christ all things are possible!

D.A. Bourne
December 13, 2006

THE FOLLOWING IS A PREVIEW
CHAPTER OF
D.A. BOURNE'S 2ND NOVEL
UN-SHAKEN
COMING IN 2008
ENJOY!

1

August 1989

The woman that I had to deliver a pizza to loved sleeping with preachers. That was the rumor among church folk in Toledo. I didn't worry about it because I was only a son of a pastor. A son of a well-known bishop, but I had no intention of following his footsteps.

Of course, many people would believe that my thoughts were foolish, but I didn't care. So what if I was Lamar Abner Davis the 3rd? Was I supposed to become a bishop because of my father and granddad? Not if I could help it. That's why I decided to deliver pizza as a part-time job. It kept me from going to mid-week services and church outings all the time. The less I heard people compare me to my father, the better.

LaWanda Francis had become one of my regular customers. Her fourteen-year old daughter Rhonda came to Friday youth nights at the church. LaWanda wasn't a church member, but she was very supportive of her daughter and our youth conferences. At the last conference, she was the first person to congratulate me for my ten-minute message about being a witness for Christ. I thought nothing of it. I delivered pizza to her apartment for the first time a month later. The lady couldn't stop talking about the sermon and comparing me to my old man. She wouldn't even let Rhonda say more than hello and good-bye. It was odd behavior for a mother, but I didn't complain. Miss Francis was a pretty woman who gave great tips.

Every Thursday since then was a stop to the Francis home. One medium veggie pizza for Miss Francis, and one medium pepperoni pizza for Rhonda. The order never changed. The tips stayed good. My best friend Victor found out from Rhonda about my frequent visits and told me about Miss Francis and her fascination for pulpit speakers. I laughed at him. Why would a fine mid-thirties woman want to sleep with a seventeen year-old?

I arrived at the entrance of the high-rise condo where they resided. I turned the engine off but left the battery on. Had to finish listening to Public Enemy's "Fight the Power." After watching Spike Lee's *Do The Right Thing*, I rushed to the store to buy the soundtrack. It was hard for a hip-hop fan not to love the scenes when homeboy toured the neighborhood with his boom box, blazing the track like it was the best tune ever. I was a hip-hop fanatic. Loved everything about it except for the cursing. Loved it even more after my parents banned it from our home. Whenever I drove my 1984 Dodge Sprint, I played my rap music like I didn't have a tomorrow. To make myself feel less guilty for listening to it, I would convert the secular choruses to Christian. It sounded corny most of the time, but it made me content. Plus I had little options. I didn't have any gospel rap to listen to. Didn't even know if such a genre existed.

I reached for the pizza bag and looked for the Francis' box. I had three deliveries to make, and there were three orders, but I was confused. Did I pick up the wrong order for the Francis'? I pulled out the box with their name and receipt on it. I didn't make a mistake, 'cause the receipt stated one medium veggie only. Rhonda wasn't home.

"Hey, sweetheart, how are you?" greeted Miss Francis with her usual sweet Southern accent.

"F-Fine, Miss Francis," I replied as I stared at her in awe.

I almost forgot what I was supposed to do. Miss Francis wore a blue and green polka dot bikini top and jean cut-off shorts. The woman was fit! I couldn't believe that I was looking at Rhonda's mother. I already knew that her face looked very much like Whitney Houston's, but I had no idea she had a body of a Sports Illustrated swimsuit model. It was the first time I'd seen her wear so little. Then again, it was the first time I'd seen her without Rhonda.

"My Lord, come inside and cool down!" she cried, pulling me into her lavish two-bedroom apartment. "Do you want some water? Hard working young man like you must be exhausted!"

I was sweating. More so after seeing Miss Francis. But the apartment was very cool, thanks to the A.C. It would be dumb for me to refuse water after coming from outside where it was still ninety degrees in the evening. I gladly accepted some H2O.

"Be right back with that and your money," said Miss Francis as she headed towards the kitchen with her veggie pizza.

My eyes were glued to her backside as she walked away. Was I at Sister Rhonda's mother's apartment or Miami Beach?

Watch yourself, Lamar! How would you like your boys staring at your mother's booty?

I gave myself a disgusted look just thinking about it. My mom was beautiful, but my friends Victor and Matt saw her as Co-Pastor Davis and a second mother.

And Mom never wore clothes like Miss Francis. And Mom didn't have a body like Miss Francis. There had to be a good amount of preachers guilty of adultery or fornication courtesy of her.

She returned with a glass of water. It was easily the most refreshing drink I had all summer. Surprisingly, it made me feel more relaxed. Must have been due to the quick prayer I said while gulping the beverage. I could look at Miss Francis and not get aroused! Word up, my God worked a miracle indeed.

The Francis home was one of the few stops that I actually took time to chat for a few minutes. Rhonda was a friend, plus I took advantage of their A.C. I asked Miss Francis where she was, and she told me that Rhonda was spending Labor Day weekend with her father in Arkansas. Miss Francis asked me if I was excited about my final year of high school.

"Yes, ma'am!" I answered with joy. "My high school days are almost over!"

"Enjoy it, sweetheart. Some days I wish I could go back to my high school days. Life was so much easier."

"That's what every grown-up tells me."

Of course, being a typical teenager, seeing high school as the easy life made no sense.

"So what are your plans after you graduate?" she asked. "Full-time ministry?"

Dang, how cliché was that question? Because I have the same name as my pops and granddad, people expect me to be their clone. What, if my ancestors were crack heads, should I be the same? No doubt the question bothered me, but I got rid of my frustration by staring at her two friends. It wasn't a godly move, but they made me smile.

"I'm actually interested in studying social work at the University of Toledo," I replied. "Or I might go elsewhere and study it at Michigan or Ohio State."

"Really?" she asked, sounding quite impressed. "Social work is a great field. I can see you being a man that helps . . . the needy."

When Miss Francis said that, she looked at me like I was BBQ chicken. Was Victor right when he told me that she wants to break me off? Yes, I was six foot one, two-twenty in weight, and could pass for a twenty-one year old, but I was only seventeen! A youngin' for crying out loud! Yes, she may like to get freaky with preachers, but she wasn't desperate. Then again, when Miss Francis said "the needy", she sounded just like Jessica from the film *Who Framed Roger Rabbit*.

"I know you have to go, but I need a huge favor," said Miss Francis, sounding normal again. "Do you have a couple of minutes to spare?"

Oh my God, a couple of minutes?

I said, "Sure . . . sure. What do you need?"

"Both light bulbs connected to the living room ceiling fan died yesterday. Usually Rhonda changes them when she's here 'cause I have a fear of standing on stools. Childhood accident, long story. Can you change them for me? If you have to go, that's . . ."

"Of course I can do it, that's no problem."

She thanked me and went to the kitchen to get a pack of light bulbs. Then I followed her to the dark living room where the only light was coming from outside. Wheel of Fortune was on the television. MC Hammer was playing lightly through the stereo. This woman didn't want to knock my boots. Stupid Victor had my mind tripping!

Miss Francis placed a footstool under the fan and I stood on it. With my left hand, I unscrewed the dead bulb. She gave me a new bulb and placed in my right hand while she took the dead one from my left. I screwed in the new bulb with my left while unscrewing the second dead bulb with my right. Had to move quick cause I didn't want to give away any free pizzas to my other customers. So, one hand was holding the dead bulb, the other screwing in the second new bulb, and a third was caressing my privates.

That when I stopped moving. The dead bulb dropped to the floor.

I looked down at Miss Francis and she was smiling at me while rubbing you-know-what like a genie bottle. What I refused to believe was actually true, and I got crazy scared. I honestly didn't know how to react.

"Do you like this, baby?" she asked.

Of course I liked it. It was about to break through my pants!

"M-M-Miss Francis, what are you doing?"

"You need to call me LaWanda, baby! Just relax, 'cause I wanna introduce you to manhood. What are you doing after work?"

"Uh, uh . . . I'm going to church."

"I need you to come back here when you're done work! We can have our own service. I want . . . I need you to lay your hands on me."

My God, she was desperate. And I was in trouble. My flesh was so ready to lose my job and get in trouble with my folks over something teenage boys could only dream about.

Miss Francis un-buckled my belt and pulled down my pant zipper.

"Do you want me to give you a sneak preview?"

That's when I lost my balance and fell backwards on the carpet. Miss Francis moved the stool out of her way and continued trying to pull my pants off. I quickly crawled backwards, but I was stopped by the screen door to the porch. I really wanted to give in, but my faith kept me on the defensive.

"Miss Francis, I really really have to go now," I pleaded as she sat on my lap.

She pressed her bosom against my chest and stared at me with eyes of seduction.

"Promise me that you'll come back tonight," she begged.

"No, Miss Francis, I can't-"

"No! All I want to hear is 'Yes, LaWanda!'"
Then she took off her top.
Oh yes, LaWanda! Yes, yes . . .
Don't do it again, Lamar!

Her twin friends were fully exposed. It was the second time in my life that I'd been so close to the naked female body. Twice in the last four weeks. Our church had a weekend youth retreat in August with another church in the state. One of their youth members brought a guest that was visiting from Windsor, Canada. I was so attracted to her that I did whatever I had to do to get her alone with me for a half hour. To make a long story short, the opportunity came and I lost my virginity. Biggest mistake of my entire life. Minutes after it happened, I repented to God and promised him that I would never have sex again until my wedding night.

"I can make this a night you'll never forget," said Miss Francis. "This tutor session won't be available once Rhonda comes back. I'll show you the right ways to minister in the bedroom with your future first lady. All you gotta say is-"

"No, Miss Francis!!!! NO!!!!"

I pushed her off my lap, pulled up my pants, and headed for the door. Whatever her veggie pizza cost, I was willing to pay for it 'cause I didn't want to wait for her cash or her tips. I had to flee like Joseph with Potiphar's wife. Obviously it was easier said than done.

"Wait, Brother Lamar!" she cried, running to the door while re-connecting her polka-dot bikini top. "Please forgive me. I've always seen you as an attractive young man, and . . . I allowed my emotions to get carried away."

"Miss Francis, I'm shocked!" I snapped as I straightened out my clothes. "I'm shocked that a woman like yourself would lower your standards and take advantage of a friend of your only daughter! How could you?"

She looked at me like I was a ghost. My words surprised her big time. Not only did I have a moderately deep voice, but I had no respect of age when I was shocked or angry. I was bold enough to tell off a little kid or a mature adult if someone rubbed me the wrong way. That's why I spent many days slapped, grounded, or stuck in detention growing up. I blamed it on my pops, a militant man who was ridiculously blunt in our home and on the pulpit.

I continued. "A fine, beautiful woman like yourself should be with a good husband. But you're not going to get a good man if you give up your body to anyone who could preach a hot sermon! I hear bad things about you, and I be buggin' 'cause I know you're a sweet lady. If you stay patient and trust God, you can have the man you're looking for, in His perfect timing!"

With that said, I bounced before she got out of her shock and kicked me out. Sped down the hallway without looking back. Got to the elevator, pressed the down button, and waited for the door to open. It was taking its own time.

"Come on! Hurry up," I snapped, pushing the button constantly like it was the remedy to bring the elevator sooner.

Sweat poured down my forehead as mixed emotions frustrated my mind.

You did the right thing, Lamar. God's gonna bless you for it.

The boss is gonna be pissed cause you have to give away free pizzas for being late!

Did I just preach to a woman who wanted to have sex with me? Lamar, what's wrong with you? You should've been her love slave! A man would be insane to turn down a body like that! She could make a gay man turn straight!

It takes real integrity to do what you did, Lamar.

Getting with Rhonda's mommy would've been a hundred times better than doing Sherelle!

"Brother Lamar?"

I didn't even hear Miss Francis approach me. She'd put on a Cleveland Indians T-Shirt over her bikini. Tears were flowing down her face.

"Here's the money for the pizza," she said softly. "Like always, keep the change."

I took the folded bill and put it in my pocket. I said nothing as I kept looking at the elevator.

"It took a lot of courage to say what you just told me," Miss Francis added. "I didn't want to hear it, but it was exactly what I needed. Thank you. You have just gained a lifetime of full love and respect from me."

I looked at her and gave a bashful smile. When I said thank you, Miss Francis told me to never change 'cause I was an extraordinary young man. My words really humbled her. Made me feel much better about the outcome even though I greatly needed a cold shower. The biggest surprise happened while I was in the elevator. I unfolded the bill. A fifty for a seven-dollar pizza!

I drove down the neighborhood streets like I being chased by police. Was way behind schedule and excited about my forty-three dollar tip. Didn't have much time to think about what just occurred or how I was going to spend the cash. I had to finish my rounds and catch church before it was over.